Glitz, glamour and happily ever after!

ROYAL
WEDDINGS

Three powerful, thrilling wedding
stories from three exceptional,
favourite authors

We're proud to present

MILLS & BOON

Spotlight

a chance to buy collections of bestselling novels by favourite authors every month — they're back by popular demand!

February 2009

The Danforths: Wesley, Ian & Imogene

Featuring

Scandal Between the Sheets by Brenda Jackson
The Boss Man's Fortune by Kathryn Jensen
Challenged by the Sheikh by Kristi Gold

Royal Weddings

Featuring

The Reluctant Princess by Christine Rimmer
Princess Dottie by Lucy Gordon
The Royal MacAllister by Joan Elliott Pickart

March 2009

The Danforths: Toby, Lea & Adam

Featuring

Cowboy Crescendo by Cathleen Galitz
Steamy Savannah Nights by Sheri WhiteFeather
The Enemy's Daughter by Anne Marie Winston

Secrets and Desire

Featuring

Best-Kept Lies by Lisa Jackson
Miss Pruitt's Private Life by Barbara McCauley
Secrets, Lies and Passion by Linda Conrad

ROYAL WEDDINGS

The Reluctant Princess
CHRISTINE RIMMER

Princess Dottie
LUCY GORDON

The Royal MacAllister
JOAN ELLIOTT PICKART

MILLS & BOON®

Pure reading pleasure™

This collection is first published in Great Britain 2009.
Harlequin Mills & Boon Limited,
Eton House, 18-24 Paradise Road, Richmond, Surrey TW9 1SR

ROYAL WEDDINGS © Harlequin Books S.A. 2009.

The publisher acknowledges the copyright holders of the individual works, which have already been published in the UK in single, separate volumes, as follows:

The Reluctant Princess © Christine Rimmer 2003
Princess Dottie © Lucy Gordon 2002
The Royal MacAllister © Joan Elliott Pickart 2002

ISBN: 978 0 263 87149 4

064-0209

Printed and bound in Spain
by Litografia Rosés S.A., Barcelona

The Reluctant Princess

CHRISTINE RIMMER

CHRISTINE RIMMER

came to her profession the long way around. Before settling down to write about the magic of romance, she'd been an actress, a sales assistant, a caretaker, a model, a phone sales representative, a teacher, a waitress, a playwright and an office manager. She insists she never had a problem keeping a job – she was merely gaining "life experience" for her future as a novelist. Christine is grateful not only for the joy she finds in writing, but for what waits when the day's work is through: a man she loves, who loves her right back, and the privilege of watching their children grow and change day to day. She lives with her family in Oklahoma, USA.

This one's for you, Susan Mallery, because you are not only a fabulous writer and most terrific friend, you can also plot circles around the best of them and you know when to give encouragement and when to come out with the gentle reminder that passion is everything.

Chapter One

A Viking was the last thing Elli Thorson expected to find in her living room on that sunny afternoon in early May.

At a few minutes after five that day, Elli parked her little silver BMW in her space behind her building and got her two bags of groceries out of the trunk. She'd had the checker bag her purchases in paper because she was short on paper bags. Possibly, if she'd gone ahead and taken plastic, everything would have turned out differently.

With plastic, she would have been carrying the bags low, by the handles. There'd have been nothing in the way of her vision. She'd have seen the Viking before she shut the door to the landing with both of them on the same side of it. Maybe, with the door standing open, there would have been at least a *chance* of escaping him.

When she got up the stairs to her apartment, she was carrying the bags high in her arms, with her purse looped over her left elbow and her key ready in her right hand. Maybe if she hadn't been ready with the key—if she'd set the bags down, dug around in her purse, and opened the door before picking the bags up again...

But she didn't set the bags down. She had her key ready. And on such small choices, the course of a life can depend.

Elli braced the right-hand bag against the door. That freed her hand just enough to work the top lock. Then, by bending her knees and twisting sideways a fraction, she was able to slip the key into the bottom lock and get it open, too. She pushed the door inward, juggling the bags back to where she had a firm grip on them from underneath.

Her apartment had a small entry area—a square of floor, really—between the living room and the kitchen. Elli spun over the threshold. A quick nudge of her heel as she turned to the right and the door swung shut and latched. Her cute little butcher-block kitchen table was right there. She slid the bags onto it.

"Ta-da!" With a flourish, she dropped her keys and purse beside the bags and spun back toward the living area.

That was when she saw him.

He stood in her living room. A man dressed all in black—black slacks, black boots, muscle-hugging black T-shirt. He was blond and scarred and stone-faced—and big. Very, very big.

Elli was no midget herself. She stood five-eleven in bare feet. But this man topped her by several inches. And all of him was broad and hard and thick with muscle. The sheer size of him was scary, even if he hadn't been standing right there in the middle of her living room, uninvited, unexpected and unwelcome in the extreme.

The sight of him so shocked her that she jumped back and let out a shriek.

The man, gazing so calmly at her through piercing gray-blue eyes, fisted a hand and laid it on his chest, right over his heart. "Princess Elli, I bring greetings from your father, King Osrik of Gullandria." His voice was deep and sonorous, his tone grave.

It was then, when he called her Princess Elli, that she realized he was, in reality, a Viking and not some buff burglar she'd just caught in the act. He was a Viking because that was what they were, essentially—the people of Gullandria.

Gullandria. Though Elli had been born there, the place had always seemed to her like something from a fairy tale, a barely remembered bedtime story told to her by her mother.

But Gullandria was real enough. It was an island shaped roughly like a heart that could be found between the Shetlands and Norway, in the Norwegian Sea—a tiny pocket of the world where the ways of the legendary Norsemen still held sway.

Elli's mother, Ingrid Freyasdahl, had been eighteen when she married Osrik Thorson, who shortly thereafter became king of that land. Five years later, Ingrid left the king forever, taking her tiny triplet daughters and returning to California where she'd been born and raised. It had been a big scandal at the time—and now and then the old story still cropped up in tabloid magazines. In those magazines, her mother was always referred to as the Runaway Gullandrian Queen.

Elli's heart was beating way too fast. So what if her father had sent this man? She had no memory of her father. She knew only what her mother had told her and what she'd read in those occasional absurd scandal-sheet exposés. Osrik Thorson seemed no more real to her than the mythical-sounding country where he ruled.

She demanded, "How did you get in here?"

The intruder opened his fist and extended his massive hand, palm out, in a salute. Tattooed in the heart of that hand was a gold-and-blue lightning bolt. "Hauk FitzWyborn, the king's warrior, bloodsworn to your father, His Majesty, King Osrik of the House of Thor. I am at your service, Princess."

She resisted the urge to shrink back from that giant hand and boldly taunted, "Was that my question? I don't think that was my question."

The huge man looked somewhat pained. "It seemed wiser, Your Highness, to be waiting for you inside."

"Wiser than knocking on my door like any normal, civilized human being?"

In answer to that, she got a fractional nod of his big blond head.

"Here in America, what you did is called breaking and entering. What's wise about that?"

This time the fractional move was a shrug.

Elli's mind raced. She felt threatened, boxed in—and at the same time determined that this oversize interloper would not see her fear.

She looked at him sideways. "You said you were at my service."

"I am bloodsworn to your father. That means I serve you, as well."

"Great. To serve me best, you can get out of my apartment."

He had those bulging, tendon-ridged arms crossed over that enormous chest and he didn't look as if he was going anywhere. He said, "Your father wishes your presence at court. He wishes to see you, to speak with you. He has...important matters to discuss with you."

This was all so insulting. Elli felt her cheeks burning. "My father has made zero effort over the years to get in touch with me. What is so important that I have to drop everything and rush to see him now?"

"Allow me to take you to him. His Majesty will explain all."

"Listen. Listen very carefully." Elli employed the same patient, firm tone she often used on stubborn five-year-olds in her class of kindergartners. "I want you to return to Gullandria. When you get there, you can tell my father that if he suddenly just *has* to speak with me, he can pick up the phone and call me. Once he's told me what's going on, *I'll* decide whether I'm willing to go see him or not."

The Viking's frown deepened. Evidently, he found the disparity between her wishes and his orders vaguely troubling. But not troubling enough to get him to give up and go. "You will pack now, Princess," he intoned. "Necessities only. All your needs will be provided for at Isenhalla."

Isenhalla. Ice hall. The silver-slate palace of Gullandrian kings....

Truly, truly weird. A Viking in her living room. A Viking who thought he was taking her to her father's palace. "I guess you haven't been listening. I said, I am going nowhere with you and you are trespassing. I want you to leave."

"You will pack now, please." Those flinty eyes seemed to see right through her and that amazingly square jaw looked set in granite.

Elli repeated, more strongly than the first time, "I said, I want you to leave."

"And once you are packed, I will do as you say. We will leave together."

There was a silence—a loaded one. She glared at him and he stared, unblinking, back at her. From outside, she heard ordinary, everyday sounds: birds singing, the honk of a horn, a leaf blower starting up, a siren somewhere far off in the distance.

Those sounds had the strangest effect on her. They made her want to burst into tears. Though they were right outside her door, those sounds, all at once, seemed lost to her.

Lost...

The word made her think of the brothers she had never known. There had been two of them, Kylan and

Valbrand. Kylan had died as a young child. But Valbrand had grown up in Gullandria with their father, the king. Over the years, she and her sisters had talked about what it might be like to meet their surviving brother someday, to get to know him.

But that would never happen now.

Valbrand was dead, too. Like Kylan.

And were her brothers the key to what was happening here? Her father had no sons anymore. And without a son, maybe his thrown-away daughters had value to him now—whether they wanted anything to do with him, or not.

Yes. She supposed that made sense—or it *would* make sense if she could even be certain that this Viking had been sent by her father in the first place.

Maybe this was a trick. Maybe this man had been sent by an *enemy* of her father's. Or maybe he was simply a criminal, as she'd assumed at first. But instead of robbing her apartment, he was here to take her hostage. He'd haul her out of here and hold her prisoner and her mother would be getting a ransom note....

Oh, she didn't know. How could she know? This was all so confusing.

And whatever the reasons for the Viking in her living room, there could be no more denials. Elli could see it, shining there, in those unwavering pale eyes. Hauk FitzWyborn—who called himself the king's warrior, who said he was blood-something-or-other to her father—*might* be at her service, but only if her desires didn't conflict with whatever orders he'd been given. He intended to take her...somewhere.

And wherever that somewhere actually was, he meant to take her today—whether she agreed to go or not.

The bottom line: this was a kidnapping and Elli was the kidnappee.

Oh, what was she *thinking*—to have stood here and argued with him? She should have hit the door running at the sight of him.

Maybe she could still escape—if she moved fast enough.

She spun for the door.

And she made it. She had the doorknob in her hand. But she never got a chance to turn it.

With stunning speed for such a big man, he was upon her, wrapping those bulging, scarred arms around her. It was like being engulfed by a warm boulder. She cried out—once. And then a massive hand covered her mouth and nose.

That hand held a soft cloth, a cloth that smelled sharp and bitter.

Drugged. He had *drugged* her....

"Forgive me, Your Highness," she heard him whisper.

And the world went black.

Chapter Two

Hauk looked down at the princess in his arms.

She was slim, but not small, with long, graceful bones and surprisingly large, ripe-looking breasts, the kind of breasts that would serve equally to please a man and nourish the children he gave her. Her mouth was full-lipped—and silent, at the moment. Silent and lax.

The compliant one, his lord had called her. And compliant she was—now. The drug had made her so. But Hauk had looked deep into those fjord-blue eyes. He'd seen the steel at the core. If his lord hoped this one might be yielding when conscious, he was in for an unpleasant surprise.

"Bring her to me," Hauk's lord had instructed. *"Tell her that her father would like to see her, to speak with her. Say that her father has many things*

*to say to her and will explain all as soon as he can
talk to her. Try to coax her to come with you willingly. My spies tell me that of the three, she is by far
the most compliant.''*

Hauk had sworn to do as his lord commanded.
*''And if she should refuse, in the end, to accompany
me?''*

There had been a silence. A silence that spoke volumes. Finally his lord had said quietly, *''Her refusal
is not an option. I wish you to bring her. But please.
Treat her gently.''*

Shaking his head, Hauk carried the woman to the
couch against the inner wall. Coaxing was for courtiers, he thought as he carefully laid her down. He
tucked a bright-colored pillow beneath her head so
her neck would not be strained into an uncomfortable
position. Then he slipped off her low-heeled shoes
and smoothed her skirt modestly over those pretty
knees.

He stood back and stared down at her, considering.
The drug would wear off shortly. She would not be
pleased when she woke, and she would make her displeasure known. He should disable her now.

But he hated to do it. She looked so sweet and
peaceful, lying there.

With some regret, he went for the duffel bag he'd
left behind the chair across the room. From it, he took
lengths of soft, strong rope and a kerchief-sized gag.

Carefully, he turned the princess on her side, so
she was facing the wall.

He was good with knots. It took only a few minutes
to bind her wrists behind her, to tie her knees to-

gether, and her slim ankles, as well. He ran an extra
length of rope down her back, connecting the ropes
at wrist and ankle, bending her knees slightly, drawing her feet up and back.

Perhaps the final rope, which would gradually pull
tighter with resistance, was overkill. But he couldn't
afford to take any chances. She would be angry when
she woke and ready for a fight, ready to do anything
in her power to escape. It was his job to see that she
had no power. He tied the gag firmly in place, taking
care to smooth the softly curling wheat-colored hair
out of her face so none of the strands were caught in
her eyes or her mouth.

The binding accomplished, he stood back from her
again.

It was not for him to wonder—and yet, he *did* wonder. If his liege wanted this woman effectively
coaxed, why in the name of the frozen towers of Hel
had he sent a soldier to do it?

The soles of her feet, turned out to him because of
his perhaps too-cautious binding, seemed to reproach
him. He bent, gently scooped her up and turned her
so that she was facing the room again. Bound was
bound and she wouldn't like it, but at least in her
current position, when she woke, she could see what
went on around her.

He noted a flicker of movement in his side vision,
tensed, and then relaxed again. It was only those two
cats he'd spotted earlier, when he'd entered the apartment. One was big and white, the other sleek and
black. They were sitting side by side beneath the table
in the kitchen area, watching him.

"Freyja's eyes," he muttered, and then smiled to himself. The oath was fitting. Freyja was the goddess of love and war. Her chariot was drawn by cats.

Hauk had more to accomplish before the darkness fell. He turned for the room where the princess slept.

Elli groaned and opened her eyes. She was lying on her side on her own couch, a rumbling ball of white fur in front of her face and a pillow cradling her head.

And speaking of her head—it ached. Her stomach felt queasy and her mouth…

She had a gag in her mouth! The gag was firmly tied and held her mouth open, so that her lips pressed back hard over her teeth. Her jaw hurt and her throat was dry and scratchy, the gag itself soggy with saliva.

And that wasn't all. Her arms and legs were tied, too.

"Rrreow?" The sound came from the white ball of purring fur in front of her face. Doodles put his damp kitty nose to her cheek and asked again, "Rreow?" Then he jumped to the carpet and trotted off toward the kitchen, fat white tail held high, no doubt hoping she would take the hint and get out there and dish up his dinner.

Elli groaned and yanked at the ropes that bound her. It didn't help. If anything, her struggling seemed to pull them tighter.

"It is best not to struggle, Your Highness," said a deep, calm voice from across the room. It was *him*— the Viking. He sat in the easy chair opposite her. With Doodles in the way, she hadn't seen him at first.

"Struggling only pulls the long rope tighter." His kindly tone made her yearn for something long and sharp to drive straight into his heart.

One of her suitcases waited upright beside his chair. Evidently, he'd done her packing for her.

"We'll be on our way soon, Princess. We're only waiting for darkness."

Waiting for darkness...

Well, of course they were waiting for darkness. Dragging a bound-and-gagged woman down a flight of stairs and out to a waiting vehicle wasn't something he'd be likely to get away with in the bright light of day.

He was silent, watching her, his expression implacable. She watched him right back, fury curling through her, banishing the thickheaded grogginess left over from the drug he'd used on her.

As a rule, Elli was good-natured and easygoing, not as ambitious as her older sister, Liv, not as brave and adventurous as Brit, the baby. Elli had always thought of herself as the *ordinary* one of the three of them, the one who wanted meaningful work that didn't eat up her life, a nice home to fill with love and, eventually, a good man to go through life beside her. They used to joke among themselves that Liv would run the world and Brit would thoroughly explore it. It would be up to Elli to settle down, get married and provide the world with the next generation.

Right now, though, looking at the man in the chair across from her, Elli didn't feel especially reasonable or easygoing or good-natured. She felt angry.

No. Anger was too mild a word. She felt a burning, growing rage.

How dare he? What gave him the right—to break into her home, to give her orders, to knock her out, to tie her up?

Her father?

So the Viking said.

And what gave her father the right? Her father *had* no rights when it came to her. He'd given them up twenty-plus years ago.

And even if her father still had some claim on her, no claim in the world made kidnapping acceptable. This was an outrage, a crime against basic human decency.

Elli wanted the ropes untied and the gag removed. And she wanted—had a *right*—to be untied *now*. She grunted and squirmed in her rage and fury.

And as her Viking captor had promised, the rope that bound her wrists to her ankles pulled tighter, until her heels met her hands and her body bowed outward beyond the outer edge of the couch cushions. Her right thigh cramped up. It was excruciatingly painful.

She let out a small, anguished moan and lay still, forcing herself to breathe slowly and deeply, to relax as best she could with her heels yanked up and pressed against her palms. Sweat broke out on her brow. She shut her eyes, concentrated on pulling her breath in and sending it out, *willing* the cramp in her thigh to let go.

The pain seemed to ease a little. She opened her eyes to find the Viking standing over her. She let out a muffled shriek as she saw the jet-black knife handle.

With an evil snicking sound, the slim, deadly blade sprang out. The Viking bent close—and cut the rope that held her hands and ankles together.

The relief was a fine and shining thing. She straightened her legs, the cramp in her thigh subsiding completely. And then, though she knew it was foolish in the extreme, she flung out her bound feet and tried to kick him.

He simply stepped to the side, collapsing the knife and kneeling in a smooth, swift motion to stow it in his boot. Then he stood to his height again.

"I am sorry to have bound you, Princess." He actually managed to sound regretful. "But your father's instructions are to bring you to him, whether you are willing or not. I can't have you trying to run away all the time—or shouting for help."

She made a series of urgent grunting sounds, shaking her head with each one.

He got the message. Reluctantly, he suggested, "You wish me to remove the gag."

"Umn, uhgh, umngh." She nodded madly.

"If I remove the gag, you must swear on your honor as a descendant of kings not to cry out or make any loud sounds."

She nodded again—that time sharply and firmly.

He was silent, regarding her. She stared right back at him, unmoving now, willing him with her eyes to take off the gag.

At last, he spoke. "You are a princess of the House of Thor. To you, honor should be all." His doubting expression was distinctly unflattering. "But you have been raised in…this." He gestured toward the glass door that led out to her small balcony. The sun was lowering now. A massive oak grew beyond the balcony and the sunlight shone through its branches, creating enchanting patterns of shadow and light.

The Viking sneered. "This California is an easy, warm place, far from the hard snows and misty fjords of our island home. You know nothing of the endless nights of winter. The frost giants, harbingers of Ragnarok, do not stalk your dreams. Perhaps you do not hold your honor precious above all else as you should."

Elli knew the Norse myths. She understood his references. Still, what he said sounded like something out of *Lord of the Rings*. She should have found such talk ridiculous. But she didn't. His meaning was crystal clear. He believed she wouldn't keep her word, that she'd scream her head off the second he took the gag away.

A minute ago, she had planned to do exactly that. But not anymore. Now, she would not scream if her life depended on it. Now, she was madder, even, than a minute ago. She was utterly, bone-shatteringly furious—which was thoroughly unreasonable, as he only suspected what she *had* planned to do.

But this was far from a reasonable situation. And Elli Thorson boiled with rage. She didn't move, she didn't *breathe*. She simply stared at him, her gaze burning through him, wishing she could sear him to a cinder where he stood.

Evidently, the hot fury in her eyes was the answer he sought. He stepped in front of her once more and knelt opposite her head. They shared another long look. And then he reached out and untied the gag. "Forgive me, Your Highness. I want you to be comfortable, but I must know that I can trust you."

"I don't forgive you," she muttered in a dry croak. "So stop asking me to." Elli pressed her lips together, ran her tongue over her dried-out teeth and swallowed repeatedly to soothe her parched throat. Finally, she said in a low voice, "Water. Please."

He dropped the gag on the couch arm and went to the kitchen, returning quickly with a full glass. He set the glass on the coffee table and helped her to sit. Her skirt was halfway up her thighs. He smoothed it down so it covered her tied-together knees. She had a powerful urge to snap at him to get his big, rude hands off her, but she pressed her lips together over the self-defeating words. She did want her skirt pulled down and since her own hands were tied, his would have to do.

Once she was upright, with her skirt where it was supposed to be, he held the glass to her lips. Oh, it was heaven, that lovely, wet water sliding down her dry throat. She drank the whole thing.

"More?" he asked. She shook her head. He was very close, his bulging hard shoulder brushing against her. She realized she could smell him. His skin gave off a scent both spicy and fresh. Like cloves and green, newly cut cedar boughs. Every Christmas, her mother decked the mantels and stair rails with cedar boughs. Elli had always loved the smell of them....

And what was the matter with her? Had she lost her mind?

He had drugged her and tied her up and as soon as

dark came, he was dragging her out of here, hauling her off to God knew where. The last thing she should be thinking about was how good he smelled.

She scooted as far away from him as she could, given her hobbled state, and hugged the couch arm.

Without another word, he set the empty glass on the coffee table, stood and crossed the room to sit again in the easy chair—as if he found it uncomfortable or distasteful to be anywhere near her. Fine. She felt the same way. On both counts.

Neither of them spoke for several minutes. The Viking was still. Elli fidgeted a little, pulling at the ropes that bound her, unable to resist a need to test them. Unlike the rope he had cut, the ones that were left pulled no tighter when she tugged on them. They didn't loosen, either.

It occurred to her that the only weapon she had at her disposal right then was her voice. Shouting for help was out. She'd sworn she wouldn't do that, and for some insane reason she felt bound to stick by her word. However, she'd never promised she wouldn't speak. And words, if used right, could serve as weapons.

She straightened her shoulders and let out a long breath. "This is kidnapping, do you realize that? In America, what you're doing is a capital crime."

He looked away, toward the kitchen, where both of her cats—Doodles and Diablo—sat side by side, waiting for the dinner that was so long in coming. Elli began to wonder if the Viking would reply to her.

And then that gray-blue gaze swung her way again.

"You will not be harmed. I will take you to your father. He will explain all."

A shriek of rage and frustration rose in her throat. She had to swallow to banish it. She spoke with measured care. "None of that is the point. The point is—"

He raised that tattooed palm. "Enough. I have told you what will happen. Make your peace with it."

Not in a hundred million years. "Untie me. I have to feed my cats."

He just looked at her, reproach in those watchful eyes.

Though it galled like burning acid to do it, she gave him the oath he required. "I will not try to escape— not while we're here, in my apartment. You have my word of honor on that."

He studied her some more in that probing, intense way he had, as if he knew how to look through her skull, to see into her real thoughts and know for certain if she told the truth or if she lied. Finally, he bent to his boot and removed the black knife. *Snick.* The blade appeared, gleaming.

He rose and came toward her again. She wriggled sideways, twisting from the waist, presenting her bound wrists.

He slid the knife between them. She felt the cool flat of the blade. A quick, annoying brush of his skin against hers—and the rope fell away. She brought her hands to the front and rubbed her chafed wrists.

The Viking knelt before her, golden hair flowing thick and shaggy to his huge shoulders. He slipped the knife beneath the rope that bound her ankles. His fingers whispered against the upper arch of her foot—and her ankles were free. He raised the knife, the steel glinting, and slid it between her knees, slicing the rope there, his knuckles making brief and burning contact with the inside of her leg. When he pulled the knife away, he gave it a flick. The blade disappeared. Swiftly he gathered the bits of rope and the soggy gag.

The knife went into his boot and he stood. He backed away without once looking up, got a black bag from behind the easy chair and stowed the cut ropes and the gag in it. Then he sat in the chair once more.

Only then did he look at her, his eyelids low, his gaze brooding. "Go, Princess. Feed your animals."

She stood slowly, expecting a little dizziness from the drug he'd used on her—and some stiffness from being tied up so tightly. But it wasn't bad. Her head swam at first, and her stomach lurched, but both sensations passed quickly.

Her cats jumped up and followed her as she went past, Doodles meowing at her to hurry it up, Diablo a silent shadow, taking up the rear. She dished up the food, covered the half-used can and put it back in the refrigerator. Then she rinsed the spoon and stuck it in the dishwasher.

Her apartment, in a four-building complex, was at one end of her building. She had a window over her kitchen sink. She lingered for a moment, looking across at the next building over, and down at the slopes of grass and the concrete walkway below. She saw no one right then, but she couldn't help wondering…

If she were to signal a passing neighbor, would that count as trying to escape?

"Princess."

She let out a cry—actually a guilty-sounding squeak—and jumped back from the window. The Viking was standing about eight feet away, by her table with her bags of groceries still waiting on it. Damn him. How did he do it, appear out of nowhere like that without making a sound?

Slowly, he shook that gold head at her. As if he knew exactly the question she'd been asking herself and had materialized in her kitchen to let her know that he still had a few lengths of rope handy for any naughty princess who insisted on breaking her word.

"Look," she snarled. "Do you mind if I at least put my groceries away?"

"As you wish."

Hah, she thought. None of this—*none*—was as she wished.

But she'd already made that point painfully clear to him. And he was still here and still planning to take her to Gullandria with him as soon as it got dark.

With a sigh, she went to the table and began unloading the bags. He stepped out of the way, but he didn't go back to his chair in the living room. Instead, he stood a few feet from the table, arms crossed over his chest, watching her put the lettuce and the Clearly Canadians in the refrigerator, the Grey Poupon in the cupboard.

Once she had everything put away, they returned to their respective seats in the living room.

The silence descended once more. He watched, she waited—or maybe it was the other way around. Doodles and Diablo jumped up beside her and settled in, purring. She petted them—the thick white coat, the velvety black one. There was some comfort in touching them, in feeling the soft roar of their purrs vibrating against her palm.

The phone rang, startling her. She'd been avoiding looking at him, but when she heard the shrill, insistent sound, her gaze tracked immediately to his.

"Leave it."

"But—" Before she could devise some really good reason why he had to let her answer it, it stopped—on the second ring. She wanted to shout at it, at whoever had called and given up too soon, *Damn you, can't you see I need a little help here? What's holding on for a few more rings going to cost you?*

Outside, it was still light. But it wouldn't be that long until night fell. When that happened, he'd be dragging her out of here by the hair—figuratively speaking.

Was she ready for that? Not. There had to be a better way.

She made herself look at him again—and then she forced her voice to a friendly tone. "Hauk… May I call you Hauk?"

He cleared his throat. "Call me what you will. I am—"

She waved a hand. "At my service. Got that. But Hauk?"

"Your Highness?"

Oh, this was all so way, way weird. "Look. Could you just call me Elli?"

The silver-blue gaze slid away. "That would not be appropriate."

Elli stared at his profile for a count of ten. Then she sighed. "Please. I think we have to talk." He turned those eyes on her again—but he didn't speak. When the silence had stretched out too long, she suggested, "What if I were to go with you willingly?"

His gaze was unblinking, his face a carved mask. "Then you would make the inevitable easier on everyone."

She added hopefully, "There would be conditions."

And that brought on another of those never-ending silences. Surprise, surprise, she thought. He's not interested in my conditions.

Gamely, she prompted, "Let me explain."

For that, she got one gold eyebrow lifted. "I need no explanations. I have my orders and I will carry them out."

"But—"

"Your Highness, all your clever words will get you nowhere."

"Clever?" She had that dangerous feeling again, the one that told her she was about to throw back her head and scream the house down. "You think I'm *clever?*"

"Don't," he said softly, and then again, in a whisper, "Don't."

She pressed her lips together hard and folded her hands in her lap, bending her head, as if in prayer.

And in a way, she *was* praying—praying that she'd figure out how to get through to the Viking in the easy chair before he tossed her over his shoulder and headed for the door.

Elli sat up straight. "Why does my father suddenly just have to see me?"

He frowned. "As I said earlier, he will explain that himself."

"But what did he tell *you*—or did he even bother to give you the order himself?"

That eyebrow inched upward again. "Are you trying to goad me, Princess?"

She opened her mouth to deny that—and then shut it before she spoke. She had a sense that to lie to this man was to lose all hope of getting anywhere with him. She said, quietly, "Yes. I was goading you." She swallowed and then made herself add, "I apologize."

He gave her an infinitesimal shrug.

She looked up at him from under her lashes, head lowered modestly, "Please. I really do want to know. Did you speak with my father yourself? Did he tell you in person to come here and get me?"

An excruciating parade of seconds went by. Finally, the Viking said, "Yes."

"And what did he *say,* when he gave you your orders?"

"I have told you what he said. That he wanted to see you, that he would explain all once you were at his side."

"But why does he want me there?"

"He didn't tell me. And there is no reason he *should* have told me. A king is not obligated to share his motives with those who serve him."

"But he must have said *something*."

Hauk had that look again, that carved-in-stone look. The one that told her she'd gotten all the information she was going to get from him.

Well, too bad. She wanted some answers. And maybe, if she handled this right, she could make him give them to her. "You've said more than once that you are at my service."

"And so I am, Princess Elli."

"Wonderful—and I want you to know, I do understand that, while you serve me, you serve my father first."

"Yes, Your Highness."

"So that would mean, if something I ask of you doesn't affect your ability to do what my father wants, you would do *my* will. You would, as you said, serve *me*." She waited. She knew, eventually, he would have to say it.

And eventually, he did. "Yes, Princess Elli."

A slow warmth was spreading through her. She knew she had him now. "And when my father gave you the order to bring me to Gullandria, did he also instruct you not to tell *me* what he had told *you*?"

"No, Princess. He didn't."

"Then, since what I ask does not conflict with my father's wishes, I want you to serve me now and tell me what my father said to you when he ordered you to come for me."

Oh, she did have him. And yes, he did know it.

He sat ramrod straight in the chair. "His Majesty's instructions were brief. I was to be...gentle with you. First, I was to ask you to come with me. I was to tell you what I *have* told you, that your father wished to see you, to speak with you, that he would explain everything once he had you with him."

She knew the rest. "And if I said no, he told you to kidnap me and bring me to him, anyway."

Hauk looked offended. "Never once did he use the word *kidnap*."

"But that *is* what he expected—I mean, it's what you're doing. Right?" For that she got a one-shoulder shrug. She sat forward. "But why didn't he at least call me? Why couldn't he ask me himself?"

"Highness, you ask of one who has no answers. As I told you before, a king doesn't concern himself with 'whys' when giving orders to his warrior. Your father has said that all will be revealed to you in time and His Majesty is a man of his word."

"But I don't—"

"Your Highness." Those frosty blue eyes had a warning gleam in them now.

"Hmm?" She gave him bright, sweet smile.

He looked as if a series of crude Norse oaths was scrolling through his mind. He said softly, "Patience is a quality to be prized in a woman. It would serve you well to exercise a little of it."

In a pig's eye. "Think about this, Hauk. Just think about it. My father told you he would prefer that I went willingly. And I am seriously considering doing just that."

"You're considering."

"Yes. I am. I truly am."

He might be the strong, silent type, but he wasn't any fool. He knew where this was headed. He said bleakly, "You're considering, but there is a condition."

"That's right. And it's a perfectly reasonable one. I want you to call my father and let me talk to him."

Chapter Three

She wanted to talk to her father.

Hauk couldn't believe it. The woman was too wily by half. She'd led him in circles until she had him right where she wanted him—with his head spinning. And then she'd made the one demand he wasn't sure he could refuse.

It was removing the gag that had done it. He never should have made such a fool's move. But his lord had tied his hands—as surely as Hauk had tied *hers*.

Bring her, but do it gently. Coax her, but use force if you must.

The instructions were a tangle of foggy contradictions. And that put Hauk in the position of abducting her—and also having to listen to whatever she had to say.

The cursed woman was still talking. "Hauk, come

on. I know you have to have a way to get in touch with him—a beeper? A phone number? A hotline to Isenhalla? It's so simple, don't you see? I want you to call the number, or whatever it is, and let me speak with my father.''

Hauk didn't know what to do, so he did nothing. He sat still in the chair and said not a word.

Silence and stillness didn't save him. Princess Elli rattled on. ''My father wants me to come to him, period. But first and foremost, he hopes I'll come to him voluntarily. And that's perfectly understandable that he would want that—any father would, after all. And if a phone call will do that, will make me agree to go, then wouldn't it be my father's will that you call him and let me speak with him?''

Why wouldn't the infernal woman shut up? Though Hauk had never before questioned the actions of his king, how, by the ravens of Odin, could he help but question them now?

The king's orders echoed in his head. First *ask* the woman to come—and then force her if she refuses. And don't forget—be gentle about it.

The king must have believed that she *would* refuse, or else why send his warrior to get her? Perhaps if she'd had need of a bodyguard...

But there had been no mention of an outside threat. Therefore, if His Majesty had truly believed the girl might come willingly, he would have chosen someone other than a fighting man to fetch her, someone with a honeyed tongue, someone who knew how to coax and cajole, someone who could outtalk the woman sitting opposite him now.

"First and foremost," the irritating princess repeated for at least the tenth time, "he wanted me to *want* to come. So what could it cost you to call? Nothing. But if you *don't* call, and later my father learns that all I wanted to come voluntarily was a chance to—"

"All right."

Elli couldn't believe her ears. Was he saying what she thought he was saying? Had she actually gotten through to him? She gaped at him. "Uh. You mean, you will? You'll call him?"

He had that black bag right beside him. He reached into it and pulled out a small electronic device—it looked like some kind of beeper. He punched some buttons on the face of the thing, stared at it for maybe fifteen seconds and tucked it back in the bag.

And then he straightened in the chair and stared straight ahead.

Elli couldn't stand it. "What did you just do? What is happening?"

He waited a nerve-shattering count of five before he answered, "I have contacted your father. Unless something unexpected keeps him from it, he will be calling here within the hour."

Forty-three minutes later, the phone rang. Elli leaped to her feet at the sound, jostling the cats, who shot from the couch and streaked off down the hall.

"Wait," the Viking commanded.

"But I—"

"Stay where you are."

Every nerve in her body thrumming with excruciating anticipation, Elli stayed put. The Viking went to the phone. He checked the call waiting display and then picked it up. "FitzWyborn here...yes, my lord. She is here. She has agreed to come with me, on the condition that she might speak to you first. Yes, my lord. As you will." Hauk held out the phone to her. "Your father will speak with you, Princess Elli."

Elli could not move.

That bizarre feeling of unreality had returned, freezing her where she stood. Surely this was all a dream. The father she had never known couldn't actually be on the other end of that line. And, now that she thought about it, how could she possibly be certain that the man waiting to speak with her wasn't an imposter? Hauk said the caller was her father, but his saying it didn't necessarily make it so.

The Viking strode toward her. When he reached her, he opened his hand. On top of the blue-and-gold lightning bolt lay her phone. She took it, put it to her ear.

"Hello?" It came out sounding awful, whispery and weak.

"Elli." The voice on the other end was gentle and deep. "Little Old Giant," the voice said, so tenderly.

Little Old Giant. Nobody called her that. Nobody. Except her mother, when she was a child...

"You're my Little Old Giant, Elli, that's what you are."

"No, Mommy. I'm not a giant. I'm way too small."

"But your name is a myth name. A name from the old, old stories that are told in the land where you were born."

"In Gullandria, Mommy?"

"That's right. In Gullandria. And in Gullandria, they tell the story of Elli, the giantess. Elli was a very old giantess—so old, she was old age itself. The Thunder god, Thor, was tricked into fighting her, though everyone knows..."

"You can't fight old age," Elli said softly into the phone.

Her father—and she knew it was her father now—laughed. He had a good, strong laugh. A kind laugh, warm and sure. He said, "Ah. Your mother has taught you something, at least, of who you are."

Elli felt the tears. They burned behind her eyes, pushed at the back of her throat. Hauk had returned to his chair, but his ice-blue gaze was on her.

She looked away, dashed at her damp eyes and asked her father, "If you wanted to see me, why did you have to do it this way?"

"I need you to come, Elli. Please. Come with Hauk. *Trust* Hauk. He will never harm you and he will keep you safe. Let him bring you to me."

"Father." So strange. To be speaking to him, at last, after all these years. "You haven't answered my question."

There was a silence from the other end of the line. Elli heard static, in the background, thought of the thousands of miles of distance between her life, here, at home in Sacramento and her father, on the island of her birth in the Norwegian Sea. What time was it there? Late at night, she thought. Was he in bed as he talked to her, or fully dressed in some high-ceilinged study or huge palace drawing room?

He spoke again. "I have lost two sons. Is it so very strange that I would yearn to meet at last a daughter of my blood?"

"But why didn't you just call me, ask me?"

"Would you have said yes?"

It was a question she couldn't have answered five minutes ago—but that was before she heard his sad, kind voice calling her by the special name only he and her mother knew.

"I would have," she said firmly. "In a heartbeat, I would have said yes."

Hearing his voice did not, by any means, make everything all right. There remained great hurt in her heart, and bitterness, too. He had, after all, treated her and her sisters as disposable children. She knew something terrible had happened, all those years ago, between him and her mother, to make them carve their family in two, to send her mother fleeing back home to America with her three baby princesses, leaving her sons behind. Elli and her sisters had tried, over and over, to find out what had caused the awful rift. But their mother would not say.

Elli turned again toward the Viking sitting in her easy chair. She gave him her most defiant stare. Really, what was this crazy kidnapping plot of her father's, if not his misguided way of fighting for a chance to make things right in their family at last? She *wanted* to go now, to meet her father face-to-face, to see the land of her birth. As it stood now, Hauk would have had to lock her up and throw away the key to *keep* her from going.

Her father said dryly, "Perhaps I was in error, not to call first."

"You certainly were," she chided him. "And what about Liv and Brit? Are you having them kidnapped, too?"

"No, Elli." She could hear the humor in his voice. "Only you."

"Why only me?"

He chuckled. "As a baby, you had curious eyes. I see some things haven't changed."

"So far, you're just like this refugee from the WWE you sent here to strong-arm me." She glared all the harder at Hauk and then accused into the phone, "You keep evading all my questions."

"Come to me. You will know all."

"That's what *he* keeps saying." *He* didn't so much as blink. He was doing what he always did, sitting utterly still, staring steadily back at her.

Her father coaxed in her ear, "Elli, I do long to see your face, to talk with you at length, to get to know you, at least a little…."

Her throat closed up again. She swallowed. "I said I would come. I meant it."

"Good then."

"But first—"

Even through the static, she heard her father sigh. "I don't think I like the sound of that."

"Father, be reasonable. I can't just…disappear. I have a life and my life deserves consideration. I have to get someone to feed my cats and water my plants. I have to call my principal at school, arrange for some family leave. And I have to see Mom and tell her—"

''Not your mother.'' Her father's voice was suddenly cold as the steel blade of Hauk's knife. ''Absolutely no.'' It was a command.

Too bad. ''There is no way I'm disappearing without explaining to her what I'm doing. She would be frantic, terrified for me. I could never put her through something like that.''

''If Ingrid knows where you're going she'll never allow it.''

''You don't know that for certain—and besides, Mom doesn't tell me what I can or can't do.''

''I do know for certain. I've already approached her on this issue. She flatly refused me.''

That was news to Elli—big news. ''You spoke with Mom about my coming to see you?''

''I did.''

''When?''

''A few days ago.''

''You...you *called* her? On the phone?''

''I did.''

''But you two haven't spoken in—''

''A very long time.''

''She hasn't said a word to me about it.''

''I don't find that in the least surprising.'' Her father's voice wasn't as icy as a moment ago—but there remained a distinct chill in it.

''I don't understand.''

''It's quite simple. I called your mother. I asked that she send you and your sisters for a visit. She refused. I tried to get through to her. I pointed out that I'm your father, that I've waited all these years and I have a right to know my daughters. She wouldn't listen. She told me that you and your sisters wanted nothing to do with me, that I was to leave you alone and stay out of your lives. And then she hung up on me.''

Elli knew for certain now that she wouldn't leave Sacramento before she'd had a serious talk with her mother. ''Father.'' The word still felt strange in her mouth. ''I'm an adult, past the age when my mother decides what I can or can't do. I make my own plans. And I plan to come and visit you. It's Monday night. Give me two days. By Thursday morning at the latest, I will be on a plane, on my way to Gullandria.'' She added, with a meaningful glance at the Viking sitting still as a statue across from her, ''You have my word of honor on that.''

There was a silence on the other end. Even the static stopped. And then her father said thoughtfully, ''Your word of honor...''

''Yes. My word of honor.''

''Put Hauk on.''

She felt irritation rising. ''Why do you need to talk to—''

''Please, Elli. Put him on.''

Elli marched over to the Viking. ''Here. Tell him my word of honor can be trusted.''

He took the phone. ''Yes, my lord...yes...yes, I do...'' He listened. His face remained expressionless, but something in the set of his jaw told her he didn't much care for whatever he was hearing. ''Yes, Your Majesty,'' he said at last and gave her the phone back.

She spoke to her father again. ''Satisfied?''

Her father answered calmly. "I think we have an agreement."

"We do?"

"That's right, my daughter. Speak with your mother if you must. And be on that plane by Thursday morning."

Elli smiled. "Great. Thank you, Father. I'm looking forward to seeing you at last."

"And I'm looking forward to seeing *you*." His voice was tender again. "So very much." Then he added offhandedly, "Hauk will stay with you. He'll see you safely to my side."

The Viking was still staring at her. Elli spun away from him, stalked back to the couch and plunked down onto it. She sent a fulminating glance across the room before she muttered into the phone, "You have my word. There's no need for—"

"Elli. He stays with you." Her father's tone was flat. Final.

She could speak flatly, too. "You know what this tells me, Father? You don't trust my word."

His tone softened and acquired a wheedling note. "Humor an old man. Please."

Her father was in his early fifties. Old, by Elli's standards—but not *that* old. "Oh, stop. I know you're working me."

"This is one point on which I cannot back down." He was all firmness again. "Accept it. You will have the time you want to do whatever you say needs doing—including visiting your mother. But Hauk will not leave your side until he's delivered you safely into my presence."

"You think Mom is going to talk me out of coming, don't you?"

"I do."

"She won't. I swear it."

"Better safe than sorry. I do, after all, know your mother."

She looked across at Hauk again. Till Thursday—and beyond—with him right there, watching, every time she turned around. "I'm really not happy about this."

"It's my only condition." He said it as if it were a tiny thing—something so inconsequential, it meant next to nothing. "Accept it and we'll find ourselves in perfect agreement."

Elli said goodbye to her father and immediately called her mother. She made that call brief. She wanted to speak to Ingrid in person about her trip—and about the call Ingrid had received from her father, the one Ingrid had failed to mention up till now.

"Are you all right?" her mother asked. "You seem…pensive."

Elli glanced across the room. Hauk was still there, in the chair, looking on.

Might as well get used to it, she told herself. She reassured her mother that she was fine and made a date with her—dinner at Ingrid's house in Land Park the next night.

After her mother, Elli managed to reach her principal at home. She spoke—somewhat vaguely—of a family emergency, said she had to leave within a couple of days. Her boss was far from pleased. Elli was in her first year with her own classes and didn't have a lot of leave built up.

He said that yes, he would call the district for her and get someone to start tomorrow. Then he asked the logical question, "How long will you be gone?"

Unreality smacked her flat again. She hadn't even considered how long her trip might last.

But it couldn't be *that* long. It was a visit. A visit lasted… "Three weeks," she said, getting up and going to have a look at her kitchen calendar. "I'll be back and in my classroom by the twenty-seventh." At least that way, she'd be there for the final two weeks of school. She reassured him that her lesson plans were all in good order. The substitute should have no trouble figuring things out. But should a problem arise, Elli would be in town for a day or two. The sub could give her a call.

Somewhat grouchily, her boss wished her well. She realized, as she hung up the phone, that this trip could possibly cost her her job.

Elli was fortunate, and she knew it. She didn't need the money. Her mother was, after all, a Freyasdahl. And anyone with any awareness of who was who in California knew that being a Freyasdahl meant you had money—and lots of it. Elli could live quite comfortably on the proceeds from her trust. But she loved teaching and she took pride in her work. It bothered her to think she was letting her school—and especially her two classes of kindergartners—down.

She glanced over, saw Hauk again, huge, bemuscled and implacable.

Well. She'd made a promise and she would keep it. Might as well put a bright face on it.

She flashed the Viking a big, fake smile. Those golden brows drew together and he looked at her sideways, his chiseled face set in suspicious lines.

"Tell you what," she said, so cheerfully it grated on her *own* nerves. "You just make yourself right at home." She dared to get close enough to grab her suitcase from where it waited, upright, beside him. "And if you don't mind, I think I'd prefer to do my packing for myself." She turned and marched away from him down the hall.

In her bedroom, she hoisted the suitcase onto the bed. She left it there, unopened, and went into her bathroom, where she took care to engage the privacy lock.

She planned to use the toilet, but somehow she found herself leaning over the sink, staring at herself in the mirror. Her eyes looked huge and haunted. Her face was too pale, except for the cartoon-red splotches of hectic color high on her cheeks.

"I want to go and meet my father," she told her slightly stupefied reflection. "I *want* to do this." At the same time, she was still having serious trouble believing any of it was really happening. Not long ago, she'd been carrying her groceries up the stairs, humming a tune that had been playing on the radio in the car, thinking about what she'd fix for dinner.

Now everything was changed. She was going to Gullandria.

She used the toilet, washed her hands, brushed her

hair and got another long, cool drink of water from the tap. She put on fresh lip gloss.

And then she went out to face the Viking—which happened sooner than she expected, as she found him standing beside her bed.

She shrieked in outrage. "Get out!"

"Princess, it is not my intention to frighten you."

It was too much—him here, in her bedroom. She made shooing motions with both hands and shouted, "Out, out, out!"

"Silence!" he boomed back, then reminded her, way too softly, "Remember your promise. No loud noises."

She lowered her voice to a furious whisper. "That was before, when you were kidnapping me. Now you are merely my...escort. And I want you out of my room."

Instead of leaving, he came toward her. Those huge, heavily muscled legs were so long, it only took about a step and a half.

She wasn't afraid of him—she *wasn't*. But she couldn't stop herself from shrinking out of his path when faced with all that size and power coming right at her. He was so tall that the hair at the crown of his head brushed the top of the doorframe as he entered her bathroom.

She moved into the doorway behind him, folding her arms across her middle to keep her fists from punching something. "What in God's name are you doing?"

He didn't even bother to answer her, just started checking things out, opening the slatted pebbled-glass window and peering down at the carports, looking in her cabinets at her towels and extra bars of soap, sweeping back the shower curtain to view the tub.

"What, you think I've got someone hidden in the tub? You think I'm planning to bust out—just take all the slats out of that window and jump onto the hood of somebody's Jetta? Oh, puh-lease."

Apparently, he had finished his invasion of her privacy, because he stood still, facing her. "My orders are to guard you closely, Princess—to stay at your side at all times, to see that you don't change your mind about your agreement with His Majesty. I'm doing that and only that. You came in here very quickly. I felt it wise to find out if there was some reason for your haste."

"I came in here quickly because I had to go to the bathroom. Is that a problem for you, if I go to the bathroom?"

"No, Princess." He stood with that huge chest thrust out, shoulders back, his arms tight to his sides, a soldier at attention.

"And let's back up here for a minute. Is that really what my father told you, to…*guard me closely, to stay at my side all the time?*"

"Yes, Princess."

"I think I'm going to have to talk to my father again."

The Viking didn't move.

"Did you hear me? I said, contact my father again. I wish to speak with him."

"I'm sorry, Your Highness. I can't do that."

"Sure you can. Just go get that beeper thingy and—"

"Princess."

"What?"

"Your father told me he didn't wish to be disturbed again. He said he was certain you'd think of an endless list of new questions as soon as you hung up the phone. He told me to tell you he would answer them all—"

She knew the rest. "When I see him in Gullandria."

"That is correct, Prin—"

"Hauk."

"Yes, your—"

"If you call me princess—or Your Highness—one more time, I think I'm going to forget all about my promise and my honor and start screaming. Then you'll have to tie me up again and that will make me very, very angry. And you don't really want me angry, now, do you?"

"No, P—" He caught himself just in time. "No."

"Well, all right then. Don't call me Your Highness and don't call me princess."

"As you wish."

"And now, will you please get out of my bedroom?"

"If you'll come with me."

She threw up both hands. "All right, all right. Let's go."

Elli went straight to the kitchen. It was almost eight by then and her stomach was making insistent growling sounds.

Of course, Hauk followed right behind her. That was okay, she supposed. She'd resigned herself to feeding him, too.

"Sit down," she told him and threw out a hand in the direction of the table. "Over there."

He took the chair that put his back to the wall. He could see down the hall and into the living room and, of course, he had a clear view of her activities in the kitchen. The man certainly took his duties seriously. How did he do it? So much watchfulness had to wear a person out.

She pulled open the refrigerator and stared at the chicken she'd brought home to roast. It would be enough for both of them, but it would also take almost two hours in the oven.

No. She was hungry *now*.

She considered a quick trip to Mickey D's or Taco Bell.

But then again, it wasn't as if she'd be allowed to just jump in her car and go. The king's warrior would have to be consulted. They'd have to wrangle over whether she could go at all. Then, if he allowed it, he'd insist on going with her. He'd decide who would drive—she was betting on herself. That way he'd have his hands free to deal with her if she broke her word and tried to leap to freedom from the moving vehicle. Then there'd be the question of whether she could actually be trusted to speak to the order taker at the drive-up window....

Uh-uh. Fast food was a no-go.

Elli tried the freezer. Ah. A pair of DiGiornos. Perfect. She glanced at the huge man in her kitchen chair again and decided she'd better cook both the three-meat *and* the deluxe.

When she set a plate before him, he frowned. "It is not necessary that you cook for me."

And what was he planning to eat if she didn't?

Better not even get into it. "It's nothing fancy—pizza and a salad. Just eat it, okay?"

He dipped his shaggy golden head. "Thank you, Pr—" He stifled the P-word, barely. "Uh. Thank you."

"You're welcome."

She had a nice bottle of chardonnay chilling. She'd grabbed it at the supermarket, thinking she'd have a glass with her roast chicken. She decided to open it now. She needed *something* to help get her through the night.

Elli set out two glasses, but when she tried to pour one for Hauk, he put his great big hand over the mouth of it. Well, fine, she thought. Be that way. More for me. She filled her own glass to the brim and sat opposite him. They ate in silence. Elli indulged in a second glass of wine.

She was feeling pleasantly hazy when she got up to put the dishes in the dishwasher. Hauk rose with her. He helped her clear off, and actually took the sponge and began wiping the counters as she rinsed the plates and put them in the dishwasher. She turned and looked at him, sponging her table, carefully guiding the pizza crumbs into his massive paw of a hand—and she couldn't help it. A goofy giggle escaped her.

He straightened—still holding the crumbs cupped in his hand—and turned to her. "You find me humorous?"

"I...uh..." She waved a hand. "Never mind. It's nothing."

He came toward her. Maybe it was the wine, but for the first time, she didn't feel particularly menaced by the sight of all that muscle moving her way. She stepped back a fraction, so he could brush the crumbs into the sink. Then she took the spray attachment and rinsed them down the drain. He handed her the sponge. She rinsed it, wrung the water from it and set it in the wire basket under the sink.

"Well," she said. "That's that."

He nodded. And then he just stood there—awaiting orders, she supposed.

It was 8:50. A little early for bed under ordinary circumstances. But ordinary had nothing at all to do with tonight. She wanted some time to herself, for Pete's sake, a few hours without the ever-watchful eyes of the king's warrior tracking her every move. And the only way to get that was to say good-night and shut her bedroom door.

"Listen." She tried a smile on him.

He gave her another nod.

She told him, "I'm just going to make up the futon in the spare room for you. You'll find fresh towels in the cabinet to the right of the sink in the hall bathroom. And if you want to watch a little television, the living room is all yours—oh, and if you get hungry, hey, if I've got it, you can eat it."

He just stood there, looking at her. She knew with absolute certainty he had something to tell her that she wasn't going to like.

"What?" she demanded.

"Your intention is that I sleep in your extra room and you sleep in your own bedroom."

"Something wrong with that?"

"It appears you haven't clearly understood the agreement you made with His Majesty."

She backed up a step, slapped a hand down on the counter tiles and glared at him sideways. "What are you talking about? I agreed to go visit him. I agreed that you could hang around in my apartment until it's time to go, keeping an eye on me so I won't change my mind. I agreed that you would be my escort to Gullandria."

"Yes, all that is correct."

"Good. So we know what I agreed to. And I'm going to bed." She moved forward. He *didn't* move aside. "Hauk. If you don't tell me what is going on here…" She let the threat trail off, mostly because she couldn't think of anything sufficiently terrible to threaten him *with*.

"All right," he growled. He looked especially bleak right then. "His Majesty instructed me to watch over you at all times. That means wherever you sleep, I sleep as well."

Chapter Four

"That's the most ridiculous thing I ever heard," the princess announced. "I never agreed to sleep with you. My father never said a word about my sleeping with you." She shook her head as if to clear it. "Why would my father want me to sleep with you?"

Hauk realized she'd drawn an erroneous conclusion. "Of course you would not sleep *with* me. But whatever room you sleep in—I will be there, also."

She blinked, and then she said, very slowly, "You think you're going to sleep in my room."

"It is of no consequence to me what room I sleep in. I'm merely informing you that it will be the same room as the room in which you sleep."

"But I don't... Did he *say* that to you, did he actually say you had to sleep in the same room with me?"

"He said not to let you out of my sight."

"Ah." She slapped the counter again. "But you did, remember? You let me out of your sight when I went to the bathroom and nothing happened. I'm still here."

By the runes, he hated arguing with this woman. She was too clever by half. "You have a right to your privacy, when it comes to…private matters. But not for hours. There are windows in every room. Given time, you could easily find a way to escape without my knowing it."

"But I *won't* escape. I gave you my word that I wouldn't."

"And I am ordered by my king to make certain that you keep your word."

Those proud slim shoulders slumped. She looked away. "I'm not going to win this one, am I?"

He wanted to say, *No, Your Highness.* But she had forbidden him the use of her title.

He also wanted to say he regretted this—all of it. But she had ordered him to stop apologizing.

And he might as well admit she was right—not about his addressing her properly. He didn't like the familiarity she was forcing on him by making him drop the appropriate form of address. But as to his regrets, well, they had no more value than a promise made by Loki, the god of dirty tricks.

It was what a man did that mattered, not what came out of his mouth. And what Hauk would do was continue to follow the orders of his king.

She asked, sounding forlorn, "Will you at least leave me alone while I take a bath?"

Hauk allowed her the bath.

But she couldn't relax. She lay in the scented water, thinking of the huge man waiting on the other side of the door, knowing that if she stayed in there too long, he'd be busting in to see what trouble she'd gotten into now. After ten minutes or so, before the water even started to cool, she got out, toweled dry, pulled on her pink sleep shirt, and quickly brushed her teeth.

He was waiting in the middle of her bedroom. He'd found some blankets and a pillow and laid them out on the carpet at the foot of her bed. Her suitcase was still there, on the bed where she'd tossed it, full of whatever he'd chosen to put in it while she lay, drugged and bound, on the couch in the living room.

"I took bedding from your closet in the hallway," he said, his head tipped down, as if he expected a reprimand.

Who cared if the man borrowed a blanket? He could borrow a hundred blankets—if he'd only take them in the spare room to sleep on them.

Elli crossed her arms over her chest—a gesture of self-protection. All of a sudden, she felt way too naked, though her sleep shirt was baggy and reached almost to her knees. She stared at the Viking, biting her lip.

Maybe she could bear it, having him in her bedroom all night, if he wasn't quite so…masculine. He was very controlled, but still testosterone seemed to ooze from every pore. And then there were all those hard, bulging muscles…

Elli hugged herself tighter and looked away from him. She stared at her suitcase.

He must have noted the direction of her gaze. "You wish to do your packing now?"

A shiver slid beneath the surface of her skin. It was all so eerie. He was her jailer. And yet, at the same time, he behaved like a loyal servant, ready to do her bidding before she even told him what her bidding was.

"No, I'll do it later. I have until Thursday, remember?" It was something of a dig. Even if he *had* almost kidnapped her, he seemed, at heart, a noble, straight-ahead kind of guy. He probably didn't like sleeping at the foot of her bed any more than she liked having him there. No doubt he hoped she'd make their time in forced proximity as short as possible, that she'd be ready to head for Gullandria as soon as she'd had that talk with her mother—tomorrow night, or Wednesday morning at the latest.

Well, okay. Maybe she *would* be ready to leave before Thursday. And maybe it would please him to know that. But pleasing the Viking in her bedroom was the last thing on her mind right then.

Stone-faced as usual, he lifted the suitcase off the bed and carried it over to set it against the wall. She smelled toothpaste as he went past. Sometime during her too-short, not-at-all-relaxing bath, he must have brushed his teeth.

What a truly odd image: the Viking in her guest bath, with a toothbrush in his mouth, scrubbing away. Somehow, when she thought of Vikings, she never imagined them brushing their teeth. Did he floss, as well? She supposed he must. Everything about him shouted physical fitness. He had to be proactive when it came to his health. Proper dental hygiene would be part of the package.

He marched by her again and returned to stand at attention near his pallet of blankets. "Do you wish to sleep now?"

As if. "In a minute. First, I need to lock up."

Before she could turn for the door, he said, "I've already done that."

"Surprise, surprise." She went to the bed and slid under the covers. Doodles and Diablo, with that radar cats seem to have for the moment when their human has settled into a soft, inviting place, appeared in the doorway to the hall. "Well, come on," she told them, and reached for the remote, which waited on her nightstand.

The cats settled in. She turned on the TV in the corner—okay, Feng Shui, it wasn't. But Elli didn't care. She loved to watch TV in bed with her cats cuddled close around her.

And a favorite program was in progress. *Law and Order: Criminal Intent.* Vincent D'Onofrio had the perp in the interrogation room and was psyching him out with skill and subtlety.

And the Viking was still standing there—awaiting orders, she supposed.

"Hauk. Go to bed."

He nodded and dropped to his blankets. A minute later, he was stretched out beneath the top blanket, his boots and belt a foot or two away. She wondered briefly where he kept that black switchblade knife when he slept—but then she told herself that where Hauk FitzWyborn kept his knife was no concern of hers. She watched the rest of her program, and after that turned to an old movie on TCM.

At the foot of the bed, Hauk lay utterly still. She could swear he hadn't moved since he crawled beneath the blanket over an hour ago.

When the movie ended, Elli switched off the television. The room seemed so very quiet. She could hear Doodles purring—and nothing else.

Could the Viking have died?

Hah. No such luck.

Had he fallen asleep? It certainly seemed that way. What a thrilling development. Hauk. Dead to the world. Dreaming whatever a Viking warrior dreamed, and for once—since the moment she'd walked in her door that afternoon—not guarding her.

Why, she might do anything. She might get up and go in the kitchen all by herself. Might walk out on the balcony and look up at the stars. Might go down the steps and along the walk and get in her car and…go for a drive.

And not to run away, not to break her word. Oh, no. Simply because she *could.*

She'd return later, after he woke and found her gone. He would be frantic. Old stone face. Freaking out.

Ah, yes. How lovely…

Elli rearranged the cats a little, pushing them gently to the side so they wouldn't be disturbed when she slid from the bed. Then she switched off the lamp and lay back to wait awhile. She could see the glowing

numerals on her bedside digital alarm clock. She'd
wait half an hour. And if she still heard nothing, she
was out of here.

Okay, maybe it was pointless and a little bit childish. But this whole situation deeply offended her. To
show that she *could* leave if she wanted to would be
something of an object lesson—to Hauk, and by ex-
tension, to her father. And maybe, if she left and came
back of her own accord, Hauk would realize it wasn't
necessary to take the orders of his king so literally.
Maybe, by tomorrow night, she'd have her bedroom
to herself.

The time passed slowly. She used it to consider her
next move. Should she creep to the foot of the bed
and have a look at him, see if he truly was in lullaby
land?

Uh-uh. No point in tempting fate—not to mention
squeaky bedsprings. Better just to ease out from under
the covers and tiptoe to the door. If it turned out he'd
been lying there for hours, stone still and awake,
she'd find out soon enough.

The minutes crawled by. There was nothing but
silence from the man at the foot of her bed.

At last, that endless half hour was behind her.

Slowly, so *quietly,* Elli eased back the covers. In
one careful, unbroken move, she swung her feet out
and over the edge of the bed. She slid her weight onto
them without a single spring creaking. Doodles,
sound asleep by then, didn't even open an eye. Diablo
lifted his sleek head, blinked at her, then laid his head
down again.

Good. Perfect. Wonderful.

Elli turned and started for the door to the hall. She was utterly silent. She wasn't even *breathing*. She made it into the open doorway.

"Where are you going?"

Elli gasped and whirled to face him. He was standing beside his blankets, watching her. She could have sworn he had never moved, never so much as *stirred*.

She gulped. "Uh, well…ice water! You know, I really want some ice water."

The big golden head dipped once—in permission, in acknowledgment, in who the heck knew what? Elli yanked her shoulders back and headed for the kitchen. She heard nothing behind her. But she didn't have to turn and look to know that he had followed.

Eventually, very late in the night, she finally dropped off to sleep. She woke after daylight to the sound of birds twittering in the forest: her alarm clock. Brit had given it to her a couple of Christmases ago. It made nature sounds instead of beeping or buzzing. Elli reached over and punched the off button. The cats were already off the bed and racing down the hall.

And the Viking…

All she could see from the head of the bed was the edge of his blankets. "Uh, Hauk?"

No answer.

He'd proven last night that he could hear her even if she didn't make a sound. So he must be up, or he would have answered. She pushed back the covers and scrambled to the bottom of the bed, where she found his blankets neatly folded, his pillow on top of the stack.

Boots, belt and man were gone.

Could it be? Had he really left—due to second thoughts on her father's part, maybe? Had Osrik beeped him late in the night, told Hauk to back off, that his daughter had given her word and the king had decided to trust her to find her way to Gullandria on her own?

The idea warmed her heart. Her father had faced a basic truth, apparently. He'd seen that in order to begin healing the awful breach in their family, he must *trust,* first and foremost, he must—

"You called for me?"

Hauk stood in the doorway to the hall, bare-chested, a half beard of shaving cream frothed over one sculpted cheek. She couldn't help gaping at his shoulders and arms, so big and hard, the muscles bulging and taut, the skin so tan and perfect, except for the occasional white ridge of scar tissue.

And his chest...

It was covered with beautiful, savage tattoos.

A lightning bolt like the one in his right palm, only much bigger, zigzagged across his bulging pectorals. Dragons and vines twisted and twined around it—and around the sword and dagger tattooed above and below it. The tail of the largest dragon trailed down his solar plexus to his navel.

His belly took her breath away. She'd never seen one like it—at least not outside of ab-machine info-mercials and superhero video games.

Elli gulped and dragged her gaze up to meet those

watching eyes. "Uh. Yes." Carefully, tugging on her sleep shirt that had ridden up much too high, she rocked back so she sat on her knees. She tipped her chin to a proud angle and tried to look dignified, though she knew her cheeks were tomato-red. "I...didn't see you," she stuttered lamely. "I was wondering where you'd gone."

He lifted an eyebrow and held up a thoroughly modern cartridge-type razor. She stared at it for a moment, thinking that it looked toylike and strange in his big hand. But what had she expected, that he'd shave with his black-handled knife?

"As you see, I am here. Anything else?"

"No. That's all." She gave him a backhanded wave of dismissal. "Go on and, uh, finish up."

Elli dressed and made breakfast for both of them. Once they'd cleared off the table, she returned to the bedroom, Hauk close behind. He sat in the corner chair as she unpacked her suitcase.

When she was finished, she set it, empty, back against the wall.

"When will you pack?"

She looked at him, surprised to hear his voice. He'd said hardly a word since she'd called him, half-shaved, from the bathroom earlier. "I'll get to it. I have plenty of time."

He didn't say anything more, but she knew he didn't like it, that it bugged him, big-time, to think she might insist on hanging around in Sacramento till the last possible minute on Thursday. Baby-sitting a princess was not his idea of a good time and he wanted to get it over and done with, ASAP.

Too bad. Let him be bugged. Let him wait and wonder when she would end their constant togetherness and agree to get on the plane for Gullandria. It might be petty—really, really *small* of her, to torture him when he was only following orders.

But he ought to know better than to follow such orders as the ones her father had given him. He ought to stand up and say, *My lord, I'm taking a pass on playing watchdog to your daughter. It's beneath me and beneath her and I'm not going to do it.*

He hadn't said that, or anything like it. So let him sleep at the foot of her bed and stand by the bathroom door whenever she went in there and march along beside her if she dared to go outside. Served him right, as far as she was concerned.

Elli called a girlfriend, Barb Ferris, at the insurance office where Barb worked. She made that call on speakerphone, at Hauk's insistence that he be able to hear both sides of her conversation.

Barb agreed to water Elli's plants, to bring in her mail and newspapers and keep an eye on her apartment. Barb even offered to feed Doodles and Diablo, but Elli said she'd get back to her on that. She was hoping to get her mother to take the cats. Barb said sure, she'd tell the other girls that Elli was taking off for a few weeks and would miss their girls' night out on Friday. When Barb asked her what was up, Elli said it was a family issue.

"Honest, Barb. It's nothing too serious. I'll be back in three weeks. Thanks a bunch for helping me out."

Next, Elli called Ned Handly, her date for Saturday night. Ned was a doctor, in family practice. They'd met through a mutual friend and Saturday would have been their second date. Hauk stood a couple of feet away, wearing his usual carved-granite expression, as she told Ned she was going away for a while.

Ned said, with real regret, "I was looking forward to this weekend."

Elli glared at Hauk. You'd think he'd have the courtesy to let her break her date in peace. But no. He had to loom right beside her, listening to every word, every disappointed sigh.

"I was, too," Elli told Ned. "I hope you'll give me a rain check."

"I thought you'd never ask. A family trip, huh?" Elli had given him no details—and not because the stone-faced Viking standing next to her might not approve. News like this would travel fast, and she wanted to be the one to break it to her mother.

Her friends often used her title teasingly, calling her "the princess," and "Your Highness." They all thought she was so wonderfully *unusual,* one of three triplet princesses, her estranged father a king in some faraway northern land. As soon as one of them heard she was off for a visit to Gullandria, they'd burn up the phone lines sharing the scoop. Her mother might get wind of it before tonight. Someone might even let something drop to the tabloids.

Then the stinky stuff would really hit the fan.

So she was keeping the details to herself. "Yes, a family thing. But I'll give you a call as soon as I get back."

"Elli?"

"Hmm?"

"You take care."

"I will." She disconnected the call and wrinkled her nose at the big guy in black. "Well, now, wasn't that innocuous and aren't you glad you heard every word?"

Hauk said nothing. He just stood there, waiting for her to make her next move.

She realized she didn't *have* a move. No one had called from the school or the district, so presumably the sub had been contacted and was, at that moment, teaching Elli's morning class, managing just fine with the lesson plans Elli had left open on her desk.

Except for packing and dealing with her mother, Elli was ready to go.

And it was only ten in the morning—ten in the morning on *Tuesday*. She looked at Hauk, who gazed steadily back at her.

Elli sighed. "Oh, Hauk. What in the world am I going to do with you?"

"Pack your belongings," he suggested softly. "His Majesty's jet awaits you. As soon as you've spoken with your mother, we can be on our way."

Chapter Five

Elli didn't pack. Her father had agreed to give her till Thursday and, for the time being anyway, she was keeping that option open. She wasn't sure why. Maybe it was simply because, with Hauk shadowing her every move, it felt like the only option she had.

She went to the spare room, where she kept her computer. Hauk sat at attention on her futon while she surfed the Net for a while and fiddled with e-mail. Then, for an hour or so, she made a valiant effort to get a little reading done.

But it was no good. She kept feeling those cool, careful eyes on her. She couldn't concentrate on a book.

They had lunch at one. By then she was aching for a little ordinary conversation. Over BLTs she tried to engage him in a nice, friendly chat.

He was the master of the one-line reply. He'd get it down to a single word if he could, or better still, a low, unpromising sound in his throat. She got a number of curt noes, a lonely little yes or two and a whole lot of gruff grunts.

Finally, she asked him about his family. "Do you have brothers—or sisters?"

"No."

"And your mother and father?"

He just looked at her.

"Your parents, are they still alive?"

"No."

"Both gone?"

"That's correct."

Well, she couldn't say she was surprised. It seemed hard to picture that he'd ever even had a father or a mother. With his huge, hard, smooth chest and his infomercial abs, his deadpan expression and his lightning-bolt tattoos, Hauk FitzWyborn seemed someone not quite mortal—someone who had never been something so vulnerable as a little boy with parents who loved him. He seemed more like a creature sprung from the Norse myths, like Odin, Vili and Ve, brought into being out of ice.

"Um, your father? Tell me about him."

He gave her the lifted-eyebrow routine.

She tried again. "What was your father like, Hauk?"

"I told you. My father is dead." He'd finished his sandwich. He stood, carried his plate and empty glass to the sink, rinsed them both and put them in the dishwasher.

She refused to give up. "I'm sorry, Hauk—that he's gone. Do you…miss him?"

He reached for the towel, dried those big hands. "He's been dead for almost a decade."

"But do you miss him?"

He hung the towel on its little hook beneath the cabinets. "You behave like an American." He made it sound like some crushing insult.

She sat up straighter in her chair. "I *am* an American."

His sculpted mouth curved. Too bad it was more a sneer than a smile. "In Gullandria, the lowliest of the low will know which questions should never be asked. In Gullandria, we do not presume to ask after the dead loved ones of people we hardly know."

Wow. Two whole sentences. The man was a chatterbox, no doubt about it. And he also had a truckload and a half of nerve, to imply that *she* was presumptuous, when he wouldn't let her make a call without listening in on her speakerphone.

She kept after him. "So. You're sensitive on the subject of your father. Why is that?"

He stood there by the sink, big and broad and silent, looking at her. But she was becoming accustomed to his eagle-eyed stare. She stared right back. And she waited.

At last, he shrugged. "My father was a Wyborn. My mother was not."

She was getting the picture. "They weren't married when you were born?"

"That's right. They were never married. I am a *fitz*. For future reference, during your stay in Gullandria, when you hear that a man's name begins with *Fitz,* you will know that man is a bastard. You might think twice before asking after his family."

"Thank you." She gave him the most regal of nods. "I'll remember that."

"The prefix *Fitz,*" he informed her in scholarly tones, "is one known to many lands. A child of King Henry the Eighth comes to mind. You've heard of Henry the Eighth, second of the Tudor kings of England?"

"Yes, Hauk," she said dryly. "Even rude Americans take history in school."

"A barmaid gave King Henry a son. The barmaid named the child for his father. Henry FitzRoy. The literal translation of *Fitz* is son of. Thus, Henry, son of—"

"—the king," she finished for him. Her mother had told her many things about her homeland. But not this painful little detail. "Is there some reason, now, in the twenty-first century, to…label a person that way?"

"In Gullandria, we treasure the family. Life can be hard and short—not so much in recent decades, since we discovered we are rich in oil and have a valuable commodity to trade for the comforts of the modern world. But it was not always so.

"Over the generations, we have learned to count on one another. Loyalty and honor always come first. Marriage is a sacred trust. Once his wife has given him children, a man cannot divorce. With so much value on the family, it is seen as an offense against the continued survival of our people to bring children into the world without the sacrament of marriage. Certain doors are always closed to bastard children.''

''But why? It's not the child's fault that his parents weren't married.''

''It's nothing to do with who is at fault. There's an old saying. *Don't bicker over blame while the house burns.*'' He came toward her. ''You have finished your meal?''

She stared up at him, feeling, for the first time, a certain softening toward him. ''What doors are closed to you, Hauk?''

He asked again, ''Have you finished?''

She looked down at the bit of uneaten sandwich. ''Sure, I'm finished. With lunch.''

He took her plate and her glass to the sink, dumped the crust in and ran the disposal. Then he rinsed her dishes and put them in the dishwasher with his.

''Hauk?''

He turned to her and folded his huge arms over his chest. The early-afternoon sun slanting in the window made his hair shine as though it were spun from real gold.

''What doors are closed to you?''

Now, instead of staring her down, he seemed to be studying her. She knew a certain feeling of warmth inside as she saw that she had found it, the key to having an actual conversation with him. If they spoke of Gullandria, if he thought he might impart to her things she would need to know as the daughter of his king, he was willing to talk.

He asked, ''Do you understand the rules of Gullandrian succession?''

"I think so." She repeated what her mother had told her long ago. "All male *jarl*—" she pronounced it *yarl,* as her mother had taught her "—and *jarl* means noble, both singular and plural—are princes, technically eligible to claim the throne when the current king dies or is no longer capable of ruling. When that happens, the jarl convene in the capital city of Lysgard and each casts a vote. The winner is the new king. The vote itself—as well as the ceremony surrounding it—is called the kingmaking."

Hauk dropped his hands to his sides. She could have sworn he almost smiled. "Very good. You have it nearly right."

"Nearly?"

"Not *all* male jarl are princes. Only all *legitimate* male jarl."

"You're saying that you, Hauk FitzWyborn, could never be king."

"That's correct. Not that I would get any real chance to be king—let alone even *want* to be king—were I legitimate in the first place. But were I not a fitz, to be chosen king would at least be a theoretical possibility."

"What about your children?"

He looked rather pleased. "Good question. As far as my children go—and still, remember, speaking theoretically—everything can be different for them."

"You mean, if you marry, then the sons your wife gives you would be eligible when the kingmaking comes around again."

"That's right—given that my wife is jarl herself."

It suddenly occurred to her that he might be married right now. That shocked her, for some reason. Nothing personal, she hurried to reassure herself silently. It wasn't about being...interested in him, as a man.

No. Of course not.

It was only that he didn't *seem* married. Just as she couldn't picture him as a vulnerable little boy with parents who took care of him, she had trouble seeing him with a wife, with children of his own.

She couldn't resist asking. "Are you? Married?"

"No. And I have no children, either. I will never have children, unless I first have a wife. That is the lesson a fitz always learns and thus, in Gullandria, bastard children are rare."

"So then," she said gently, "you'll never be king. But your children might."

"They might. But again, it's not likely. Families hold tight to ground they have gained. The sons of kings tend to become kings. They are groomed from birth with the throne in mind. Your brother, Prince Valbrand..." Hauk paused, fisted a hand at his heart and briefly bowed his head in what was clearly a gesture of respect for someone greatly valued and tragically lost. "Your brother was born to rule. He was wise beyond his years, a good and fair man. Gullandria would have prospered under him as she has thrived under His Majesty, your father." Something had happened in Hauk's cool eyes. For the first time, Elli saw that he did have a heart and that he had admired—even loved—her brother.

Her own heart contracted. "He was...good? My brother?"

"Yes. A fine man. The Gullandrian people felt pride that someday he would rule. Jarl and freeman alike knew a steady confidence in the future he would make for us all."

"And my other brother, Kylan?"

Hauk shrugged. "He was a child when we lost him. Barely in his fifth year."

"But...did you ever see him? Do you remember anything about him?"

After a thoughtful pause, he said, "Young Prince Kylan was strong and well made. He had the dark hair and eyes of the Celts—as did Prince Valbrand, as does His Majesty, your father."

Strong and well made, dark hair and eyes...

It was all so sad. Both of them, her fine, strong, dark-eyed brothers, lost now, one to a fire, one to the sea the Gullandrians loved. Lost to Elli and her shattered family. Lost to the country they might have ruled and ruled well.

Hauk approached her again. She looked up at him. "So sad..."

"Yes. A great double tragedy. For your family. For our land."

His words had so exactly echoed her thoughts. She gestured at the chair across from her. "Sit down. Please." He took the chair. "Tell me more. About Gullandria."

Hauk talked for a while, quietly. He told her that the North Atlantic drift made Gullandria's seacoasts warm for that latitude. He spoke of the famous Gullandrian horses, with their flowing white manes and long, thick white coats to protect them against the northern winters.

Elli asked, "And with my brothers gone, who do you think will be the next king?"

Hauk spoke then of a man who had been her father's friend since childhood, the man second in power only to King Osrik himself: the Grand Counselor, Medwyn Greyfell. Medwyn was several years older than Osrik, and unlikely to live to succeed him. But Greyfell had a son, Eric. The younger Greyfell was the most likely choice.

"Still," he added, shaking that golden head, "none can say with certainty how the jarl will vote when the kingmaking again comes around."

They left for her mother's house at a little after six in Elli's BMW. Hauk filled the seat beside her. His knees were cramped against the dashboard and his head touched the ceiling. They'd reached a sort of understanding in the past few hours. At least they'd found something to talk about: the land where he would soon be taking her, the land that he loved.

But looking at him, sitting there in the passenger seat, she was struck all over again with that feeling of extreme unreality: Elli and her Viking bodyguard, on their way to dinner at her mother's house...

The house where Elli had grown up was three stories, Tudor in style, on a wide, curving street lined with gorgeous mature oaks and maples. As a child, Elli and her sisters had sometimes lain on the emerald slope of the front lawn and stared up at the thick canopy of leaves overhead, smiling at the blue sky beyond, watching the clouds up there, drifting by.

The driveway was on the west side. Elli drove under an arching porte cochere to a back parking area. She stopped at the farthest door of the four-car garage.

"We'll go in the back way. I have a key, if we need it."

Hauk frowned. He looked almost comical, crammed into her sporty little car, hunching those massive shoulders so that he could fit. "It would be wiser, I think, to go to the front door, to knock."

"Oh, please. I was raised here. I don't have to knock."

"But I do."

She sighed. "Listen. I don't intend to explain *everything*. If my mother hears how you broke into my apartment, how you tied me up and planned to kidnap me, how Father has set you on me as a round-the-clock guard, she'll hit the roof. So we'll let her think you're my guest, okay? I can always bring a guest home. My mother would never object to that."

"I am a stranger here. A wise stranger enters by the front door."

Elli threw up both hands. "Will you save the platitudes? You hardly entered *my* house by the front door—and if you were really so damn wise, you would have let me come here on my own, because we both know that explaining *you* is going to be almost as difficult as convincing my poor mother to accept where I intend to go."

"I have told you, my orders—"

"I know what your orders are. And *I'm* telling *you,* I'm no stranger and you're with me, so there's no reason we can't just—"

He showed her the lightning bolt in the heart of his hand. "Someone comes."

The door to the back service porch opened and her mother's housekeeper emerged.

"That's Hilda Trawlson," Elli told Hauk. "Hildy's been with us as long as I can remember. She came back with us from Gullandria." Elli rolled down the window on Hauk's side. "Hi, Hildy!"

Hilda came down the steps and up to the car. "Elli." Her dark gaze flicked once over the Viking in the passenger seat. Then she looked again at Elli. "You've brought a guest." Her voice was flat.

"Hildy, don't be a sourpuss. This is Hauk."

The housekeeper and the warrior exchanged cautious nods.

Elli could see that Hilda already suspected Hauk had not come from Cleveland. So she announced, "Hauk is here from Gullandria."

Hilda took a step back.

Elli leaned on her door and got out of the car. "We have some things to talk about with Mom." She kept a smile on her face and her tone light. The whole idea here was to make her mother—and Hilda—believe that the coming trip was completely her choice.

And it *was* her choice. They didn't need to know that choosing *not* to go wasn't an option.

Hauk took his cue from her and pushed open his own door. Swinging those powerful legs out, he planted his big boots on the concrete and unfolded himself from the passenger seat. Hildy was giving him the evil eye. He stared back, stoic as ever. Neither deigned to speak.

"Can we just go in?" Elli asked wearily.

"Certainly." Hilda turned sharply on her crepe heel and headed toward the back door. She led them across the big service porch with its terra-cotta floor and profusion of potted plants, and from there, through the wonderful old kitchen where the green marble counters gleamed and the cabinets were fronted in beveled glass and something good was cooking, down the central hall to the family room.

"Your mother will join you shortly," the housekeeper said as she ushered them into the room.

"Is she still at work?" Elli's mother owned an antique shop downtown in Old Sac.

"She came in a few minutes ago. She only went up to change. Is there anything I can get you before I go?"

"Oh, Hildy. Will you stop it? Don't I even get a hug?"

Hildy's stern face softened slightly. "Come on, then." She held out those long arms. Elli went into them, pressing herself close to Hildy's considerable bosom, breathing in the housekeeper's familiar scent of Ivory soap and lavender, thinking that those smells, for all her life, would remind her of home.

"Everything's fine, honestly," Elli whispered to the woman who was like a dear aunt or a grandmother to her.

Hildy said nothing, just gave her an extra squeeze

before letting her go. "I'm in the kitchen, if you need me."

"I think what I *need* is a drink," Elli muttered as soon as Hildy had left them. "And don't give me that look."

Gold brows drew together over that bladelike nose. "Look?"

"Yes. There. That one." She turned for the wet bar on the inner wall. "It's almost like all your other looks, since pretty much your expression doesn't change. But there are...minute shifts. The one I just saw was the disapproving one." She found a half-full bottle of pinot grigio in the fridge and held it up. "You?"

"No."

"Now, why did I sense that was what you would say?"

"You are distressed."

She turned to look for a wineglass. "Yep. *Distressed* is the word. This is not my idea of a real fun time, you know? My mother is not going to be happy about our news. And I wish she had told me that my father had called, that he'd asked for my sisters and me. And I..." She let her voice trail off and shook her head. "You're right. Wine is tempting, but overall, a bad idea." She put the bottle away and then lingered, bent at the waist, one hand draped over the door to the half fridge, staring down into the contents. "Hmm. Diet 7UP, Mug root beer. Evian. But the question is, where are my—"

"Your Clearly Canadians are in the back, second shelf." It was her mother's voice, smooth as silk, cool as a perfectly chilled martini. She was standing in the open doorway to the hall.

"Hi, Mom." Elli flashed her mother what she hoped was an easy smile. "Hauk? What can I get you?"

"Nothing. Thank you."

Elli pulled out the tall pink bottle, shut the refrigerator and stood, her smile intact. Her mother, tall, blond as her daughters and stunningly beautiful in a crisp white shirt, a heavy turquoise necklace and black slacks, did not smile back.

"Mom, we were just—"

Ingrid wasn't listening. "Who is this man?"

What to do? How to handle this? There was just no right approach to take.

Elli gestured with her bottle of fruit-flavored sparkling water. "This is Hauk FitzWyborn."

Hauk whipped his big fist to his chest and lowered his head. "Your Majesty."

There was an awful moment of total silence.

Then her mother said, too softly, "Hildy was waiting for me at the foot of the stairs. She told me. But I refused to believe it." Ingrid was looking at Elli again, blue eyes gleaming dangerously. "Let me guess. A warrior, right? One of Osrik's goons, his...Viking berserkers?"

"Mom." Elli set the unopened bottle on the bar and went to her mother. "Come on." She took Ingrid's elbow. "Let's not—"

"Don't." Ingrid jerked free. "I want to know what's happening here. I want to know why you've brought one of your father's thugs into my house."

Chapter Six

So much for the faint hope of giving this explosive subject the delicate introduction it deserved.

Elli made it short and simple. "Hauk is here to escort me to Gullandria. I'm leaving sometime in the next two days. Father has—" What to call it? "—invited me. And I've said I will come."

Ingrid's mouth had dropped open. "I don't... You're not... Surely, you can't—"

Elli reached for her mother's arm again. "Oh, Mom. Here. Sit down." She made a shooing motion at Hauk, who still loomed nearby, hand to chest, head down, blocking the nearest chair.

Hauk got the message. He moved to the other end of the big room and pretended to stare out a window, giving them as much privacy as he could without actually leaving them alone together and going against the orders of his king.

Elli eased her mother down onto the cushions. "Mom. Please." She knelt, took Ingrid's trembling hand. "It's not the end of the world. It's...something you had to expect might happen someday, that one of us would want to go there, to meet our father face-to-face."

Ingrid was shaking her head. "No. I never in a thousand years expected that. I'd always believed I made it clear to the three of you. To go back there is a bad idea. A very, very bad idea."

Elli squeezed her mother's hand. "He *is* my father."

Ingrid leaned close. "He gave you up." She spoke low, with a terrible intensity. "Gave you up as I gave up our sons. And look what happened to them, to my little boys." It hurt to see it, the way heartache could twist such a beautiful face. She gripped Elli's hand more tightly. "Isn't it enough that both of them are dead? He has no right, *none,* to summon you now."

"But I *want* to go."

"You don't know what you're saying."

"Yes, I do. It's important to me, to know my own father, to find out for myself what he's like."

"I can't believe he's done this. I told him no. I told him absolutely not, under any circumstances." Ingrid didn't seem to realize what she'd just let slip.

Elli prompted, though she already knew the truth, "You're saying you spoke to him recently?"

Ingrid blinked. And then confessed, "Yes. He called last Friday."

"You didn't say a word to me. You didn't tell me—"

"Of course I didn't tell you." Ingrid wrapped her other hand around their joined ones. "There was no need to tell you. He called and he asked me to send you—all three of you. When I refused, he started giving orders. When giving orders didn't work, he offered me a bribe."

Elli stiffened. Her father hadn't mentioned any bribes. "You're not serious. He wouldn't—"

"Oh, yes, he would." Ingrid was nodding, her mouth a thin line. "He mentioned a figure. A large one." She added, more to herself than to Elli, "As if I need his money, as if money means a thing to me when measured against my babies."

Elli supposed, now that she thought about it, that she could see her father trying just about anything to get her mother to let him see his remaining children. "He's got to be desperate. And so very lonely now. He's lost two sons."

Ingrid made a feral sound deep in her throat. "*He's* lost two sons! It's *my* loss, too. *Our* loss, all of ours. Yours and mine and Brit's and Liv's. My sons, your brothers. Gone. Dead. And no one will ever convince me they died purely by accident. A fire in the stables and a five-year-old loses his life horribly, his poor little body burned almost beyond recognition. Wasn't that enough? Evidently not. Because now there's been a storm at sea—Valbrand washed overboard, survivors reporting they saw him swept away.

"No. There's more than misfortune at work here. In Gullandria, the rules of succession make life much too hazardous for the sons of the king. The jarl are forever forming their alliances, plotting and planning. Deep in my heart, I'll always suspect that your brothers didn't die purely by accident.''

Shock had Elli staring. "You've never said anything like that before."

"Of course I haven't. I've always prayed I'd never have to."

Elli found she was determined, now, to speak with her father, to learn all that he knew about the circumstances surrounding her brothers' deaths.

Ingrid stared into the middle distance. "I kept my word to your father. One son dead all those years ago. And then, last summer, the other vanishes. Sometimes it was like a knife, buried deep, turning cruelly inside of me, but I did what I had to do. I stayed here, in America, with you girls. I couldn't save what was gone, but I kept my promise to your father. And I kept you three safe." She shifted her burning gaze to Elli. "Please. I am begging you. Don't go there. I'm afraid for you to go there."

Elli realized her father had been right to fear she might be swayed by a visit to her mother. Ingrid was very convincing. Her arguments not only made sense, they plucked hard and hurtfully at Elli's heartstrings. Elli loved her mother. Greatly. The last thing she wanted was to see Ingrid suffer and know she herself was the cause of it.

Over by the window, Hauk turned—just enough to meet Elli's eyes. Something flashed between them: an insight, a *knowing*. Elli saw that the warrior understood exactly what she was feeling, that he had been warned by his king to expect it. It was why he guarded her so closely, why she had not been allowed to come here, to her mother, on her own.

Elli pushed her doubts aside. She had made an agreement with her father. And she would keep it.

Mustering her arguments, she spoke to Ingrid again. "It's only a visit. Three weeks. And you just said it yourself. If there is *any* danger, it's to the *sons* of a king." A king's daughter might be the only female jarl to claim the title of princess, but that didn't make her eligible for the throne. "A princess is never even considered when the *jarl* gather for the king-making."

"First time for everything," Ingrid said bleakly.

"It's not going to happen. You know it's not. And we've had no proof that Kylan and Valbrand were victims of foul play. Even the scandal sheets never hinted at anything like that."

"That doesn't mean it isn't possible."

"Mom, please look at this logically. There's no way I can be in any danger, because I am a threat to no one. I'm a kindergarten teacher from Sacramento and I'm going for a visit, that's all. In three weeks, I'll be back home where I belong."

Ingrid made a scoffing sound. "You aren't listening. You haven't heard a thing I've said."

"Yes, I *am* listening. I do understand."

"Elli, he gave me his *word,* all those years ago. He kept my sons to bring up as kings. And I got you girls. It was a vow, between us—that neither would ever try to reclaim what was lost. And you know how highly a Gullandrian holds his vow. But what's hap-

pening now?'' Her voice gained power—and volume.
''Our sons are dead. And he wants his daughters. His
vow is nothing. He's a liar and a cheat.''

Elli could see Hauk. He stood very still, in profile
to them, presumably looking out over the side yard.
He had heard every word, of course. And he revered
her father. Elli had the sense that if anyone else but
his king's runaway queen had dared to utter such
slanders against the ruler he served, Hauk would have
been on them and it would not have been pretty.

Her mother had more to say. ''Osrik and his Grand
Counselor, Greyfell, have been plotting. I know it. I
can feel it in my bones. Something more than a father-
and-daughter reunion is up here. Something political.
Something to do with who will end up on the throne.
And you are the pawn at the heart of his game. That's
why he wants you, why he's taking you away.''

''It's a *visit,* Mom. Nobody said anything about
taking me away.'' Well, actually, they *had.* Hauk, after all, had started out to kidnap her. But no way Elli
was going into that part of the story—especially not
now, with her mother looking so desperate and wild-
eyed.

Ingrid let out a cry. ''Oh, my God. What about Brit
and Liv? Is he after them, too?''

''No. Absolutely not. He hasn't contacted them.''

Ingrid glared down at her. ''How do you know?''

''He told me so.''

Her mother made that scoffing sound again. ''And
you *believe* him?''

''Yes. I do.''

''Then you are stone-blind.'' Ingrid gestured at the

phone on the side table a few feet away. "Give me that."

"Mom—"

"Give me the phone."

With a long sigh, Elli rose and got the phone and handed it to her mother.

Ingrid punched a number from autodial and pressed the phone to her ear. After a minute, she demanded, "Liv? Is that you?" She put her hand over the mouthpiece. "Well. At least she answered." She spoke to Liv again. "Yes... No... I just... Oh, Livvy, Elli's here. Your father has contacted her.... Yes. That's right. That's what I said.... He wants her to visit him in Gullandria. She tells me she's going. She's got some big Gullandrian savage with her.... Yes, yes. Insane... You're so right. And I need to know. Have you heard from him? Has he summoned you, too?" Ingrid let out a relieved-sounding breath. "Thank God for that, at least." Ingrid cast a sharp glance at Elli, then said to Liv, "Yes. I told you. She's right here... All right." She held out the phone. "Talk to your sister. Maybe she can make you see reason."

Elli took the phone. She tried a light approach. "Hey, there. How's torts?" Liv was a law student at Stanford.

She was also ever the "big" sister, at fifty-nine minutes Elli's senior. She started right in with a lecture. "Ell, are you crazy? There is no way you can do this."

"Liv—"

"In the first place, you'll break Mom's heart if you go. And why would you even *want* to go, to take off out of nowhere for that throwback misogynistic block of ice in the Norwegian Sea? Step back. Get a grip on yourself. Ask yourself what's really happening here. Who's to say what that long-lost father of ours has in store for you once he gets you there and under his control?''

''Liv—''

''I don't like this. It scares me. It—''

''Liv.''

''I don't—''

''Liv!''

There was a silence, a hostile one. Then Liv finally grumbled, ''What?''

''I've talked to Father. And I've made up my mind. I *want* to do this. I *want* to meet him.'' She sent a glance at her mother, who stared back at her through anguished eyes. ''Mom is going to accept this, eventually.'' Passionately, her mother shook her head. Elli said slowly and clearly, ''I don't believe for a minute that Father would ever do me—or any of us—harm. I'm going to be fine. I'll be back in three weeks and I want you *not* to worry.''

Liv swore under her breath. ''You're so easy most of the time. It was always Brit and I fighting over who got to run things. You'd just go along. But every once in a while, you'd decide to take a stand for your own way. And whenever you did…''

''That's right. You two couldn't budge me. One time in a hundred, we'd do what I wanted. And this is that one time.''

''It *is* strange, you have to admit it. He doesn't

know any of us. He's made no *effort* to know us. Why now—and why did he pick on you in particular?''

''Why now? I think it's obvious. With Valbrand gone, he can't help but think of the daughters he's never known.''

''Then why you?''

''I don't know. But I intend to find out, I promise you that.''

''If anything happens to you in that place, I swear I will kill you.''

Elli couldn't help smiling. ''I love you, Livvy. I'll be fine.''

''You'd better keep in touch on this.''

''You know I will.''

Ingrid took the phone again to say goodbye. The minute she disconnected the call, she tried Brit's apartment in L.A. Brit's machine answered. Ingrid left a message. After that, she dialed Brit's cell, and then her *other* cell—Brit was forever losing her cell phones.

Increasingly frantic, Ingrid tried the numbers she had for three of Brit's friends. The third one finally picked up the phone. She suggested Ingrid try to reach Brit at work.

Brit was a licensed pilot. She'd eaten beetles and jumped from a skyscraper on *Fear Factor*. She'd trekked the Amazon and the New Zealand wilderness. She'd also dropped out of college after only two years. Like Elli and Liv, Brit had a hefty regular income from a well-managed trust, but Brit was forever giving her money away and inevitably ran short before the next check came in.

So she worked. At a series of menial jobs.

Currently, she was waiting tables at an Italian restaurant on East Melrose, where the owner was Greek and all the cooks were from south of the border. Everybody hated to call her there. The owner did a lot of shouting whenever Brit used the phone.

But Ingrid was desperate. She dialed the number—and sighed in relief when Brit came on the line.

Ingrid asked her youngest daughter the same questions she'd asked Liv. She got the same answers. Brit was fine, too. No sign of any Vikings in her life. And she wanted to talk to Elli.

So Elli took the phone and explained what she'd already explained to Liv, while in the background, the owner of the restaurant yelled at Brit to get to work and Brit had to pause every couple of minutes to shout at him to get off her back.

"Just stay in touch, okay?" Brit demanded, echoing Liv.

"I will. I love you. Don't work too hard."

"Hah. Like I've got a choice in this place. It's a hellhole, I'm telling you."

The call to Brit seemed to get Ingrid more upset than before. But Ingrid always got upset when it came to her underemployed, fearless, free-spirited youngest daughter.

Elli tried again to soothe her mother, promising over and over that she'd be all right, she'd keep in touch.

Hilda finally called them to dinner. They sat at the big table in the formal dining room—and Ingrid turned her fear and fury on Hauk.

"What is going on between you and this man, Elli? Why did you bring him here? He watches you—'' she gave a frantic laugh ''—like a hawk.'' The laughter died in her throat and she glared at Hauk. "You behave like a bodyguard. Is there some reason my daughter needs a bodyguard?''

Elli spoke up. "Of course I don't need a bodyguard, Mother. I told you why Hauk is here. He'll escort me to Gullandria. I invited him to dinner because it seemed the polite thing to do." Yes, it was an outright lie. But what help would the truth be at this point? In the end, in spite of her mother's endless and convincing arguments, Elli intended to keep her word and go to her father.

She said softly, "I realize now it was probably... unwise to bring him to dinner. I'm sorry."

Hauk let Elli's answer stand for him. He was not a stupid man. He must have understood that anything he said would only make matters worse.

In the end, Ingrid seemed to realize that nothing she could do would stop Elli from going to Gullandria. She agreed to care for the cats and extracted a promise from Elli that she would call as soon as she reached her father's palace.

At a little after nine, Ingrid stood in the driveway, waving, a brave smile on her lips, as Elli and Hauk drove away.

"I think you should pack now," Hauk announced right after Elli unlocked her apartment door and let them both inside.

Elli didn't want to pack. She didn't want to do

anything right then, except maybe sit on the couch in the dark and watch something mindless on TV and pretend that she hadn't told all those lies to her mother, pretend that she hadn't heard all the troubling things her mother had said about her father and her brothers and the land where her father lived.

Hauk stood before her, huge and unmoving and waiting for her answer.

"You think I should pack, huh?" she asked provokingly.

"I do."

"Well, what you think is your business. I'm not packing now." She dropped her purse and keys on the table.

Hauk said, "The royal jet is ready and waiting, with the crew on call, at Sacramento Executive Airport. If you pack, we can leave tonight. The Gulfstream has its own bedroom suite. You will be comfortable. You can sleep in flight."

Elli had wandered into the living room and picked up the remote. She tossed it back down again. "I was just thinking that what I'd like to do more than anything right now is watch TV and forget everything that's happened around here since you showed up yesterday and turned my whole life upside down. But just this moment, I realized, that if I watch TV, I won't be able to forget anything. Because you'll be here, sitting in that chair, watching me, guarding me against the possibility that I might do something *I* want to do rather than what my father wants. I have to tell you, Hauk, I find that upsetting. You could say that it really ticks me off."

"You should pack. We should leave."

"I'm not packing now. I'm not *leaving* now. And you have nothing at all to say about that, because it's not Thursday and I have until Thursday if I *want* until Thursday."

"There is no need to linger here."

"Not to you, maybe."

"Other than to pack, you're ready to go now."

"You're not getting it. I may be ready, but I'm not *ready*." She turned for the hall, then paused and turned back to him. "I'm taking a bath. This time, I'm staying in there awhile because it's the only place I can go right now where you *won't* be."

He had that soldier-at-attention look he liked to get when he wasn't quite sure what she was going to do next—let alone how he ought to *handle* what she was going to do next.

She glared at him. "I want an hour. To myself. Is that understood?"

"Yes."

She went to her room and from there to her bathroom and the second she got in there, she shut the door. Hard.

Sixty minutes later—she had a travel clock she kept on the bathroom shelf, so she was able to time herself—she emerged from the bathroom. Hauk was waiting, boots off and bedroll at the ready, by the foot of her bed.

She considered heading into the living room to channel surf in the dark for a while as she had threatened to do earlier. But he'd only follow her. Might as well channel surf from the comfort of her bed.

She climbed under the covers and the cats came and cuddled in with her. Hauk continued to stand, staring off toward the door.

"Is there some problem?" she demanded sourly. He wasn't in the way of the TV, but he was distracting in the extreme, just standing there. It was like having a giant statue at the foot of her bed.

The statue spoke. "You are upset about the visit with your mother and that has put you in a contrary frame of mind. It's possible you will rethink your decision to go to bed at this time. I see no reason to become comfortable if you're only going to go elsewhere."

"Comfortable? What are you talking about? You never become comfortable. You never even *sleep*."

"I sleep. Perhaps not as you would perceive sleep to be. I am capable of maintaining a state of readiness while technically sleeping."

"A state of readiness."

"Yes."

She resisted the urge to hurl the remote at him. "Hauk."

"Yes?"

"Lie down."

He dropped to his blankets, disappearing from her view.

She petted her cats, watched back-to-back *Buffy* reruns and told herself she was ignoring him. A state of readiness. Oh, *fershure*.

At eleven, she turned off the television and rolled

on her side. By midnight, she couldn't stand it. She sat up and turned on the lamp and grabbed the phone.

"Who are you calling?" His voice came from the foot of the bed. She couldn't see him. He hadn't even sat up.

"My mother. And I'm not putting it on speakerphone, so don't you dare try to make me." She clutched the phone tightly, ready to whack him with it if he rose up from below the footboard.

She thought she heard him sigh. "All right. Keep your word. Say nothing to endanger your visit to your father."

"I hate you, Hauk."

"Make your call."

Her mother answered on the first ring. "Elli?"

"I love you, Mom. I'll be fine. Please don't worry."

There was a silence, then Ingrid said, "I won't." They both knew it was a lie, but a *good* lie, a loving mother's lie. "Thank you, darling. For calling. I've been lying here thinking of you."

"I know. I was thinking of you, too."

A low, sad little chuckle came over the line. "Isn't it ironic? Liv is so headstrong. And Brit? Well, we all know Brit is the type of daughter to make her mother prematurely gray. But you? An excellent student, always so reasonable. You were the one I went to when I needed help convincing one of your sisters not to do something dangerous or harebrained."

"Mom..."

"Oh, I know, I know. This is something you feel you have to do. And it's your choice to make."

"That's right."

"Hilda will be over tomorrow to pick up Diablo and Doodles."

"That should work."

"Elli."

"What, Mom?"

"Have a good trip. A *safe* trip."

"I will, Mom. I'll be back before you know it and…our lives will go on."

"Good night my own sweet Little Old Giant."

Elli whispered, "Good night, Mom," and hung up the phone.

From the end of the bed, there was silence.

"Hauk?"

"Yes?"

"I don't really hate you."

"I know."

Elli turned off the light and rolled onto her side. Within a few minutes, she was asleep.

Hauk lay awake.

Wide-awake.

As a rule, he possessed considerable discipline when it came to the time for sleep. He'd been trained and trained well. Sleep, like good nourishment and regular physical exercise to muscular exhaustion and beyond, was a main building block of superior performance. He could sleep in a snow cave, in subzero temperatures with enemies on every side—and be ready to snap wide-awake at the smallest strange movement or sound. As he'd told Elli—

He caught his own dangerous thoughts up short. Not simply Elli. Never simply Elli.

She was the princess. Her Highness. *Princess* Elli. But never her name by itself.

From thought sprang action. And he couldn't allow his thoughts to become too familiar. It was unacceptable. More than unacceptable.

It was forbidden.

He wanted her on that plane. He wanted her safe with his liege and out of his hands.

But she *would* balk, would stall—would keep insisting she had until Thursday and she wasn't leaving until then. The more he tried to get her to go, the more determined she became to stay.

Dangerous, the games she played. For more reasons than she allowed herself to understand. Not only was *she* stuck with *him,* every moment, as she never seemed to tire of reminding him; *he* was stuck with *her.* He could go nowhere, do nothing, without keeping her in sight.

This was the kind of assignment that, under most circumstances, he could do with one eye closed and a hand tied behind his back. Second nature. To watch. To guard. To remain detached and yet vigilant. Over the years, he'd delivered a number of important personages—and dangerous prisoners—into the proper hands.

But this, he was learning, was *not* most circumstances. This was the daughter of his king. And something was happening to him, in this period of forced proximity with her. Something that had never happened to him before.

He let himself think it: *She draws me. I want her....*

He could hardly believe it. He'd thought himself well beyond such ridiculous weakness. A warrior, in particular the king's warrior, learned early to effectively sublimate physical needs—especially sexual ones, which were no use at all to a soldier in his work.

And yet, in a mere twenty-four hours, it had happened. This troublesome princess had somehow managed, all unknowing, to get under his skin.

He found himself doing things he despised. Noticing the fresh, flowerlike scent of her. More than noticing. May the three Norns of destiny curse him, he was constantly sniffing the air when she was near. And he watched her. All the time. Yes, it was his duty to watch her. But he was not supposed to take such pleasure in the task.

It was hopeless, this growing hunger he felt for her. Counterproductive in the extreme. The woman was so completely beyond his touch. So far above him that his king had not even bothered to remind him to keep his hands off.

Hauk didn't know for certain what scheme his king was hatching, but he knew that Queen Ingrid was right. His lord had plans for Princess Elli. And those plans did not include her lying down with her father's bastard warrior. It would be a huge and unpardonable betrayal of honor and his king's trust for Hauk to lay a hand on her, except as required in the furtherance of his duty.

Still—in spite of how wrong it was, no matter the complete lack of discipline it showed—the woman enchanted him. She wove a spell over him, with her huge eyes and soft mouth, her clever tongue and quick mind. And her heart.

Yes, that was surely her most alluring feature. That seeming contradiction of softness and strength only found in a woman with a true and loving heart. She would be a prize beyond price to the man who claimed her.

And he would never be that man.

Yet his orders forced him to this—to spending the nights at the foot of her bed—scenting her, listening to her small, sweet sighs as she dreamed.

It was the purest kind of torture. A taste of Valhalla. A visit to Hel.

And there was no way to make an end to it until she gave up and agreed to go—or until Thursday came at last.

Chapter Seven

When Elli woke in the morning, Hauk was gone from his place at the foot of her bed.

But this time she had no illusions that he might have given up and returned to Gullandria without her. She tossed back the covers and went into the bathroom to wash her face and get dressed. When she got back to the bedroom, there he was, dressed in a fresh black shirt and black slacks, his square jaw smooth from a recent shave.

Waiting.

Elli sighed. "Let's get some breakfast."

"As you wish."

Over scrambled eggs and toast, he suggested again that she pack so that they could leave.

Elli just looked at him, a long look. She knew a

bleak satisfaction when he was the first to glance away.

Hilda came knocking at a little before noon. She scowled when she saw that Elli had a houseguest.

"Why is he here? He doesn't need to be here."

Elli finessed an answer. "I told you, he's my escort. We're leaving together tomorrow."

Hilda never stopped scowling the whole time she was there. Elli put the cats in their carrier and Hauk helped her haul all the cat supplies down to Hilda's 4×4.

"Do I get a goodbye hug?" Elli asked the housekeeper just before she drove away.

Hilda relented enough to bestow the hug, but kept her scowl in place. And of course, about fifteen minutes after she and the cats departed, Ingrid called.

"You didn't tell me that thug was staying at your apartment."

"Oh, Mom. It's no big deal. I have a spare room." Too bad Hauk refused to sleep in it unless she did.

"Still, he has no right to—"

"Mom. Let it be. Please."

A silence echoed down the line. Then her mother murmured, "Yes. I suppose you're right." She wished Elli well again and reminded her to call.

"I will. I promise."

They said goodbye. Elli hung up.

Hauk was right there, maybe three feet away. Watching. Listening.

Elli decided she might possibly go insane if she had to stay cooped up in her apartment all day with two hundred-plus pounds of Viking observing her every move. She reached for her purse. "Come on."

He frowned at her. "You wish to leave now?"

"That's right."

"You have yet to pack your belongings."

"You are so very, very observant."

He might have flinched at that one. But if so, it was a tiny flinch—so small it probably hadn't really happened at all. "You don't wish to take anything with you?"

"To Gullandria?"

"Yes. To Gullandria."

"Well, as a matter of fact, I do intend to take a few things to Gullandria."

"Then hadn't you better pack them?"

"Not now."

He looked at her steadily, his expression especially bleak. He knew by then that she was up to something.

And she was. "We're not going to Gullandria. Not yet, anyway." She waited. She wanted him to ask, *Then where are we going?* But apparently, he'd decided not to give her the satisfaction. Fine. She told him anyway. "We're going to a movie."

"A movie. Why?"

"Because it's Wednesday. Because I *can*."

She took him to the latest James Bond thriller. Who could say? Maybe he'd be able to relate. At the snack counter, she bought a jumbo tub of popcorn drizzled with butter flavoring and a large Sprite.

"We can share the popcorn," she told him. "Want a Coke or something?"

"No, thank you."

She accepted her Sprite from the guy behind the counter, who kept shooting sideways glances at Hauk. Elli supposed she wasn't surprised. Hauk was hardly your average Joe. He stood at least a head taller than anyone else in the sparse weekday-afternoon crowd around them. And then there were all those muscles, that proud military bearing—not to mention the shoulder-length golden hair. Even with his shirt on, so you couldn't see the blue-and-gold lightning bolt that blazed across his chest, Hauk could have walked right off a martial arts movie poster.

Elli realized she might actually be starting to enjoy herself a little. She grinned. Oh, yes. *Enter the Viking.* Or maybe *Warriors of the North.*

"You're smiling. Why?" Hauk's voice was low. Somehow, it sounded right next door to intimate.

Elli felt a shiver run beneath her skin. How odd. "Oh, nothing. Here." She shoved the tub of popcorn at him. He took it and she got herself a straw and a handful of napkins and led the way up the ramp to the little stand where the ticket taker waited.

There were thirteen theaters in the building. Each of them had Dolby sound and big, comfortable seats, like easy chairs, well padded with high backs and plenty of room between the rows. Still, in deference to Hauk's massive frame, Elli chose the row in back, which had an extra-wide aisle between it and the next row down.

Once they were seated in the dark, he offered her the popcorn tub. "Oh, you go ahead and hold it," she said.

"I don't care for any."

She started to take it from him. And then a naughty whim took her. "Hold it anyway—because I am your princess, right? Because, after my father, you serve me."

He looked at her for a long time, his eyes shining at her through the darkness. "That's right. I serve you."

A small tremor went through her, a quivery feeling. Her heart beat too fast and her cheeks felt warm.

Was something happening here?

Oh, of course not.

The dark screen lit up and the preshow snack-bar advertisements of dancing paper cups and singing candy boxes began.

The movie was your usual James Bond flick. Fast-paced, fun to watch, with lots of drop-dead-gorgeous women and Pierce Brosnan, the perfect James Bond, dark and sleek, killer handsome, delightfully urbane.

Elli sipped her Sprite and intermittently munched her popcorn and wished her silly heart would stop pounding so fast every time she reached over and grabbed a handful out of Hauk's lap.

Okay, she'd blundered. She should have taken the tub when he tried to give it back to her. She should have thought about how awkward it was going to be, how…intimate, to keep groping for fistfuls of popcorn while he was holding the container.

Intimate.

It was the second time that particular word had come to mind since they'd entered the theater complex.

But what was so strange about that?

Not a thing. Not considering the way it was between them, the way she had to be with him virtually round-the-clock. Even though they weren't *really* intimate, it was hard not to think of the word. Intimate, at least in part, meant to be physically close. And *that* they were.

Oh, yes, they were.

She could feel the heat coming off his big body. And the outer side of her upper arm touched his, just barely, all the time. And then there was the scent of him, that scent of cedar and spice and…maleness. That scent that she did find so dangerously attractive.

He whispered, out of the side of his mouth, "You're not eating your popcorn." She could have sworn she heard humor in his voice.

Humor.

And intimacy.

She looked at him sharply. He was staring at the screen.

And wasn't that the main reason she'd dragged him here? To give him something else to stare at but her.

She hadn't thought it through, though. Hadn't considered that they'd be sitting so close their bodies brushed, that she'd have the bad judgment to make a big deal of ordering him to hold the popcorn for her.

She whispered, "Um, are you sure you don't want any popcorn?"

"Yes. I'm sure."

"Then I guess I'll just hold it myself."

He leaned a fraction nearer, heat and size and maleness pressing in. "Are you certain? I am willing to serve." His voice was low and soft and…silky.

Elli's mouth went bone-dry. She gulped. "I…yeah. I'm certain."

He handed her the tub, the pads of his big fingers brushing hers. A bullet of heat went shooting through her, so thrilling it was painful—from where his fingers grazed hers, straight up her arm—and right to her chest, which contracted sharply, so that she almost gasped.

They were staring at each other. The Dolby sound swelled around them and images flashed on the big screen, reflecting at them, so that Hauk's chiseled profile gleamed alabaster in the darkness. His hair shone, not gold, not platinum, but some rare color in between.

He was the one who looked away, back at the screen. And this time she felt no triumph that he did. This time, she felt it as a tearing sensation, that he ripped something, left tattered raw edges, when he looked away.

She stared at him for several bewildered seconds, thinking what she shouldn't be thinking: that he was so very wonderfully male. That it would be a lovely, thrilling thing to have his big hands on her, to press her mouth to his…

When they came out of the movie, it was a little after three. Hauk pushed the glass door open for her and she walked out, across the covered ticket booth area and into the bright sunlight of a beautiful afternoon. Overhead, the sky was clear and powder-blue.

And she wasn't ready—not yet—to go back to her place and be cooped up in there with Hauk. She headed for Land Park.

Hauk saw they weren't going where he'd assumed they'd be going. "Where are we going now?"

"To Land Park."

"You wish to see your mother again?"

"No. Not to my mother's house. Just into the park. I want to walk by the duck pond." She added, turning to give him a sarcastic smile, "Is that all right with you?"

Their gazes collided. A shimmer of heat went through her. "Return to your apartment," he said softly. "Pack your belongings. I'll take you to the plane."

Elli yanked her gaze back to the street in front of her. She had to be careful. She could get them in an accident. "No. Not yet."

"This is foolish."

And it was. She knew it. Something more than a James Bond flick had happened in the darkened movie theater. They'd emerged into the sunshine with everything changed between them—or if not changed, at least mutually acknowledged.

Looking back, it seemed that maybe there had been attraction between them almost from the very first. She'd denied it. That hadn't been difficult. What self-respecting woman would ever willingly admit that her kidnapper made her heart go pitter-pat? Not Elli.

But time had done it, made her see it. Time and the forced closeness that they shared. She was coming to know him a little, coming to understand that though she despised the job he was doing, she didn't—she *couldn't*—despise the man himself. She knew there was goodness in him. That honor and loyalty meant more to him than life. How could she help but admire that? How could she help but let down her guard with him, at least a little?

Now it seemed terribly dangerous to imagine the night to come, should she continue to insist on remaining in Sacramento until the last possible moment her agreement with her father allowed.

She should do what Hauk kept trying to get her to do. Pack. Get on that plane.

And yet, she held back. Beyond this impossible attraction to the man her father had sent to kidnap her, she had other issues here.

The more she thought about this whole situation, the more suspicious she became of her father's motives. What if her mother was right? *Could* she be walking blind into some ugly palace plot?

Her doubts ate at her. True, she *was* going. Hauk would make certain of that. But she saw no reason to rush headlong into the jaws of a possible trap.

Who knew what might happen in the next eighteen hours or so? It didn't seem particularly likely, but some new and valuable piece of information just might come to light. Maybe everything would become clear, after all.

Right, whispered a knowing voice in the back of her mind. *Everything might become clear. Oh, certainly. Anything might happen....*

Now, that did ring true. Anything might happen, all right—between her and Hauk.

Elli tossed her head. "I don't care. I don't want to go yet. I'm not sure I want to go at all."

She waited for the man beside her to tell her that she had no choice. She'd vowed to go and she *would* go.

He said nothing.

Land Park boasted its own outdoor amphitheater across from a children's amusement area called Fairy-tale Town and not far from the zoo. Below the amphitheater, sparkling in the afternoon sun, lay the duck pond.

Elli parked the car above the amphitheater, to the side a little. A steep, tree-shadowed, grass-covered hill swept down to the pond. They got out and Elli took off at a run down the grassy slope. Maybe she'd leave him behind.

Yeah, right.

Elli kept running anyway, not looking back, almost tumbling head-over-heels once or twice, but somehow managing to keep her feet.

Hauk followed close behind. She could *feel* him there. Never once did he stumble. And she knew he wasn't running full-out, that he effortlessly paced himself to keep a few yards back.

She reached the base of the slope, where the ground leveled out, drawing to a halt on the asphalt path that encircled the perimeter of the pond. Ducks and geese glided on the sun-sparkled surface and oaks and sweet gums grew at intervals along the bank, inviting wooden benches waiting beneath them.

Slightly breathless, she turned to Hauk. "It's pretty, isn't it?"

His sky-blue gaze darkened. "Beautiful."

She knew what he meant and it wasn't the duck pond. Her mouth was dry again. She swallowed.

He looked away from her. "What now?"

Good question. "Let's, uh, walk."

He started walking. Fast.

"Hey, wait up."

He stopped where he was. She hurried and caught up.

They stood on the path, facing each other. He was looking at her again—gazing at her as if he would eat her up. And she *liked* it, to have him look at her that way.

He said, as if it hurt him to tell her, "You *will* have to go. I will have to make you go."

"I know. But not till tomorrow. You won't make me go…until tomorrow."

"You enjoy this? Pushing the boundaries? Tempting the fates?"

Anger sizzled through her. "I'll tell you what I *don't* enjoy. Being kept in the dark. Knowing that if I break my word, you'll make me keep it anyway."

"You are jarl. High jarl. A princess."

"Did you think I'd forgotten?"

"You are a princess and a princess keeps her word."

The ducks drifted, elegant and easy, on the pond. The tree branches swayed in the slight breeze. A hundred yards away, on a swath of green across the street, a woman and a small blond child sat on a pink blanket beneath an oak, eating ice cream. The cars rolled past on the street, each one observing the speed limit. Everything seemed peaceful and perfect. Idyllic.

Except between Elli and Hauk. Between them, the air crackled. With hostility. And with heat.

She demanded with a low voice, "Do you know more of what drives my father than you're telling me?"

"No."

"If you *did* know more, *would* you tell me?"

"I can't say. It would depend."

"On?"

"What I knew. What I was ordered to keep to myself, what I thought *wise* to keep to myself."

"So, I can't really trust you, then. You could be lying to me now. You *would* lie to me now—if my father had ordered you to lie, if you thought you *should* lie."

"You knew that from the first. And you *can* trust me. To take you where you need to go, to keep you safe."

"Where *I* need to go?"

"Yes. By your own vow, I will take you where you need to go."

She was recalling the things her mother had said. "Do you think it's possible that my father hopes I might somehow claim the throne of Gullandria once he's gone?"

"No."

He had replied almost before she had the question out of her mouth. She couldn't hold back a sharp little laugh. "Well, you had no trouble answering that one."

"You think like an American."

"You said that before."

"And it remains as true now as it was then. There will be a kingmaking when your father is gone. And a prince will be chosen to succeed him. A prince. Not a princess. And certainly not a princess raised across the sea, a woman not even brought up in our ways."

She looked at him sideways. "You could use a woman ruler. You might learn a few things. You could get out of the Dark Ages and start treating women as the equals they are."

"A woman may never sit on the throne of Gullandria. But that doesn't mean a woman doesn't have rights—more rights, in some cases, than a man."

"Rights like...?" She began walking along the path.

Hauk fell in step with her. "She can own property. She is equal, as an heir, when a parent dies."

"Equal in terms of property rights. Well, good. That's something. But you said *more* rights."

"Yes. Our marriage laws give the woman the power. You'll recall I told you that a man can't divorce after his wife gives him children?"

"I remember."

"I didn't tell you that a woman *can* divorce her husband. A woman has the right to divorce at any time, simply because she believes the marriage is unworkable."

"I assume there is some reasoning behind that."

"It is thought that a woman is more responsible in

matters of hearth and home, that she would be less likely to break the vows of marriage for frivolous reasons."

Elli hated to say it—but she did, anyway. "I don't agree with that. I think men and women should have the *same* rights. I don't think one—either one— should have more power than the other."

"You have plans to change our laws?"

"It was just an opinion."

"There's an old saying. *An opinion means only as much as the power and intention of the one who owns it.*"

She arched an eyebrow at him. "Are you implying my opinion doesn't mean much?"

She could have sworn he almost smiled. "It's only a saying. Take what you will from it."

Ahead of them on the path, an old man tore at a loaf of bread and tossed the pieces into the pond. The ducks gathered, nipping up the soggy bits. Bold pigeons scrambled around at his feet, gobbling the crumbs that fell to the walk from his hand.

Elli paused. "You think maybe my father plans to marry me off to someone, then?"

Hauk paused, too, and they faced each other once more. "It is not my place to think. Not about the intentions of my king."

"You've said that a hundred times. But I mean, you know, go with it for a minute. What would be gained, if he married me off to some prince or other?"

Hauk lowered his head, a gesture she had come to realize was meant to display his subservience. "I cannot play this word game with you. I have already said more than I should have.''

"Why? We're just…talking. Just sharing opinions." She gave him a grin. "Minus power. And intention.''

"You have a fine mind. And a devious one.''

"Hey. I guess I'll fit in just great at my father's court.''

"I think you will—and I cannot help you scheme against my king.''

"I'm not scheming. I'm only—''

"Enough.'' He walked on. The old man saw him coming and stepped out of his path. The pigeons scattered.

Elli had to hurry to keep up.

A short time later, they went back to the apartment where Elli found two messages on her machine. One from a girlfriend and one from a guy she'd known a couple of years ago, while she was still in school at UC Davis.

Hauk stood right there as she played the messages back. He shrugged. "Just leave them. You can answer them when you return.''

"Well, that's reassuring. You seem to think I *will* return. Too bad my own mother fears otherwise.''

He had that locked-up-tight look he got whenever he decided that responding to her would get him nowhere.

He was right to get that look. She said, "I'll answer them now, thank you very much.''

He made her return the calls on speakerphone. He

stood there, listening to every word as she told her girlfriend she couldn't do lunch this weekend and asked for a rain check, then told the old school friend, David Saunders—in town just for a couple of days on business—that she wouldn't be able to meet him for a drink. She was leaving town tomorrow. A family trip. David said maybe next time.

"That would be great. Give me a call."

"You know I will."

She hung up and glared at Hauk. "You enjoy this? Listening in on my private conversations?"

"No."

"Then maybe you should stop doing it."

He turned away, shaking his golden head.

And that angered her.

More than angered her.

All at once, she was utterly furious with him. She grabbed his arm.

He froze.

Beneath her hand, his silky flesh felt as it if had been poured over steel. Her palm burned at the contact, her fingers flamed. The heat seemed to sizzle along her arm, blazing on, up over her shoulder and down into the center of her, making a pool of molten fire in her lower belly.

She let go, brought her hand to her mouth—and it was like touching him all over again, pressing her skin that had been on *his* skin against her lips.

She lowered her hand, slowly. Carefully. She felt shaken to the core—and ashamed of herself, too. "I…uh…sorry. Honestly. I got so angry. It was stupid. I shouldn't have grabbed you like that."

His eyes seemed to bore holes right through her. "Pack. Now."

She bit her lip, shook her head.

"You will destroy us both," he whispered.

"No. That's ridiculous. It's an...attraction, that's all. It happens between men and women. It's natural. We don't have to act on it. And if we did—which we *won't*—it would be nobody's business but yours and mine."

He was scanning her face again, his gaze burning where it touched. "You understand nothing."

Fury flared again within her. She ordered it down. "Well, then." She spoke calmly. Reasonably. "I guess you'd better explain it to me."

He didn't reply—not right away. She started to think he *wouldn't* reply. But at last, he said, "I am assigned to bring you to your father. That is all the extent of the contact you will ever have with me. Whatever your father has planned for you, I am not a part of it. I could never be a part of it, not in any way."

"My father told you that?"

"He had no need to tell me. It's fact, pure and simple. It's true that if fortune smiles on me, the daughter of some minor jarl might agree to reach out and clasp my hand in marriage. But no king would willingly give his daughter to a bastard. Some doors, as I told you, are forever closed to me."

"Not to me, Hauk. Never to me. I'm the one who decides who I'll be with, not my father. He has no rights at all when it comes to my private life."

"That may be. I am in no position to say. However,

your father does have rights over me. He has *all* rights. I live and breathe for him. All my acts are acts in his service. I am *his* warrior. It is a high honor. And a sacred trust.''

Chapter Eight

By tacit agreement, there was silence between them.

Hauk went where she went within the apartment. In the living room, she sat on the couch and he sat in the easy chair. She read—or she tried to read, though she continually lost her place and had to go back and reread whole passages to have any idea what she was reading about. She could feel his eyes on her the whole time—or so it seemed.

But then, when she couldn't stand it a moment longer and glanced up, he would be looking not *at* her, but beyond her, into the distance. His body would be so very still and straight. She would stare at his chest, wondering if he was even breathing.

Eventually, he'd draw himself back from whatever distant meditative state he'd put himself in. He'd meet her eyes.

And she'd know that he had been there all the time, watching—and yet not watching. Across the room from her. And a million miles away.

Around five, she gave up on her book and went into the spare room. She tried to pretend Hauk wasn't sitting on the futon behind her as she paid a few bills to get them out of the way and answered a few last e-mails, then put her various listserves on No-mail.

By seven or so, she was starting to get that frantic feeling—that feeling that if they remained alone in her apartment, just the two of them, for much longer, she would do something unforgivable.

Start screaming like a maniac. Start throwing things—favorite figurines, a lamp or two.

Climb him like a big tree, grab him close and kiss him, force him to put aside everything he believed in and make love with her.

Oh, how had this happened? How had this gone so dangerously far so very, very fast?

She honestly wasn't some sex maniac. Okay, she wasn't a virgin—but she was no wild thing, either.

Serious relationships? She'd had a few—well, if you included her two high-school boyfriends. One in sophomore year and one when she was a senior. At the time, she'd been certain she would love each of those boys forever and ever. But she'd grown up and so had they.

Surely this crazy attraction to Hauk was like her schoolgirl crushes—destined to flare high and hot and then, soon enough, fade away. It was the lure of the forbidden. And they'd both get over it.

Maybe he was right. She should throw some stuff

in her suitcase and tell him she was finally ready to head for Gullandria.

But somewhere deep inside, she had a true stubborn streak. She wasn't leaving until she *had* to leave and she didn't have to leave until tomorrow. She shoved the chicken she'd never gotten around to roasting into the freezer and told Hauk they were going out for dinner.

He didn't argue. He didn't say anything. He kept his sculpted mouth shut and his expression closed against her, as he'd been doing for hours by then.

She took him to a restaurant over in Old Sacramento, where the food was excellent and so was the service. The steward brought the wine list. She waved it away.

Yes, a glass of wine or two would have soothed her frayed nerves right then. But she couldn't afford to be soothed. When they went to bed tonight, she would need all her inhibitions firmly in place—and not because she feared that Hauk might make a move on her. He had way too much self-control to do that.

No, he wasn't the one she was worried about. It was herself. She would need to fight her own wayward, hungry heart and her yearning body, too, if she planned to get through the whole night without doing something they would both later regret.

Hauk spoke with the waiter briefly but politely. He *didn't* speak to Elli, not the whole time they sat at that table. Anyone watching them probably would have guessed that they'd either been forced against their will to share a meal—or they were locked in some private battle, some intimate tiff, and currently refusing to speak to each other. Both speculations would have been right on the money.

Too soon, the meal was finished. It was only 8:15. She didn't want to go back to her apartment, not yet. She wanted it to be late—after midnight at least, when they got there. She wanted to be really, really tired.

But every nerve she had was humming. She felt as if sleeping was something she would never do again. And she'd made the mistake of drinking two glasses of water with her meal.

She had to use the ladies' room.

Hauk stood outside in the hall. She hoped it embarrassed him, to lurk there by the ladies'-room door. She used the facilities and she washed her hands, glancing now and then at her unhappy face in the wide mirror above the sink.

She was blowing her hands dry when the small window over the center stall caught her eye. It was a single pane of pebbled glass, roughly a foot and a half on each side, hinged at the top. To open it, you undid the latch and pushed it outward.

She was reasonably certain there would be an alley on the other side. It wouldn't be that difficult to hoist herself up there, to slither through it and...

What? Run away? Go into hiding and terrify her mother and Hilda and her sisters, too? Go to the police? Tell them that her father was having her kidnapped and she needed protection?

After they sorted it all out, they might even believe her. And just maybe they'd be able to protect her. It was a good chance, with all the publicity that would ensue, with her face and the faces of everyone in her family splashed all over the tabloids, that her father would back off, give up on whatever scheme he was hatching.

Hauk would be disgraced for letting her get away. And she would stay right here, in Sacramento, where she belonged. She would not see Gullandria—or her father, after all. And she would never see Hauk again.

The dryer had turned itself off. The ladies' room seemed very quiet.

Behind her, the door to the hallway swung open. She turned. It was Hauk. He looked at her and he looked at the window above the center stall and then at her again.

"So all right," she muttered. "I was tempted. But notice I'm still here."

"Ahem. Do you *mind?*" A short, cute redheaded woman had appeared in the open doorway beside Hauk. She craned her neck to look up at him. "Read the sign on the door. *Ladies.* That is *so* not you."

Hauk retreated and the redhead came forward. The door closed with him out in the hall. The redhead pretended to fan herself. "Is that *yours?* Oh, my, my…"

Elli let a smile answer for her. She hooked her purse over her shoulder and went out to join her jailer.

Out in the parking lot, the attendant brought her car. She tipped him and got behind the wheel. Hauk hunched himself down into the passenger seat.

Elli drove—out of Old Sac, out of town, beyond the city lights.

More than once, she felt Hauk's brooding gaze on

her. She knew he was wondering where they were going. But he didn't ask.

Which was just as well, since she didn't know, anyway. She held the wheel and watched the road ahead and kept on driving.

They ended up on the river road, rolling through a string of sleepy little one-stoplight towns. When she was in her teens, she and her sisters and their friends—or sometimes she and one of those two boys she'd thought she loved so much—would come out here.

With a boyfriend, she'd end up parked by the levee, in the shadows of the cottonwood trees, kissing until her lips hurt, moaning and sighing and declaring undying love—all, of course, without going all the way.

Back then, Elli and her sisters would talk about sex all the time. They were young and they were curious about all the new and bewildering yearnings their bodies could feel. They had one girlfriend who'd gotten pregnant and had to leave school. And another who had tested positive for HIV.

Sex was so tempting. And yet they understood it could also be dangerous, that it had consequences, serious ones. They had formed a pact, the three of them. They called themselves the NATWC—the Never All the Way Club. Whenever one of them would go off to be alone with a boy, a sister was always somewhere nearby to raise a fist in the air and announce with pride, "NATWC!"

It had worked. They all three remained full-fledged members of the NATWC—at least until college and then...

Well, even triplets, at some point, have to make their own decisions about love and sex and how far to go.

Elli made a turn, toward the river. She parked beneath a cottonwood and she got out and climbed the levee. Hauk, of course, got out, too. He followed in her wake, a shadow—always with her, never speaking.

The mosquitoes were still out. As usual, they found her delicious. She slapped at them now and then. Sometimes she got them—and sometimes not. The ground beneath her sandals was soft. The wild grasses, still moist and green in early May, brushed at her ankles as she climbed.

She reached the crest of the levee. It stretched out, a wide path, in either direction. Below, by the light of the fading last-quarter moon, the river looked dark and oily, flowing easily along. There were dangers, beneath the surface. Swirling currents. Undertows.

But from here, it looked so serene and slow. Hauk stood beside her. As usual, he made no sound. She couldn't even hear him breathing.

She turned in the opposite direction and started walking. He came along behind her, but several yards back, as if he wanted to give her as much space, as much leeway, as he could and still follow the orders he'd been given by his king.

She stopped. Looked at her watch. Ten o'clock.

Hauk came up beside her. She sent him a sad smile. "I know. It's not your fault. None of this. You can't be who you are and behave any differently."

He said nothing. He stared out over the smooth-moving water.

"Come on," she said. "We'll go back now."

When they got to her apartment, the princess wanted a bath. She asked nicely for an hour to herself in the bathroom.

Hauk wanted to shout *No*. He wanted to order her to come with him. Now. Out of here, to the airport, to the jet that awaited her.

But he'd demanded that they leave so many times already. She always refused. And then there was nothing more he could do. He had no rights here. He was to wait and to watch. And then tomorrow, if she continued to balk, he was to use force to see that she went where she'd agreed to go.

In answer to her request for time alone in the bath, he gave her a grunt and a shrug. He wasn't talking to her, hadn't for hours now. Talking to her only led to trouble.

She was too good with that mouth of hers. Whenever he let himself engage in discourse with her, she always got him thinking things he knew he shouldn't let himself think. She would lure him close to doubting the wisdom of his own king, to questioning the way things were and had always been.

And beyond the dangerous questions she had him asking himself, there was that other problem, the one that kept getting worse: the way she roused him, as a man. Whenever she spoke, he would watch her full lips moving and wonder what else she could do with that soft mouth and that clever tongue.

She went into her bathroom and he turned for the guest bath. He emptied his bladder, washed his hands and cleaned his teeth. He returned to her bedroom and rolled out his bedding. And then he stood, waiting, all too aware of the scented moistness of the air, constantly turning his mind from the light beneath the bathroom door, from images of her, naked. Wet. That wheat-colored hair curling and damp from the steam that rose upward off the warm water...

By Odin's one eye, he was doing it again.

He ordered his mind off the thought of her, naked.

He pondered the morning, when her time for stalling, for lingering here, would run out. Would she force him to bind her and gag her again, to toss her over his shoulder and carry her out of here as he'd started to do two days and a lifetime ago?

And the larger question: Would he do it if she did?

That he even asked himself that question spoke volumes about what was happening to him. Something had shifted—inside him. Something had changed. Something in his very self, in who he was.

He'd earned, over time, an inner contentment. Born from high stock, but a bastard, he'd been cast down. Both his mother and his father had past kings in their lineage. Had his mother agreed to marry his father, as a child of two old and powerful families, he would have been high jarl. Had his parents been married, he could now look at Princess Elli eye-to-eye. Even should her father have plans to marry her to another, Hauk would still be her equal, he could still court her. He would have a chance at her hand.

But though his mother succumbed to her passion

for his father, she would not marry. She was kvina soldar: a woman warrior. If she married, she would have been forced to give up her warrior status. For a wife to be a warrior was not done. And, as a result, she condemned her son to start from less than nothing.

A warrior's training was brutal. But Hauk had been born with his father's size and his mother's natural physical skill. He'd fought his way forward to the front of the pack. In recent years, he'd thought that he could see his future and that it was good. He'd believed he brought honor to his bastard name.

He had eight more years in the king's service, and then, when his commission was up, there would be money enough. He'd ask a good woman, one only slightly above him—legitimate and jarl, but low jarl, from an unimportant family, a family only a generation or two up from freeman—to marry him.

And his sons and daughters would have a better start, a better chance than he'd had. Thus, the error of one generation found correction in the next. It had all seemed fitting. Right. Good.

Until now.

Until he'd been sent to kidnap the king's daughter.

And ended up trailing after her wherever she went, looking into those deep-blue eyes, listening to that warm, musical voice. Sitting beside her in a darkened theater, across from her at her own table—and in that restaurant tonight…

There had been a candle on the table tonight. In the warm light, her skin had glowed, soft as the petal of some rare pink rose. He had sat and stared and admired up close what such as he should never see except from a careful, formal distance.

It was all a mistake. A huge one, an error in judgment on the part of his king. His king had trusted him.

And no matter that Hauk had yet to touch the woman intimately—would *never* touch the woman intimately—he had betrayed that trust in his heart and his mind.

Betrayed his king. And thus, betrayed the man he had always believed himself to be.

The door to the bathroom opened. The princess emerged wearing the big pink shirt she liked to sleep in. A cloud of sweet steam came out with her. Her face had a clean, scrubbed shine to it. Her hair was slightly damp at the temples, little tendrils of it curling along her soft, moist cheeks.

Desire was a lance, turning in his flesh, twisting ever deeper.

If only she had never dared to speak of it—to talk of it so calmly, in her easy American way. Her words had seared themselves into his brain.

It's an…attraction, that's all. It happens between men and women. It's natural. We don't have to act on it. And if we did—which we won't—*it would be nobody's business but yours and mine….*

She had him thinking, oh yes, she did. Thinking that to have her would be worth everything—his commission, his pride. Possibly even his freedom and his life. Just one night, to touch her everywhere, to put his mouth on all her most secret places, to hear her call out his name.

What was his life, anyway? Who was he? Less than nothing. Fitz. Bastard. With his small hopes of an insignificant future.

The wife he hadn't found yet was ruined for him now. In the distant, empty time to come, he would look down into her face when they mated and think of the woman standing in the doorway now.

Her Highness said, "You can get comfortable. I'm going to bed."

Hauk pulled off his boots and his stockings and went down to his blankets to wait out the endless night.

Chapter Nine

Somehow, though she never expected she would, Elli did go to sleep. If she dreamed, she didn't recall those dreams when she woke. Her eyes popped open at a few minutes after seven on Thursday morning and her first thought, as she stared at her silent bedside clock, was that she'd forgotten to turn on her alarm.

Her second thought was of Hauk.

Hauk. A warmth spread through her. A longing.

She ordered that longing to get lost. Today, they were leaving. By tonight, she'd be in Gullandria. He'd made it clear that once he delivered her to her father, they might never see each other again. And if they did, it would only be in passing. A quick glimpse, from a distance, in some echoing palace room. That, at most. Nothing more.

She sat up. And found him sitting in the straight chair opposite the end of her bed. He had his boots on and his face was just-shaved smooth.

Elli raked her tangled hair back off her forehead. "Imagine running into you here."

"It is Thursday morning."

Irritation sizzled through her at his preemptive tone. "No kidding."

"Rise. Dress and gather your things. The time to go has come."

She folded her hands on top of the blankets and looked down at them. She was thinking that she ought to just do as he said.

Too bad when she raised her head what came out was, "Think again."

As usual, he sat absolutely still. "Why do you insist on playing these endless mind games?" His eyes were like a pair of lasers, slicing through her, cutting deep.

"This is no game. It's only seven. It will be Thursday morning for five more hours."

His expression showed very little. Yet somehow he seemed to seethe where he sat. There was a long, heated moment during which they glared at each other.

Then he stood. "Five hours then. At noon, you will be ready. At 12:00 p.m., exactly, we will walk out your door."

She yanked her shoulders back and shot him her most defiant scowl. "And if I'm *not* ready?"

"Then I'll bind you hand and foot, stuff a kerchief

in your mouth to still your cries and carry you out.''
He turned on his heel and left.

Elli gripped the blankets and told herself she would
not, under any circumstances, jump from the bed and
chase him down the hall screaming obscenities at the
top of her lungs.

Hauk stood in the hall, composing himself. He
wanted to march back in there, wrap his fingers
around her smooth neck and squeeze the defiance
right out of her. But if he touched her, he knew it
wouldn't be strangling she'd get at his hands.

The most important thing, the goal above all, was
to last until noon without laying a finger on her. Then,
one way or another, he'd take her to the airport. The
Gulfstream could make it nonstop to Gullandria.
Within hours, he'd be turning her over to her father,
the king. Once he got free of her—once she wasn't
there every moment, her very presence like a taunt, a
constant reminder of what he'd never have—he could
begin to purge himself of this impossible hunger for
her.

Through the most recent long and sleepless night,
he'd pondered deeply. And by dawn he'd almost convinced himself that, over time, he would again find
the man he had been before Monday—before two
brief days and three cruel nights of following his
king's beautiful daughter everywhere she went. He'd
almost made himself believe that the day would come
when the prospect of the life that lay before him
would be enough to satisfy him again.

Already there was a bright spot to focus on. Never

again would he be forced to spend a night lying so near to her, forbidden to touch.

Elli got dressed, washed her face, combed her hair and brushed on a little blusher and mascara. Hauk was waiting for her in the hallway when she emerged from the bedroom.

She couldn't seem to stop herself from sneering at him. "There you are again. How can I miss you if you won't go away?"

He fell in step behind her. "You will soon have your wish."

She stopped, turned. And all her anger just melted away. There was nothing left but longing.

"Oh, Hauk. I didn't say it was my wish."

They stared at each other. Always a mistake, for them to stare at each other...

Elli sucked in a trembling breath. "Breakfast," she said. "We need breakfast."

"Yes," he said. "Breakfast."

Neither of them moved.

"Go on," he said.

Somehow, she did it. She turned from those eyes of his and went on down the hall.

The dishwasher was full of clean dishes. Hauk emptied it and set the table. Elli made the coffee, fried the last of the bacon and whipped up some batter for pancakes.

They ate in silence.

And not an angry silence, either. Just a cautious one—cautious and a little bit sad. Elli let her gaze stray out the window to the patch of blue sky between the buildings.

She looked back at Hauk, who was so carefully not looking at her.

Oh, really, he was very dear. He was true and good and…straight-ahead. Not to mention absolutely thrilling to look at. She remembered the little redhead in the restaurant last night. *Is that* yours? *Oh, my, my…*

Elli agreed with the redhead. What woman wouldn't want to make love with Hauk? All that beautiful bronze skin and those big, hard muscles. And those eyes…

Once she'd thought his eyes cold and hard. But she'd learned better in the last two days. His eyes were clear. Unflinching. They spoke of the honesty and strength within.

And it wasn't only that just looking at him made her want to throw herself into those huge arms of his. There was also an odd and lovely… comfortableness, between them. Or at least, there was whenever she let down her guard and stopped manufacturing anger to keep her feelings for him at bay.

Really, other than held tight in his arms, there was no place she'd rather be than right here, at the breakfast table, with Hauk sitting across from her.

How could that have happened, in little more than two days? How had he gone from a terrifying stranger, her kidnapper—to this? The man most likely to turn her knees to jelly, the man she wanted so much to kiss. The man who could clear her table and empty her dishwasher any time, no questions asked.

She set down her fork. "Hauk?"

He allowed himself to look at her.

"Why are we doing this?"

"Because you refuse to give up your stalling and pack your—"

"No."

He looked at her sideways, suspicious.

"Hauk, I don't mean that. I don't mean my going or not going. I mean…you and me. I mean, well, that I *care* for you. A lot." He stared—and he blinked. She waved a hand. "Oh, I know. It sounds crazy, to say that, considering why you came here in the first place, considering that it's only been a couple of days since we met. But so what if it's crazy? It's also true. I do care for you. And I think you care for me." He was gaping at her. He looked utterly stunned. She continued. "I don't see why we can't just—"

"Enough." Hauk dropped his own fork. It clattered to his plate.

"But I want you to—"

His chair screeched across the floor tiles as he surged to his feet. "I have told you. I know you have heard. There can be nothing between us. Ever."

She looked up at him unblinking. "That is so ridiculous."

"To you, perhaps."

"No. Not only to me. To any…thinking individual."

"Now you insult my intelligence."

"No, I'm not. You know I'm not. And we both know what *you're* doing now. You're trying to drum up some fake reason to be angry with me—and I don't blame you for doing that. I mean, it's not as if

I haven't been doing it, too. But we both know it's all just an act, just a hopeless attempt on both our parts to keep from admitting how we really feel about each other.''

He fell back a step—as if he needed all the distance from her he could get, as if he feared she might actually reach out and touch him.

She did no such thing—she didn't even move. ''You think of me as a princess, as someone far above you, someone out of your reach. But that's…all in your mind. I'm no princess. Not really. You're always telling me that I think like an American. Well, that's because, as *I* keep telling you, I *am* an American. I might have been born in Gullandria, but I've lived all but the first ten months of my life right here, in Sacramento. The laws and customs of Gullandria don't apply to me. At heart, where it matters, I'm just Elli Thorson. And I think, honestly, that we might have something here, you and me. Something really powerful. Something so good…''

Apparently, he didn't agree with her. He stood to attention now. He was just waiting for her to be done with him. Waiting so that he could go.

''Oh, Hauk,'' she said in a low voice.

''Are you finished?''

She bit her lip, gave a small, hopeless shrug.

To get away from her, out of the kitchen, he had to go past her. It was his undoing.

She caught his wrist as he tried to get by. ''Oh, Hauk. Please…''

He froze. The air seemed to shimmer around them. Heat radiated from the point where her flesh touched his. That heat was spreading out, all through her body. Arrows of longing zinged straight through her heart.

She had a split second—even less than that—and he would shake her off. She didn't give him time to do it. She swept upward, out of her chair, throwing her arms around his neck, pressing her body against his big, hard chest.

It was too much for him. His resistance broke. With a low moan he gathered her close.

Stunned that she'd gotten exactly what she'd yearned for, Elli stared upward, into his wonderful, square-jawed, determined face.

Oh, my. This was a lovely, lovely place to be, held so close against his heart, those huge, strong arms wrapped around her.

He whispered, "You should not have touched me."

"Oh, right. Ask me not to breathe, while you're at it."

"You should not—"

"Shh." She slid one hand up between their bodies, put two fingers against his mouth. "Stop that," she chided, oh so tenderly.

His mouth moved. She felt his breath flow down her hand. His lips parted slightly and his lower teeth scraped her finger pads.

Elli shivered—with delight, with excitement. "Oh, see? See, this is how it *ought* to be...."

His big hand was in her hair. He cupped the back of her head. "A mistake. This is all a dangerous mistake."

"Stop that. You stop that right now. This is no

mistake. I just told you what this is. This is how it ought to be.'' She was pressed very close to him, close enough to feel his arousal—and to revel in it. In her own most intimate place, she felt...hollowed out, moist and needful and longing to be filled with him. She gasped. ''Oh, Hauk. Kiss me. Kiss me, please.''

Her eyes drifted closed.

Hauk looked down at that beautiful mouth, the mouth she offered, the mouth she wanted him to have.

Damned, he thought. *I am damned to the bitter cold and unending night of Hel, to do this.*

But right at that moment, he didn't care. He thought, *Just the taste of her. Why shouldn't I have that? She wants me to have that. Only a taste....*

Her head tipped back, her mouth tipped up. She loosed the sweetest, tiniest sigh.

He thought, *Only that. One kiss. And that sigh, inside me, all the rest of my days.*

He brought his mouth down over hers.

Her lips parted. The sweetness within nearly finished him—right there, in her kitchen, in the bright light of morning. He tasted the slick inner surface beyond her soft lips and he thought he was dying.

An acceptable sacrifice, the loss of his life. He was glad to go, though Valhalla would be lost to him— ah, the shame of it.

The king's warrior, dead in a kitchen of a woman's kiss...

He held her more tightly, his hands roaming her slim back, pressing that softness, that female warmth all the closer. Those full breasts of hers pushed against his chest. She moaned and her breath, sweet and hot and scented of coffee, flowed into his mouth. He sucked it in all the deeper, down into his soul. He would keep it forever, along with her sigh.

Her soft fingers danced at the nape of his neck, threading into his hair, caressing outward, across his shoulders, then sliding back to clasp around his neck again. Her tongue, shy at first, grew bolder, darting into his mouth, flicking along the top of his own tongue, pausing there, darting back.

She made a small, hungry sound, like a kitten seeking strokes. He groaned in response. And he swept his hands downward, over the incredible twin swells of her bottom, tucking her into him, his manhood pressing her most secret place.

He was so hard. His body commanded him. To lay her down, to make her his...

He curved the slim length of her backward over his arm, and he lost her mouth in order to gain the petal-soft flesh of her sweet chin, to run his tongue down the glorious stretch of her long, satiny throat.

"Oh, Hauk. Oh, yes, yes..." She pressed her hips up against him, in invitation, in a promise of something he knew he couldn't take.

Yet still, she promised. She promised him everything. She murmured sweet encouragements, she drove him on with sighs.

He kissed the twin points of her collarbone, pausing there, where her pulse beat in the hollow of her throat, to breathe deep, to suck in the womanly, flower-sweet scent of her, adding it to the treasures he'd already claimed—that sigh before he kissed her, that later breath. Breath upon breath, he would have them all.

Those soft hands of hers were at his waist, fumbling with the shirt he wore, gathering it, sliding it upward. She caressed the bare skin over his ribs, scratching him lightly, tauntingly, with her fingernails.

He nuzzled the fabric of her light cotton blouse, burying his face in the soft swell of a breast, finding her nipple beneath the layers of clothing.

He teased that nipple, drawing it up to a point, then closing his mouth over it, sending out a focused breath of air across it, biting at it, lightly, feeling it pebble up more firmly, as if it begged for more.

She'd forgotten her task of removing his shirt. Her hand splayed in his hair now, pressing him closer, against her offered breast. He latched on, sucking, soaking the fabric over her nipple as he toyed with it.

"Oh, yes," she moaned, pulling him ever closer. "Oh, yes, yes, yes, yes…"

He brought one hand between them, laid it in the center of her chest, against the glorious fullness of those proud breasts.

"Yes…" She urged him on, soft lips against his ear, warm breath against his skin. She captured his earlobe, teased it between her teeth. "Yes, Hauk. Oh, yes…" Her hips moved against his, promising untold delights.

Offering everything.

All of her. All she was, all she had. So much. More than he had ever dared to dream of in his bastard soul.

A prize beyond measure. Worth any price. He found the first button on her blouse, captured it between his thumb and his forefinger.

"Yes," she whispered, one more time.

And then the phone rang.

Chapter Ten

The jarring bleat of the phone ruined everything.

Hauk went still as a statue in Elli's arms.

She gripped his big shoulders and begged him, "Oh, please, just let it ring."

But he was already taking her hands, gently peeling them away, his face flushed and regretful, shaking his head. "We must stop. You know that."

"No, I don't know that. I don't know that at all."

He stepped back from her. She had that feeling of something tearing again, as in the movie theater the day before. Only worse. A thousand times worse.

He said softly, "Answer the phone."

She wanted to scream, to throw something. "No."

"Don't behave like a spoiled child."

He was right and she knew it.

Not about having to stop—never, ever about that.

She had given up fighting this lovely, impossible magic between them. And she was furious with him all over again, to look in his face and see his jaw was set—like his mind—against her, against what might be between them, against all they might share.

But acting out wouldn't solve anything. She went to the counter and punched the button that answered the call on speakerphone. "Hello?"

"Elli. Oh, sweetheart..."

"Aunt Nanna." Like her daughters, Elli's mother had been one of fraternal triplets. Elli's Aunt Kirsten lived in San Francisco. Aunt Nanna lived in Napa. There had been a brother, too, but he had died when Elli and her sisters were babies.

Nanna made a worried noise, low in her throat. "I was afraid..."

"Afraid of what?"

"That you'd already have gone."

Elli shut her eyes and tried to collect her scattered wits, to concentrate on what her aunt was saying instead of thinking of what hadn't quite had a chance to happen between her and Hauk. "I, uh, take it you've been talking to Mom?"

"Oh, Elli. I just got off the phone with her."

Elli opened her eyes and there he was, watching. She turned away, toward the window, so she wouldn't have to look at him. "I'll be leaving in a few hours."

"Oh, honey, are you absolutely sure about this?"

"Yes. I'm positive." And she was. Positive about a lot more than just the trip to meet her father.

"Ingrid's so worried for you. I am, too. You don't really understand the way things work in that place.

I'm sorry to say it, but your father is not a man anyone should trust. He broke your mother's heart, you know, he broke—''

Elli had heard it all before. "Nanna, what, exactly, did he *do* that's made you all hate him so?"

Nanna took a moment to answer. Elli could just see her, pursing up her mouth. Finally she said, "You'll have to speak with your mother about that."

"That's what you always say. And when I ask Mom, I get nothing. So let's just leave it, okay? Accept the fact that I have to meet him, to decide how I feel about him for myself."

Nanna made a small, frustrated sound.

Elli said firmly, "I want to do this, I sincerely do."

Nanna sighed. "Your mother warned me that there'd be no way to change your mind."

"And she was right—how's Uncle Cam?" Her uncle was a total type A. He'd had a quadruple bypass a couple of months ago.

"Elli—"

"Come on, Aunt Nanna. I'm going and that's all there is to it. So how's Uncle Cam?"

The silence that followed told Elli her aunt was debating with herself—to let it be as Elli asked. Or to press on with her warnings and her worries.

Nanna let it be. "Your Uncle Cam is doing well. We've got him eating low-salt and low-fat. He's taking his medication...."

They talked for a few more minutes, about her cousins, Nanna's son and daughter, who were both in high school, about Elli's two classes of bright-eyed kindergartners. Elli promised she'd make it over to Napa at least once during her summer break.

"Take care," Nanna said at last. "Be safe."

"I love you. I will."

The line went dead and after a second or two, the dial tone buzzed. Hauk was the one who reached out and pressed the button to cut off the sound. Elli turned from the window and met his eyes. Distant eyes now. Once again, he had barricaded his heart behind a shield of watchfulness. Looking at his stern, unforgiving face, she wanted to throw herself against him, to beat on his broad chest, to demand that he show her his real, tender self again.

Her shirt was wet, where he'd put his mouth to her breast. She looked down at it, at the moist circle over her right nipple. Then, proudly, she lifted her head.

"Guess I'd better change my shirt."

"Pack," he said. The single word echoed harshly, like a door slamming shut.

What more could she say, except, "Yes. I guess I'd better do that."

For once, he didn't fall in behind her as she turned for the hall. Great, she thought. She could use a break. A few precious minutes to herself, to get past her shameless disappointment at losing her chance to get lost in his arms.

Elli paused in the doorway to her bedroom. She leaned her forehead against the doorframe and shut her eyes and wished it didn't have to be like this.

Maybe she should just look on the bright side. At least for a few unforgettable minutes there, she'd had a taste of what it might be like to be Hauk Fitz-Wyborn's love....

Elli drew herself up. Really, looking on the bright side just wasn't going to cut it. She unbuttoned the shirt that was still wet from his kiss and went to the bathroom to toss it in the hamper.

Okay, so he'd been saved by the bell. This time.

In her bedroom, she pushed open her closet door.

He still had a commitment to escort her to Gullandria. And after they got there, she might find ways to see him, to be near him.

She took a jewel-blue silk shirt from a hanger, put her arms in the sleeves and buttoned it up.

Why not think positively? She wanted him, she *cared* for him. And as hard as he kept fighting it, she believed in her heart that he wanted and cared for her, too.

He'd let down his guard once. It could happen again. Maybe she'd get another chance to show him just how strongly she felt for him. And maybe next time, he wouldn't push her away.

She got her big suitcase and hoisted it to the bed, laying it open. Standing very still, she listened. She heard nothing. Hauk could move so quietly. He might be standing in the doorway right now.

She shot a glance over her shoulder.

Empty.

Good. She listened some more and ended up deciding she felt reasonably certain he'd yet to leave the kitchen. He didn't want to be near her right now. He needed a little time to marshal his defenses against her.

Suited her just fine.

She went to the tall dresser by the inner wall and pulled open the top drawer—all the way open, so she could get to the very back of it.

Her hand closed on the box that she'd pushed in there a few months ago. She'd been dating someone then, on a regular basis. She'd thought that maybe it might become more than it was.

But the relationship had cooled before it ever really heated up. In the meantime, though, she'd bought the box of condoms, just in case.

Right now, with Hauk, it was much more than a *just in case* situation. If a miracle happened and he held out his arms to her, she would run to him, eagerly. Better safe than sorry, if her dreams did come true.

At ten-thirty, she was ready to go. She got her passport from the desk in the spare room. She was slipping it into her purse when Hauk appeared in the doorway.

"Are you ready?"

She thought of the box of condoms and she almost let out a wild little laugh. "Um-hm."

"Your suitcase?"

"In my bedroom."

He turned toward the door to her room.

She followed behind him. "I packed my overnighter, too. And I can carry both bags myself, honestly. The big one has those rollers and…" She let her voice trail off. There was no point in saying more.

He slung the strap of the smaller bag over his

shoulder and he grabbed the handle of the big suitcase and headed for the front door.

Fine. Let him haul it all down the stairs by himself if he wanted to. She checked the lock on the patio door and made sure all the lights were out. He waited for her by the front door, laden with her bags and that big black duffel of his, too.

She opened the door and gestured him out ahead of her. At the base of the stairs, she turned for the carports.

"No," he said. "Follow me." He led her out another way, to a side street and a black van.

"Tinted windows," she remarked. "An absolute necessity when it comes to kidnapping unwilling princesses."

It was a bad joke and it fell flat. He didn't bother to respond.

She just couldn't leave it at that. "I suppose you'll want me to drive. You'll need your hands free to keep me under control. Then again, who knows? If I'm behind the wheel, I could go wild, decide to make a break for Bakersfield."

He was already turning for the driver's door himself. "Just get in."

Her father's Gulfstream jet had a roomy pressurized cabin furnished with six high-backed leather seats, teak tables beside them. There were also a collapsible dividing wall and a full-size bed that could be pulled down to make the divided-off space into a flying bedroom.

"Does Your Highness wish a nap?" the attendant

inquired. She was a tall blonde in a slim black skirt and a crisp white shirt. She had a blue-and-gold lightning bolt embroidered on her pocket as well as on the crest of her jaunty-looking red garrison cap.

"No, thanks." Elli took one of the high-backed leather chairs as Hauk, shoulders hunched, golden head grazing the ceiling, moved farther down the cabin.

"Refreshment?"

"Not right now." Elli's mind wasn't on food. She resisted the urge to lean out of her seat and look back at Hauk. He'd been depressingly silent on the drive to the airport—not that his silence was anything all that new or different. It only seemed that way, after those beautiful, too-brief moments in his arms.

"Fasten your seatbelt," said the flight attendant. "We'll be cleared for takeoff soon."

Elli nodded and smiled and the attendant left her alone. She looked out the window as they taxied along the runway. It all seemed so…civilized, the attractive attendant, the beautifully appointed jet. She couldn't help wondering what the attendant might have said to her had Hauk brought her on board all tied up with a gag in her mouth.

Probably nothing. The woman would have pulled the collapsible divider across the cabin and brought down the bed and Hauk would have dropped Elli on it without anyone asking if she'd care for a nap.

It would be a long flight, but it would be nonstop. Hauk sat in his seat and tried not to stare at *her* seat in front of him. The sky out the window was clear. Fat white clouds drifted below the wing.

It was over—their time together. In the end, his sense of duty and his understanding of his place in the world had triumphed. He hadn't succumbed to the desperate hunger that would have caused her nothing but shame and heartache and cost him more than he cared to contemplate. He told himself he was glad it had gone no further between them.

An indiscreet embrace and a few passionate kisses—more than he should have allowed to happen. But not total disaster. Thanks to a ringing phone, he'd stopped it in time.

He was weary. Of everything. Hauk shut his eyes and allowed himself to disappear into the first deep sleep he'd known in days.

He woke, startled, when the plane dropped several hundred feet and then slammed against an air current below.

The attendant, in a chair down near the cockpit door, wore a bright, professional smile. "A little turbulence. Nothing to worry about."

He took her at her word, at first. But the going got rougher, the plane rising and dropping like a toy in the hands of a brutal child. Rain drove against the windows. The sky beyond the insulated panes was black a few feet from the glass—except when Thor threw his hammer and lightning in ragged fingers lit the blackness with a golden-green light, followed not long after by the deafening crack and roll of thunder.

Hauk got up and worked his way forward. He

paused by the seat of the princess—after all, it was his duty to check on her. To keep her safe.

She looked up at him. "Kind of rough, huh?"

"You're all right?"

She gave him a nod. "I'm good." It was another reason among the thousand reasons that she was a woman any man would covet—she didn't frighten easily.

Lightning speared through the blackness outside again, its eerie glow suffusing the cabin. Thunder boomed. The plane dropped sharply, then bottomed out hard against the fist of a rising air current.

And through it all, he stared at her and she looked up at him, her face pale and calm and so beautiful it felled him like a deathblow from an enemy's ax. "I'll check our status with the pilot."

She nodded, shifted that haunting gaze away. He staggered on toward the cockpit.

The pilot told him what he'd already deduced. There was no fighting through this mess. They no longer had the fuel to make it all the way to Gullandria. They would have to land, refuel and then wait for the storm to blow itself out.

It was, to say the least, a rocky next few hours. Elli was never so grateful as when Hauk told her they'd gotten the go-ahead to land at a private airstrip just outside of Boston.

The landing was one of those lurching, scary, hope-I-never-do-this-again kind of experiences. But they made it and they made it safely. As soon as the plane taxied to a stop, Hauk went forward a second time to speak with the pilot.

He came out looking bleak. "The storm shows no signs of abating. This will be an overnight stop."

"Will we just stay here, on the plane?"

He shook his head. "I'll arrange for suitable lodging."

Lodging. A triumphant little thrill shot through her. Hauk wouldn't be rid of her quite as soon as he'd hoped.

And so very much might happen, in one more night alone together....

Half an hour later, Elli looked out the window and saw a long, black limousine rolling across the tarmac toward the jet.

"Will you have need of both your suitcases?" Hauk asked, his tone carefully formal.

Elli had flown enough to be prepared for situations like this. "Just the smaller one."

"Your Highness." The flight attendant presented her with a big black umbrella at the cabin door.

"Thanks." The rain was coming down in sheets, the wind gusting hard.

Halfway down the steps, the umbrella turned inside out. Hauk, right behind her, took it from her hand. He shouted against the gale, his voice hearty with sudden good humor, "Speed will serve you better than this." He held the ruined umbrella high. Already, that golden hair was plastered to his head. Water ran off his bladelike nose. His eyes gleamed. Apparently, he liked wild weather—enough that he'd even forgotten for a moment to treat her like the princess he didn't dare to touch. "Run!"

She took off down the final steps and sprinted across the streaming pavement to the open door of the limousine. Hauk ducked in right after her, pulling the door shut, tossing the useless umbrella to the floor. They waited a moment or two, while the necessary bags were stowed in the trunk. And then they were off.

Their hotel suite was on the thirty-fifth floor, with a view of the harbor where the storm was tossing all the boats around. There were two big bedrooms, each with its own bath, a living and dining area between. Elli suppressed a knowing smile when she saw there was a second bedroom. Wishful thinking on Hauk's part. The poor man. Duty bound to sleep wherever she did.

Oh, yes. It could turn out to be a very interesting night.

They ate dinner in the room. Elli hadn't realized how hungry she was until the bellhop wheeled it in. She'd ordered the pheasant. It was absolutely wonderful.

For dessert, she had amaretto crème brûlée. It was practically sexual, how delicious it tasted. She ate every last creamy bit.

Hauk, on the other hand, seemed to have little appetite. He mostly sat and watched her. He was looking broody again.

She could almost feel sorry for him.

A whole night of temptation ahead. How *would* he get through it?

Ah, well. She'd do her very best to help him with that.

She sent him a bright smile. "Does my father know we're going to be a day late?"

He nodded. "The message has been sent."

Via the mysterious black beeper thingy, no doubt. "Well, good. I wouldn't want him to worry."

Hauk narrowed his eyes at her. "You are much too cheerful."

She toasted him with the last of her wine—he, of course, wasn't having any. "You'd rather I scowled and brooded like you?"

"You have some scheme you're hatching."

"You are just so suspicious."

"Not without good cause."

"What can I tell you? I was born in Gullandria and Osrik Thorson is my father. Scheming comes as naturally to me as…tying people up does to you." She drank and set the empty glass down.

He said, thoughtfully, "It takes study and practice to master the secrets in a strong length of rope."

She looked at him sideways. "Now, why did that sound like some kind of veiled threat?"

He drank from his water glass. "I am your servant. Never would I threaten you." He set the glass down and pushed back his chair. "I bid you good night."

It took her a moment to absorb what he'd just told her. He'd already grabbed that black duffel of his from where he'd left it in the corner and strode to the door of one of the bedrooms before she stopped him.

"Hauk."

He turned, put his fist to his chest and dipped his head. "At your service."

"What are you doing?"

"Going to bed."

"But I'm...not ready for bed yet. I want a long bath first."

"By all means, have your bath. Watch the television from your bed as you enjoy doing. This is America. There's a television in every room."

She didn't like what she thought might be happening here. "Then we are, uh, sleeping in separate rooms tonight?"

"Yes."

She had an awful, sinking feeling. All her glorious and naughty plans to seduce him were destined to come to nothing, after all. Disappointment had her dishing out a mean-spirited taunt. "You do serve me. I could command you to sleep at the foot of my bed."

"Yes. But that would be needlessly cruel and you are not that kind of woman."

Her throat felt tight. She swallowed. "Hauk?"

"Yes?"

"You would rather take a chance that I might run away than sleep in the same room with me tonight?"

He didn't answer. He didn't have to.

She felt ashamed. "I won't run away—wherever you sleep."

There was a long moment where neither of them spoke. Rain beat against the wide window that looked out on the lights of Boston and the harbor beyond. Lightning jumped and flashed across the black sky.

Elli felt that something very precious, a onetime
chance that would never come again, was slipping
away.

"All right," she said at last. "Good night, then."

He turned and went through the door to the bedroom, closing it quietly behind him.

Hauk tossed his duffel on the bed and strode to the
bathroom, pulling off his clothes as he went. He
turned on the shower and stepped into the stall with
the water running cold.

It wasn't cold enough. It could never be cold
enough. The ice-crusted Sherynborn—the river that
ran through the Vildelund at home—in dead of winter
wouldn't be cold enough.

He stayed in there for a long time. It didn't help,
not in any measurable way. It didn't cure him of the
yearning that was eating him alive. But the beating
of the cool water on his skin provided something of
a distraction, at least.

When he got out, he toweled dry and then he spent
an hour on the dragon dials, a series of strenuous
exercises consisting of slow, controlled movements
combined with precise use of the breath. He'd learned
the dials at his mother's knee. There were, after all,
some benefits to being born the bastard of a well-
trained and highly skilled woman warrior. Fighting
women took great pains to develop control and flex-
ibility in order to make up for their lesser physical
strength. A woman warrior sometime in the 17th century had created the discipline of the dials.

All his life, the dials had served him well. They

brought him physical exhaustion and mental clarity, always.

But not tonight. Nothing seemed to help him tonight.

He showered again—quickly this time—to wash off the sweat. Then he stood in the middle of the bedroom and stared at the shut door to the central living area and tried not to think how easy it would be to pull it open, to stride across the space between his room and hers.

A knock and she would answer. She would open her arms to him. She had made that so very, very clear.

Somehow, he kept his hand from reaching for the door. He climbed naked into the bed with thoughts that were scattered. Wild.

He stared toward the window opposite the foot of the bed. He'd left the blinds open. The rain beat against the single wide pane, streaming down in glittering trails, like veils of liquid jewels. When the lightning speared through the sky, the room would flash as bright as day. He tried to concentrate on that, on the beauty of the storm.

But he was not successful. Images of the woman kept haunting him. He arrived, constantly, at the point of thinking her name.

He'd already deliberately disobeyed his king, left her to her own devices for this entire night. She might turn and run. He'd have to track her down, or it would not go well for him.

But she'd said she wouldn't run. And in his heart, he believed her.

The chance she might flee was not the true problem here. His climbing from this bed and going to her—that was the problem.

His own mind, usually a model of order and discipline, betrayed him now. It mattered not what orders he gave it, it *would* continue straying to forbidden thoughts of what it might be like, for just one night, to call her his love.

He lay there and he stared into the darkness. He listened to the storm raging outside and he tried not to see her face, not to think her forbidden name.

And in the end, it was as if all his efforts to deny her had only conjured her to come to him.

There was a soft knock at the door.

It fell to him to call out, *Go away.*

But he said nothing. He lay there. Waiting.

Slowly, the door opened and there she was in her big pink shirt.

He sat up. And he said the word he'd vowed to himself that he would never say—her name, unadorned.

"Elli."

Chapter Eleven

Elli.

It was the first time, ever, that he'd called her by her given name alone. Her chest felt too small, suddenly, to hold her hungry heart.

The light from the room behind her spilled in across the bed. The blankets covered him to the waist.

He was...so beautiful and savage to her civilized eyes, with his broad smooth chest and the lightning-bolt tattoo slashing across it through a thicket of vines and dragons and swords. And his eyes... Oh, they were the saddest, loneliest eyes she'd ever seen.

"Hauk, is it all right if I come in?" Even now, after he'd at last dared to call her Elli, she more or less expected him to send her away.

But what she dreaded didn't happen. Instead, he flicked on the lamp beside him and held out his hand.

With a glad cry, she ran for the bed and scrambled up onto it, aiming straight for his arms. He wrapped them around her with an eagerness that warmed her to her soul. He stretched out on his back and she settled against him, cuddling close, with only his blankets and her big shirt between them now. She laid her head against his heart and noted with a surge of slightly silly joy that it seemed to beat right in time with hers.

She felt his lips brush the crown of her head. And she snuggled even closer with a long, happy sigh.

"Maybe I'll never move," she threatened tenderly. "I'll just lie here, forever, holding on to you...."

Hauk made a low sound in his throat and kissed her hair again. Most important, he kept those warm strong arms around her. How absolutely lovely. To rest in his embrace, to feel his kiss in her hair, his heart beating a little fast like her own, but steady and true, too, under her ear.

She spoke dreamily, without lifting her head. "Hauk, you probably won't believe this, but I came in here to *talk* to you."

"Ah," he said. "To talk. Always a danger, when *you* want to talk."

She faked an outraged cry and lightly punched his arm.

He stroked her hair. "Go ahead then. Say what you came to say."

She lifted her head. "I want to suggest something to you. And I want you to really think about it before you tell me it's not possible...." He was looking at her. And she was looking back at him. And suddenly what she'd intended to say was the last thing on her mind. "Oh, Hauk..."

He said her name again, "Elli..." The sound thrilled her.

With a hungry cry, she scooted up the glorious terrain of his big body to claim those beautiful lips.

Lightning flashed and thunder rolled as her mouth touched his. Elli didn't know or care which storm—the one outside or the sweeter, hotter one between them—had caused the bright pulsing behind her eyelids, the lovely, echoing, booming crash that seemed to shake her to the core. She kissed him harder, longer, deeper.

And he didn't hold back. He kissed her tenderly, passionately. He made her stomach hollow out and all her thoughts melt away to nothing but joy and a longing to be his. She rubbed herself against him, shamelessly eager, and she felt his response to her, knew that he was ready, so ready, to be hers.

But then he was capturing her chin, making her look at him. "We are foolish, *worse* than foolish."

She couldn't argue fast enough. "Oh, no. That's not so. Everything will work out. Just you wait and see."

His fine mouth curved upward. "You are, truly, an American."

She was so delighted to see his expression, she forgot to be irked at his superior tone. "Oh, Hauk. Look at that. I swear that's a smile you've got on your mouth."

"What man wouldn't smile after kissing you?"

She touched his lips, so soft when the rest of him

was anything but. So soft and so perfectly designed for kissing…

"Oh, Hauk…" Her eyes drifted closed and she lifted her mouth to him.

But just before her lips touched his and all rational thought could fly away, she remembered that she had something important to tell him. Her eyes popped open. "Wait."

He actually chuckled. "What?"

She kissed the ridge of a crescent-shaped scar on his chin, because she couldn't resist the temptation. But then she did pull back enough to say, "I was lying in that big, lonely bed in the other room, thinking…"

He raised his huge arms, laced his fingers behind his head and lifted one eyebrow. "About?"

She canted up on an elbow and laid a hand on his smooth chest, right in the center, where the lightning bolt zagged and a dragon reared, breathing fire. "My father."

He didn't move. That one eyebrow was still arched, yet it seemed to her that his rare lighthearted mood had vanished as swiftly as the sun sliding behind a dark cloud. Lightning flared again, a blinding glare through the room, and somewhere out in the storm-dark sky, thunder boomed and rolled away.

"Just listen to what I have to say." She touched the hard line of his jaw. "Please."

"I'm listening."

"Everyone—my mother, my sisters, Hildy, Aunt Nanna and you, too—you all seem to think my father has something else planned for me. That there's more going on here than a father's desire to meet a daughter he's never really known.''

''I never said—''

''Bear with me. Please?''

He gave her a curt nod.

She spoke briskly. ''So, then, what could it be, this other reason he's sent for me?''

''We've spoken of this.'' His gaze slid away. ''I've told you I don't know.''

She reached up again, this time to touch his cheek. ''Don't look away….''

He unlaced his fingers and dropped one hand at his side. The other hand he rested in the curve of her back—but very lightly, as if he didn't plan on keeping it there for long. ''All right.'' He was frowning. ''I'll say it once more. I can't tell you what His Majesty has planned for you, if anything, beyond what we already know—a time to speak with you, to see your face, to know the splendid young woman his infant daughter has become.''

''Splendid, huh? I like the sound of that.''

''It's only the truth.''

She trailed her hand down, so tenderly, and rested it once more against the dragon's heart. ''I think you do suspect his plans, Hauk.''

''It is not my place to—''

''Don't say it.'' She put her fingers to his lips. ''I don't need to hear it again. I sincerely do not.''

He moved his head, to free his mouth from her shushing hand. ''What do you wish me to say?''

''Nothing. Just listen.''

He gazed at her coolly now. She wondered if this

conversation would cost her the precious night to come.

No. She wouldn't think that way. Once he heard what she had to tell him, he would cradle her close and kiss her, again and again. They'd hold back the dawn together.

And morning would find them all wrapped up in each other's arms.

"Hauk, I think my father has plans for me—wedding plans. I think you think so, too, and—" She cut herself off with a tiny cry of distress. "Oh, don't do that, don't…get that hard and distant look."

"Why say such a thing?" His voice was ragged. "Why say it now, except to remind me that I betray my king—and that you and I have nothing beyond this moment, this moment that shouldn't even be?"

"No. No, you don't understand. You have to let me finish."

"What do you want from me?" He dragged himself up against the padded headboard, took her by the shoulders and pushed her carefully away from him.

"I said, let me finish." Elli had gathered her legs beneath her. She knelt beside him, her hands folded tightly on her thighs. He didn't want her to touch him right then, that was painfully evident in every line of his face, every tense muscle in his beautiful body. Clasping her hands together was the only way she could make them behave.

"All right, then," he said way too quietly. "Finish."

"Oh, don't you see? Why would he send you here, why would he force us to be together every minute?

Unless he's hoping I'll see just what I see in you, unless it's *you* he's hoping I'll learn to love and want to marry?''

When she said that, Hauk's hurt and anger melted away like the snowfields over Drakveden Fjord in the spring.

He almost smiled again. No matter that this woman was his king's daughter, in her heart she was American. American to the core. She saw what she wanted to see. She made the world over to fit her own idea of it.

Those deep-blue eyes of hers were shining. By all the roots of the guardian tree, he hadn't the will or the heart to remind her of the facts. Somewhere in that sharp mind of hers, she had to know the truth. That he'd first been sent to take her quickly and bring her straight to his king. That it was *she,* with her insistence on speaking to her father, on striking a bargain, who had made it necessary for Hauk to assume the role of round-the-clock guard.

Why point out the obvious when she so clearly didn't want to see it? Why be wise now, when for once in his life, all he wanted was a chance to play the fool?

The mighty Thor, her family's namesake, most beloved of all the gods, had given him this night of driving rain and rolling thunder, had forced her father's ship out of the sky. Sometimes, the whims of the gods might favor a man.

For an hour. Or a night.

A man might, however briefly, hold in his arms his greatest desire.

In the morning, there would be time for wisdom, for acceptance.

For regret and for anger.

And for shame, as well.

She whispered, "Are you going to send me away?"

It was the moment to tell her, to make her understand that her wild, bright American dreams would not change what was. If her father did have plans for her to marry a Gullandrian, it wouldn't be his low-jarl bastard warrior he intended for her. It would be the man King Osrik thought most likely to be king himself someday. That way the Thorson bloodline would continue to hold the throne. That way, even if His Majesty had lost his sons, the day might come when his grandson would rule.

"Oh, Hauk…" Those eyes of hers begged him to see what she saw—the two of them, united, His Majesty, her father, blessing the match.

He knew he should make the truth clear, that he should tell her what would really happen if they shared this stormy night and His Majesty found out.

At the very least, Hauk would lose his position, be stripped of all honors. He could be banished or even sent to Tarngalla, the tower prison where murderers and those who committed crimes against the state were kept. It was highly unlikely that what they were doing might cost him his life—not in this modern day and age. But anything could happen when the most trusted of soldiers dared to betray his king.

He knew if he told her all that, she would scoff.

She would call it impossible, barbaric, medieval. She would say it was wrong and unfair and an outrage.

And then she'd return to her own room. Even if she didn't want to believe him, she wouldn't let him take the risk.

Hauk cared nothing for the risk. She was here. She wished to stay. And he was through battling. The war inside him was over—at least for this night. For the brief, lightning-struck hours to come, he would hold this woman in his arms.

She sat there, on her knees, her fine face flushed and hopeful—those slender hands clasped. "Hauk, I..."

"Yes? Tell me."

"If you let me stay..."

"Yes?"

"Well, if you do, then I confess..."

She seemed to need more urging. He gave it. "You confess..."

"Since this morning, when you kissed me and then sent me to my room to pack, I have...thought of this. Hoped for this. Prepared for this."

"Prepared?"

The blush on her cheeks flooded outward, suffusing her entire sweet face with color. "You said you'd never have children until you had a wife."

By the breath of the dragon, he'd said exactly that—and meant it. He'd also taken a blood oath to give undying loyalty to his king. But look at him now.

"I'm a responsible woman." She was earnest now, enchantingly so. "I'd never ask you to go against your beliefs. I have contraception."

Contraception. Of course. American to the core.

She looked so very sincere about this. And so beautiful.

He told her simply, "That's wise." There were other things he might have said. But anything else would have brought questions he saw no need to answer right then.

He wasn't a total thief. He'd only take the taste of her, her deep, warm sighs, the touch of her skin to his. There'd be no risk he'd put a bastard in her belly. She'd understand that, soon enough. They didn't need to talk it over now.

She slid up his chest again and pressed her sweet mouth to his—quickly, this time. And firmly. "I'll go then. I'll…get them." She pretended to glare. "You stay right here."

"Your wish is my command."

She jumped from the bed and hurried to the door, pausing there briefly to send him a tender look. Then she was gone. He lay back, thinking that he loved the lightning. It had always pleased him. And it seemed all the brighter the dimmer the room. He switched off the lamp.

A moment later, she returned, a small box in her hand.

She set the box by the bed.

He whispered, "You don't need that big pink shirt. Not now. Not for the rest of the night."

She hesitated, hovering there beside the bed, the wedge of light from the open door behind her casting her face into shadow, making a halo around her golden hair.

Lightning flared. He saw her face clearly—uncertain and sweetly shy. The light went out. Thunder boomed.

She took the bottom of the shirt, whipped it up and over her head. And tossed it away.

Chapter Twelve

Hauk held back the blanket. Elli slid in beside him. He wrapped the blanket around her and he looked down at her, a look so tender—and yet also somehow infinitely sad.

Apprehension rose within her. "What? What's the matter?" She brushed two fingers along his brow, wishing her touch could soothe away his frown. "Hauk?"

Instead of giving her an answer, he lowered his mouth to hers. His lips touched her lips and her apprehension vanished as if it had never been. And his sadness? Surely, he couldn't be sad now. There was no such thing as sadness—not when he was kissing her, not when they held each other close.

He clasped her waist with his big hand and he kissed his way over her chin and down her throat.

Pushing back the blanket, he raised up over her, resting on an elbow. He looked down at her—at all of her. She gloried in that, in having him look at her. She felt no shyness, no embarrassment. It seemed right that he should see her. She *wanted* him to see her.

It seemed that she could actually feel his gaze, that where he looked, he touched. She shivered in blissful response.

Slowly he lowered his head to her left breast. His hair trailed on her skin. She felt the touch of his tongue—one long, wet swipe, deliciously abrasive, against the yearning flesh of her nipple. And then he blew where he'd licked.

Elli moaned in delight.

He lifted his head again. She looked at him from under lowered lashes and saw his white teeth flash in the darkness—a rare smile.

She smiled back, her mouth trembling a little. "Oh, Hauk..."

And then he dipped his head once more and took her nipple in his mouth.

Elli gasped and bowed her body up for him, offering herself, offering all she had to give as he caressed the aching bud, drawing on it, suckling her. She tossed her head against the pillow.

His hand strayed over her belly—and lower. He dipped a finger into the curls where her thighs joined. She cried out in excitement. Anticipation shimmered through her.

He raised his head from her breast and moved up a little, so his face loomed above hers. A blaze of lightning cut the night and she saw the feral gleam in his pale-blue eyes.

Thunder rolled and the room was dim again. Still, his eyes shone at her through the shadows. "I want to bring you pleasure, Elli."

"Oh, Hauk. You do. You *are*."

He brushed a kiss on her brow.

And below, very gently, he eased the curls aside, finding the slick groove of her sex. She gripped his big shoulders and whispered his name.

His finger moved. One long, shockingly intimate stroke and no more—right then. He took his touch elsewhere, sliding his rough and tender palm down the vulnerable inner surfaces of each of her thighs.

She sighed and let her legs ease open.

He was kissing her again. Kissing his way down the center of her. Elli lay beneath him, awash in pleasure, a willing victim of his mouth and his seeking tongue that dipped into her navel and played there. She gasped as she felt his teeth, lightly nipping. She moaned with the wonder of it—moaned and then moaned again.

Lower and lower, down over the tender skin below her navel. He put his lips there, against her mound, not delving in, just pressing his mouth, open, upon her.

And he let out a long, warm, focused breath of air.

Several bolts of lightning struck in quick succession, each followed by that rolling, booming sound. Elli was tossing her head on the pillow, muttering words she hardly knew the meaning of.

"Yes" and "Oh" and "Please" and "There…"

Gently, he moved her thighs wide apart and positioned himself between them. She dared to open her eyes, to gaze dreamily down the length of her own yearning body. His mouth was on her, now. And his tongue was...

His tongue was...

Elli groaned and the room lit up with wild stormy light. There was the thunder. And the hollow pounding, like a continuous sigh, of driving rain.

She clutched his golden head and she moved beneath his mouth and the soft explosion of fulfillment lifted her up, above the world, into the dark wet storm-shattered sky.

The only word she had was his name. And she said it. Over and over and over again.

For a while, they held each other and whispered and gently touched. It was a lovely time, a time for learning all the curves and hollows, all the tender places.

Each caress was a whisper. A question that found its answer in a sigh.

She traced the path of the lightning bolts—the one on his chest, the smaller, hidden one, in his palm. And the shape of the biggest dragon, the way its naughty tail curled down and down.

He said, "A wise woman never toys with the dragon...."

She closed her hand around him, so large and thick and wanting her. And she looked up into his eyes as she held him and the lightning blazed in the room.

He made a long, surrendering sound, a sound that

rolled low beneath the rumble of distant thunder. And he said her name, "Elli…"

And then she did for him what he'd done for her, first with long, slow strokes of her tongue and her hand and then more fully, her hair brushing his hard thighs, her mouth around him, drawing him into her, urging him on.

The hours went by in bursts of bright heat and shimmers of slow pleasure. More than once, she reached for the box on the bedside table.

Each time he caught her hand before her fingers could close on it. He took those empty fingers to his lips and he kissed them, one by one, drawing them slowly into his mouth, caressing them with his teeth and his tongue, then turning her hand over, laying his lips in the heart of her palm.

The third time he stopped her from reaching for the box, she took his hand and she kissed it chastely, then held it to her heart. "Why, Hauk? Why won't you let me—"

"Shh." He pulled her close.

He caressed her in long, slow strokes, running his hand down her back, over the twin curves of her hips and inward to find her wet and ready. Within minutes she was clutching him frantically, mindless with pleasure.

She didn't reach for the box again. She thought, as his wonderful hands and his talented mouth worked their magic on her hungry flesh, that it didn't matter, that maybe it was better this way—that she didn't have to be so greedy for everything all at once.

There would be time for them, together, for his body within hers. It seemed impossible to think it now—in some ways she felt she knew him better, even, than she knew her sisters—but she had to remember...

Four days ago, she hadn't even known he existed. Three days ago she'd found him, a total stranger, waiting in her apartment—to kidnap her—when she got home.

And here she was in a bed in a Boston hotel room, climbing all over him, thinking of words like *forever* and *I do*. Thinking of having his babies, of making a life with him.

Was that crazy or what?

He saw her dreamy smile and he asked her what had caused it.

She thought, *I think I love you*, but she didn't say it.

Like the box on the bedside table, the words of love could wait.

Some time after two, exhausted and deliciously satisfied, Elli dropped off to sleep in Hauk's arms.

When she woke, it was daylight. The storm had passed. The sky beyond the window across the room was cloudless. And she was alone in the bed.

She pushed back the covers, grabbed her pink shirt from where she'd thrown it on the floor and pulled it on over her head. Then, smiling the smile of a happy woman, she went to find him.

He hadn't gone far. She pushed open the door to the other room and there he was, fully dressed, sitting in a chair near the big window that took up half of one wall.

Out there beyond the glass, the harbor waters lay calm, the boats gently bobbing, a few of them, small pleasure craft, with sails as white as new snow. The orange ball of the rising sun lit up the clear blue sky.

Elli looked in his face and her happy smile faded. She knew that expression—that distant, composed look. She couldn't believe she was seeing it. She *refused* to believe she was seeing it.

"Hauk?" She ran to him—and then she drew herself up short. She wanted to reach for him. But somehow, she didn't quite dare. "Oh, Hauk, what's wrong? What's happened?"

His expression didn't change. "I have contacted the pilot. The plane is refueled and ready. Shower if you'd like, and get dressed. We need to be on our way."

Four days—going on five now—that she'd known him. Yet it felt like forever. It felt as if there had never been a time when Hauk FitzWyborn wasn't in her life. She knew him well enough to know that when he got that look, that tone to his voice, there was no reaching him, no hope that he might tell her what was going on inside him.

Still, she couldn't stop herself from trying. "I don't understand this." She spoke quietly. She wanted to be reasonable. She didn't want to start crying and begging and throwing herself on him, though that was exactly what she felt like doing. "What can have changed so much? Why are you so…far away? Last night, I thought that the two of us were—"

He put up a hand. She stared at the lightning bolt. Only hours ago, that hand had touched her in all her most secret places, giving her the kind of pleasure she'd never known before. And now he was using it to keep her at bay. "Last night was last night. It's over and done with."

"But I don't—"

"Enough." He stood. "Dress. Gather your belongings. I will take you to His Majesty, your father, where you belong."

She could feel anger rising, prickling the back of her neck, making her blood rush faster through her veins. "What are you saying, 'Where I belong'? I don't belong with my father. I don't even *know* my father. I'm going to visit him, and that's all. If I belong with anyone, I belong with—"

He put up his hand again. "Don't say it."

A furious shout rose in her throat. Somehow, she swallowed it and asked very quietly, "What have I done, for you to treat me like this?"

Something flashed in those pale eyes. It might have been pain. But he hid it quickly. Again, his face was stern and impassive. "Nothing. You have done nothing. Last night I was weak. And you were a beautiful, impossible dream I had—a dream that's over now. We won't speak of it again."

She whirled from him—she had to, to keep from flinging herself against him. She took two steps and then realized she had no idea where she was going. So she hovered there, with her back to him, not sure what to do next.

From where she stood she could see through the

open doorway to the tangled sheets of the bed where they'd spent last night. She could also see the night table, and the box that still waited, unopened, upon it. It all became pitifully clear to her, when she looked at that box.

She spun back to face him. "You *knew*." It was an accusation. "You knew last night that you'd do this in the morning. That's why you stopped me every time I tried to…" Her voice trailed off. There was no need to finish. The bleak look in his eyes said it all.

He confessed, so softly, "Yes. You understand. You have it right."

Oh, she saw it all so clearly. She *did* know him. They were worlds apart. He lived by codes and rules she couldn't begin to comprehend. Still, she knew him, knew how his mind worked, had seen down into his secret heart.

She whispered, "Because contraceptive devices are fallible."

"Yes."

"Because the only way to be certain conception won't happen is never to do what makes babies in the first place."

"That is correct."

"You are…saving yourself, aren't you? For the woman who will one day be your wife?"

"I wouldn't call it that."

"Then what *would* you call it?"

He gave a tiny shrug of those huge shoulders. "Protecting the rights of my children, making certain that when they're born, they're born legitimate. And protecting you, as well—protecting *your* children, who have the right to a father who's able to claim them.''

"So you'll only make love all the way with your wife.'' An absurd thought popped into her head—and she let it right out her mouth. "Why, Hauk. You're a charter member of the NATWC.''

His brows drew together.

"NATWC,'' she said again, as if it was going to mean anything to him. "The Never All the Way Club.''

Now, he looked completely confused. "This is an American institution?''

She let out a wild laugh. "Hardly.''

"Ah,'' he said uncomfortably. "A joke. It's a joke.''

"Sort of. I guess.'' She felt foolish, to have even brought it up. "It's just…something my sisters and I used to say to each other.''

"It makes no sense to me.''

"I know. Never mind. It doesn't matter. What matters is that there's no chance the woman you marry will ever be me. You won't let her be me. You won't let yourself even imagine the idea of a marriage to the daughter of your king.''

His mouth moved. She knew with absolute certainty he was about to say her name. But he didn't. He closed his lips over the word before it escaped him. And he started again. "This is not about what I might imagine.''

"Then what is it about?''

"There can never be more between us. Accept it.

You are a princess and I am far beneath you. That's how it is. That's how it will always be.''

"But *why?* Why does it have to be that way? Why do you have to…limit yourself that way?''

"Questions,'' he muttered. "With you, the questions never end.'' He sounded weary. And strangely tender, too.

She stared at his mouth. She was thinking, *How can he be telling me it's over when it's hardly begun?*

How could anything so wrong be happening?

And where had her anger gone? It had left her, completely, just melted away. She missed it. Anger was so much better than this sad, empty feeling. "You should have told me last night—that it could never go anywhere, that last night was all we'd have.''

"No. What I should have done was to send you away. But I didn't.''

"And now everything's changed.''

"Nothing is changed. I'll do what I have been ordered to do. I'll take you to your father.''

"And then?''

"I'll ask for three weeks' leave.''

Her throat closed up on her. She swallowed to make it relax. "Three weeks—that's how long I plan to visit.''

"That's right.''

It hurt, just to look at him and to know that if she reached out to him, he would step back. She stared past his shoulder, at the boats on the water with their white, white sails. But the sun was so bright.

She blinked and sun dogs danced at the corners of her eyes. "I feel…so much for you."

"You're young. What you feel will pass."

"Oh, please. That's a lame one and you know it. How old or young I am has nothing to do with how deeply I feel or how long it will last."

He stood so still and straight. She knew he was only waiting for her to give up this talk that he saw as pointless, to go and get dressed and get her things together so they could leave.

"I can't…reach you, Hauk. Not if you won't reach back."

"I can't reach back."

"That's not true."

"It *is* true. We're not the same, you and I. You see possibilities where I know there are none. We are what we are—and I am not the one for you."

"Only because you won't let yourself be. You won't give us a chance, won't even let yourself try."

"There's a line from an old Norse poem, *The length of my life and the day of my death were fated long ago.*"

"That may be. But it's what you'll *do* with your life, however long or short it may be, that we're talking about right now."

He chided gently, "Such a clever, clever tongue you have."

"I don't care what you say. You *can* reach back. You simply choose not to."

"All right. Have it your way. I choose not to."

Chapter Thirteen

It was early evening when they reached Gullandria, though the day, as yet, showed little sign of dimming. The flight attendant told Elli that at the summer equinox, which was a month and a half away, the sun would stay above the horizon for close to twenty hours, gradually fading into a long twilight.

"On a clear night in Gullandrian high summer," the attendant explained, "it never gets dark between sunset and sunrise."

They approached the island across the endless blue of the sea. At first, it all blurred together. Elli saw the rough shape of it, patches of green and black, puddles and fissures of deepest blue that were lakes and the major fjords. Then, as they got close, she had her first view of Lysgard, the capital, a harbor city low on the western shore, where the land curved sharply inward on its way to the southernmost tip.

As they flew in, Elli saw a jumble of steep-roofed compact houses that seemed to crowd each other on the fingers of land extending into the cobalt waters of the harbor. The close-packed dwellings clung to the green hillsides and perched above the steep black rock walls of Lysgard Fjord.

The attendant joined her at the window, pointing out the gold dome of the Grand Assembly, where freeman and jarl alike met to argue law and decide on matters of importance to the public at large. "The Grand Assembly is similar to the British Parliament, which, of course, owes its beginnings to the earliest assembly of its type—the Althing, where the Vikings of Iceland once gathered to make their laws."

She made special mention of the tall, proud spires of the largest churches. "Many think we worship the old Norse gods. But we say that we learn from them, that we take to heart what our earliest cultural myths have to show us. We in Gullandria are good Christians, of course—and look there." She pointed at the magnificent silver castle with its turrets and spires and glittering jewel-paned windows that crowned a jut of land above the city. Parkland like a green blanket fell away beneath it.

Elli found the sight enchanting. "It's like something from a fairy tale."

"Yes. Everyone says the same thing the first time they see His Majesty's largest palace. Isenhalla was built in the sixteenth century of rare silver Gullandrian slate. The slate has splendid reflective properties. It shines in the sunlight almost as if it were carved of ice.''

The urge came on Elli as it had several times during the flight, to turn in her chair, to ask Hauk some eager, touristy question. *So how's the fishing here? I understand it's always been one of the major industries.* Or *What about the oil refineries? Where are they? From what I've read, oil is the main export now....*

She did no such thing. Once or twice since they boarded, she'd dared to look at him. He'd stared back, unblinking, as if he were looking right through her. She'd felt like a naughty child at the gates of Buckingham Palace, trying to get one of those expressionless guards in a tall furry hat to crack a smile.

He was one hundred percent the king's warrior again. The man who had held her and kissed her and brought her to the heights of ecstasy the night before might never have been.

Her father wasn't there to welcome her when they touched down. He'd sent an entourage, though. She stepped off the plane and there they all were, including a color guard of ten proud soldiers in the red-and-black uniforms of the Gullandrian army. They carried the Gullandrian flag, which showed a red dragon coiled around a red tree on an ebony ground. The tree had thick, gnarled roots. Elli knew it represented Yggdrasill, the guardian tree of Norse mythology that anchored the cosmos, growing through all the nine worlds, from the underworlds up through Midgard, where men and giants walked, and on into the upper worlds of the gods and the light elves. There were other flags whipping in the wind, foremost among them the Thorson banner with its lightning bolt and hammer.

A small brass band played the national anthem and an aide stepped forward to read a long, flowery welcome speech from a device that rolled open like a modern-day version of a parchment scroll. Several yards away, a hundred or so Gullandrian citizens cheered and waved small flags, calling out, "Princess Elli, Princess Elli! Welcome! Welcome home!" There were reporters, too, and a news crew with the camera rolling. Guards kept them all behind a temporary barrier.

Elli played her part, waving and smiling and calling out, "Thank you! Oh, thank you!"

A limousine, more banners flying, rolled toward them. When it stopped, the aide who had read the welcome speech stepped forward and opened the door. With a final wave, Elli ducked inside.

The aide hustled in behind her. Elli looked back at the plane as they drove away, unable to stop herself from hoping for one last glimpse of Hauk. Maybe he'd be disembarking now she was safely in the car and on her way.

She saw the soldiers and the flags whipping in the wind and the people still cheering and waving. But no Hauk.

A black car with black-tinted windows rolled in behind them. Elli faced front and saw another car perhaps twenty feet ahead. Maybe Hauk was in one of them....

"May I say, Princess Elli, that it is an honor to escort you to the palace of His Majesty, your father." The aide, sitting down the long leather seat from her, was a tall, slender man in a dark, expensive-looking suit, attractive in a slightly fussy way.

"Thank you." He'd introduced himself a minute ago. And already she'd forgotten his name. She'd been thinking of Hauk, of last night, thinking that she couldn't believe it; that it couldn't be possible she would never see him again, never speak with him, never match her wits against his determination—and never, ever feel his kiss.

The aide looked at her hopefully. She put a little effort into recalling his name. Something beginning with prince. But then, in Gullandria, all the men's names started with prince—as long they were jarl and legitimate, anyway.

"It is only a short ride, under twenty kilometers, to Isenhalla," said Prince Whatever.

Elli gave the man a vague smile and looked out the window and wondered what Hauk might be doing now.

Three black Volvo sedans had been waiting at the edge of the airstrip when the royal jet landed. Two carried armed guards assigned to accompany the princess's limousine to the palace.

While Her Highness was busy listening to that endless welcome speech, Hauk had slipped off the plane and into the third car. Thus, at that moment he was on the way to the palace himself, well ahead of the royal limousine.

Perhaps the king would wish to speak with him today. Perhaps not.

If not, Hauk would busy himself in the stables. He was good with the stocky, white longhaired horses for which his country was famed, and he often helped with their training. But whatever he did—train horses or men, work up a sweat in the training yard himself, gamble with off-duty soldiers from the palace guard—until the king summoned him to hear his report, Hauk's real job would be to wait. When the king did send for him, he would make use of the audience to request leave.

Hauk sat in the back seat and stared out the window at the emerald-green fields and the karavik—hardy fat-tailed Gullandrian sheep—grazing on the slopes of the hills. To the north, the Black Mountains, gateway to the Vildelund, loomed tall and dark and capped with snow.

They were reaching the outskirts of Lysgard when Hauk's contact device, which he'd stuck in his boot for the flight, began vibrating. He asked the driver for a phone and placed the call to his king.

"Your Majesty. Hauk speaking. Her Highness, Princess Elli, is at this moment on her way to you."

"Yes, I know. She is well, in good spirits, from what my observers at the airport have told me."

"Yes, sire. She is well."

"I commend you, Hauk."

"I live only to serve, Your Majesty."

"I would have a word with you before I welcome my daughter in person. Come immediately to my private audience room."

* * *

When Hauk entered the royal chamber, King Osrik stood before the wide diamond-paned window. He stared out at the capital city below and the jewel-blue waters of the harbor beyond. It was 2100—nine in the evening American time—and outside the long twilight had begun. Also in the room, but in the corner near a bust of Odin, was a tall, gaunt figure with wise gray eyes, thinning white hair and a gray beard. He was the king's Grand Counselor, Prince Medwyn Greyfell. Prince Greyfell, who was second only to the king in power and influence, granted Hauk a small nod. In respectful response, Hauk put his fist to his heart and dipped his head.

The king turned from the window, knowing dark eyes warm with welcome. "Hauk. Hello." He held out the hand on which the ring of state gleamed.

In four strides, Hauk had crossed the big room. He swept to one knee and pressed his lips to the huge bloodred ruby that crowned the ring.

"Rise," said the king. "Sit with me." With a sweep of his hand, he gestured at two red velvet chairs with carved ebony arms, one on a small dais, the other placed lower, on the floor.

Hauk knew how to sit before his king, how to orchestrate the act of sitting, so that his liege always stayed slightly above him.

"There," said the king, once they had taken the chairs. He was smiling.

King Osrik had a good smile. It was open and confident, a smile that made people trust him. He was tall—not as tall as Hauk, but taller than most. His brows were dark and thick, his black hair streaked with silver. A handsome man, still strong and straight in his early fifties. Yes, there was sadness in those dark eyes sometimes. He had, after all, lost his greatest hope, his two sons. But he was a wise ruler and he knew that in front of his subjects, too much display of sadness spoke of weakness. And though a king no longer went a-Viking or carried a sword into battle as in days gone by, even in modern times, a king must never be thought weak.

"Tell me of my daughter," the king said, while from the corner the Grand Counselor listened and watched.

Hauk had a little speech prepared. "My lord, she is all a father could wish for in a daughter, all a king could wish for in a princess. Quick of mind and good at heart. Strong and beautiful. Raised American, of course. But she has studied the great myths. She has some background in our ways." Not as much as she *should* have, Hauk was thinking, though of course, he didn't say any such thing.

The king chuckled. "Quicker of mind than we had anticipated, I think."

Hauk dipped his head in acknowledgment of those words. "She drives a good bargain, sire."

"And with the queen, how did that go?" The king's smile had vanished.

"Her Majesty was…not pleased, that Her Highness would visit her father. But Her Highness held firm."

"She looked well?"

It took Hauk a moment to realize the king referred to his runaway queen. "Yes, sire. Very well."

The king insisted on hearing the details of the meeting with the queen. Hauk trotted them out, telling the story as briefly as possible, from the housekeeper's initial hostility, through the queen's distress at the news that the princess would travel to Gullandria, on to the calls to Princess Liv and Princess Brit, through the grim meal that he, the queen and the princess had shared, capping it all off with the queen's final acceptance of the inevitable.

"And it was Tuesday night, that my daughter went to the queen?"

"Yes, sire."

"She had that much more to do, in America, that she couldn't leave until the last minute we'd agreed on?"

"Sire, from my observation, after her visit with the queen on Tuesday night, all was in readiness for the princess to leave California."

"Yet she lingered there?"

"She insisted you had agreed she could stay in California until Thursday and she was not leaving until then."

"And what did you make of that—of her stalling?"

Hauk hesitated. He never felt comfortable when the king asked for interpretations of the motives of others. He always preferred to stick with the facts—especially now, when they were talking of the woman he had touched in ways that one such as he should never so much as dream of, when he felt certain that any moment he would betray himself as he had betrayed his king. That the king would sense the turmoil within him and want to know what was bothering him.

And that when the king began questioning him more pointedly, he'd answer bluntly, admit that he'd touched the king's daughter intimately, that all he longed for was to do it again.

He'd throw it all over—the life he'd built, all he'd worked so hard to earn, the bastard name he'd sought to make whole and proud. He'd throw it over because right now it all meant less than nothing to him. Right now it was empty as wheat chaff after threshing, of so little substance it was easily blown away by the wind.

Right now, he could almost open his mouth and confess what he'd done, redeem a shred of his tattered honor by taking whatever punishment the king saw fit to mete out.

But the thought of *her* kept him from that.

He couldn't say what it might cost her if her father learned where she'd spent the previous night. Perhaps little. Perhaps much.

At the very least, she would be shamed, diminished in her father's eyes. *That* he did care about. That made it imperative he keep the truth to himself.

The king sighed. "Ah, Hauk. Never mind." He spoke more briskly. "So. You left California yesterday morning, as agreed. And then a storm dragged you out of the sky and held you overnight in the city of Boston."

Hauk kept his eyes down and ordered the sudden, stunning erotic images out of his mind. "Yes, sire."

"But at last, here you are." The king rose, Hauk along with him. "Well done, my warrior."

Hauk stepped back and saluted. The interview was

almost over. He'd made it through without throwing his life away. The only thing left was to request leave.

The king spoke first. "A week from tomorrow is May Fair." There were three major fairs in the warm months: May Fair, Midsummer's Eve and Summer's End. "This year, in honor of my daughter, I'm planning a special celebration. War games and displays of horsemanship in the morning and afternoon. And along with the battle games and horse races, the usual festival, with music and poetry, games of chance and a bazaar. And then a feast. And then, at midnight, we'll set a ship ablaze in my daughter's honor.

"Notice has been sent out to all the fighting clubs." Gullandrian men liked to form fighting clubs. They would practice the old, wild ways of battle, and often stage fight shows at the local fairs. "As my warrior," said the king, "you will fight in my name."

There was only one response. "Your Majesty honors me."

"As you bring honor to our name. That is all, then."

Hauk hesitated again, unsure when he'd get another chance to ask for some time away from the palace. He was in a special position in regards to his orders. He took them only from the king.

The king gave him his opening. "You have more you wish to say, Hauk?"

"A request, Your Majesty."

"Name it."

"I'd like to take some leave, sire."

"When?"

"Right after I represent Your Majesty in the games next week."

"Is there some pressing reason you'll be going?"

He should have thought up a good story in advance. But he wasn't an effective liar, never had been. And lying always galled him, anyway. "No, my lord. I'd merely like some time to myself."

"No...personal difficulties?"

"None. Just holiday leave, my lord."

"Will a month do it?"

Three weeks, effective immediately, would have been better. That would have covered the entire length of time she planned to stay. But that wasn't possible. He must fight for his king.

And it should be all right. He felt reasonably certain he could avoid contact with her for the week to come. The king would keep her busy with tours and parties. And Hauk would stay near the stables and the training yard. It would all be so new to her. If she had a thought or two of him, she'd have no idea how to seek him out.

"I thank you, Majesty."

The huge ruby glittered as the king waved his hand. "Fight well for me. Then take your month and enjoy it. We have no crises brewing. There's a good chance your holiday will be uninterrupted."

Elli's limousine rolled into the huge paved court at the grand front entrance to her father's palace. The black escort cars kept going, down a side driveway and out of sight.

The aide led her up the wide steps, between the

intricately carved pillars, past the stone dragons and the statues of Odin and Freyja and Thor and turned her over to a phalanx of beautifully dressed young women who fisted their pretty hands to their designer-clad hearts and bowed their lovely heads.

One, a tall, graceful redhead with freckles across her patrician nose, stepped forward. "We are your ladies, Your Highness. I am Kaarin Karlsmon, first among those who will serve you." Kaarin was wearing a particularly fetching ensemble of midnight-blue silk with a pencil-thin skirt and a short, tight little jacket that showed off her trim figure. All the women wore beautiful jewels, to go with the gorgeous clothes.

Elli smiled and nodded and murmured hello over and over as each of the ladies introduced herself.

Finally, they led her inside, up a sweeping stone staircase and down a number of hallways to a set of wide carved doors. A pair of guards in red-and-black uniforms stood at attention, flanking the doors.

Elli's heart leaped in glad excitement. At last. She would meet her father.

But when the guards pulled the doors wide, she found herself looking through a marble-floored entrance area to a huge, beautifully decorated high-ceilinged drawing room—and no sign of the king, or anyone else for that matter.

"Your rooms, Your Highness," Lady Kaarin announced.

Elli was becoming a little tired of all the pomp and circumstance—not to mention the absence of the one person she'd come here to see. "Where's my father?"

Lady Kaarin smiled brightly. "He eagerly awaits you. But first, we are honored to make you comfortable, to see you bathed and suitably attired."

Elli thought, I'm clean and I'm ready. But she decided that announcing as much probably wouldn't sound very regal. She leaned close to the tall redhead and asked in a whisper, "I wonder...may I just call you Kaarin?"

"Certainly, Your—"

"And you'll call me Elli."

"Absolutely, Elli." Kaarin's soft mouth bloomed in a delighted smile.

"Kaarin, I must admit..."

"Anything, Your, er, Elli. Feel free to confide in me."

"Right now, I'd like a...reduction in my retinue. Say, just you. Could that be arranged?"

"Of course." Kaarin turned to the others. "Thank you all. The princess wishes her privacy now."

Dainty fists flew to chests, followed by a flurry of fawning farewells. And a minute later, Kaarin and Elli entered the spectacular drawing room alone.

Even Elli, who'd been raised in wealth and privilege, was impressed. The drawing room was big enough to use as a ballroom. More double doors led to a smaller sitting room. There was a fully equipped kitchen off the sitting room for any time she might have a sudden desire to whip herself up a little something to nosh on.

Kaarin laughed at that idea. "Of course you wouldn't, er, 'whip something up' yourself."

"I wouldn't?"

"A cook will be sent to you. And a chambermaid, of course. Cook and maid will be at your service at all times."

There were two baths. The largest, off the bigger of the two bedrooms, included a whirlpool large enough to swim in and a sauna, double sinks and dual showers. Each room had huge fireplaces, with mantels of stone or dark wood intricately carved with dragons and Viking ships and scenes from the myths. The fireplaces all had beautiful inserts. Kaarin explained that they now burned gas. Gullandria was rich in oil, which meant that gas heat was more economical than burning wood or coal.

With a sweeping gesture, Kaarin indicated the whole huge suite. "Will it do?"

"It's lovely. Now, when will I see my father?"

Elli's father, at that moment, was closeted with his Grand Counselor.

Beyond being his top advisor, Medwyn was also Osrik's closest—really his only—friend. The two had been bloodbound forty years before, when Osrik was a boy of twelve and Medwyn a bachelor and scholar of twenty-seven. At first, Medwyn had been Osrik's mentor and teacher. But time had made them equals. When the kingmaking had put Osrik on the throne, he'd risen above his friend.

Except when they were alone. To be bloodbound, after all, was to be closer than brothers, to share undying loyalty and support, each to the other. Osrik and Medwyn were bloodbound in the truest sense.

When Osrik was alone with his friend, all the formalities that set him apart as royalty could fall away.

The two were discussing Osrik's recent interview with the warrior.

"There seemed," remarked Medwyn thoughtfully, "something amiss with him. And much between the lines."

Osrik shrugged. "With Hauk, it always seems that way. The man is a true soldier. He'll never say two words where one will do. If we'd wanted conversation and clever analysis, we should have sent Finn Danelaw." Prince Danelaw was a notorious charmer—handsome and cunning, a master of intrigue. He owned a honeyed tongue and a tender manner no woman could resist. He bowed to no one but his king, to whom he was always unfailingly loyal.

Had they sent Finn to collect Elli, he would have had detail upon detail to share with them when he returned—what pleased Elli, what made her frown, what political positions she took—and what she yearned for in her most secret heart.

Also, Finn would have had a wealth of information about Ingrid....

But, no. There had been the possibility that Elli would have to be taken by force. Hauk was the best man for that.

And the choice of Danelaw would have presented one completely unacceptable risk.

Osrik said, "In the end, I still believe we were wise to decide against young Danelaw. He's *too* good with women. Elli most likely would have ended up in love with him—as all the women do. We'd have had a royal mess on our hands.''

Medwyn was nodding his white head. "The warrior has done the job assigned him. He's brought your chosen daughter safely home.''

"I will get to know at least one of my lost girls at last.'' When he thought of that word, *lost,* Osrik felt sadness like a dark cloud pressing all around him.

A wife. Three daughters. One son and then the other. He had lost too much. It was time he took something back. "Eric?" he asked. "Still in the Vildelund?''

Like their fathers before them, Eric Greyfell and Valbrand Thorson had been bloodbound. Medwyn's son had been groomed all his life to walk in his father's shoes, to step up as Grand Counselor when the jarl declared Valbrand king. Both fathers had felt an inner peace that the future was as assured as any future could be.

All that was gone now.

Lost.

Eric—until then the most reasonable young man it had ever been Osrik's joy to know—had been crazed with grief at the disappearance of his friend. He'd insisted on striking off by sea to find out the truth of what had happened to Valbrand. He was determined to learn if vengeance was called for—and if so, to carry it out.

He'd returned a month ago having achieved little satisfaction in his quest. Everyone told the same story. There had been a storm and Valbrand was washed overboard. Eric could find no evidence of treachery.

Still grieving, still unsatisfied with the explanations of his friend's death, Eric had stopped only briefly to see his father, then headed straight for his family's village in the Vildelund—the wild country beyond the Black Mountains. Eric, like Valbrand, was much beloved by the people, but like his father, he owned a Mystic's heart. He found solace in the wild.

Medwyn was nodding. "I'll send for him, at your command."

"Give him time," said Osrik. "It would be better if he came on his own, better if it all happened... naturally. You know how young people are. Giving them orders only makes them determined *not* to do what's best for everyone."

"He's become something of a recluse since the tragedy last year. A command may be necessary to get him here."

"Still. We can wait awhile. And right now, I want to get to know this daughter of mine."

The two men regarded each other. There was no need to say more.

From all reports, Elli Thorson was a woman of integrity and strength. She was intelligent and beautiful, yet yielding, too. Not as driven and career-obsessed as her older sister, not as wild and contrary as the younger. Of Osrik's three daughters, Elli would make the best queen—especially, since, of the three, his spies had told him that Elli was the one who talked of marriage. Of children.

The fathers had it all planned. When Elli met Eric Greyfell, each would see the value in the other. Marriage would follow. When the time for the kingmaking came around again, Eric would be chosen.

And Elli would be his queen.

And if the gods smiled but for a moment on King Osrik Balderath Crosby Aesir Harald Einer Thorson, the day would come when his grandson would sit on the throne of Gullandria.

Chapter Fourteen

Kaarin insisted Elli take a long, hot bath. "And a sauna, too," Kaarin suggested. "There is nothing so effective at cleansing the body of toxins and impurities."

"Right. So does that mean you'd like a sauna yourself?"

"Your Highness, nothing would delight me more."

Before she saunaed with Kaarin, Elli called her mother. She got lucky and found Ingrid at home.

"Are you all right? You arrived safely?"

"Mom. I'm here. I'm fine. The palace is beautiful."

"Your father…?"

"I'll be seeing him soon. Call Brit and Liv, will you? Tell them I got here without a hitch and everything is all right."

"Nanna told me you left yesterday. I heard about that big storm on the east coast. Did you—"

"We had to land and wait it out in Boston." And it was the most perfect, incredible night of my life. "And now I'm here in Gullandria. Safe and sound."

"You'll call me, immediately, if you have a single…worry."

"Oh, Mom. Stop it. I'm fine and I'll *be* fine."

By the time Elli said goodbye to her mother, the chambermaid had appeared. She took charge of Elli and Kaarin's discarded clothes and offered huge white towels. Elli and Kaarin went into the wooden room together.

Ten minutes later Elli insisted she'd had enough. So they got out and stood under an icy shower spray, both of them shivering, Elli making whimpering sounds that had Kaarin giggling.

At last, Elli was allowed to climb into a scented bath and float for a while. That was nice. Soothing. Elli lay back and watched the steam trail up toward the arched stone ceiling and tried not to wonder what Hauk might be doing now.

After the bath came a real shower—in civilized warm water. Then Elli dried her hair and put on her usual light makeup. In the bedroom, the maid had laid out a hot pink number of lustrous silk that rivaled the one Kaarin wore. Elli put it on. It fit as if it had been made for her—which, she realized, it probably had.

"I think you are ready now to meet His Majesty." Kaarin was back in her blue silk and looking fantastic. She led the way.

It was a long walk, up one corridor and down another. At last, they turned a corner and came to another set of tall guarded doors.

"I'll leave you now," said Kaarin. "For this first meeting, your father wishes to see you alone."

Elli had hoped he would wish just that. "Thank you. For everything."

"It's my pleasure, Your Highness. I'll return in an hour. You'll find me waiting to escort you to your rooms when the visit is through." Kaarin set off down the hall and the guards opened the doors.

And there he was.

Her father.

So tall and handsome, in a beautifully cut designer suit, with eyes as kind as the voice she remembered from their phone conversation four days—and what seemed like a lifetime—before. The doors closed behind her and they were alone.

"Little Old Giant," he said.

The fond words did the trick. With a glad cry, Elli ran to him. He caught her in his arms and he held her close.

"I'm so glad you've come." He squeezed her tighter and rocked them both from side to side.

"Oh, Father. So am I."

Dinnertime had passed hours ago, but she'd had no chance to eat. In consideration of that, he'd had a simple meal laid out near one of the tall windows. They sat down across from each other.

Oh, he *was* kind. She could see it in his wise eyes, hear it in his gentle voice. Everything about him spoke of goodness. Now she'd finally met him, she couldn't comprehend why her mother had left him, what the deep, dark secret could be that had torn the two of them—and their family—apart.

As she looked at her father, Elli realized that in spite of everything—her mother's fears, her sister's warnings, in spite of losing Hauk when she'd barely managed to find him—she was glad she'd come.

Osrik asked her about her mother and her sisters and her life in Sacramento. She answered honestly and in detail and more than once had the feeling he already knew what she was telling him.

She supposed that didn't surprise her. Looking at him now, she knew in her heart that he'd never really given them up—not her, not her sisters. And not her mother, either.

He would have kept tabs on them over the years. And that didn't offend her in the least. He was her father, after all. Of course he'd want to know how his family was doing.

She longed to question him about Hauk—if he'd asked for leave, if he was gone on a new assignment now. But she also felt a definite reluctance to mention the warrior's name.

After all, Hauk was no fool. And he'd seemed so certain there was no hope for them, that what had happened between them should never have been.

Elli had trouble understanding why he felt that way, why he put himself beneath her and insisted that was where he had to stay. But then, she hadn't been brought up in Gullandria. As he was always telling her, she thought like an American.

She knew she had to be at least a little cautious. She needed to come up with some clever way to find

out where he was now—and yet not reveal anything
that might put him in a bad light with her father.

She set down her silver fork and picked up her
water goblet. "Father, I have to tell you, I'm still a
little upset with you."

Her father frowned. "But why?"

She drank and set the glass down on the snowy
tablecloth. "For having me kidnapped. Where I come
from, kidnapping is a crime."

He tried to slough it off. "What does it matter
now? In the end, you decided you *wanted* to come."

"Yes, I did. But that doesn't make what *you* did
acceptable."

Osrik's frown had turned to a scowl. "What's happening here? All of a sudden, you're lecturing me."

"I'm just trying to make you see that—"

He set down his own fork. "Elli, let me remind
you. No one lectures the king."

"We're alone. No one's listening. I'd like to think,
for now, we're just a daughter and her father, spending a little quality time together."

Her father reached across the table and patted her
hand. "I like the sound of that. Let's not spoil it with
an argument."

Elli kept pushing. "It was wrong, what you did. I
was terrified at first."

He fell into her trap. "Did Hauk mistreat you?"

Elli ate a string bean, delicately, taking time to
chew and swallow before answering. "Of course not.
He was very gentle with me. And I know he only did
what you ordered him to do." She had to watch it.
Or she'd be smiling like a dreamy fool. Hauk, after

all, had done a few things her father would never in a million years have ordered him to do.

"Well." Osrik's voice had turned gruff. "Forgive me then. And let's put what's done behind us."

Elli assumed an injured expression. "You should never have done that. You should never have—"

"We discussed this on the telephone four nights ago." Her father's voice was soft. And utterly unyielding. "There's no need to go into it again."

"No need for you, maybe."

"Elli," he said. Just her name and then dead silence. There was no kindness in those dark eyes now. He looked every inch the king. And the king was leaving this subject behind.

"This lamb is delicious," Elli said.

Her father's expression softened. "Yes. The meat of the karavik lamb is the most tender on earth. And the wool, as you've probably heard, is greatly prized. Our sheep, our horses, the fruits we pluck from the sea. These are the Gullandrian's pride."

"And your oil. Don't forget that."

"Our oil is our prosperity."

"I'll drink to that." She raised her wineglass. Her father raised his. They both drank. As she set her glass down again, Elli suggested, "You know, now you've got me thinking of him, it seems to me you ought to give Hauk FitzWyborn something." She was careful, to use his last name, to speak lightly, to keep the longing from her eyes.

Her father looked vaguely puzzled. "Give him something?"

"A reward. For a job well done. It wasn't exactly

a piece of cake getting me here. At first, I was absolutely determined not to come. I'd say, now I think about it, that it was kind of a minefield of an assignment, you know? To get me here no matter what—and to treat me like a princess while he did it.''

Her father cut another bite of lamb. "He's asked for leave. I've given it."

Her heart sank. So. He was gone. Still, she spoke as if she hadn't a care in the world. "Leave? But wouldn't he get that anyway?"

Her father finished chewing and swallowed before he answered. "You may be right. I'll think about it. A week from tomorrow, he'll fight for us. He'll win. He always does. When I crown him the victor it's customary that he will claim a prize. Perhaps I'll grant him some attractive property—something with a few good buildings, with promising mineral rights and a large flock of karavik.''

Elli was stuck back there at the word *fight*. "Fight for us?"

Her father chuckled. "Next week is an annual celebration, May Fair. We always hold it in the parkland, below the palace grounds. This year, in your honor, we're adding a few extra events to the festivities.''

"Extra events that include fighting?"

"Picture a medieval fair. With battle reenactments and horse races—well, not precisely battle 'reenactments.' This will be more a battle *game*. Each man for himself, as it were.''

"I'm confused. I thought you said you'd given him leave.''

"Him?"

"Hauk. FitzWyborn."

"Ah. Yes, I did. But not till after the celebration. He's my warrior, after all. He fights in my name."

As soon as Osrik's daughter left the room, Medwyn slipped from his hiding place behind the heavy drape in back of the bust of Odin.

Osrik turned to his friend. "It went well, don't you think?"

Medwyn nodded. "She is lovely. Intelligence shines from her eyes."

"And good at heart, as well. You noted how she thought of FitzWyborn, how she was concerned that he receive his due?"

Medwyn didn't answer immediately.

Osrik chuckled. "I know that thoughtful look, old friend. Speak up. What's bothering you?"

But Medwyn only waved a long, pale hand. "It's nothing, nothing at all. My son is a lucky man."

The heavy curtains were drawn at all the windows, making it as dark as it would have been at home, where the sun set and true night followed.

But Elli couldn't sleep.

She couldn't stop thinking of Hauk. She missed him terribly. And the idea that she'd see him only once more, from a formal distance, while he did whatever he did when he fought in her father's name…

Well, she wouldn't accept that.

It wasn't right. It hurt too much.

Something had to be done.

But then again, what if she'd read him all wrong?

What if he didn't feel for her as strongly as she felt for him? Maybe even if he *could* give himself permission to love her, he wouldn't. Maybe she simply wasn't the woman for him.

That *was* possible. Though in her soul, she didn't believe it.

But it could be the truth. It might have to be faced—and to do that, to face that, she had to *see* him, to *speak* with him.

She just couldn't stop hope from springing up inside her, from whispering in her ear that there had to be a way.

And for more than just a private moment.

A way for the two of them. A way that they could be together—proudly. And openly. If he only wanted that, *yearned* for that, as she did.

Damn it, this was the twenty-first century. The woman tenth in line to the British throne claimed no title, had a stud in her tongue and had lived openly with a commoner boyfriend. And that was a good thing, the way Elli saw it. A woman ought to be able to live her life without everyone around her bowing and scraping and calling her "Princess." A woman ought to be allowed to follow her heart. And no honest man should have to turn away from a woman he could love simply because some cruel cultural stigma declared him beneath her.

That morning, in Boston, Hauk had taken her totally off guard. She'd been too stunned and hurt to muster her best arguments. He owed her another chance to state the case for love.

And Elli Thorson intended to see to it that she got what he owed her.

She spent the sleepless night making plans.

First of all, she needed to get in touch with him. And she didn't have a clue where to go to look for him. She considered confiding in Kaarin, asking her if she knew where the king's warrior might be found.

But on second thought...

Kaarin seemed nice enough, but she was so clearly an aristocrat, a little bit formal, very aware of her place. Elli's instinct was that it would be unwise to share secrets with her. And at this point, really, all she had were her instincts.

Maybe she could befriend the chambermaid or her cook. Elli had no doubt both of them would have the information she sought—or would know where to get it.

Elli had grown up with servants around her. Besides Hildy, who was really like one of the family, there were always a couple of maids and often a chauffeur living in the apartments over the garages at the house in Land Park.

"Never underestimate the knowledge of your servants, girls," her mother had told her and her sisters when they were only children. "They know everything about you. They know all the secrets you don't want to admit they've learned. Treat them with respect and fairness always, and as a rule they'll repay you with loyalty and hard work. Treat them shabbily and they will sell your secrets and never think twice about it."

But to befriend the servants would take time. She

only had a week. She would have to watch and listen—see if she got a sense that either the cook or the
maid might be someone who would help her get to
Hauk.

Oh, this was all so...difficult. Was she making too
much of it? Should she simply do what she'd do if
she were home in Sacramento? Ask anyone who
might have information—Kaarin, her father, the
chambermaid, the cook? And take it from there.

Her instincts kicked in again. And they told her no.
They told her to proceed with caution.

For two days, Elli learned nothing about where to
find Hauk. She thought she would go stark, raving
head-banging nuts—longing only for a word with
him, and getting instead formal audiences with her
father and numerous princes and well-born ladies, en-
during extended tours of the Grand Assembly chambers and the harbor area, of a farm outside the city
and a huge, hangarlike workshop where talented
craftsmen still built the sleek, narrow Viking-style
ships for pleasure use and for racing.

And feasts. They had huge dinners both nights, followed one night by music and dancing and the other
by long renditions of a couple of the lesser-known
Norse myths as recited by a leading poet/minstrel, or
skald.

The night they had dancing, she was led out onto
the floor by a number of handsome princes. One she
thought especially good-looking—and probably a
danger to any girl whose heart wasn't already otherwise engaged. Finn Danelaw was his name. She

would have enjoyed flirting with him if she were capable of flirting with anyone right then. In fact, she could almost have been angry with Hauk for that, for stealing away her pleasure in the company and conversation of other men.

Finally, Sunday night, as she lay in bed, awake as usual, doubting she would ever speak to Hauk again, she figured out how to find him. It was so simple, she couldn't believe she hadn't thought of it earlier.

Monday morning, she requested an extensive tour of Isenhalla and the grounds and parkland surrounding it. Her father thought it was an excellent idea. He had matters of state to attend to, however, and couldn't take her around himself. He assigned the job to the prince who'd met her at the airport.

She and Prince What's-it spent the morning and early afternoon inside the palace, touring the endless, echoing rooms. Elli expressed fascination with all of it—the precious antiques, the Austrian crystal chandeliers, the huge tapestries in the formal audience hall that had come from France and were over five hundred years old.

The prince finally led her outside. They wandered through the formal gardens. She admired the tennis courts and the green swathe of velvet-textured grass where the courtiers played croquet.

Her heart knocking harder in hope and anticipation, she asked to see where the soldiers of the palace lived when off duty. Though Prince Whoever-he-was clearly didn't approve, he took her to the long, high-roofed barracks. He even allowed her a quick look at the yard and the enormous, fully equipped gymnasium where the men trained.

Elli saw a lot of soldiers. But not the one she sought.

Next they went to the stables so she could have a look at the famed longhaired white Gullandrian horses.

And there he was.

In a round pen, working with a young and spirited mare.

Elli's pulse went racing and her whole body felt suddenly light as a sunbeam. She balanced on air.

She turned a blinding smile on Prince What's-his-name. "There's Hauk FitzWyborn. My escort here, to Gullandria. I have to say hello."

"Uh," said the prince, for once at a loss for words. "Oh, well. Of course, Your Highness. Whatever you—"

She didn't hear the rest. She had eyes and ears for one man only and that man stood in the center of the pen, working a long lead, guiding the plucky mare to prance in a circle and toss her snowy head, her long mane and silky coat streaming in the breeze.

He saw her as he guided the horse around to where she stood. He never paused in working that lead, in coaxing the horse on in a circle. But for a split second, his gaze met hers.

The world was in that second. The universe in that shared look.

She knew then with absolute certainty that the problem was not that he didn't want her.

The prince came and stood beside her. She stared

at Hauk, smiling. Waiting. Absolutely calm—at least on the surface. Inside she was all quivers and needles and pins.

In the end, he had no choice but to lead the mare from the pen and hand her off to a groom. He came toward them, so stunningly male all the breath flew right out of Elli's body and every last drop of saliva dried up in her mouth.

"Your Highness," he said, removing his rawhide gloves, then bringing his big fist to his chest and dipping his gold head. "Prince Onund."

Elli swallowed to moisten her bone-dry mouth and resisted the urge to remind Hauk playfully that she'd given him an order a week ago and she expected him to obey it. He was never to call her Your Highness again.

But his beautiful light eyes had warnings in them. *Say nothing too casual, betray nothing of what has been.* She heard them as if he spoke them aloud.

"Hauk. Good to see you." She held out her hand. He had no choice but to take it. She saw his eyes narrow—just a fraction—when he felt the tiny folded square of paper she passed him. But his face, as always, remained carefully controlled. He bowed over her hand and released it. Her skin flamed where his had touched it.

She granted him a cool smile. "I hope you are well."

"My health, Princess, is excellent."

Princess. Your Highness. She could see that gleam in his eyes. He was *enjoying* the opportunity to disobey her command.

Prince Onund spoke up, putting clear emphasis on the first syllable of Hauk's name. "*Fitz*Wyborn works frequently with the horses. He seems most comfortable in the company of livestock."

Elli had learned a few things at her mother's knee. One was how to deliver *the look*. *The look* was designed to put upstarts in their place. *The look* clearly said, *If you don't watch it, you'll never do lunch in this town again.*

She turned *the look* on the prince. That shut him up. She turned back to Hauk. "I guess I never mentioned while you were…making sure I arrived here safely, that I love to ride."

Okay, it was a serious exaggeration. She'd never be the horsewoman her sisters were—Liv because she had to do everything well, Brit because riding a horse, like flying a plane or mountain biking, came as naturally to her as breathing. But Elli *had* ridden. Aunt Nanna kept horses at her vineyard in Napa. All three girls had learned to ride as children. "I think, tomorrow, I'll go riding. I'm sure I can dig up some suitable clothes." There were clothes for days in the huge closets in her dressing room. It only made sense that riding gear would be among them. "Since you're the expert around here when it comes to horses, I'd like you to ride with me, Hauk. Would you mind?"

He looked at her coolly. Distantly. She wondered if she had it all wrong after all, if he really wanted nothing to do with her—if he'd felt only relief once he got her off his hands last week.

But then he said what he had to say. "I would be honored, Your Highness."

"Thank you. In the morning, I think. Early. That way I won't disrupt whatever schedule my father has planned for me. Say, eight? I'll meet you right here."

"As you wish, Princess."

"Great." She turned to the prince. "Well, Onund. Why don't we go on in and have a look at the stables?"

The prince's worried expression brightened considerably. "Certainly, Your Highness."

"And then maybe we could check out the progress they're making on the preparations for Saturday's big celebration."

"Absolutely." The prince offered his arm. Elli took it. "This way," he said.

They turned for the stables.

Hauk put his fist to his chest and lowered his head. He didn't look up until the prince had led the princess through the open stable door. Then he stuck his fist in his pocket, letting go of the small square of paper she had passed him.

He wasn't going to take it out. Ever. He would forget it was in there. To him, it would be as if it didn't exist.

Hah.

And while he was at it, he'd forget to draw his next breath.

He lasted less than an hour. Then he flung himself down under a birch tree out in the horse paddock, near the clear, narrow creek. There was no one nearby. A gelding and a pretty mare nibbled grass over by the fence. They weren't the least interested that the king's warrior had lost so completely what he once prized most: his self-control.

Hauk shut his eyes and leaned his head back against the tree trunk—hard. The impact should have knocked some sense into him. But it was no good.

His blood whispered her name as it ran through his veins—her true name, her given name: *Elli, Elli, Elli, Elli...*

His hands shaking like those of a palsied man, he took out the little bit of paper and spread it open on his thigh.

It read, *Meet me. Here. Tonight at midnight.*

Chapter Fifteen

As far as Elli was concerned, there were way too many hours to live through until midnight. Every one of them seemed to take a lifetime to go by.

At eight that evening, she and her father had dinner again in the private audience room where she'd met him that first night. She was glad for some time alone with him. She had questions she needed to ask—about her lost brothers, about whether he thought their deaths were really accidental.

Her father answered thoughtfully. ''There's always the possibility that treachery was involved. In both cases. But our best people looked into Kylan's death—police and the NIB.''

''NIB?''

''National Investigative Bureau—similar to your FBI in America. They found no evidence that the fire was set. And all our reports about Valbrand are the same. No foul play. There was a storm. He didn't survive it.''

He spoke with sad conviction. Elli found she believed him—or at least, she believed that *he* believed what he told her. If either of her brothers had been murdered, she was certain her father didn't think so. Osrik must have insisted that the investigations be thorough. And he honestly seemed satisfied that they'd turned up nothing suspicious because there was nothing suspicious to find.

He'd spoken so frankly of her brothers, she dared to ask the other question that had troubled her all her life—the question her mother would never answer.

"What happened, between you and Mom? What made her take me and my sisters and leave here forever?''

He looked away. "Your mother will have to answer that one.''

That was all he would say—the same thing her aunts always said. Elli found herself wondering if she'd ever learn what had ripped her family apart all those years ago.

At a little after ten, she left her father to return to her rooms. She walked back alone. As she'd become more accustomed to the layout of the palace, she'd been allowed to find her way around on her own now and then.

Of course, when she got to her suite, the two guards were waiting. She was reasonably certain they'd have reported to her father if she hadn't shown up, that they'd be reporting to her father if she left again. She doubted there was much Osrik would do with that knowledge—unless he heard she'd gone somewhere he didn't approve of.

Like maybe out to the stables to get it on with a guy whose name began with Fitz.

Elli was beginning to see now that the fitz thing was a big problem. She'd heard it more than once— in the way that jerk Onund had said *Fitz*Wyborn, in any number of casual, cutting remarks. "Hopeless as a fitz," was a favored Gullandrian pejorative. "Bastard son of a fitz," was another—meaning that one's father (or mother) hadn't learned his lesson by being born in shame, but had gone ahead and produced a few fitzes of his own. And "fitzhead." Now, there was a colorful one.

It all seemed utterly ridiculous to Elli. But it must have been terrible for Hauk, growing up. The constant abuse had to be killing.

It was a miracle he'd turned out as he had, honorable to the core. So very strong. And good.

The guards opened the doors for her and she entered her rooms. The chambermaid was waiting. Elli thanked her and told her she wouldn't need her until seven the next morning. The girl smiled slyly, dropped a curtsy and left. There was a boyfriend. Elli had seen them, in the shadows on the back stairs, sharing kisses. Elli was glad her maid had found a special guy. It was one less pair of prying eyes to worry about when midnight came.

Elli's cook, who had a real fondness for schnapps, would already have retired to her room with her bottle. No worries there.

Elli went looking for her own clothes, the ones she had brought from home. After a ten-minute search, she found what she needed, a pair of jeans, a dark T-shirt and her trusty comfy sneakers. She pulled her hair back into a ponytail and put on the blue visor she always took with her on trips—not because it would be bright outside, but because maybe, if someone happened to see her, they wouldn't guess who she was.

She had the way scoped out: down the back stairs. The stairs led to a long, narrow hall on the ground floor. At the end of that hall, there was a servants' entrance. From there, it wasn't that far to the stables.

Elli found it kind of funny that her father would take such care to place guards at her door—and then leave the back stairs unattended. But then, as far as he knew, she had no reason to sneak around at night. And maybe the cook and maid were supposed to keep an eye on her. Who could say? Maybe the guards were only for her protection—or their presence was simply part of palace protocol. It didn't matter. No one would see her leave if she could help it.

At eleven-forty, she slipped out the door in the kitchen. She met no one on the dim, narrow stairs. A guard patrolled the area outside the back door. But luck was with her. His back was to her. She slipped across the short space of grass and into the cover of the trees.

A gap in the garden hedge was her gateway into open parkland. She ran across the damp grass that shimmered in the faint glow of deepest twilight. She reached the stables and the training pens within minutes and ducked quickly into the shadows cast by one of the long, steep-roofed buildings.

From there, she had an unobstructed view of the round pen where she'd found Hauk training the high-stepping mare that morning. He wasn't there.

She took off her visor and smoothed her hair. It was still a few minutes till midnight. Maybe—

Right then, a big hand closed around her mouth. She was yanked back against a hard chest.

She knew instantly who held her—knew the feel of him, the scent of him. He took his hand from her mouth and turned her to face him.

''Oh, Hauk...''

He gestured for silence and grabbed her hand.

She followed him willingly, a silly grin on her face, around the end of the building and through the open door into the stable. From a few of the stalls she heard soft whickering sounds. He pulled her on, between the rows of stalls to a door at the back. They went through it. He shut the door behind them and flicked a switch on the wall. A bare low-wattage bulb suspended from the rafters popped on.

It was a tack room, windowless, with straw on the floor and bits and bridles hanging on pegs. There were rows of saddles and shelves stacked with blankets.

He led her over to a long, rough pine bench. ''Sit down.''

She obeyed him, dropping her visor next to her and folding her eager hands in her lap so that they wouldn't get too bold and start grabbing for him.

He loomed above her, looking down, his expression depressingly grave. "You shouldn't be here. This is wrong."

"Lovely to see you, too."

"I told you there could be nothing more, ever, between us. I told you—"

"I don't want to hear it."

"You're a fool and I'm—"

"—here," she finished for him. "You're here. You came."

"Because I—"

"Oh, don't say it. Don't tell me any lies. We both know why you're here and it's nothing to do with my wish being your command."

"There can be no more between us."

"Oh, stop," she hissed in an impassioned whisper. "Stop right now." She shot to her feet and he backed up a step. "You'll never convince me you mean that—and if you believed it yourself you wouldn't have to keep saying it over and over and over again."

"Keep your voice down."

"All right, fine," she whispered. "My voice is down. But I will talk. I will say what I came here to say."

"Oh, you'll talk," he muttered. "I know you will. You'll use that clever tongue of yours until you have me convinced that black is white and up is down."

That hurt, for some reason. She dropped back to the bench. Gripping the edges of it, she looked down at the straw beneath her sneakers. "I just...I want tell you. I *have* to tell you." She looked up, into those eyes she wanted to look in for the rest of her life. "I love you, Hauk. I'm *in* love with you."

He blinked. His face went utterly blank—a stunned kind of blank, the way a man would probably look right after an enemy shoved a knife between his ribs.

Her heart was breaking. "Oh, please. Don't look at me like that. It can't be as bad as that."

"Elli…"

Her name. *Her first name.* He had said it. He had said as if it was all he ever thought about.

Joy leaped like a hungry flame within her. She gripped the bench harder. It seemed very important not to fling herself at him, not to force an embrace when he wasn't ready for one.

"I love it when you say my name," she whispered. "You do it so seldom."

"It's not appropriate."

She couldn't keep from scoffing. "As if I care. As if that matters in the least. As if what's appropriate has a damn thing to do with—" She cut herself off. To rant at him was not the way. She sucked in a calming breath and she tried again. "Hauk. Listen. Could you…do you think it might be possible that you could love me back?"

"What I feel means nothing."

She felt her anger rising. She put all her will into keeping it down. "What are you talking about? What you feel is half of it—half of what we need, to start building something, together, you and me." She swallowed hard and she lifted her head high and she told him what she wanted. "Hauk. I know I'm rushing this, but you've boxed me into a corner here. There's no other way but to tell you now, to…say it all, now. This may be my only chance."

He started to speak.

"Please," she said.

He gave her a tight nod.

And she told him. "I want us to be married. I know what this is, between you and me. I know you're the man I've been looking for. I want *you*. I want to be the woman you finally make love with all the way. Because I want to be your wife. I want my babies to be *your* babies. I'll...take your name proudly. As our children will. Please. Won't you just consider it?"

For a moment, in his eyes, she saw that he wanted exactly what she wanted.

And then he denied her again. "You don't understand. You refuse to see. Some things are never done."

"You mean, because you're illegitimate?"

"A fitz can only be allowed to reach so high."

"You're saying it's *never* happened? No one like you has *ever* loved someone like me?"

"Certainly it's happened. And those lovers either gave each other up. Or it ended badly. In mutual bitterness. Or worse. Men—and women—who reach too high tend to die in mysterious ways."

"I won't believe that. My father would never—"

"Elli." His voice was so tender. All the love he wouldn't declare was there in it. "I didn't say the king would have me killed. I don't believe that either." For a split second, his eyes shifted away and she wondered if maybe he *did* believe exactly that. And then he was looking straight at her again. "I don't know what would happen to me. I doubt, other than the shame of dragging you down, that it would be anything I wouldn't survive. But I know, unequiv-ocally, that you would be disgraced to stoop so low.''

She jumped to her feet again. ''No. No, you don't know that.'' She drew herself up. ''All this...*fitz* thing, it's nothing to me. If people look down on me for loving you, then those are people whose opinions I don't give a damn about. Oh, Hauk. Maybe I don't get it. Maybe I don't understand how really powerful this thing is, this judgment of a person by what his parents did. Maybe I'm asking for disaster. But then again, maybe you underrate yourself. Maybe you've been trained since childhood to see yourself as so much less than you are. Maybe if we went to my father, together—''

He didn't even let her finish. ''No. It's no good. I want you to go back, now. To your father's house. Tomorrow, when you come to ride, someone else will be assigned to ride with you. You won't see me. Please don't ask for me. Don't look for me anymore.''

She stared at him. It seemed impossible that he was doing this—sending her away like this. Forever.

She couldn't stop herself. She tried one more time. ''Just...think about what I said. Think about it. That's all. Because deep in your heart, you have to know that love is never wrong. If you never...come to me, I truly hope that someday you'll find someone. That you'll love her as you won't let yourself love me. That your life will be a good life, a happy one. A full one.

''And for myself, I hope the same thing. That I'll get over you. Find someone else. Make myself the kind of life I've always wanted, with a good man.

And our children. But that isn't going to happen for a long time. So if you change your mind—"

"I won't."

She felt the tears gathering. She swiped them away and turned briefly to grab the visor she'd left on the bench. It took her a minute to collect herself, a minute in which she fought, as she'd fought since he'd brought her into that windowless room, to keep from throwing herself on him, to keep from crying like a baby, begging him to give her—and all they might share—some kind of a chance.

Finally, when she thought she could speak without bursting into tears, she said quietly, "I'm just telling you. I'm here. I'm ready. If you dare to reach for me, I'll be reaching back. I won't disappoint you. I'll never let you down."

Chapter Sixteen

Hauk stood by his word. The next day, when Elli went out to ride, a captain of the guard was waiting for her. She smiled and greeted the man politely and mounted the sweet-natured gelding he'd already saddled before she got there. By ten, she was back in her rooms. She showered and changed and then went down into the city with Kaarin and a few of her other ladies. They shopped. They did lunch.

The days went by in a whirl of tours and endless state dinners with dancing afterward. Elli tried to smile through it all, to forget about Hauk and enjoy her visit to her father's land. It wasn't easy. But most of the time she thought she managed pretty well.

She and Osrik shared a third private meal on Friday night. He asked her if she was troubled. He said he'd noticed that sometimes she seemed a little sad.

Elli lied. She told him there was nothing important, that it was all pretty overwhelming, being here, being pampered and photographed and constantly in the limelight. But really, she was having a wonderful time.

After dinner, Kaarin joined her in her rooms to give her a few instructions about the part she would play in the various ceremonies at May Fair the next day. Kaarin left around eleven.

Elli dismissed the maid and went to bed. She slept well, for once. She woke in the morning feeling surprisingly rested, thinking that over time, she would be all right.

Today would be rough. She'd have to see Hauk again—probably give him the victor's token if he won in the mock-battle as her father seemed certain he would.

But once she got through that, it would truly be over. He'd be gone. She wouldn't have to wait and wonder if maybe he'd change his mind and come to her. Or if maybe she'd just happen to run into him somewhere and have to exercise all her self-control to keep from saying or doing something they'd both regret.

When he returned from his leave, she'd be home in California. Slowly, over time, she'd get used to the idea that she'd loved him and he couldn't let himself love her in return. Her heart would heal.

Over time.

By one in the afternoon, Elli had been introduced to more prosperous freeman merchants than she cared to count. She'd been photographed with her father and her ladies, with various adoring princes and a phalanx of elected officials called assemblymen, who were roughly equivalent to congressmen in America.

It was a beautiful day, breezy and cool in the morning, slightly warmer now the afternoon had come. The parkland was lush with spring green, the leaves of the aspen trees quivering sweetly in the slight sea-scented wind. The sky overhead was cloudless, a clear, cool blue.

Like Hauk's eyes, she couldn't help thinking, though she knew that such thoughts did her no good at all.

"Princess Elli, Princess Elli! Best oatcakes in Gullandria," called a merchant from a nearby booth. Elli led her chattering ladies over there. She took a bite of the offered oatcake, chewed, swallowed and announced, "Outstanding." Though of course, she wasn't really any kind of judge of a good oatcake.

"Princess Elli! This way!"

Obediently, Elli turned to the cameraman, making certain the proud merchant would be in the shot with her.

"Have another bite!" shouted the cameraman. Elli bit into the oatcake as the merchant beamed with pleasure and the cameraman got his shot.

An hour or so later, when Kaarin whispered that it was time to meet His Majesty again in the royal box at the edge of the area designated as the battlefield, Elli was glad to go.

Though her chest felt tight and her stomach unsettled at the prospect of seeing Hauk for the last time, it was a relief to escape the endless photo-op for a minute or two. The past week in Gullandria had brought her a true understanding of the ambivalence of public figures toward the press. They could suck a person dry with their cameras and their shouting and their constant demands.

She climbed the steps to the high box and took the seat next to her father. He smiled on her fondly, caught her hand and brought it to his lips. The rows of people across the open field from them and in the stands around them cheered at the sight.

The fight was nothing like she'd expected it to be. It was absolutely wild, with no order or discipline that Elli could see. The men poured onto the field at a run and then turned without ceremony and began hacking away at each other. Elli watched with her heart in her throat.

Battle garb included leggings and soft boots. Some wore light chain mail, "Called a *byrnie*," Kaarin, who sat behind her, whispered in her ear. "Or Odin's shirt, or a battle-cloak..." Some wore rough shirts that ended above the knee and were belted at the waist. Some wore breeches belted with a sash—and nothing above the waist. "The king's berserkers," Kaarin told her with pride. "They fight bare-chested."

Hauk was one of those. The sight of him stopped Elli's heart dead in her chest—and then sent it racing triple-time.

Kaarin said, in a throaty, excited whisper, "He's magnificent, isn't he? The king's warrior? Too bad he's a fitz.'' Elli felt her blood rising. It took all the self-control she possessed not to turn in her seat and inform the Lady Kaarin that Hauk was the finest man she knew and this whole narrow-minded prejudice against people who'd had the misfortune to be born to unmarried parents made her sick to her stomach.

If she could be certain that was all she would say, she might have done it. But her emotions rode a razor's edge right then. She might say anything. She might blurt out that she loved him. For herself, that wouldn't matter. She'd be proud to announce her love to the world.

But she hadn't forgotten the way Hauk's gaze had slid away the other night, when he'd said he didn't believe her father would harm him if he knew what they felt for each other. There seemed no reason, since what they felt for each other wasn't going anywhere, to put her father to the test.

Somehow, she stayed facing front—and luckily, she didn't have to look composed.

Nobody did. The spectators shouted and stomped and called out coarse encouragements.

Weapons were axes and spears and heavy double-edged swords. Each man carried a brightly painted round shield. Along with all the shouts from the stands, the men on the field yelled and cursed and let out wild, mad-sounding shrieks. Add to all that the clanking and thudding of weapons—blade to blade, ax to shield.

Blood flowed—but not *too* much of it. Elli kept telling herself it was all just a show.

But then, near the center of the melee, the first man

went down. He shouted in pain, dropped, sprawled—
and lay still.

Elli let out a sharp cry of dismay.

Her father patted her hand. "They train fiercely to
make it a good show. Watch closely. When a weapon
touches a man at a vital spot, he has to go down."

"You mean he's not dead?" Another man fell,
right then. Elli stood and peered closer. Then she
dropped to her chair again. "You're right. I think he's
breathing."

Her father chuckled. "My daughter, in this battle,
all the dead still breathe."

One by one, the men fell. When a man went to the
ground, he stayed there, unmoving, until the field was
littered with the breathing "dead."

The spectators quieted as the fight wore on. And
fewer men fighting meant the blows seemed to ring
out louder, the individual battle cries seemed all the
more powerful, all the more fraught with deadly intent.

Hauk fought on. Elli couldn't take her eyes from
him. He was so beautiful, the dragon rearing, the
lightning bolt striking, laying low all who dared to
challenge the sharpness of his sword. The powerful
muscles of his arms and back gathered and flexed
with each blow. He'd been cut, here and there, and
his body ran sweat. His smooth skin gleamed in the
sunlight, streaked with red.

In the end, as her father had predicted, all the men
had dropped to the field save one. And that one was
Hauk.

He stood in the center of the wide grassy space

now littered with the fallen and he turned in a slow circle, raising sword and shield as he moved.

The crowd went wild, screaming, "The king's champion! The king's warrior! The victor!"

The wild shouts faded. Someone started clapping. Within seconds, the others joined in, clapping in a steady rhythm.

One loud voice shouted above the clapping, "Hauk!" And the name became a chant. "Hauk, Hauk, Hauk, Hauk!"

Hauk made a full circle until once again he faced the royal box. He lowered his weapon, his shield— and his head. The chant from the people died, the clapping stopped.

And a stream of young barefooted women dressed in gauzy white gowns ran onto the field. Each knelt by a fallen warrior and helped him to his feet.

"To Valhalla," shouted the spectators. "To Valhalla and the glorious feast!"

The young women, Elli knew, represented the Valkyries, the battle maidens who took the honored dead from the battlefield and led them to Odin's great hall, there to feast and fight for eternity.

The white-gowned girls led the slain warriors away. Hauk was left alone on the field, sword and shield lowered, head bowed.

Elli knew what to do. Kaarin had drilled her the night before. She slid a hand into her pocket and her fingers closed around the king's token—a silver charm of Thor's hammer on a heavy silver chain. She watched her father and stood when he did.

Her heart was rising, too. Oh, it really did feel as if it had lodged in her throat.

The crowd fell silent.

Her father called out in sonorous tones, "Come forward, my warrior!"

In long, proud strides, Hauk came toward them. When he reached the royal box, he dropped to one knee.

"Rise, warrior," her father said, as Kaarin had told Elli he would.

Hauk stood. For a split second, his eyes met hers. Elli felt the contact like a blow to her soul. But then instantly, his gaze shifted. He faced her father.

She felt bereft, empty. It was just like the other night, in the tack room at the back of the stable. She wanted to burst into tears.

Of course, she did no such thing. She was made of sterner stuff than that.

Her father spoke again. "You bring our daughter home to us. And here, today, you bring honor to our name in the game of battle. It is your right to claim a prize. What will you have?"

Hauk was to say what Kaarin had told her the victor in the games always said at that moment, *Whatever my king will grant me.* And then her father would name the prize and Elli would present the token.

But Hauk didn't say what the victor always said. He faced his king proudly and he said out loud and clear, "I would have Princess Elli to be my wife."

You could have heard an aspen leaf whisper its way to the ground. Every man, woman and child in the stands and in the boxes sat stock-still, gaping. No one believed the warrior could possibly have said what they had all heard him say.

Elli was aware of the huge hole of silence. But only vaguely.

Hauk was looking right at her now. His eyes asked the question. Would she stand by her own words of the other night?

Had she really meant what she'd told him?

If you dare to reach for me, I'll be reaching back....

Elli knew what to do then—and it had nothing to do with Kaarin's instructions. She stepped to the railing of the box. And she reached down her hand.

Hauk's strong fingers closed over hers.

"Yes," Elli said. "Yes, yes, yes, yes."

Chapter Seventeen

For a brief and shining moment, Elli reached down and Hauk reached up and there were only the two of them, hands clasped tight, her answer echoing between them.

But her father must have signaled for his men. They came running.

"Elli. Let go," her father commanded low and furiously.

The hell she would. She held on tight, and she scrambled to get over the too-high railing and into the strong arms that waited for her.

It was Hauk who stopped her. "No," he said. "He's right. Let go."

"No way." She held on tighter, craning down frantically toward him. "I told you. I'll never—"

He cut her off. "Let them take me. Stand firm. So will I."

"But I—" She got no chance to finish. The red-and-black coats were all around him. They dragged him back. She lost her hold.

He didn't struggle. He let them march him from the field.

The crowd had watched all this in total silence.

But as they saw the champion led away, the silence ended.

It started with a whisper that shivered through the stands. A whisper that built to a shout. The people rose from their seats and flooded the field. Someone threw a punch and someone hit back. And all of a sudden, there was a riot going on.

Elli couldn't tell whose side who was on. She couldn't tell if most of them were thrilled at what Hauk had done—or outraged.

Maybe, she decided, the people didn't know, either. The mock battle had laid the fire. And the sight of the champion being led off by the guard had struck the match. The blaze had gone instantly out of control.

Her father grabbed her arm. "This way. Now."

She supposed it would prove nothing to shake him off. She went where he took her, through an opening at the back of the box—along with Medwyn Greyfell, a couple of doddering old princes, Kaarin and two other ladies who'd been with them in the royal seats. They ran under the stands and came out on the grass about twenty yards from the trees. Her father's men materialized around them and led them on to safety.

* * *

They entered the palace through a service entrance similar to the one Elli had used the other night. The guards in the lead, they thundered up the narrow stairs and emerged into a wide hallway.

There, her father took charge. He sent the ladies and the elderly princes on their way. They fled eagerly, all too happy to escape a distinctly sticky situation. Within seconds, only Elli, her father, the Grand Counselor and the soldiers remained.

Her father turned a thunderous look on her. He spoke coldly to the guards. "Escort my daughter to her rooms. And see that she stays there."

Talk about medieval. What did he think? That she'd meekly allow them to lead her away? He should have asked Hauk about how well she took being held prisoner. The first guard dared to touch her sleeve.

"Get your hands off me."

The guard ignored her. He took one arm. A second guard moved in and took the other.

Before they could haul her off, Elli shouted, "Wait!" It worked. For a second, everyone froze. Elli spoke directly to her father. "Send them away. Give me a minute. Let me say what I have to say. Please."

The guards waited, still holding her.

At last, when she felt certain her father would bark out a curt order that would have the soldiers dragging her off, he raised a hand. "Release her."

The guards let her go.

"Leave us."

The guards—every one of them—tromped out through the door that led to the back stairs.

Finally, it was just Elli and her father and the Grand Counselor.

Elli didn't waste her chance. "Father, you're making a mistake," she said quietly. "There's no way you can make a prisoner of me—not if you imagine I'll ever speak willingly to you again. Not and have a prayer my mother might someday forgive you for whatever happened between you two all those years ago. This is the truth. I love Hauk. I want to marry him, and he's finally seen the light and admitted he wants to marry me. Give up whatever big plans you had for me. Let me go to the man that I love."

Her father's face now revealed nothing beyond a terrible composure that reminded her of Hauk. The wide hallway seemed to echo with her words—and with his tightly leashed fury.

She waited for him to shout for the guards again. But in the end, he only said softly, "Go to your rooms. Allow me a little time to…consider this situation."

She turned without another word and left him there.

"Admit it, old friend." Medwyn stood near the bust of Odin in Osrik's private audience room. "Your warrior has outfoxed us."

Osrik was still fuming. "My warrior. My *bastard* warrior."

"He is a fine man," said Medwyn, "bastard or not."

Osrik grunted. "Never in my wildest, most impossible imaginings would I have thought him a threat to our plan. Always, Hauk has known his place."

Medwyn chuckled. "That was before he met your daughter."

Osrik was pacing. He stopped and whirled on his friend. "You find this whole damnable mess amusing?"

"Wiser to laugh about it."

"My people are rioting."

"A good brawl, nothing more. It's probably over by now."

"There has to be a way to—"

"No."

"Medwyn, try to remember no one tells the king no."

"No one but his bloodbound, lifelong friend."

"And his own daughter." Osrik loosed a string of oaths.

When he fell silent, Medwyn said, "We are beaten, admit it. You saw the look that passed between them. *Inn makti murr.*" Medwyn said the words from the old language solemnly. "'The mighty passion.' No use in fighting *inn makti murr.* And Eric would never be a party to such a thing, anyway. We both know how he is. He'll never accept a wife who pines for another."

Osrik peered at his friend more closely. And then he stepped back. "I recognize that look. You knew. You knew all along."

Medwyn shrugged. "I suspected."

"Since when?"

"The night she came to this room to meet you for the first time. She expressed an excess of interest in your warrior, I thought."

"You said nothing." It was an accusation.

"I wasn't sure. And besides, I knew that if my suspicions were correct, we'd lost this gamble, anyway."

"Not necessarily. If you'd warned me before he declared himself so publicly, we might have—"

Medwyn waved his pale hand. "Doubtful. Fitz-Wyborn is almost as beloved by the people as your son was. As my son *is*. Were he to…disappear, there could be questions, investigations we'd never be able to control completely. And then there'd be your daughter to contend with. She's quite formidable. I doubt she'd simply accept that the man she loves has vanished."

"I was thinking a mission, a top-secret assignment…"

"Old friend, it's over. You know it. And you know you couldn't really do it, have FitzWyborn… eliminated. You're too fond of him."

"This is more important than my own petty emotions."

"Accept it. We've lost this battle. Declare Hauk high jarl, elevate him to legitimacy. Only the king can do it and you are the king. The Wyborns will love it. He does their name proud."

"I had hoped—"

"It is wiser, my dear friend, to put hope in a place where it will do you some good. Let Hauk go to the Wyborns, let him demand of them his marriage sword. Start planning a wedding fit for a treasured daughter." Medwyn laid a hand on Osrik's shoulder. "Consider it from this perspective. From what we know, the three sisters are very close. I doubt one of them would miss the wedding of another.''

Osrik shook his head. He could still see Elli, standing so proudly before him, demanding to be taken to the man that she loved. ''What a queen she would have made.''

''Be of good cheer,'' suggested Medwyn. ''You still have two other daughters. Both of them are unmarried. And nothing brings a woman running faster than a big wedding.''

Chapter Eighteen

In Gullandria, the wise couple marries on Friday as Friday is Frigg's day and Frigg is the goddess of hearth and home. As it happened, the summer solstice fell on a Friday that year. Osrik and Medwyn decided to combine a royal wedding and the annual celebration of Midsummer's Eve.

Thus, Elli married her Viking on June twenty-first, six weeks and four days after she'd first found him in her living room.

The vows themselves were exchanged in a broad, green field down in the palace parkland. A Lutheran minister presided over the vow-saying—after all, Gullandrians are good Christian folk.

Though tradition didn't call for attendants, Elli had two: her sisters. Brit and Liv had flown in from America for the event. Ingrid had ranted and railed at first, but then she'd finally realized that her daughter was in love. She'd ended up giving Elli her blessing and sending lavish gifts and her sincerest regrets that she wouldn't be at the wedding. Long ago she had vowed never again to set foot on Gullandrian soil.

Before the vow-saying, there was the presentation of swords, one provided by Osrik, one by the Wyborns to symbolize the traded power of the families. Then came the ceremony of the rings—exchanged, in true Viking style, on the ends of the marriage swords.

After the exchange of vows, the wedding party raced to the palace. Hauk, as tradition declared, arrived first. He barred the door with his marriage sword until his bride appeared and they could cross the threshold together.

In the great hall, the ceremonies continued: Hauk proved his strength by driving his sword into the heart of a tree trunk that had been cut and brought inside for the occasion; the new couple shared their first loving cup of ale. And Hauk set Mjollnir, Thor's hammer, in Elli's lap, a blessing said to ensure many strong, healthy children.

After the ceremonies, there was feasting and dancing and tale-telling by the best skalds in the land. Elli's sisters had a grand time. Many noted that both young women danced often with Finn Danelaw who seemed equally taken with each of the tall, proud American-raised princesses. It was remarked that young Prince Greyfell remained absent from the palace, though his father had contacted him and as good as commanded that he come to see his king's daughter wed.

Finally, well after midnight, the bride was led upstairs to the wedding chamber by her sisters and her ladies. Once she'd been properly prepared and lay beneath the covers in the wedding bed, the men—their way lit by torches—carried Hauk in. They stripped him of his wedding tunic and his fine, ruffled shirt and pulled off his boots and stockings, leaving his feet bare.

"Enough!" he boomed out once they got him down to only his black wedding breeches.

No one was going to argue with the king's warrior when he spoke so forcefully. They dragged him to the bed and pushed him down on it.

"Out," said Hauk. "Now." So at last, with much laughter and an excess of tasteless wedding-night advice, the men and the ladies left the bride and groom alone.

Hauk got up and locked the door behind them. He turned back to Elli, who looked like something straight out of the myths, her hair falling to her shoulders, her nightgown white as new snow.

"Wife," he said softly.

She threw back the covers and ran to him.

Their kiss was long and achingly sweet. When he raised his head, he said tenderly, "Tell me this is real and not just some dream I'm having."

She beamed up at him. "If it's a dream, we're both having it. If it's a dream, I ask only one thing."

"That we never wake up."

She laughed and nodded. "That's it. All I wish for."

He asked, "Are you sure you'll be happy as the wife of a soldier?"

She resisted the urge to roll her eyes. "Haven't we been through this about a hundred times?" She had decided to move to Gullandria. Hauk would finish out his commission. Already her father had offered her a number of positions, most of which included lots of glad-handing and photo-ops. She'd put Osrik off. She wanted a little time to get to know her new country without the added pressure of playing the princess— and to enjoy herself as a bride. "I am proud to be your wife," she said. "We'll figure it all out, day by day."

He still wore a too-serious expression. "I know you loved your work as a teacher."

She reached up and smoothed her fingers lightly over his furrowed brow. "Hauk. Stop it. I never make choices that I don't *want* to make. And anyway, I have a feeling I'll be teaching again someday."

"And your mother. I know you wanted your mother at your wedding."

"Yes, I did. But she didn't come. I'm not going to be sad about it. I'm only going to hope that someday she'll change her mind about returning here." She stood on tiptoe and pressed a kiss on his square chin. "This is no time for sadness, or for regrets. This…right now, is for you and for me."

A hot red light glowed from beyond the windows.

She grabbed his hand. "Come on. They've done it. They've set the ship on fire. Oh, come on, I have to see it."

She dragged him to the window. He stood behind

her, his strong arms around her, cradling her close to him, and they gazed down at the parkland behind the palace. Her father had ordered a proud Viking ship hauled into the open field where a month before Hauk had won the day and asked for his bride. The flames from the burning ship leaped high in the twilit sky. The long, graceful hull and the shape of the dragon's head at the prow could still be seen, gleaming golden, in the heart of the fire. Around it, people danced in joyous celebration.

"It's so beautiful," she whispered.

She felt his lips brush her hair.

And she couldn't wait a moment longer. She turned in his arms, slid her hands up that massive chest and clasped them around his neck. "Is it time, now, at last? Can we do...what married people do?"

His answer was a long, deep, soul-shattering kiss.

When he lifted his head, it was only to scoop her up high against his chest and to carry her back across the room to the bed.

He laid her down on it and he came down with her, fusing his mouth to hers, drinking her sweetness, stoking the fires between them to a white-hot blaze.

He kept kissing her, kept his mouth on her mouth, as he pulled away enough to get two handfuls of her gown. He gathered it in his fists and slid it up and up—until their kiss was broken.

But only for as long as it took him to drag the gown over her head and toss it to the rug beside the bed.

He claimed her mouth again, in hunger. In the need of a man for the woman he loves, the woman he has sworn to build a life with, the woman who will bear his children.

The children of a legal, consecrated union.

She fumbled at the lacings that tied his breeches, got them undone and off. And at last, they were both naked. Naked in their marriage bed, while the red-gold glow from the blazing ship and the soft glimmer of twilight bathed the room in burning light.

He kissed his way down her body, tasting a trail along the center of her, pausing to dip his tongue into her navel and then moving on....

Down...

She took his head in her hands as he pleasured her, as he did the things he did so well he had her writhing and begging and calling out his name.

And then, just at the moment when she knew she was finished, that she was on her way to fulfillment and there was no way to hold back, he slid up her body and seated himself within her in one clean, deep thrust.

Elli cried out.

The pleasure was so intense, the sensation so perfect, so exactly what she longed for. And he was there, with her. His face above her, his big body covering her, inside her—all hers.

She rolled her head on the pillow, drowning in a river of liquid fire, in a hot pool of purest erotic sensation.

"Elli." His voice was low, hoarse, dragged up from the depths of him. "Let me see your eyes."

She obeyed his command with a moan.

His eyes were waiting. He said, in a whisper of

passionate agony, "Elli. I love you. I love you. My wife…"

And then the rolling wonder began, up from the center of her, spreading out like a flame along every nerve ending, a fire in the heart of her, fire everywhere….

Her body closed around him, claiming him utterly. She called his name and he answered, "Elli."

And that was the best thing, the most beautiful thing of all.

That he could say her name now. Simply. With love.

At last, there was stillness.

Two cats—one black, one white—brought from California by Elli's sisters, cautiously emerged from beneath the bed where they'd scrambled to safety at all the shouting and laughing over the bedding of the bridal pair.

The cats jumped onto the bed, and sat together near the footboard. Diablo gave himself a bath. Doodles looked dreamy and purred with enthusiasm.

Hauk and Elli lay limp and satisfied, arms and legs entwined. Elli traced the thunderbolt and the tail of the dragon.

He whispered, "Forever."

She tipped her head back to look in his eyes again. "Oh, yes. Forever."

And then once more he kissed her, a kiss that started out so slow and sweet and then grew hotter, deeper, the banked fires licking higher, into flame.

Elli felt her heart rise up, into the endless twilight,

into the red glow from the ship that burned below them on the wide green field.

Born a princess, raised a happy, healthy American girl. But always wondering, always wishing, imagining what it might be like. If her mother hadn't left her father. If their family hadn't been torn apart.

Somehow, all that didn't matter quite as much anymore. She and Hauk were a family now. And *their* family would stay whole.

Love was what mattered. Love was what gave life order and dignity, beauty and meaning.

And for Elli Thorson Wyborn, love was right here. In her warrior's arms.

* * * * *

Princess Dottie

LUCY GORDON

LUCY GORDON

met her husband-to-be in Venice, fell in love the first evening and got engaged two days later. They're still happily married and now live in England with their three dogs. For twelve years, Lucy was a writer for an English women's magazine. She interviewed many of the world's most interesting men, including Warren Beatty, Richard Chamberlain, Sir Roger Moore, Sir Alec Guinness and Sir John Gielgud.

In 1985 she won the *Romantic Times* Reviewers' Choice Award for Outstanding Series Romance Author. She has also won the 1990 Romance Writers of America RITA® Award in the Best Traditional Romance category for *Song of the Lorelei*.

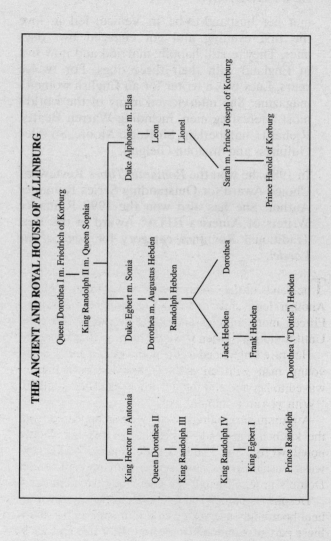

THE ANCIENT AND ROYAL HOUSE OF ALLINBURG

Queen Dorothea I m. Friedrich of Korburg

King Randolph II m. Queen Sophia

King Hector m. Antonia

Duke Egbert m. Sonia

Duke Alphonse m. Elsa

Queen Dorothea II

Dorothea m. Augustus Hebden

Leon

King Randolph III

Randolph Hebden

Lionel

King Randolph IV

Jack Hebden

Dorothea

Sarah m. Prince Joseph of Korburg

King Egbert I

Frank Hebden

Prince Harold of Korburg

Prince Randolph

Dorothea ("Dottie") Hebden

Prologue

The hands of the clock crawled toward nine o'clock. Another long shift over, Dottie thought thankfully. Fifteen more minutes and she'd be out of the café. Until tomorrow, when it would be time to start again.

Her face brightened as the door opened and a beefy young man with an amiable expression, came in, waved to her and slid into a corner seat. She mouthed, ''With you in a minute.''

A plump, dark-haired young woman appeared from the kitchen and made a beeline for the lad, Dottie noted wryly. She knew Brenda fancied Mike, and wasn't ashamed to make a play for him right under Dottie's nose, although she knew they were engaged.

Despite its name, The Grand Hotel was a down-at-heel boardinghouse with a café to match, in the shabbiest part of London. Dottie ran the café, and Jack, the elderly owner, had bestowed on her the title of manageress to cover the fact that she was a maid-of-all-work, who slaved long, tiring hours for a small wage.

Yet Dottie was happy. She had a fiancé she loved and a future to look forward to. Mike might not be glamorous, but he was kind, hardworking and devoted to her. True, his brain lacked the quicksilver alertness of her own. Unkind persons had been known to describe him as thick. Dottie would have been up in arms at that slander, but when her own mind went dancing away she sometimes wished he could follow her, instead of just saying admiringly, "You sound grand when you talk like that, Dot."

Mike was proud of his fiancée: proud of her petite figure and fluffy blond prettiness, proud of her quick tongue, her shrewdness and her ability to laugh at herself. But he never pretended he could keep up with her.

As Dottie cleared away, Jack appeared and began to cash up. "Has it been a good evening, Dorothea?" he asked kindly.

Dottie made a face. "I wish you wouldn't call me Dorothea."

The old man grinned. "Perhaps I should call you Ms. Hebden, then?"

"You do and you're dead," she told him amiably. "Dottie's good enough for me."

"There's a few hamburgers left over," Jack said. "If you fancy them."

She scooped them up eagerly. This was a valuable perk for people who were living on nothing so that Mike could save up for his own garage. She bid Jack good-night and headed for the corner table, tapping Brenda firmly on the shoulder.

"Hands off! He's mine!" But she said it with a good-natured smile.

Brenda grinned back. "Bet he's not. Bet I could have him off you."

"Bet you couldn't!"

"Bet I could!"

"Oi!" Mike objected mildly. "D'you two mind not talking about me like I wasn't here?"

He allowed his fiancée to shepherd him to the door, only pausing to call back, "Better check your food for arsenic tomorrow, Bren."

"Well if I do poison her it'll be your fault," Dottie said when they were outside. "Serve her right for putting her head so close to yours."

"It was just gossip," Mike protested. "She's been reading that magazine again. *Royal Secrets.*"

"Her and her royal scandals! That's all she thinks of. What is it this time?"

"The king of Elluria can't be the king 'cos his parents weren't properly wed."

Dottie yawned. "Well, they'll find another one. Come on, I've got some free hamburgers."

"Good for you! I'm starving."

Chapter One

The avenue of lime trees stretched into the distance, the tips faintly touched by the crimson of the setting sun. Randolph regarded with indifference a scene he'd watched a thousand times before. It was as useful as listening to the conversation going on behind him, which he'd also been through a thousand times before—or at least it felt like it. And while he kept his back to the room nobody could study his face.

He was wearily used to that study. Ever since he'd been barred from the throne of Elluria barely hours before assuming it, the world was curious about his feelings. Sometimes he felt like a caged animal, staring back at faces pressed against the bars, all watching him for some sign of weakness. And he would die before he revealed such a sign.

These days his expression was habitually grim. He was a serious man who normally found little in life to make him laugh, although he secretly envied those who could. Recently heaviness had overcome him completely. Those who might have been his subjects had known what to expect from him, gravity and devotion to duty, tempered with a quiet, stern kindliness. Now they were almost afraid of him.

The prime minister, Jacob Durmand, approached him nervously. "Your Royal…Your Highness…oh dear!" He lapsed into confusion at having used the term "royal" to one who could no longer be described that way.

Randolph turned, forcing a brief, reassuring smile. It wasn't Durmand's fault. "It's a trial to all of us," he said. "Don't worry about it."

"Thank you. Oh dear, this is all very difficult. If only—"

"If only my dear, scatterbrained father hadn't fallen in love with an actress when he was young," Randolph said wryly, "and been persuaded to go through a marriage ceremony when he was too drunk to know better. If only he hadn't believed those who said it wasn't binding. And if only he'd made sure of his situation before marrying my mother. But you knew my father, Durmand. He was the kindest man in the world, but he had this fatal habit of hoping for the best."

"And if only Prince Harold hadn't discovered that your parents' marriage was bigamous," the prime minister sighed. "Once he knew, he was bound to pounce, hoping to take the throne himself."

"And get his hands on Elluria's mineral reserves," Randolph said angrily. "How long would it take him to strip the country of everything? He's got to be stopped. Dammit, this family must have some off-shoots left somewhere in the world.''

He was interrupted by an elderly man scurrying into the room, his arms full of papers, his face full of excitement. He was Sigmund, the royal archivist.

''I've found something,'' he said.

They all crowded around the table while he spread the papers out.

''It goes back to Duke Egbert, who married an English lady in 1890,'' he explained. ''She was an heiress, and he had heavy gambling debts. They went to live in England.''

''Are you saying there are descendants there?'' Durmand asked.

''One, as far as I can gather. And I'm afraid the family has come down in the world—gambling again. The duke had one daughter who married a man called Augustus Hebden. It's his great-great-great-grand-daughter who concerns us. It's been carefully checked. The line is unbroken.''

''Did Egbert really leave no other descendants?'' Randolph asked.

''The family was almost wiped out in two wars,'' Sigmund explained. ''In the end there was only Jack Hebden left, plus his sister, who never married. Jack had one child, Frank, who fathered the lady with whom we are concerned. Ms. Dorothea Hebden is next in line to the throne of Elluria.''

''Do we know anything else?'' Durmand inquired nervously. ''Has she encumbered herself with a husband and a brood of children?''

''Fortunately no,'' Sigmund said, too deep in papers to notice that Randolph had stiffened. ''Exhaustive inquiries have failed to turn up a marriage certificate. She is only twenty-three, but has already risen to the position of manageress of an establishment called The Grand Hotel.''

"This looks encouraging,'' Durmand said. "This young woman must be talented, hardworking and educated with an orderly mind.''

"That doesn't mean she'll want to come to Elluria,'' Randolph pointed out.

"To have risen so high, so young she must also be ambitious,'' Durmand said hastily. "She will welcome the chance to broaden her horizons.''

"My dear Prime Minister, you're creating a fantasy figure to suit yourself,'' Randolph said sharply. "You have only to add that a hotel manageress's training is the ideal basis to become queen of Elluria.''

"In so far as it requires elegance and authority, that may be true,'' Durmand defended himself.

Randolph sighed. "Perhaps I can't blame you. We're all hoping for the best. Let us hope that she is the paragon of your imagination.''

"There's only one way to find out,'' Durmand said. "She must be sought out and brought here without delay.''

When he left the room Randolph headed for the elegant apartment that was reserved for Countess Sophie Bekendorf when she was visiting the palace. She'd been there often recently, preparing for the wedding that would make her Randolph's princess, and eventually his queen. Her life too had been overturned, he reminded himself. She was five years his junior, and their marriage had been planned in her cradle. He admired her and knew how perfectly she would have adorned a throne.

She smiled and rose when he entered, crossing the floor quickly, looking into his face. Her tall slim figure had been tautened by hours of riding. Her face was beautiful, though marred by a slight hardness in her eyes. Her manners were elegant and commanding. She knew who was worthy of her smiles, and who not.

She was all anxiety, taking Randolph's hand. "Was it very bad, my poor dear?" she asked gently.

"Worse than I can say. The heir turns out to be a hotel manageress in England. Her name is Dorothea Hebden."

"It's impossible!" she said violently. "A servant."

"Not quite. She seems to have achieved some authority—"

"Tradesman's authority. A servant."

"I suppose we mustn't judge without seeing her. We might be able to make something of her."

"You don't mean you're considering this monstrous idea for one moment?"

He led her back to the window and looked out over the great park. This way it was easier to voice his thoughts.

"It's not a matter of what I will agree to. My authority ended the moment we discovered that I was illegitimate. Now I'm not even royal. Dorothea Hebden is the rightful heir to the throne of Elluria."

"Have you thought she might be married?"

"Sigmund seems sure that she isn't."

"I see," Sophie said quietly.

Something in her tone made him put his arms around her. "I left soon after that because I could see the way Durmand's mind was working, and I didn't like it. My dear, how can I forget that when I offered to release you from our engagement, you refused, and stood by me so steadfastly?''

''You thought I'd turn my back on you because you had no crown to offer?''

''If I did, I was wrong,'' he said tenderly. ''No man could ask for more courage and loyalty that you've shown me—''

''But you may have to marry this other woman,'' she interrupted him. ''Perhaps it will be you who breaks our engagement, for duty. I understand, and you are free. But if it doesn't come to that—'' she broke off, her voice husky.

Randolph was confused and embarrassed. From the country's point of view the ideal solution was for him to marry Princess Dorothea, ''this interloper'' as he thought of her. Then, under the guise of being her consort, he would rule Elluria as he had been raised to do, and nobody would care about his feelings for Sophie, or hers for him.

He'd never pretended to be in love with her, but they were friends, and he was furious at being required to behave badly toward her. It offended his sense of himself, and there was much haughty pride in it. But there was also much generosity. The situation was very bitter to him, and not merely on his own account.

He wasn't a conceited man, but now it seemed to him that Sophie had more true feeling for him than he'd suspected, and that touched his conscience. Perhaps she knew this, and was pleased. She was a very clever woman.

Sophie's brother Dagbert sauntered in. He was in his early twenties, strikingly like his sister, except that too much self-indulgence was already beginning to show in his face.

"So what are you going to do?" he demanded when Randolph had outlined the situation. "Pity it's not a century ago. We could have had her assassinated."

"That wouldn't make me legitimate," Randolph pointed out. "I intend to bring her here, and see how we can make the best of it."

"You mean you'll marry her and carry on as before," Dagbert said sharply.

"He means that we shall all do our duty," Sophie said. "Whatever it may be."

Randolph pressed her hand in gratitude, and made his escape. He found Dagbert's callow vulgarity oppressive.

When brother and sister were alone the young man regarded her through narrowed eyes. "What deep game are you playing, Soph?"

"I don't know what you mean."

"Yes you do. Why cling to the engagement? You ought to be hunting bigger game."

"What makes you think I'm not?"

Dagbert gave a crack of laughter. "I see. Keep him on the string just in case."

"What have I got to lose? This English servant won't come to anything. Randolph is still the biggest 'game' in Europe."

"Except for Harold."

"Harold's marrying that woman with the millionaire father."

"That's been put on hold," Dagbert murmured. "Harold thinks his prospects are improving every day. But you're right. Keep your options open—just in case.''

Randolph's trip to England was made incognito. His secretary made a reservation at The Grand Hotel in the name of Edmond Holsson, and a special passport in that name was hurriedly produced by the Ellurian Ministry of the Interior. Thus armed, Randolph flew to London, and took a taxi straight to the hotel.

He had often visited friends in England, but they lived in the great country houses that were like palaces, or in Mayfair, the most expensive part of London. He'd never ventured to the shabbier parts of the city, and didn't even know where they were. So the hotel's address, in an area of London called Wenford, set off no alarm bells in his head. But as the cab took him farther away from the city center and his surroundings grew poorer and more dreary the alarm bells began ringing with a vengeance. When the driver sang out, ''Here it is!'' he stepped out and regarded the place with horror.

The Grand Hotel was a narrow, three-floor building of peeling paintwork and red brick that needed repair. It was evening and the pink neon sign was on. Some of the letters were missing, so that the sign actually read The Gran Hot.

Inside was a poorly lit hall and a reception desk, but no receptionist. Randolph rang the bell and an elderly man in shirtsleeves emerged from some inner region.

''Good evening,'' Randolph said politely. ''I have a reservation. Edmond Holsson.''

''Right,'' Jack said, eyeing the stranger's expensive clothes and air of breeding. ''If you'll just sign here, sir, you're in Number 7. It's all ready—that is—'' a thought seemed to strike him and he added quickly, ''would you be wanting something to eat? The hotel restaurant closes in half an hour. It's an excellent place. My manageress takes personal charge of it.''

''Would that be Ms. Dorothea Hebden?'' Randolph asked cautiously.

''It would indeed, sir. Have you heard of her?''

''Of the excellence of her work,'' Randolph confirmed.

''Well, just go through that door over there. The porter will take your bags up.''

With deep foreboding Randolph passed through the connecting door and found himself in a café whose chief merit was its cheerfulness. The tabletops were laminate, in a truly vile shade of red. Worse still was a small palm tree made of plastic that was clearly meant to dress up its surroundings. Randolph gazed at the palm, dumbstruck at its sheer awfulness.

The waitress, a dainty blonde with fluffy hair and the face of a mischievous imp, called out to him, ''Sit down, love. I'll be over in a minute.''

Randolph didn't want to sit down in this place but his knees were threatening to give way with shock, so he found a corner table that was partly concealed by the palm, and tried to be inconspicuous. It was hard because, surrounded by men in shirtsleeves and overalls, he was the only one in a proper suit.

Where was the high-class establishment of his imagining? A mirage. Instead, this. *This!* And he'd committed himself to spending the night in the place. He'd told himself that no sacrifice was too great for his country. Now he began to wonder if he'd been wrong.

The waitress was gathering plates vigorously. At the table behind her a young man leaned across and patted her behind, making her turn with a little squeal and a reproving, "Hey, watch it!"

"Sorry," the young man said, grinning. "Couldn't help myself."

"Looks to me like you *were* helping yourself," she riposted. "Keep your hands off or I'll set Mike on you." She was laughing as she eased away from him, wriggling gracefully to avoid his hand again.

A good-natured young woman, Randolph thought, but hardly the person he sought.

Another waitress bustled out from the kitchen. She was dark, comely and extremely well built. She called out, "Dottie, do you want me to do the corner table?"

"No thanks Bren, I've grabbed him," the blonde sang back. She waved at Randolph and called cheerily, "You don't mind me grabbing you, do you love?"

"Not at all," he replied politely, trying to conceal his growing dismay. Dottie! Dorothea? *This was Princess Dorothea?*

At that moment one of the men at the table whispered something to her and she went into peals of laughter. It was a delightful sound, rich and resonant, full of the joy of life. But princesses did not laugh in that unrestrained way.

She scurried over to Randolph, and sat down at the chair opposite with a sigh of relief. "Okay if I sit down to take your order? It's been a long day and my feet are killing me."

A flash of inspiration came to Randolph. He assumed an air of hauteur to say, "As a matter of fact, it's not 'Okay.'"

She rose at once. "All right, all right, keep your hair on."

"Keep—my—hair—on?" he echoed in bewilderment, feeling the top of his head. "Are you impertinent enough to suggest that I'm wearing a wig?"

Again her laughter bubbled up. "Blimey no! It's just an expression. It means don't get worked up. Keep your hair on."

"But why hair?"

"I don't know. It's just, well, you're not English, are you?"

"Is that a crime?" he asked sternly.

"No, it's just that it's an English expression and, well, you're not English, so you don't understand it." She made a wry face. "I think I've said enough."

"More than enough," he said coldly. "Now, if you don't mind, I should like something to eat."

"Sausage and beans? Sausage and fries? Sausage and bacon? Sausage and eggs?"

"Do you do anything that doesn't come with sausage?"

"Hamburger with beans? Hamburger with fries, ham—"

"Thank you, I get the picture," he said hastily. "You'll pardon me for saying that the cuisine hardly lives up to the place's name."

"Cuisine? Oh, posh food. No love, nothing posh about us."

"So I gather," he murmured heavily.

"Pardon?"

"Nothing. Down here it says 'liver and bacon'—"

"Sorry, liver's off. It's the end of the day. We ran out an hour ago."

"Rabbit stew?"

"We ran out of that two hours ago." She checked her watch. "And you'll have to be quick. We close soon."

"Close? With an unsatisfied customer?"

"Well, if we could find something you like—"

"But I've already found two things that I like, and you said they're both off," he said, trying to sound peevish. He was really getting into the skin of the part now, seeking the point where her patience would fray. Turning the screw a little further, he added acidly, "This hardly seems a very well-run establishment."

"It's a little backstreet café, not the flamin' Ritz," she protested. "I know what my customers like and I cater for it."

"You're not doing so well with me."

"But you're not like the others. You *should* be at the Ritz. Are you sure you came to the right place?"

"Unfortunately, yes," he responded in a hollow voice.

"So what'll it be?"

"Since it all looks equally disgusting," he snapped, "you'd better bring me anything that isn't 'off.' That is, if you can find something."

That should test her temper to the limit, he thought. But when he looked up she was regarding him with quizzical amusement.

"You've had a hard day too, haven't you?" she asked kindly.

"Yes," he said, suddenly dazed. "Yes—"

"What's the matter?"

"I—nothing."

"Why are you staring at me like that?"

"I'm not. Just bring me the first dish you lay your hands on."

He was glad when she left. He needed a moment to come to terms with his sudden sense of shock. It was nothing that could be precisely defined, just a strange sensation when he'd surprised that odd kindness on her face.

Suddenly he was a child again, with his Aunt Gertrude, his father's sister who'd raised him after his mother died. The boy had been throwing a temper about some childish tragedy. And when he'd kicked the furniture and shouted unforgivable things in his frustration and misery he'd looked up, expecting anger, but encountered instead his aunt's understanding smile.

"Why don't we just forget all about it?" she asked tenderly. And he'd known that she was the kindest person in the world. As well as the prettiest.

He could see Aunt Gertrude now, her pixie face with its halo of soft blond hair, so like the waitress's. There could be no doubt about it. Impossible as it seemed, this was a member of the Ellurian royal dynasty, bearing the family face down through the generations.

His rudeness hadn't fazed her, and he had to give her high marks for her patience and self-control. But oh, her voice! Her laugh! Her way of calling him "love"! And this woman was the rightful monarch of Elluria! He could have wept for his country.

She returned with a plate of pie and peas.

"Sit down," he said, indicating the seat opposite. She gave him a wary look and he nodded. "I'm not consistent, am I? But I'm a stranger here and I'd like to talk."

"All right," she sat down with a sigh of relief.

"It must be a hard job," he said sympathetically.

She groaned. "Tell me about it!" Then she laughed. "But I enjoy it. You meet people."

"Do you live on the premises? I understand you're the manageress."

She giggled. "Manageress! Honestly! That's just one of Jack's harmless daydreams, like calling this place The Grand. I mean, look at it. He's a sweet old boy, but you've got to admit it's hilarious."

Randolph, who was feeling anything but amused, agreed that it was.

"So you don't live here?" he continued valiantly.

"I've got a room a few streets away."

"You're not married?" Randolph asked cautiously. He no longer dared rely on any of Sigmund's information.

"Not yet, but Mike and I will be setting the day soon. That's him, over there."

Randolph followed her gaze to the stocky young man who was just coming through the door. From his stained overalls he seemed to be a mechanic. He waved at Dottie, then settled down in a corner table.

"No other family?" Randolph persisted. "Father? Mother?"

"My parents died years ago."

"Brothers or sisters?"

"No."

"Ex-husbands?"

"No. Excuse me," she said with sudden determination, "I've got some urgent business to attend to."

She jumped up, hurried over to the young man, just getting there ahead of the dark-haired waitress, and planted a firm kiss on his mouth. "Push off," she told Brenda. "Find your own feller."

"You can talk." Brenda addressed herself to Mike. "She's been all over that bloke behind the palm. Can't see his face but his clothes are posh."

"Eee, Dot," Mike said, awed, "have you got a rich admirer?"

"Could be," Dottie agreed.

"He's been asking her all sorts of personal stuff," Brenda went on. "Like, has she got any family?"

"What's he want to do that for?" Mike asked, puzzled.

"White slavery," Brenda said dramatically.

Dottie stared. "You *what?*"

"He's the front man, luring innocent girls into his net, then selling them on," Brenda said with relish. "He's probably stocking a harem. He's asking all those questions because he wants to know if anyone will be looking for you."

"Then why isn't he asking you questions?" Dottie wanted to know.

"There's a better market in blondes. He's probably got your purchaser already lined up."

Mike was impressed. "Hey, Dot, do you think he'd give me two camels for you?"

"You cheeky blighter!" she said indignantly. "What do you mean, two? Three, or you're dead."

"Well, tell him I'm open to offers. Three camels would just about pay the deposit on that garage."

This sent Dottie into gales of laughter. Still shaking, she made her way unsteadily back to Randolph's table, and collapsed into her seat.

"What's so funny?" Randolph demanded, fascinated. He'd only caught odd scraps of the conversation.

It took her some time to get the words out between chuckles, but when she'd finished he gave a reluctant grin. Despite his gloomy mood he found her sunny approach to life infectious.

"I'm afraid I'm not anything as interesting as a white slaver," he said.

"Pity," Dottie said, making a face. "I could sell you Brenda at a discount. That would make her leave my fiancé alone."

"She's certainly making eyes at him. And he doesn't seem to mind."

"Oh, Mike's an innocent," Dottie said cheerfully. "He needs me to look after him."

"Shouldn't he be looking after you?"

"We look after each other, we always have, ever since we were at school. On my first day, someone knocked me down in the playground and he picked me up and stopped them doing it again. And I helped him with his sums."

Yes, Randolph thought uncharitably, the bumpkin looked like someone who would need help with his sums.

"Is that all you want out of life," he asked, "to settle down with a garage mechanic?"

"What's wrong with him being a garage mechanic?" she fired up.

"Nothing," he said hastily, reading dire retribution in her eyes. "I just thought you might have been a bit more ambitious."

"Why?" she asked, honestly baffled.

"Because a girl as pretty as you could take her pick of men."

"Do you really think I'm pretty?"

"Ravishing," he said, adding shamelessly, "With that tiny waist and those smoky blue eyes, you could be a model."

"You *are* a white slaver," she said triumphantly. "I must tell Mike. He said you could have me for three camels."

Randolph felt all at sea. Nothing in his previous life had prepared him for a woman who turned everything into a joke.

"Why does he want three camels?" he asked, grasping at straws.

"When he's sold them he can afford the deposit on a garage."

"I'm not sure how much three camels would fetch," he mused, keeping gamely up with her.

"Well if it's not enough we'll throw Brenda in as well, for another two."

"Only two?"

"Well, she's not worth as many as me," Dottie said with such indignation that he laughed. "He's not just a mechanic," she added. "He's going to be an owner."

"And who'll do the sums?" Randolph asked, touched by her eagerness.

"Me of course. Mike's genius is in his hands."

"And did you, by any chance, put the idea into his head?"

"I may have done."

"And who found the garage?"

"Well, me."

"And who's been talking with the bank? Mike?"

Dottie crowed with laughter and thumped him on the shoulder in a familiar way that nobody had ever dared do before. For an instant he stiffened, but then he remembered he was incognito and forced himself to relax.

"It's no use you trying to make me think Mike is thick."

"I can see that," he murmured wryly.

"Anyway, I don't care. He's mine."

The sudden softening of her voice, and a glow in her eyes made Randolph ask quietly, "You really love him, don't you?"

"Heaps and heaps," Dottie said with a happy sigh.

"So you wouldn't be interested in my nefarious intentions?"

"Nef— What?"

"It means 'up to no good.' That's what you think of me?"

"I've got to, while you're in that posh gear," she said cheekily. "The last bloke who came in here dressed like that was arrested as he went out the door. Got five years for fraud."

"Then since my clothes have given me away, you'd better tell me something about yourself so that I can decide whether you're worth three camels."

That made her crow with laughter, and to his ears it had a pleasant sound.

"My name's Dottie Hebden," she said, unwittingly sinking his last hope. "It's short for Dorothea. I ask you! Fancy saddling someone with a name like Dorothea!"

"Perhaps it's a family name."

"Funny you should say that because as a matter of fact it is. According to my grandpa, anyway. If you believed him we come from a grand family, years and years ago."

"Did he ever tell you anything about this family?"

"I'm not sure. The trouble was, he was a terrible man for the drink, and when he was tipsy everyone stopped listening. No, it was just Grandpa spinning pretty tales."

"Haven't you ever wished that they were true?"

"Heavens no! What, me? Swanning about in a tiara and acting grand? Don't be funny!"

Her smile died as something attracted her attention. Randolph followed her gaze and saw that Mike was talking into a mobile phone, looking as annoyed as his good-natured face would allow. He finished the call, shrugged helplessly at Dottie and rose to his feet.

"Sorry, love," he said, coming across. "Gotta go out and see to a breakdown. Important customer. It sounds like a long job, so I won't see you tonight. Never mind. Tomorrow's half day. Meet you in the park as usual."

He kissed her cheek and departed.

"Oh heck!" Dottie sighed. "Just when we're about to close. Brenda, come and help me clear up. Brenda? *Brenda?*"

"I'm afraid she's gone," Randolph told her. "She slipped out straight after Mike."

"The lousy, rotten… She's not supposed to leave until I say so. You wouldn't believe it, but I'm supposed to be the manageress here." Dottie stood in the middle of the floor, raised her fluffy head to heaven and cried, "I am Authority, with a capital *A*. Underlings tremble when I talk to them." There was a cheer from the other customers, evidently used to this, and she reverted to normal. "But for all the notice she takes of me I might as well be the dogsbody. In fact,

I *am* the dogsbody, because now I've got to clear up on my own.''

"I'm afraid that's the price of scaling managerial heights,'' Randolph said sympathetically.

Dottie pointed a sausage at him. "*You* can hush!''

She went around the tables collecting money, and the café slowly emptied. As she started the washing up a wall phone buzzed. Under cover of taking his crockery to the counter Randolph shamelessly eavesdropped, but it gained him little. Dottie's face, full of exasperation, was more revealing.

"I'll strangle Jack,'' she said, hanging up. "Someone called Holsson made a reservation for tonight and Jack forgot to tell me, so I've got to get his room ready before I go. Oh blast Jack. I hope his milk curdles and his socks rot. And the same goes for Mr. Holsson, whoever he is.''

Chapter Two

"I'm afraid you have to go now," Dottie said. "I'm locking up."

"Can't I help you clear away to atone for my crime?"

"Crime?"

"I'm the awkward Mr. Holsson," he confessed.

"Oh heck!" She clasped her hand over her mouth, looking so much like a guilty child that he had to laugh. "Me and my big gob! I'm always doing it."

"Don't worry. I won't tell anyone if you don't."

"I'm not usually this disorganized."

"It's not your fault if nobody told you."

"Thanks. That's nice of you. Just give me a minute and I'll be over there to make you comfortable."

Randolph felt that nothing short of a miracle could make him comfortable in this nightmarish place, but he held his tongue. He was growing to like Dottie.

She was loudmouthed, over-the-top and totally unsuitable to be a queen, but she had a rough good nature that appealed to him, and her ability to laugh in the face of her dreary life touched his heart.

She was just finishing the cashing up. "This is supposed to be Jack's job," she sighed.

"But tonight he's giving you a wide berth," Randolph reminded her. "That way you can't complain about his 'high crimes and misdemeanors'."

"His whaters?" Dottie asked, her eyes on the till.

"His failure to pass on the message."

"Oh, I see. Why not say so in English?"

"It *is* English," Randolph said, suppressing a desire to tear his hair.

"Not where I come from."

He drew a long breath. It was her language, wasn't it? If he could speak it, why couldn't she?

But he abandoned the subject as fruitless. "Since this is partly my fault, why don't you let me help you clear up?" he suggested.

She agreed to this readily, and within a few minutes they had finished. She vanished into a little room at the rear to remove her waitress uniform, and returned in a blouse that looked faded from much washing, and shorts that revealed a pair of dazzling legs.

He had a sudden aching memory of his much loved but erratic father, a "leg man" and proud of it. Gazing at Dottie's shining pins Randolph wondered if he had more in common with his wayward parent than he'd suspected.

She locked up, turned out the lights and together they went next door, where, despite Jack's promise about a porter, Randolph's bags were still standing in the hall where he'd left them. It was a measure of how far he'd traveled in the past hour that this didn't surprise him.

Room 7 came as a nasty shock. With his first step he had to hold onto the door frame as a loose floorboard wobbled underfoot. The wallpaper was a sludgy green that suggested it had been chosen to hide stains, the mattress seemed to be stuffed with cabbages. The curtains were too small for the window, and the drawers beside the bed didn't shut properly.

An inarticulate sound behind Randolph made him turn to see a pile of sheets and blankets walking around on Dottie's legs. He guided her inside and removed the top layer, unblocking her view.

"Sorry," she said, dumping everything on the bed. "The furniture's a bit…a bit…"

"Yes, it is," Randolph said with feeling.

"Jack buys it secondhand, you see. Never mind. It's clean, I see to that."

"I believe you. Let me help you make up the bed."

This wasn't a success, except that his efforts reduced Dottie to tears of laughter. "I'll do it," she said when she'd recovered. "It'll be quicker."

She proceeded to attack the bed in a wild frenzy of efficiency, punching seven bells out of the pillows until they took on some sort of shape.

"I still feel I should atone for making your life difficult," he said. "Let me take you for a meal."

"But you've just had a meal."

He looked at her.

"No, I suppose not," she sighed. "You didn't really touch it, did you? But you don't have to—"

"I should like to. Please." When she hesitated he

added shamelessly, "Just think of Brenda making up to your fiancé."

"Right," she said, setting her chin firmly. "Let's go."

At his suggestion she used his mobile to call a cab to collect them in Hanver Street.

"Why Hanver Street?" he asked. "Is this a pedestrians only area?"

"No, but cabs don't like coming here because of all the one-way streets," she explained as they stepped outside. "Hanver Street is just on the other side of Hanver Park."

The little park was at the end of the road. A tiny place, just a stretch of greenery, a few swings and a little wood, it was an unexpected delight in this dingy neighborhood. It lay on a gentle slope, and as they descended the broad steps Randolph's attention was taken by two figures on the grass verge. They wore black jeans and sweaters. Their hair was completely covered by black woolly hats, and their faces were painted dead-white. Silent and mysterious, they were gravely miming a little scene. Their manner was gentle, and occasionally they smiled at the odd passerby who stopped to regard them. They might have been young men or young women. It was impossible to tell.

Randolph took out some coins, but the two performers threw up their hands in horror, seeming genuinely shocked.

"You don't want money?" Randolph asked.

As one, they laid their right hands over their hearts and bowed graciously, as if to say that it was their pleasure to give. Randolph was charmed. He would have watched them longer but Dottie had seen their cab at the far gate, and seized his hand.

Her eyes widened when he gave the driver their destination.

"I can't go to The Majestic," she said, scandalized. "It's posher than the Ritz. I've never been anywhere like that before."

"Then it's time you did."

"Don't be daft, I can't go like this."

"Get in," he said, taking her arm and urging her into the cab.

It swept them away from the dreary surroundings and off to central London, where the store windows shone and the restaurants glittered. Dottie pressed her nose to the window, eyes shining in a way that made Randolph wonder how often she had any kind of treat.

He'd discovered so many new things that day that he regarded his horizons as fully enlarged, and was beginning to think there was no more for him to learn.

He was wrong.

The Majestic offered him an experience that he'd never known before and if he never knew it again until his last day on earth it would still be too soon.

As they pulled up before the luxurious restaurant the cab door was opened by a doorman in an extravagant livery. He bowed, his face wreathed in obsequious smiles that vanished when he saw Dottie.

"I am very sorry, sir," he said, addressing Randolph as if Dottie wasn't there, "the restaurant has a dress code. Ladies must wear skirts."

The habit of years made Randolph say impatiently, "Nonsense."

"I'm afraid the rule cannot be broken, sir."

Only a lifetime of thinking before he spoke stopped him announcing who he was. Prince Randolph went where he pleased and restaurant owners groveled for his patronage. Now he was being told that he wasn't good enough, or rather, his friend wasn't good enough. The sight of Dottie's face gave him a nasty shock. She was smiling, but not in her normal joyous way. This smile had a forced brightness that told him she was hurt.

He was suddenly full of anger but it was directed at himself. She'd tried to warn him and he'd ridden roughshod over her.

"Come on," he said, taking her arm gently. "This place doesn't suit our requirements. We'll find somewhere better, that does."

That made the doorman swell like a turkey.

Dottie walked along the street in silence. Randolph was about to say something comforting when she began to laugh. "His *face!*"

"It was worth seeing," he admitted. He was thinking of some women he knew who would have said, "I told you so," and sulked until they thought he'd been punished enough.

Being offended was the last thing on Dottie's mind. She was in seventh heaven, enjoying the first fun outing she'd had in years. She recalled the last time she'd been in London's glamorous West End, as a child, when Grandad had brought her to see Santa Claus in one of the stores.

This felt much the same. The way her companion had whisked her away and brought her to this glittering street gave him much in common with Santa. Of course he was young for the part, and far too handsome, but she clung to the analogy because it left her free to admire him without feeling guilty about Mike.

They found somewhere a little farther along, different from The Majestic in every way except for its prices, which were even higher. This was an emporium of nouvelle cuisine, bright, modern, chic, sexy.

"All right for us to come in?" Randolph asked the man in jeans and shirt leaning against the door.

"You got the bread, man?" He indicated the exorbitant prices.

"He's got the bread," Dottie said, seeing Randolph's baffled expression.

"Bread?" he asked as they made their way to the table.

"Money." A horrid thought struck her. "You *have* got the bread, haven't you?"

"I think I can manage a loaf or two."

The waiter led them to a table by the window, through which they could catch a glimpse of the River Thames. He pulled out a chair for Dottie, who seemed disconcerted.

"I can't sit down," she protested to Randolph. "He's holding it too far away."

"Just sit," he advised. "Trust him, he'll move it into place as your legs bend."

She tried, and seemed relieved when she landed safely.

"Obviously you don't know the story of the Empress Eugenie," Randolph said, amused.

"Who was she?"

"She lived in the middle of the nineteenth century, and married the French emperor Napoleon III. But she was a *parvenu.*"

"A *what?*"

"An upstart. She wasn't born royal. She had to learn. In her memoirs she told how she and her husband once shared a box at the opera with Queen Victoria, and when they sat down she looked behind her to see the chair. But Victoria didn't look back. She *knew* the chair would be in place, because for her it always had been. Eugenie said that was when she understood the difference between a true royal like Victoria, and a parvenu like herself."

"I know how she feels," Dottie said. "Life's always waiting to kick the chair away. Now me, I'd just fall straight on my ass."

Randolph winced.

"You sound like Brenda," Dottie continued. "She's got a thing about royalty. Just now she keeps on talking about Elluria and how they've lost their king 'cos he's illegitimate, or some such thing."

"How did she know that?" Randolph asked quickly.

"This magazine she reads, *Royal Secrets*. All the dirt."

And the magazine would certainly have contained a picture of himself, he realized. He could only be grateful for the plastic palm in the café that had prevented Brenda from seeing him well enough to blow his cover.

"Do you also read *Royal Secrets?*" he asked apprehensively.

"Not me. Well, it's all cobblers, isn't it?"

"Cobblers?" he asked, his eyes starting to glaze.

"Rubbish. Royalty! Who needs it these days?"

"What about the British royal family?"

"Oh look, I don't mean them any harm," Dottie explained hurriedly. "I don't want to see them exterminated or anything—just pensioned off."

The waiter was hovering expectantly. After studying the menu with bafflement Dottie accepted Randolph's suggestion that he order for her.

"Do you have any preference about wine?" he asked, knowing the answer.

"A half of beer will do me," she said.

"I'm not sure that they do beer. How about—?" He named a French wine, not telling her that it cost nearly one hundred pounds a bottle, and Dottie smiled and said she guessed that would do.

When the food arrived she made slow progress because she seemed unable to talk without gesticulating, and her hands were seldom free to eat. But after a while she seemed to be enjoying herself.

"You're not English are you?" she said between mouthfuls. "You've got a funny voice. No, I mean— not funny exactly…"

"It's all right," he said, rescuing her. "I do have an accent." He tried to sound casual. "Actually, I come from Elluria."

"What, that place we were just talking about?"

"The very same."

"Cor! Fancy that!" She giggled. "You're not royal, are you?"

"No," he said quietly. "I'm not."

It was true, he told his conscience. It had been true for several weeks now.

"I don't know anything about Elluria," she admitted. "Not even where it is."

"It's in the center of Europe. It's quite small, about three million people. The traditional language is German, but everyone speaks English as well because it's the language of trade and tourism, and these are important to us."

"Is that why you're here?"

"In a sense. You might say that I've come on a fact-finding expedition."

"But why Wenford? Why The Grand? You're completely out of place there."

"Thank you."

"Sorry, I didn't mean to be rude. I speak first and think later. Always have, and I guess I always will. Too late to change now."

"Don't you think you could try?" Randolph ventured.

She gave a worried little frown. "Are you mad at me?"

"No, speaking first and thinking later is charming in a young woman, but there are times and situations when it could be damaging."

"You mean when I'm an ugly old battle-ax?" she asked cheerfully, spreading her hands wide and forcing a waiter to swerve around her.

"I can't imagine that you could ever be ugly," he said truthfully.

"But a battle-ax, right? Mike says it's like being with a dictator sometimes."

"And you don't mind him saying things like that?"

She chuckled. "Oh, if he steps out of line I just give him a long, lingering kiss, and then he forgets everything else."

That was wise of her, he thought. A kiss from those lips wouldn't just be about sex. It would be about laughter and sunshine, wine, sweetness and all the good things of life.

"Guys never give me any trouble," she added blithely.

"You give them all long, lingering kisses?" he asked, startled.

"No need. A smile usually does it. But you're quite right. The day'll come when they're not trying to get me into bed—"

"Would you mind keeping your voice down?" he begged, conscious of the waiter just behind her.

"And then I'll have to watch my mouth," she finished.

He reddened. "That's not really what I said."

"Well, it's what you meant by 'damaging.' Me coming out with something daft isn't going to damage anyone but me, now is it? Kingdoms aren't going to rise and fall because Dottie Hebden opened her big gob—"

"Aren't they?" he murmured grimly.

"—and that's lucky because she's always blurting out something stupid. A really daft cow, that's what everyone says. Well, Mike doesn't say it because he doesn't dare but...oh heck, I'm sorry!"

"It's perfectly all right," said the waiter, rubbing himself down. Carried away by her own eloquence, Dottie had made a wildly expansive gesture right across his path. He'd gone straight into it before he could stop, with disastrous consequences to the artistic creation in his hands.

A wail from behind him indicated that the chef had arrived on the scene, and it wasn't all right with him. "My masterpiece," he moaned, regarding the mess on the floor.

"I shall naturally pay for any damage," Randolph declared with a touch of loftiness. It was maddening to have this interruption when he was getting a glimpse into Dottie's mind, even though what he found there made him deeply apprehensive.

"Damage? Damage?" shrilled the chef. "It took me an hour to get it perfect. Do you really think that you can—?"

"I never think," Dottie said penitently. "Oh, I'm so sorry. How could you ever forgive me?"

She'd risen from the table and taken the chef's hands in hers, smiling up into his eyes. He was a foot taller, so that Randolph was able to see straight over Dottie's head, and observe the precise effect she was having on the man. From avenging angel to trembling jelly in three seconds flat, he thought in admiration. The chef was almost burbling, assuring her that there would be no further trouble, she wasn't to worry herself...

"That was very clever," he said when they were alone again. "How long did it take you to perfect it?"

"Hey, c'mon, I wasn't being cynical." Her tone suggested a crime.

"Be fair. You were just boasting about how you could reduce Mike to a quivering wreck any time you liked—"

"I was not boasting," she said firmly. "Mike *loves* me, which is why it works."

"With him, maybe, but what about the others? 'A smile usually does it,' is what you said. You knew exactly what you were up to just then, Dottie."

"Oh well." She gave a wicked chuckle. "I didn't do badly, did I?"

"No, they're not even going to charge for the 'masterpiece' you ruined. One flash of your eyes and he buckled at the knees."

"But that's not being cynical," she said earnestly. "That's being nice to people. I did spoil his masterpiece, so I just said sorry and...and...that's all there was to it.''

She meant it, he realized. Dottie might talk about playing off her tricks, but the truth was she preferred being nice to people. The smile sprang from her kindness and honesty, which was why it was dynamite.

Encouraged by Randolph, Dottie chatted about her family, which seemed almost nonexistent. Neither her parents nor her grandparents were still alive, and he gathered that she'd been alone since she was sixteen. She told this part of the tale without conscious pathos. She'd fended for herself and survived with her humor intact. No big deal.

She knew how to tell a funny story, and a woman who could do that had never been part of Randolph's experience. All the strains and tensions of his life seemed to fall away as he rocked with laughter at her description of her grandmother coping with her grandfather's numerous flirtations.

'''Course she knew he loved her really, and she loved him, but she was always chucking pans at him, and if she really thought he'd blotted his copybook she'd be after him like a ferret up a drainpipe.''

"Pardon me?" he said, startled. "Ferret? Drainpipe?" These too, were outside his experience.

"Sorry. Don't suppose you've ever seen a ferret, have you?"

"No," he said thankfully.

"Grandpa wanted to keep some, as pets, but Grandma said over her dead body, and he said not to tempt him.''

She finished the meal with an exotic ice cream and another glass of wine.

"It's my third," she said guiltily. "Ought I?"

"Wine as good as this can be drunk safely," he assured her. "And I promise you're quite safe with me."

"No funny business?"

"No funny business."

The word, "pity," flitted through her head and was gone before she could be sure it had ever been there. The man across the table was regarding her with kindly amusement. His eyes were warm and suddenly she felt as though the two of them were the only people left in the world. She wondered why she hadn't realized before just how handsome he was.

She seemed to see him more clearly than before, and it occurred to her that he was two different men. He had the body of an athlete, broad shouldered, tall and powerful, as though his whole frame had been made hard and taut by a life in the outdoors. His hands were a rare combination of size and grace, as though he could hold anything in them, with no appearance of effort.

Yet his face told a different story. It was lean, almost austere, with fine features and dark, expressive eyes: the face of a thinker, a scholar, perhaps a poet. This was something Dottie had never seen in her life before, yet she recognized it at once, and felt a faint stir of response.

Then she laughed at herself. What could she do with a man like this? A man she couldn't read.

"Are you a soldier?" she asked impulsively.

"Why do you ask?"

"Just...something about you," she said helplessly. Life in a family with a small vocabulary hadn't left her equipped for this.

"I did a stint in the army," he said truthfully. It had been part of his training.

"But not anymore? I mean, you didn't want to make a career of it?"

"No, but it's not impossible that I might return," he said with a wry grimace. She made no answer and he saw a vague look in her eyes, as though she had gone into a trance. "Dottie?"

She came back to earth. She'd been watching his mouth, the way the lips moved against each other as he spoke, or used them expressively.

"Yes?"

"What were you thinking?"

"That this is the best night out I've ever had."

"Doesn't Mike take you out?"

"Yes, we go dog racing sometimes. It's great."

"What do you want, Dottie?" he asked suddenly. "I mean, out of life."

"But you know what I want. I'm going to marry Mike and we're going to have the garage."

"And live happily ever after," he finished wryly. "Nothing else?"

"Lots of kids."

"But don't you ever want to soar into the heavens?"

"In an airplane? With me it was always boats."

"How do you mean?"

"Grandpa used to take me to see the River Thames. I loved it. I watched the boats and thought about far-away places." She glanced through the window to where the river flowed, shining under the shore lights and those from the occasional boat.

"Why don't you show me?" Randolph suggested, signaling to the waiter.

In minutes they were outside, making their way toward the water. It was quiet along the embankment, and they could hear the soft lap of the water. For a while Dottie had nothing to say, until at last she rested her arms against the stone ledge overlooking the river with a sigh of deep contentment.

"I didn't really mean soaring in an airplane, Dottie," Randolph said, taking up the thread of their previous conversation. "I meant, inside you."

"People don't soar in Wenford," she said with a faint sigh. "It's not a soaring sort of place."

"But what about the 'faraway' you mentioned? What about the lands of your dreams? Don't you ever have dreams? You've got your café and your garage mechanic, and that's it?"

"You're having a go at poor Mike, aren't you? Look, I know he's not the answer to every maiden's prayer—"

"That depends what you think the maiden was praying for," he said wryly.

She gave a choke of laughter. "Well, this maiden was praying for someone who was kind and good-natured, and who'd let her look after him."

"That's what you like? Looking after people?"

"Of course," she said, sounding surprised, as though it was a matter of course. "It's wonderful to be needed. I used to think—"

"Go on," he said when she stopped.

"You mustn't laugh."

"I promise."

"Well, at first I wanted to be an actress. But then I used to think I'd like to be a children's nurse."

"Why would I laugh at that?"

"Well, honestly! Me! I'm too dumb. I never passed any exams at school. In fact I never took any. There

was just me and Grandpa by then and he was always
sick so I bunked off school."

"But that doesn't mean you're dumb, just caring.
If there'd been someone to care for you, you'd have
done well."

"I did have someone to care for me," she said
firmly. "Grandpa loved me. It's just that things got
on top of him a bit. Anyway, I couldn't be a nurse.
It's not in my stars."

"You read horoscopes?"

"No, not that sort of stars." In a sudden expansive
gesture she flung a hand up to the night sky. "Fate,"
she said dramatically. "Destiny. There's a niche waiting for you somewhere in the world, that only you
can fill."

He'd once thought the same. His niche had been
clear, and he was well prepared for it. But then it had
turned out not to be his at all. "That's a dangerous
doctrine," he said somberly.

She sighed and went back to gazing over the water.
"You're right. It's not good to dream too much. It's
better to be a realist."

"Maybe reality will turn out to be stranger than
you think," he murmured.

She looked at him. "You sound as though that
meant something particular."

"Nothing special," he said hastily, trying to make
his face and voice blank so that his pain wouldn't
show. Mostly he kept that pain under stern control,
but this disconcerting young woman had touched a
nerve.

A cab rumbled by and he hailed it. "Let's go
back," he said.

The lamps were still on in Hanver Park, and as they

climbed the broad steps Randolph became aware of something very curious. But for themselves the park was empty, yet the two mime artists were still there, earnestly gesticulating, oblivious to the fact that nobody was watching them. They seemed completely happy in a world of their own, where no audience was needed.

They stopped to watch. The entertainers continued in serene silence, their white faces ghostly under the lamps. After a while Randolph looked away from them, to Dottie.

She was entranced, oblivious to him, her eyes gleaming with the colored lamps, her lips parted in a half smile of delight. He wondered when he'd last been so happily unselfconscious, but he couldn't remember it. Perhaps never.

Dottie's radiant innocence was like a blow to his heart. She was so candid and trusting, so sure the rest of the world was as honest as herself. How could she realize that the man with her was the serpent in Eden, plotting to destroy her happiness? He would take everything away, first the world in which she was at ease, then the lover who meant so much to her. And in their place he offered wealth, grandeur and a kind of power—all of which, Randolph was increasingly convinced, would mean nothing to her.

She looked up at him suddenly. "What's the matter?"

"Nothing. Nothing's the matter."

"Yes it is. You were thinking about something that made you sad."

Her shrewdness caught him off guard and for a moment he floundered.

"Is it me?" she asked. "Have I done something wrong?"

"No Dottie," he said gently. "You've done nothing wrong. You've been delightful, all evening."

The two artists had stopped miming and were watching them intently, looking from him to her, and back.

"Yeah, well, I gave you a laugh, anyway."

"More than that," he said seriously. "I think you're one of the nicest people I've ever known."

A soft breeze had sprung up, making her hair drift about her face. Randolph couldn't take his eyes from her.

"It's been a lovely, lovely evening," she sighed. "Like magic."

"Yes. A kind of magic. That's just what it was."

Dottie became aware of the anxious gaze from the two white faces. "What's up with you two?"

"I think they want me to kiss you," Randolph said, and putting his fingers under her chin, he lifted it and bent his head.

He made no attempt to put his arms around her, and his lips barely touched hers. It wasn't passion that she felt in him, but tenderness, a continuation of the enchantment that had pervaded the whole evening. When he lifted his head he saw that she was smiling. He smiled back, then, turning to the two mimes he said, "Thank you."

Their response was to jump for joy, dancing around Dottie and Randolph. He took some money out and again tried to give it to them. "Won't you let me show my gratitude?"

But, as before, they shook their heads. Then they

turned and ran away, hand in hand, until they vanished into the darkness of the trees.

"Why did you thank them?" Dottie asked, speaking as in a dream.

"Because without them I wouldn't have dared to kiss you."

"I'm glad they wouldn't take money," Dottie said. "That would have spoiled it somehow."

"Yes," he said, in quick appreciation. "It would."

Dottie didn't say anything, but stood looking at him in unutterable content. This was part of the glory of the whole evening. It was as though time had been suspended for a few hours. Later it would start again and she would become her real self once more. But nothing would be quite the same.

They wandered on out of the park until they reached the hotel, which was in darkness.

"Got your key?" she asked.

"Later. I'm walking you home."

"It's only two streets away."

"A gentleman doesn't let a lady walk home alone."

And the spell could last a little longer, she thought happily. They walked the two streets in silence and stopped outside a shabby brick house, three floors high.

"Good night, Dottie. Thank you for a lovely evening."

"It should be me thanking you. I've never—" she laughed and sought for words. "I've just never…just never…"

"Never drunk white burgundy?" he said, smiling. "Never eaten nouvelle cuisine?"

''Never talked like that,'' she said. ''It was nice to fly.''

''Don't you want to keep on flying?''

She shook her head. ''But it was nice to do it once.''

''You're so certain that it will never happen again?''

He thought for a moment that she would answer, but then she backed off like someone who'd seen danger. ''I've got a real life to live. You can't do that flying.''

''But—''

''I have to go in now,'' she said hurriedly. ''Good night.'' She ran up the short path to the front door.

''Good night,'' he said regretfully and turned away. But before he'd gone more than a few steps she called out to him. ''Yes?'' he said hopefully.

''Don't forget to miss a step as you go into your room. Otherwise you'll hit the wobbly floorboard.''

''I'll remember.''

''Have a good night, and I'll bring you a real English breakfast in the morning.''

''Thank you,'' he said, trying to conceal his feelings at the prospect of this treat. ''Good night.''

Just before she went to sleep Dottie spoke to a photo of Mike that she kept by her bed. She often did this, and not for the world would she have admitted that it could be more rewarding than talking to the real man.

''It was just a meal—not an actual date or anything—a bit like being taken out when you were a kid. It's not like I fancied him. Well, maybe just a bit...all right, a lot. Okay, Okay, so he kissed me.

And I wouldn't have minded if he'd done it again. But you're the one I love. Honest. Anyway, what were you up to with Bren?''

She turned out the light.

Chapter Three

Thursday was the great day of the week, the day when Dottie finished work early, and met Mike in the park. As two o'clock neared she hurried away from the café, rejoicing in the knowledge that all was right with the world. The sun was shining and heaven, in the shape of a chunky garage mechanic, was just around the corner. The fantasies of the night before were no more than colored dreams, like being taken to the movies. It was easier to think like this because there'd been no sign of Mr. Holsson this morning. She'd done him a good English breakfast, as promised, but had persuaded Jack to take it up.

She entered the little wood that fringed the park, and at first she had to stop and blink as the trees blotted out the light. Then her sight cleared and she realized that she wasn't alone. A man stood leaning against a tree, only half-visible through the slanting sunbeams.

Today he was in slacks and shirt, with the sleeves rolled up past his elbows. He didn't see Dottie at first and she was able to study him, trying to recapture the way he'd seemed the previous evening. But in the morning light she saw only a man whose arms were heavy with muscles, and whose torso beneath the light shirt was lean and hard.

Last night he'd kissed her, but only softly, on the lips. He hadn't put those strong arms around her or drawn her against him. Of course it was better that he hadn't, but for a moment her head spun with the thought. Behind the gentleness of his mouth she'd sensed something else, a tension, an urgency, even an anger, that she'd never known before in a man's kiss.

Her experience was limited: overeager boys whose wishes had exceeded their skill, and whom she'd had to put firmly in their place. And Mike, well-meaning and affectionate, always glad to please her.

But now she'd encountered something different, not a boy but a man, with the power to excite her mysteriously. She closed her eyes, and when she opened them again something had changed. The sun struck him at an angle that made him seem enclosed in a golden light, and for a moment it was like seeing an apparition; a benevolent apparition that hinted at a glorious future that might tantalize her for a moment before vanishing.

He looked up to where she stood. But although his eyes were fixed on her she had a feeling that it wasn't herself he was looking at, but someone else. The impression was so strong that she turned to look behind her. But then he smiled, and she knew it was just for her.

Randolph had awoken with a strange sensation, as though the new world he'd glimpsed last night was still there, inviting him to enter again, because she was there. She had the gift of spring, he thought, and was startled at himself, because such a poetic thought had never crossed his mind before. All his training urged him to avoid such ideas, but when he saw her again he smiled despite himself.

"Was your breakfast all right?" she asked, coming closer to him. "You didn't eat it all."

He nearly said frivolously, "That was because you didn't bring it up to me." But he pulled himself together. He was here on serious business.

"It was excellent," he said, "but a little more than I normally eat. The tea was—" he hunted for the word, "very strong," he said at last.

"Round here we say tea's not tea unless you can stand the spoon up in it."

"So I gathered," he said with feeling.

It was better to keep the talk light, and so avoid the swirling undercurrents.

"Are you exploring the neighborhood?" she asked as they fell into step.

"No, I was waiting for you."

The sudden gravity in his voice made Dottie's heart beat faster, as though she was faced with unknown danger.

"I warned you about that floorboard," she said quickly. "If you want to complain—"

"I have no complaints," he said, taking hold of

her arm to halt her. "There are things we need to talk about. Last night—"

"Last night was lovely but..." she shrugged helplessly, "it was last night. Today I'm me again."

"And who were you then?"

"I don't know. Someone I'd never met before. Someone who could fly." Meeting his eyes she saw an understanding that disconcerted her. It was as though he knew everything she would say before she'd thought of it herself. It made her laugh self-consciously. "Whoever she was, it's time she went her way and let me go mine."

"Was she the one who kissed me?"

"She didn't," Dottie said, trying to be firm. "It was you... Oh, I don't know anything anymore."

"I've been a bit confused myself," he admitted. "But I think it was something like this."

He leaned swiftly down and laid his mouth over hers. He knew there was danger in it, because springtime was always dangerous to a man who'd never known it before. But his caution had deserted him. He must kiss this one woman or regret the loss all his life.

He'd moved too swiftly for Dottie to prevent him. She instinctively put her hand up, but it merely fell on his shoulder. He almost seemed to be hypnotizing her so that her will died away, and she could do only what he was telling her. Obeying those silent instructions, she failed to protest when he put his hands gently on either side of her face.

She hadn't known that a man's lips against hers could feel like this, tender and coaxing, yet impossible to deny. She had a strange feeling that she was kissing him with all of her, not just her mouth. Certainly all of her was responding, from the top of her head, down the length of her suddenly tingling body, right to her curling toes.

Her hands had become rebellious. They wanted to rove over his body, across the hard muscles of his arms and chest and discover the flatness of his stomach, the power of his thighs. She knew that these things were true about him because the movements of his mouth against hers were silently telling her.

Somewhere in her consciousness doors and windows opened wide, showing vistas of far horizons, stormy seas, endless blue skies. The world was so much bigger than she'd dreamed, and was full of so many unsuspected things. There was exploring to do, and it would take her far beyond the comfortable little world in which she'd planned to contain herself and Mike—

Mike!

The word was like a thunderclap in Dottie's brain. Shocked at herself, she drew sharply back and stared at him. Then she wrenched herself out of Randolph's arms and ran deeper into the wood.

"Dottie!" he called and ran after her. "Don't go, please. I'm sorry, I didn't mean to offend you."

"No," she said, turning back to him and managing a shaky laugh. "This is so silly. It's just...just..."

"Spring makes people do silly things," he said hastily. "I got carried away."

"You?" she echoed with such naïve astonishment that he had no doubt how he looked to her: a man who couldn't let himself be spontaneous. And she was right. When had it last happened? Never before he met her.

"Perhaps it's because I'm a tourist," he impro-
vised. "People go mad when they travel abroad—"

"And they make other people mad too," she
agreed, frantically rewriting history. She was in love
with Mike, so she hadn't kissed this man. At least,
she *had* but she hadn't really enjoyed it—not as much
as she thought she had.

"I have to go now," she said. "It was nice seeing
you again but—" suddenly the words came out in a
gabble, "I really must go."

She rushed away without a backward glance, eager
to find Mike and the safe, cozy world she knew with
him. There was nothing safe or cozy about this
stranger. He made her think of lightning and fire, and
she needed to get away from him.

Just beyond the trees she found Mike sitting on a
wooden bench, munching a sandwich. He was startled
out of his contented reverie by Dottie's arms about
his neck as she flung herself down beside him.

"Careful, Dot," he protested. "You'll get peanut
butter over me."

The last words were lost in the most fervent kiss
she'd ever given him. He abandoned the sandwich
and embraced her back, despite his surprise.

"Have you been taking something?" he demanded
when he could breathe.

"Yes, I'm drunk with spring," she said idiotically.
"And I wanted—" she took a deep breath, "the most
wonderful kiss in the world."

"And you reckoned I could give you that?" Mike
asked, awed. "Eee, Dot!"

"Of course. Who else? You're the one I love."

She said this so fiercely that Mike stared at her in
alarm. Randolph, a short distance away, behind a tree,

couldn't see him clearly, but he could sense the reaction. What did Mike understand of a woman like this? In the few moments it had taken him to brush his mouth against Dottie's he had discovered the banked fires of passion waiting for the one man to bring it forth. And that man wasn't this well meaning oaf, whatever she believed.

Her next words gave him a nasty shock.

"Mike, when are we going to set the date?"

"Whenever you like, Dot. But I thought we decided to wait until we had the deposit for the garage."

"I've changed my mind. I'm going to snap you up fast, before Bren gets her claws into you."

"Aw, c'mon. You know I love you Dot. I couldn't care about anyone else, any more than you could."

Dottie's voice was suddenly high and breathless. "Of course we couldn't, but let's not take chances. You—you never know what's going to happen."

"All right. Whatever you say."

"No, it shouldn't be just what I say. It should be what *we* say." She sounded suddenly despondent. "Don't you *want* to marry me?"

"Course I do. I said yes when you proposed, didn't I? All right, don't hit me."

From behind the tree Randolph could hear a scuffle and laughter that ended very suddenly. He resisted the impulse to lean out and see what was happening, but the silence went on longer than he liked.

"Are we going to have a honeymoon?" Mike asked at last.

"Sure. How about a Caribbean cruise?"

"Yeah, I'd like one of them."

"Price no object," Dottie said grandiloquently.

"Three thousand, four thousand, or there's a top flight cruise at seven thousand."

"Let's have that," Mike said. "Only the best for us."

"Luxury class."

"Money to burn."

"Our every whim catered for," she cried to the blue sky.

"We'll eat off gold plates."

Hand in hand, they considered this for a moment.

"Unless you'd prefer a month in Hawaii," Dottie offered.

"Is that the one where you get sexy maidens meeting you on the beach with garlands?"

"On second thought, forget Hawaii."

Mike gave his easygoing chuckle. "Anything you say, Dot." He squeezed her hand as they left the brightly colored dreams behind. "Mind you, if you go off the cruise idea, Uncle Joe's always said we could borrow his caravan for a long weekend."

"That would be lovely," Dottie said.

She sounded as enthusiastic about the cheap caravan as the luxury cruise that existed only in her lively imagination, and Randolph had to admire her spirit. It might be nice for a man to share his life with such a funny, gutsy lady. It was the same spirit that he admired in Sophie, he reminded himself. Not that Sophie's lofty mind would have indulged in that crazy fantasy.

With regret he remembered that Dottie's fantasies too, must be dispelled. He had lingered as long as he dared. Now it was time to claim her for his country, and her duty. He stepped out from behind the tree, treading on a twig, its snap making Dottie look up quickly.

"Are you following me?" she demanded.

Then Randolph, the severe and practical man, was truly inspired.

"Yes," he said. "I am following you—both of you. I had to be sure that you were suitable for the prize. A stay in a luxury hotel as guests of the Ellurian gov—tourist authority."

"Elluria?" Dottie echoed, wrinkling her brow. "That's the place you were telling me about."

"We're trying to promote it as somewhere to take the vacation of a lifetime," Randolph said. "It's never been done before, which is why so few people think of traveling there. But we have everything, magnificent scenery, great art, history—"

"Disneyland?" Mike asked eagerly.

"No," Randolph was forced to admit, "we don't have Disneyland. But we have Lake Bellanon, with its beautiful beaches. I think you'll both like it there."

"Us?" Dottie asked suspiciously.

"It's been my task to find two people who would make best use of the prize. It has to be a young couple, so that as well as enjoying our hospitality you can tell us what Elluria needs to attract other young people. It will be everything you've dreamed of—money to burn, gold plates, your every whim catered for."

If only, he thought, Mike didn't say, "Eee, Dot!" But he did. Randolph ground his teeth.

"It's too good to be true," Mike went on.

"Right! Too good to be true," Dottie said, showing an astuteness that dismayed Randolph. "In real life, things just don't get handed to you on a plate like this. I'm suspicious."

"He can't be stocking a harem, Dot," Mike pointed out. "Not if he wants me as well."

"You don't know that. He's probably covering all the angles."

"Pardon?"

"Never mind," she said hastily. Randolph's lips were twitching. He'd divined her meaning at once, while Mike was still floundering around trying to believe she'd meant what he thought she'd meant.

"I promise you, it's all on the level," Randolph said smoothly. "Wouldn't you like a free vacation, spending money, new wardrobe?"

Dottie drew a long breath at the thought of new clothes, but she was torn two ways, trying to equate this with his behavior to her earlier. Randolph understood her perfectly and his conscience smote him.

"It could be our honeymoon," she said at last.

"No," Randolph said hastily, "we have to leave at once."

"But if we got a special license…"

Seeing disaster staring him in the face Randolph became even more inspired.

"I must make a confession, Ms. Hebden. The fact is that you two are replacements. The original prize winners had to drop out at the last minute. The celebrations are all arranged. When I return to Elluria tonight I must take you with me or I'll probably lose my job."

"Tonight?" Dottie squealed. "And what about *our* jobs?"

"I promise to settle everything with your employers. The Ellurian tourist authority will provide temporary replacements, at their own expense. Generous expense. Your employers will gain on the transactions.''

''But we don't have passports,'' Dottie pointed out.

''You will travel on Ellurian diplomatic passports.''

''A whole month's free vacation,'' Mike mused. ''It's a pity it couldn't have been our honeymoon.''

''But it can,'' Dottie said triumphantly. ''We can get married out there. Think what terrific publicity for tourism that will be.'' She beamed at Randolph. ''You'd like that, wouldn't you?''

''Of course,'' he said in a hollow voice.

It seemed that as he avoided one pitfall another opened at his feet. His conscience was troubling him more every minute. But he had no choice. At all costs, he had to get Dottie to Elluria, or his country would be at Harold's mercy, and that mustn't be allowed to happen.

''We can be married at once,'' Dottie was murmuring, almost to herself. ''Oh but look, it's nonsense. Things don't happen like this. We have to be realistic.''

''Perhaps you can be too realistic,'' Randolph pointed out. ''Take the chance life holds out to you.'' The cunning of the serpent made him add, ''Just think how mad Brenda will be when she finds out! Of course, by then it will be too late.''

''Oh, if only I could be there to see her face,'' Dottie breathed.

''But you won't,'' Randolph reminded her. ''You'll be in Elluria, with Mike.''

''Let's go,'' Dottie said at once. She jumped to her feet, her face shining with joy. ''Oh Mike, Mike!''

She threw her arms about him and they hugged each other exuberantly. Randolph suddenly looked away. When he looked back he found Dottie regarding him, and he could have sworn there was accusation in her eyes.

Like all crown princes of Elluria, Randolph had spent some time in the army. There he'd learned lessons about tactics, strategy and intelligence gathering that stood him in good stead now.

Certain things were simple, like arranging two diplomatic passports. Sorting matters with Mike and Dottie's employers were tasks for embassy attachés. But keeping his two quarries in protective custody without arousing Dottie's suspicions further, demanded the skills of a policeman, a magician and a mother hen, and taxed Randolph's ingenuity to the fullest.

Whatever organizing skills Dottie displaying at the café seemed not to carry over into her personal life. Her packing was an exercise in chaos, and the number of times she stopped to remember, "just one more thing," drove Randolph nearly demented.

Finally she made her appearance dressed for traveling in what she called "comfortable clothes." These turned out to be a pair of short shorts which would give her future prime minister heart failure, were he to see them. Luckily Randolph had prepared for this disaster by having suitable clothing waiting on the aircraft.

At last he had them in a car on the way to the airport, and their attention was occupied by the excitement of the trip.

"What happens when we get there?" Mike asked.

"We get married," Dottie said firmly.

"What, today?"

"It will take a few days for the paperwork to be complete," Randolph said hastily. "In the meantime, why don't we celebrate with champagne?"

He produced glasses and a bottle of Bollinger from the car's mini bar, and the moment slid past. At the airport they were whisked through their passport checks with the minimum of fuss, and then onto the small luxuriously appointed aircraft, with its soft armchairs in a pale biscuit color.

"Where are the other passengers?" Dottie asked.

"You are Elluria's honored guests," Randolph informed her. "This is a special plane, part of our hospitality."

It was, in fact, the royal plane, which had been on standby, ready to leave at his command.

Dottie regarded him wryly. Something about this was all wrong, and she was growing more uneasy by the minute. But once they took off she became entranced with gazing out of the window at the sea, and then the coast as they reached France.

"Hey, look at that," she breathed to Mike. Receiving no answer she turned and found Mike missing.

"He's in the cockpit," Randolph explained, coming to sit beside her. "Knowing that he was interested in things mechanical, the captain invited him."

"You fixed that," Dottie said. It wasn't a question. She already knew that this man was a great fixer.

"Yes," he admitted. "I needed to talk to you alone. Please Dottie, it's very important." Having created his chance he found he couldn't use it, and was silent a long time.

"So important that you can't find the words?" she suggested.

"Exactly that. What I have to tell you is so extraordinary that at first you may not believe it. In fact, you won't believe it."

"If I'm not going to believe it, it doesn't matter what words you use," she said, trying to be helpful.

"Oh it matters. A lot hangs on this. You may blame me for...for various thing—"

"Well, I have a few things to blame you for, haven't I?" she said quietly.

She couldn't name the obscure sense of hurt that had troubled her since this morning. Nor would she say aloud that he'd deluded her with false magic, but the unspoken reproach was there in her eyes, and he colored.

"Please hear me out before you judge me," he said.

When she didn't reply he took out a copy of *Royal Secrets* and put it into her hands. "Read page 8," he said.

Frowning she opened at the page, and the first thing she saw was a large picture, captioned, Prince Randolph, The Deposed Heir.

At first she didn't believe what her eyes told her. It was impossible for this to be the man sitting opposite her. But gradually the truth of the likeness became impossible to ignore.

"But...you're Mr. Holsson."

"I'm afraid he doesn't exist. I am—I was Crown Prince Randolph of Elluria. Until recently I was heir to the throne. Then it turned out that my father had never been properly married to my mother. In short, I am a bastard, and incapable of inheriting."

"But what's that got to do with me?"

"Let's say you did your grandfather an injustice. Those tales weren't just the drink talking. You're a direct descendent of the royal house of Elluria."

"Oh, get away with you. This is a windup, isn't it? Any minute now a bloke's going to start filming me for *Candid Camera*."

"Dorothea, I am trying to be serious. This is not a 'windup.' Your royal descent goes back over a hundred years, to Duke Egbert, who was the king's brother. He married an English lady and went to live in England. They had one child, Dorothea, who married a man called Augustus Hebden, and you're their great-great-great-granddaughter."

"So we're both called Dorothea. It's a coincidence."

"It occurs in every generation, and we've had two Queen Dorotheas. It's a common name in the Ellurian royal family, and in yours I believe?"

"Well, there was my great Aunt Dot... How did you know?"

"Because I've checked the Hebden family and there's no mistake."

"So if I'm descended from a duke, how come I'm running a greasy spoon?"

"Egbert was a spendthrift. He got through his wife's money, but managed to marry his daughter to a wealthy man on the strength of his royal connections. Then he spent his son-in-law's money, too. After that it was downhill all the way. And you are *not* running a greasy spoon. That's in the past. Now you are Her Royal Highness, Princess Dorothea, heiress to the throne of Elluria, and my fifth cousin."

"We're related?"

"Very distantly."

She stared. "You're serious aren't you? You staged this whole thing—"

"To get you to Elluria. Don't expect me to apologize. Without you the next heir is Harold of Korburg, and it makes me go cold to think of what will happen to my country if he gets his hands on it. Elluria is rich in minerals and Harold is greedy. He would sell the ground out from under us, and spend nothing on the people. You *must* become the queen. Anything else is unthinkable."

"For you, maybe. Who gave you the right to kidnap me?"

"I didn't—"

"Oh yes you did. Don't play word games with me. You talked me onto this plane with a pack of lies."

"Yes, I did," he admitted. "That's how desperate the situation is. Dorothea—"

"Don't call me that. I'm Dottie."

"Not anymore. For the past ten minutes we've been in Ellurian air space, and in this country you are Princess Dorothea."

"Then listen to me, buster. Princess Dorothea demands to see the British consul."

Randolph had grown pale. "Her Royal Highness's commands will be obeyed as soon as we land. In the meantime, I've arranged for some more elegant clothing to be on board. May I suggest that you attire yourself suitably for your first appearance before your people?"

Dottie looked at him and a hint of mulishness crept into her eyes. "You've got a nerve, dictating my clothes for me. I'll arrive as Dottie Hebden, because that's who I am. And if that's not good enough for you, the sooner you send me home, the better pleased I'll be.''

A steward appeared and addressed Randolph. ''Sir, the captain says we'll be landing in a few moments.''

Randolph thanked him, and as soon as he departed said urgently, ''There isn't much time. Please put the dress on. I promise you, it'll suit you. And your people will expect you to look the part.''

''Meaning that I don't look the part now.''

''No,'' he said, suppressing a shudder.

''Good. Then they won't get any ideas about my staying here. I'll go as I am.''

''But Dottie—Dorothea—''

''Dottie will do. Shouldn't Mike be coming back here if we're landing?'' She heard Randolph's sound of exasperation and said, ''It wouldn't work, honestly. I couldn't carry it off. Giving people orders—''

''Is this the woman who wanted to be 'Authority with a capital *A*'?''

''In that tatty café, yes, but I couldn't give orders in real life.''

Before he could reply Mike returned from the cockpit, full of the things he'd seen and eager to share them with Dottie.

''Yes, love,'' she said kindly. ''We'll talk about it later. I want to tell you what this joker's up to.'' Briefly she outlined what Randolph had told her, but with an ironic tone, managing to imply that only a madman would believe a word of it.

''We're going to be landing in a minute,'' she said, ''and there'll be all sorts going on.''

''What are we going to do?'' Mike asked.

She took his face between her hands. ''Mike darling, don't say anything. Just leave the talking to me."

As she delivered the order she caught Randolph's ironic eye on her.

To Dottie's relief their arrival passed off quietly. The plane came to rest in a discreet corner of the airfield, steps were rolled up, and she descended, firmly holding onto Mike, straight to a waiting limousine. As soon as Randolph had joined them the journey began.

The light was fading and she could see little through the car's darkened windows. Even so, the sight that met her eyes after twenty minutes was breathtaking.

"That's the royal palace," Randolph said, following her gaze.

The classically elegant building was nearly a quarter of a mile long, and was reached by a long avenue of ornate fountains. Two Z-shaped staircases led up the front. Wherever she looked Dottie saw windows filled with faces, proving that her arrival was already known. It was a relief when the car swung around to the side of the building, and a more discreet entrance. To her awe a footman stepped forward and opened her door, bowing slightly.

This was her, Dottie Hebden, being bowed to. Any minute she would wake up.

She allowed Randolph to lead her into the building, and had advanced some yards before she realized something was wrong.

"Where's Mike?" she demanded.

"My aide is looking after him. I give you my word, he'll come to no harm."

"As long as he's ready to leave, with me, first thing tomorrow morning," she said with more firmness than she felt.

As he spoke they were rising in a small elevator.

"It's the quickest way up to the state apartments," he explained.

Dottie set her chin but said no more. When the elevator stopped she found herself in a small corridor, with three dark oak doors leading off. Randolph opened the largest.

"This is the rear entrance to your apartment."

She found herself in a set of luxurious rooms that took her breath away. There was the royal reception room, the royal bathroom, the royal dressing room and the royal bedroom. This last one was like a small cathedral, with a ceiling that soared high above them.

"I'll bet this is murder to heat properly," Dottie muttered.

"My mother always said the same thing," Randolph agreed. "That's why you'll be glad of the four poster bed. The drapes keep out drafts. Now, allow me to present your maid, Bertha."

A strongly built young woman with a cheerful face advanced and, to Dottie's horrified fascination, dropped a curtsy. Confused and distracted by this, Dottie obeyed the dictates of good manners and curtsied back. Bertha was aghast.

"I shouldn't have done that, should I?" Dottie muttered.

"Never mind," Randolph whispered back.

"Can't you make her go away?"

"You have Her Royal Highness's permission to leave," Randolph announced, and Bertha fled.

"Now do you believe that this will never work?"

Dottie said in despair when they were alone. "When do I see the British consul?"

"You don't."

"Ahh! I knew it. It's a con."

"Your Royal Highness cannot deal with a mere consul," Randolph explained. "The British ambassador will attend you."

For some reason, that was the moment when she began to believe that this was really happening. The last of her disbelief vanished a few minutes later when the tall, elegant figure of Sir Ambrose Philips entered the room, and bowed to her. He was splendid in evening attire, glittering with ribbons and medals.

"My apologies for not being here earlier," he murmured. "I was attending a dinner."

"I'm sorry I dragged you away from it," she said, suddenly horribly conscious of her shorts.

"On the contrary. I am honored to attend Your Royal Highness." Sir Ambrose gave her a courtly bow.

"I'll leave you now," Randolph said. "I'm sure you'd prefer to talk alone."

As soon as the door had closed on him Dottie whirled on the ambassador. "What's going on here? Do you know?"

"Randolph has apprised me of the situation," he admitted. "I need hardly say how glad Her Majesty's government was to discover that the heir to Elluria hails from the United Kingdom. The understanding between our two countries—"

"Speak English, will you?" she said frantically.

He abandoned his lofty mien. "Elluria is an important country, both in its position and its wealth. Some of the minerals to be found here are as valuable as oil. We have mining agreements that are vital to manufacturing in our country, but Harold of Korburg would tear them up and sell to the highest bidder. He has to be kept out and you're the person to do it.''

''Says who? There must be other heirs.''

''Perhaps there are, but nobody's found them yet. If you walk out, Harold will take over next day.''

''You say that, but I bet I'm not free to leave.''

''You are totally free. But if you leave, your country will suffer.''

''Which one?'' Dottie asked urgently.

''Both of them.''

''And if I stay here, just for a while?''

''Then you would find the British government eager to reward you suitably.''

''Enough to buy a garage?''

''I'm sure there wouldn't be any problem about that.''

She drew a long breath, feeling herself on the brink of an abyss. If only there was someone to hold out a helping hand. But the only face that came into her mind was Randolph's, and she could no longer trust him.

''Oh well,'' she said with a shaky laugh, ''I used to think I'd like to be an actress. It can't be that much different.''

Chapter Four

"May I ask if you've made a decision?" Randolph asked when he returned and found her alone.

"I'm nearly there. What have you done with Mike?"

"He's in his own apartments."

"I want you to take me to him."

"Wouldn't it be better if—"

"Now, please."

"Is this the woman who couldn't give orders?" Randolph asked wryly.

She gave him back gaze for gaze. She understood now that this was a man of whom she must beware. He'd charmed her, but underneath he was pursuing his own agenda, and pursuing it all the more ruthlessly because it was driven by his duty.

"I'm just keeping my end up," she said, defying him with her eyes. "And I need to, otherwise you lot will swamp me. Well, I won't *let* you swamp me. You thought I was an airhead who'd jump on command. Boy were you ever wrong! This is a tough cookie, and you may end up sorry you tangled with me.''

''Bravo, Dorothea!'' he said at once. ''With just such an attitude your ancestors led their people through times of crisis. And those who tangled with them ended up sorry.''

''Don't you smooth talk me. It doesn't work. Now let's go and find Mike—if you can remember where you've put him.''

''At Your Royal Highness's command.''

''I've warned you…''

Instead of leading her to the main door Randolph pressed a tiny knob in the carved panel on one wall, and a door clicked open.

''A secret passage,'' Dottie breathed, forgetting royal dignity in childish delight.

''Not secret. There are a rabbit warren of these passages linking all the main rooms. It's quicker than going by the public corridors. And, of course, more discreet.''

It seemed to Dottie that he led her up hill and down dale before they reached one door that looked exactly like all the others, and Randolph opened it.

''You might have put him a bit closer to me,'' Dottie observed. ''But you weren't taking any chances, were you?''

''No,'' Randolph said firmly, opening the door. ''I wasn't.''

They found Mike confronting a splendid dinner, dressed in a silk robe that seemed to swallow him up. He beamed at the sight of Dottie.

''I was wondering where you were, love. This is

grand. Mind you, this place is a bit big for me. I keep getting lost. But we've really fallen on our feet.''

''That's what they want you to think,'' Dottie said urgently. ''But it's all a huge con trick.'' She looked at Randolph, regarding them, took Mike's arm and pulled him into a corner.

''It's not a joke after all. They really think I'm going to be their queen,'' she said in a low voice.

''Get away!''

''That's what I said. But they mean it. Mike, what am I going to do?''

''Well, you don't have to do it if you don't want to, do you? Just tell them no. But not yet. Let's have that holiday we were promised. We're living in grand style.''

''But if we stay too long I might be trapped here.''

''Nah, not you Dot! You always get people jumping to do what you say.''

''Keep your voice down,'' she muttered, conscious of Randolph's sharp ears. ''And it's not true.''

''Yes it is. What about that time—''

''Never mind that,'' she said hastily. ''All right. Just for a while.''

Randolph approached discreetly. ''Why don't we leave Mike to get ready for his night out? Some army officers are eager to entertain him. Good night Mike. Have a pleasant evening.''

Dottie followed Randolph back to her apartment in silence. Once there she asked. ''So what happens next?''

''Some refreshment. And a brief meeting with your chief ministers, at which you can receive their loyal greetings.''

"I can't really do that in shorts, can I?" she conceded with a sigh.

"Your Royal Highness is most gracious."

"Oh no, not you too," she protested. "There's got to be one person here who doesn't talk to me like I'm the fairy on top of the cake. It's Dottie."

"Very well, for the moment—Dottie. Bertha will bring you some clothes, and Aunt Liz will help you with them. She's actually the Countess Gellitz, and I think you'll like her."

The countess arrived a few minutes later. She was middle-aged, motherly and elegant, despite being plump. Dottie was soon calling her Aunt Liz, like everyone else.

The sense of unreality increased when she found herself wearing a simple, elegant white dress, plainly expensive and like nothing she'd ever worn before. Then Bertha got to work on her face and hair while Aunt Liz explained that in future this would be the prerogative of her personal beautician and her personal hairdresser. They must be appointed without delay to prepare her for future big occasions, but as today's meeting was urgent, Bertha would do a "rush job."

To Dottie's awed eyes Bertha's rush job was the equal of the expensive London salons where she'd pressed her nose against the window and dreamed. The woman looking back at her from the mirror had huge, subtly made-up blue eyes, perfectly lined lips and a flawless, peachy complexion. Her eyebrows had mysteriously developed an aristocratic arch, while her short hair had been teased into sophisticated curves.

Obscurely, she could feel herself being transformed into another person, and she tried to cling on to herself, which was hard because she was slipping away. Besides which, the other person looked as if she might be fun to be, and temptation was undermining Dottie's resolve.

I will be strong-minded, she told herself. I will not be seduced by all this. Well—not for long, anyway.

She realized that a dispute was taking place over her head. Aunt Liz had selected gold jewelry, while Bertha preferred diamond-studded platinum. The argument raged while Dottie looked from one to the other like a tennis spectator, ignored by both. Randolph, who'd left the room while she dressed, returned in time to witness the moment.

"I prefer gold," she ventured to say at last.

"You see?" Aunt Liz cried triumphantly. "Her Royal Highness has excellent taste."

Bertha glowered. Dottie mouthed, "Next time" to her

"Well done, Dottie," Randolph murmured. "You have the soul of a diplomat."

At last she stood and regarded her coiffured, manicured, made-up and gilded self in the mirror. There was no doubt that the woman staring back at her looked good. But who was she?

"It's time to meet your ministers," Randolph said.

He positioned her in the middle of her reception room. The double doors were thrown open and a troop of middle-aged men streamed in. Each of them threw her a sharp, curious look before bowing. Randolph introduced them, Jacob Durmand, the prime minister, Alfred Sternheim, chancellor, Felix Andras, minister for Foreign Affairs, Bernhard Enderlin, the minister of the Interior. There were several others, but she lost count.

"Gentlemen," Randolph said gravely, "allow me to present to you Crown Princess Dorothea, heiress to the throne of Elluria."

As he spoke he moved away from her side and joined the men facing her. He was the first to bow, but a little stiffly, as though it came hard to him. Then it hit her. Randolph was openly proclaiming that he was one of her subjects. The thought disconcerted her more than anything else had done in that whole incredible day.

The prime minister stepped forward. "On behalf of your people and your parliament, may I have the honor of welcoming Your Royal Highness…"

It went on for several minutes, during which Dottie pulled herself together and worked out what she was going to say.

At last Jacob Durmand finished and everyone was looking at her expectantly. She took a deep breath.

"I'm grateful to all of you for wanting to make me your queen, but the fact is, it's not on. You're so anxious to find an heir that you've pounced on the first person who looks likely, but there's got to be someone better suited than me. I'm not queen material, honest."

By this time her entire council was staring at her, aghast. Dottie hurried on before she could lose the thread.

"I know you need me around just now, because of Harold. Okay, here's the deal. I'll stay for another few weeks, just to hold the fort against him."

"And when the few weeks are up?" Randolph inquired.

"By then you'll have found another heir. Yes, you will," to forestall their protests she held up her hand in an unconsciously imperious gesture. "You will, because you're going to go on searching. When you've found someone, I'll go home."

"You don't know what you're talking about," Sternheim said scathingly.

Dottie regarded him. "In the meantime I think you should address me as Your Royal Highness," she declared coolly. She then spoiled the effect by muttering to Randolph, "Or do I mean Your Majesty?"

"Not until after your coronation."

"In that case," she told Sternheim, "you should have said, 'You don't know what you're talking about, Your Royal Highness.'"

Sternheim was rendered speechless.

"What are we going to do?" the chancellor groaned.

"We're going to do what our princess suggested," Randolph said.

"You see?" Dottie said sunnily. "I'm right."

"I didn't say you were right," Randolph repressed her. "I said we were going to do it your way—for reasons of realpolitik."

"Pardon?"

"It means you hold all the cards," he said wryly. "But if you're going to be convincing you have to play this for real. As far as the world knows you're here to claim your throne. Let Harold get a hint to the contrary and he'll be at our doors."

"But I don't know how to be a princess."

"At this stage you only have to look like one," Randolph assured her. "Receptions and receiving lines." He added slyly, "The hardest part will be the hours you'll spend being fitted for your new clothes."

"New clothes?" Dottie murmured.

"Your royal dignity demands that you don't wear the same outfit in public twice, so it means a lot of work. But I know you'll do your duty for the sake of the country."

She considered. "Well, if it's my duty, I suppose I might."

"You'll find that—what was that noise?"

"That's the royal stomach rumbling," Dottie muttered. "You promised me something to eat and I haven't had it yet."

"The audience is over," Randolph declared hastily.

Everyone filed out, but Dottie noticed that each man stopped in the doorway to give her a final, doubtful look.

"They know I can't do it," she told Randolph when they were alone.

He whirled on her. "Never, *never* say that," he said fiercely. "Never speak it again, never even think it."

"All right, all right," she said, alarmed by the change in him.

He calmed down. "Forgive me. I didn't mean to shout at you, but this is more important than you can imagine. You must be convinced that you can do it, convinced to your depths. The essence of being a princess is to believe in yourself as a princess. Otherwise how can anyone else believe it?"

She was too tired to argue with him. She watched thankfully as two footmen wheeled in a table, already laid.

"Only for one?" she queried. "Aren't you going to stay?"

"I have urgent business to attend to. You have a

full day tomorrow, so when you've eaten, go straight to bed.''

''Your Royal Highness,'' she reminded him mischievously.

''Go straight to bed, Your Royal Highness.''

She climbed into the four poster as soon as she'd eaten, and found it more comfortable than she'd expected. But her thoughts were in too much turmoil for her to sleep, and after lying awake for half an hour she put on the light and began to explore the royal apartments.

The bed could have slept five. It stood on a raised dais that was reached by three steps, so that she had no choice but to look down on the rest of the world, which didn't suit Dottie's ideas at all.

She examined a bookshelf, but its contents were in German, except for a few English magazines about horse breeding. It seemed she had nothing to help her through the long night.

Then she remembered *Royal Secrets*. She'd glanced at the magazine just long enough for Randolph to make his point, then stuffed it into her bag, where it still lay. She pulled it out and curled up in bed for a good read.

It was clearly designed for the semiliterate, which Dottie reckoned was why Brenda read it. Text was kept to a minimum, and pictures covered each page. Many of them were of Randolph, ''the dispossessed heir.'' In flashy accents the magazine described his life. Thirty-two years old, raised to inherit a throne, instructed in military matters, statecraft, diplomacy, then abruptly deposed when his parents' marriage was found to be bigamous.

There were pictures of Randolph as a child, accom-

panied by a coolly correct looking woman who turned
out to be his mother. There he was in his teens, this
time with his father, the late King Egbert III, the man
who'd so cruelly let him down by making a secret
marriage and forgetting about it. Studying his face,
easygoing, amiable, weak but lovable, Dottie felt that
if she met him in life she would have liked him, even
though she, like Randolph, had to suffer for his way-
wardness.

More pictures: Randolph in army uniform, in white
tie and tails, Randolph attending parades, in the royal
box at the opera, dancing with a beautiful woman in
his arms. The woman was unusually tall, Dottie observed from the dismal depths of five foot one, almost
tall enough to look her partner in the eye. The caption
said she was Countess Sophie Bekendorf, Prince Randolph's fiancée.

Here the magazine outdid itself, describing the love
story in throbbing accents.

Who can see into the hearts of these lovers,
reared to occupy a throne together, now seeing
their fortunes shattered? Once a great man in his
country, Randolph is now no more than an illegitimate commoner. The Bekendorfs have always raised their daughters to be queens. Will
Sophie stay true to the man she loves? Will he
hold her to her bargain, or be strong enough to
release her?

A strange feeling came over Dottie as she realized
that the cardboard cutout in this purple prose was the
flesh-and-blood man she'd met in Wenford. This was
"Mr. Holsson," who'd helped her make up the bed

and laughed at his own awkwardness, who'd charmed her until her head spun.

And all the time he'd known something that she didn't. He'd deceived her. She'd been hurt and angry about that, but now a glimmer of understanding, even sympathy, came to her. What had it been like for him to come and find her, bring her back to Elluria, offer her the throne that was rightfully his? He'd done it smiling, with no hint of what it must have cost him, because it was his duty. For his people he'd sacrificed himself. For their sake he would be no less ruthless in sacrificing her.

Dottie yawned and rubbed her eyes. The clock said two in the morning, and she supposed she ought at least try to sleep. But when she'd turned out the light the room was filled with moonlight, and she couldn't resist going to the window and looking out over the great park that surrounded the palace. The moon picked out the tops of the trees and bushes, and turned the lake into a sheet of silver.

Then she became aware that two figures were walking under the trees beside the lake. One was a tall man whose familiar outline made Dottie grow very still. The other was a woman almost as tall as himself. Together they glided by the water, his arm around her waist, his head bent down toward hers. Dottie watched as they stopped suddenly and turned to each other. She held her breath while there was a sliver of light between the two faces. Then they began walking again, and were soon lost in the blackness of the trees.

Dottie turned away, feeling uncomfortably as though she'd pried into something that was none of her business. After all the new impressions that had assaulted her senses that day, this was one too many.

Leaving the window open, she began to explore again. She'd briefly glimpsed the bathroom before, but now she studied it properly. It was a magnificent creation with a thick cream carpet, elegant tiles and a circular bath sunk into the floor.

"Like Cleopatra," she murmured.

She thought of the bathroom back in Wenford that she shared with five other people, with constant squabbles. The next moment she'd run the water and plunged in. It was bliss and she enjoyed herself for half an hour before emerging to dry herself off on a towel and look around for a bathrobe to snuggle into.

She couldn't see what she wanted, but she caught a glimpse of herself in the tall mirrored doors of the bathroom wardrobe. It was almost the first time she'd seen herself like this, full-length. Both her home and the place where she now lived were too crowded for dancing around naked.

"Hmm!" she murmured, turning slowly, while trying to look over her shoulder. "Pity I'm not taller, but I suppose I'll do."

Not finding a robe, she pulled open one of the doors to the wardrobe. Here too, there was luxury, with the same thick carpet, its own soft lighting, and enough room for her to step inside. She did so, and walked the length, but it was completely empty. She sighed, and decided to go to bed.

Then she discovered a problem....

Randolph was awoken next morning by the sound of someone pounding on the outer door of his apartment. He was sleepily aware of the murmuring of voices, then his valet hurried into the room, his face tense.

"She's gone," he said aghast. "The princess has vanished from her room."

"Impossible," Randolph said testily. "What were the footmen doing?"

"Sir, there have been four footmen outside Her Royal Highness's room all night. They swear she hasn't gone out that way. Nor can she have used the concealed door, because that seems to be locked from the other side."

Randolph knew that this was true, having secured it himself the night before. He'd done the same with the concealed door in Mike's room. He was taking no chances.

He dressed hurriedly and almost ran to the state apartments. Once there he began to be seriously worried. The only possible escape was through the window, which, alarmingly, stood wide open. It was two floors up, and although he told himself that even Dottie wouldn't be crazy enough to escape that way, an inner voice whispered that he had much to learn about her.

He became aware of a flutter among the maids. "What is it now?" he demanded.

"Sir, there's a funny noise coming from the bathroom."

Randolph strode into the bathroom and listened. From behind one of the huge mirrored doors came the unmistakable sound of soft snoring. He pulled open the door and they all stared down at the sight of the crown princess, naked as the day she was born, fast asleep on the floor.

Dottie opened her eyes and favored everyone with her sunniest smile. Randolph instantly tore off his jacket and arranged it around her, throwing a curt dismissal over his shoulder to the interested crowd.

"Dottie," he said, controlling himself, "why are you sleeping on the floor in the—in here? I assure you, it isn't the custom."

"Ouch," she said, moving her stiff limbs gingerly. "Help me up." She reached up her hands and he took them, drawing her gently to her feet while trying not to let the jacket become dislodged. It slipped and he only managed to keep it in place by pulling her against him. To his relief everybody had now left.

"Go and put something on," he commanded in a tight voice. "I'll join you in a minute."

He needed that time to himself to shut out the vision of her entrancing nakedness. She was daintily made and completely perfect, slender but rounded, with cheeky uptilted breasts that he had to fight to exclude from his mind. It was even harder to ignore the fleeting sensation of her enchanting little body pressed against his own.

Only when he was sure he was in command of himself did he join her. She was dressed in her own clothes, slacks and sweater, and for an appalled moment he had the impression that they'd become transparent. He took a deep breath.

Dottie seemed not to notice anything odd in his manner. She was too delighted over the arrival of her breakfast table.

"Oh lovely! I'm dying for a cup of tea."

"Perhaps first you will tell me what happened?" He spoke coldly, for he was under a lot of strain. "Is this some old English tradition that Elluria will have to grow used to. Will sleeping on closet floors become the fashion in society?"

"Don't be silly. Last night I had a bath and went in there looking for a bathrobe, and the door clicked shut behind me. When I tried to open it I found it had locked itself, and I couldn't get any of the others open, either. I thumped and yelled but nobody heard me. I got a bit panicky, but then I realized there was no real problem. When people came in next morning I'd yell and they'd find me. So I settled down to sleep. What's happened to the tea?"

"There isn't any. It's coffee. But you didn't yell, did you?"

"Well, I would have done if I hadn't overslept. How do I get some tea?"

"I'll give orders for it. It's lucky for us all that you snore. Otherwise we wouldn't have found you."

"How dare you say I snore!"

"If you didn't snore you could have been there all day. I was going to send out search parties."

"I see. Bring her back, 'dead or alive.'"

"Just alive," he snapped. "Dead would be no practical use."

"You're all heart," she complained.

"Dottie, don't push me. Right now you're talking to a man who's had a bad fright, and it hasn't left me in the best of moods."

"And you're talking to someone who's spent the night on the floor wearing only her birthday suit."

"There's no need to go into details." he said desperately.

"It hasn't left me feeling that everything's tickety-boo either, especially," she came to her real grievance, "since I can't get a cup of tea. What's the point of being a princess if I can't get a cuppa? I'd be better off in Wenford."

"Where I'm strongly tempted to send you."

"Can't be soon enough for me."

In the seething silence that followed Randolph pressed a bell in the wall, and when Bertha appeared he said, "Her Royal Highness prefers tea with her breakfast. Please see to it immediately."

"Yes, sir. Should that be China tea, Indian tea—"

"Just make sure that it's strong enough to stand the spoon up in," Randolph growled, assailed by memories of breakfast in Wenford.

Bertha curtsied and departed.

Silence.

"Well, you got that right, about the spoon. I'll make an Englishman of you yet," Dottie said, trying to lighten the atmosphere. From the look he threw her she knew she'd failed.

"Where's Mike?" she asked. "I think we should be eating together."

"You can call him on the internal phone. Room 43."

Dottie dialed and was answered at once by an unfamiliar male voice.

"Mike?" she demanded.

"Mr. Kenton is unavailable at the moment. This is his valet."

"His *valet? Mike?* Never mind. Haul him out of the bath. Tell him the love of his life wants to talk to him."

"Mr. Kenton is not in the bath, Your Highness. He has been invited to drive a Ferrari and will be away for the rest of the day."

"I guess I can't compete with a Ferrari," Dottie murmured wryly, hanging up.

"It was only kind to keep him happy while you're

occupied with more weighty matters,'' Randolph said. He'd recovered his poise now, and could only hope that Dottie hadn't guessed the reason for his edginess.

The arrival of strong tea helped the atmosphere. Dottie offered him some, but he declined with a shudder.

''Since you've disposed of my fiancé, I suppose I'm all yours for the day,'' she remarked. ''What's the agenda?''

''Your appearance, clothes, hairstyling etc. After a couple of days of intensive preparation there'll be a press conference.''

''What do I say at that?'' she asked in alarm.

''Absolutely nothing.''

''Pretty pointless press conference, then.''

''Others will do the talking. You will smile and look regal. The point is that you should be seen.''

''Seen and not heard?''

''Exactly.''

''Come to think of it, they'll get a shock when Princess Dottie opens her mouth.''

''Princess Dorothea,'' he corrected her. ''Dottie makes you sound crazy.''

''Well, I am crazy. Always was.''

''You *can't* be Princess Dottie!''

''Fiddle!'' she said firmly. ''I'm Dottie. If they don't like it, they can send me home.''

''We'll address this problem later,'' he growled, adding under his breath, ''among many others.''

Dottie concentrated on her breakfast, refusing to answer this provocation.

''You also need to meet various persons of the court,'' Randolph continued, ''including your future ladies in waiting.''

"Must I have ladies in waiting?" Dottie asked plaintively. "After all, I'll be gone soon. You *are* looking for someone else, aren't you?"

"Diligently," Randolph said. He'd ordered that no stone should be left unturned, in case she carried out her threat to leave. "But as far as the world knows, you've come to stay."

She couldn't resist giving him an impish look. "Now there's an unnerving thought!"

He met her gaze. "Quite. I wonder which of us is more appalled by it."

Her lips twitched. "You probably."

That came too close to home. He turned away from her sharply, pacing the room. And that was how he noticed *Royal Secrets* lying open.

It was the copy he himself had given her and it was entirely reasonable for her to read it, but logic was useless against the revulsion that rose in him at the thought of her learning his most painful secrets in this vulgar way. He had to walk away to the window because he couldn't bear to look at her.

In London she'd charmed him, but that had been another world. Here, where she was taking over his birthright, it was hard for him to regard her without hostility.

He turned, meaning to tell her coldly that her humor was inappropriate, but he met her eyes, fixed on him, and saw the small crinkle of bewilderment in her forehead. She looked smaller, more vulnerable than he remembered, and his anger died. It wasn't her fault.

"Eat your breakfast," he said more gently. "Then Aunt Liz will attend you. She knows all there is to be known about clothes. I suggest you appoint her as your Mistress of Robes, but of course that decision is yours.''

The countess was in an ebullient mood, having spent a hugely enjoyable night making plans for Dottie's appearance. She mourned Dottie's lack of height but praised her dainty build.

''We'll have clothes made to measure, but for your appearance this afternoon we will apply to a boutique, fortunately an extremely exclusive establishment. Once we've purchased the garments, they will withdraw them from their range, of course.''

''Of course,'' Dottie murmured. ''It'll be interesting to visit some of the shops.''

''What are you thinking of? You can't go to a shop.''

''Well, it won't come to me, will it?''

Aunt Liz was scandalized. ''Of course it will.''

Within an hour four young women, trooped in, curtsied and proceeded to display an array of clothes that almost made Dottie weep with ecstasy. She spent two blissful hours trying on, discarding, trying again, changing her mind, going back to the one she'd first thought of. And not once did anyone grow impatient with her.

More young women. Shoes. Underwear. Finally Aunt Liz chose three dresses, ''Just to tide you over while your official wardrobe is being made.''

''What about paying for them?'' Dottie muttered, conscious of everyone looking at her expectantly.

''These matters are dealt with by your Mistress of Robes.'' The countess paused delicately.

''In that case, Aunt Liz, will you do the honors?'' She had made her first appointment.

A hairstylist appeared and transformed Dottie's

shortish hair into more sophisticated contours. While she was still in rollers she took a bath, and emerged to find her underwear and hose laid out ready.

The dress was simple, cream silk, with a high waistline. The shoes matched it exactly. About her neck she wore a pearl necklace that, Bertha said, had been a gift from the Tsar of Russia to Queen Dorothea I in the eighteenth century. Dottie gulped.

At last she was ready. Everyone curtsied their way out, leaving her to wait for Randolph, who would escort her to the reception. Now she felt good, full of confidence knowing that she looked terrific. She wondered if Randolph would think so.

She wandered out onto her balcony that overlooked the deer park. There was the lake she'd seen last night, blue and beautiful glinting in the afternoon sun. She could pick out the exact spot where the man and woman had walked.

There was a woman standing there now. She didn't move, but stood, looking down into the water, as though sunk in thought, perhaps dreaming of the man, and the intimate moments they'd shared. Suddenly she began to walk purposefully back toward the palace. As she neared the balcony she stopped and raised her head, looking straight at Dottie. It was a direct, challenging gaze, almost angry, and it revealed her face clearly enough for Dottie to recognize her from the magazine photographs.

This was Sophie Bekendorf, Randolph's fiancé, and perhaps the woman he loved.

Dottie sensed that Sophie was looking her over. She was getting used to that, but there was something disagreeable about this woman's manner, and the slightly scornful smile that touched her mouth before she moved on and vanished from sight.

A moment ago she'd felt full of confidence and courage. Now she saw herself for what she was, an impostor, playing a role that was beyond her, and making herself ridiculous. With a sinking heart she went to survey herself again in the mirror. She even looked different, she thought dismally. Everything was wrong.

Randolph found her in this mood. "It's no use," she sighed. "I can't be a princess."

He laid his hands on her shoulders, and spoke gently. "Why ever not?"

"I'm too short."

He frowned. "I beg your pardon?"

"I'm too short. Princesses should be tall and elegant, looking down their noses at everyone, and I'm..." she made a helpless gesture, *"short."*

His lips twitched. He tried to control it but with her wicked little face gazing at him control was impossible.

"What are you laughing at?" she demanded.

"At you, and your scatty way of thinking."

"Well there you are. If people are going to laugh at me I can't be a princess, can I?"

"I won't let anyone laugh at you," he promised.

"Except you."

"Except me."

"But I'm still too short. You couldn't fix me another six inches, could you?"

"Dottie, I would fix you anything you wanted in the world, but I'm afraid that is beyond me. You'll just have to be a short princess. Now stop fretting. I've brought something to show you."

He laid out before her a small painting, in the style of the eighteenth century. It showed a woman of about thirty, at the height of her beauty. On the top of her elaborately arranged hair was a diamond tiara. More diamonds hung from her ears and around her throat was a magnificent diamond necklace, the same one that Dottie was wearing now. They were jewels for a queen, and she wasn't surprised to read, at the foot of the portrait this had been Queen Dorothea I. What did astonish her was the woman's face.

"But...that's me," she gasped.

"It's a family likeness that has carried down through the generations," Randolph agreed. "There is no doubt that you are her descendant, and it will smooth your path as queen." When she didn't answer he frowned slightly. "Dottie? Did you hear me?"

"Yes," she said vaguely, her eyes fixed on the portrait.

Almost in a dream she went to the mirror to look at herself, then back at the picture. It was happening again, the feeling of morphing into somebody else. From a great distance she could hear the voice of Dottie Hebden saying, "I can't do this. Me, a queen? Don't be funny."

Against that she set her own face looking back at her from the portrait. The lips never moved, and yet it spoke to her in a voice she knew, silently telling her that this was where she belonged.

Chapter Five

"Don't try to take it all in," Randolph advised Dottie in the last few seconds before she met the members of her court. "Just smile at everyone."

"I can't smile," she gasped. "My stomach's full of butterflies."

"Trust me."

It was too late for her to say anything more. The heavy gilt doors were being pulled open in front of them, and she was staring along the length of a room that seemed to go on forever. Down the center was a long crimson carpet, leading to a dais, at the top of which was a chair upholstered in crimson plush. A crimson canopy, bearing the royal coat of arms, rose high overhead. The room was lined with faces.

Randolph took her hand in his, holding it up, almost to shoulder height. She wondered if he could feel that she was shaking. Strangely it felt as though he too was shaking. She gave him a quick, disbelieving glance, but he was staring straight ahead. "Lead with the left foot," he murmured. And they were off.

As they walked slowly along the carpet the faces came into focus, so that she could discern bafflement, hostility, but mostly curiosity.

Nearing the dais she murmured to Randolph, "That chair…is it?"

"Yes, it's the throne."

She gulped. "Blimey!"

Randolph's voice was low and fierce. "Dottie, I beg you not to say 'Blimey!'"

"What can I say?" she asked frantically.

"If you must express surprise, 'Goodness me!' would be appropriate." There came a suppressed choke of laughter. *"Dottie!"*

"Well, I can't keep a straight face. I've never said 'Goodness me' in my life."

"Then start saying it now."

During this urgent, whispered conversation they had reached the canopied throne. Dottie turned to confront the people who had moved forward to crowd around the base of the steps, and she felt as well as saw their shock as they gained their first clear view of her face. There was a ripple of astonished recognition. Dorothea.

As before, Randolph made a speech presenting her, and signaled for her to take her place on the throne, while he remained standing. One by one her courtiers advanced and bowed or curtsied while Randolph introduced them. As he'd advised, she didn't try to take it all in, but one name stood out. Sophie Bekendorf.

The tall beauty came forward and looked up at Sophie. It was the same look, defiant, scornful, as she'd seen barely an hour before. And now she realized the full splendor of Sophie's looks. Her skin was pale porcelain, without blemish, her eyes large and dark, her features regular and her chestnut hair glossy. But it was her mouth that would draw everyone's attention, Dottie thought. It was petulant, willful and sensual, a mouth to make a man dream of kissing it, and then dream afterward of how the kiss had felt. How could Randolph not be in love with her? How could he ever love anyone else?

Everyone knew the story and was watching the meeting of the two women with interest, waiting for Sophie to curtsy. But she stayed motionless for so long that a thrilled whisper ran around the crowd. At the very last possible moment Sophie dropped the very smallest possible curtsy, and passed on, her head high.

If Sophie aroused Dottie's dislike, Sophie's brother made the hairs stand up on her spine. Dagbert was handsome, but everything he did seemed naturally insolent, so that the disagreeable effect was stronger than his good looks. He flicked his eyes over Dottie and gave a little dismissive smile. Indignant, she raised her chin and looked over his head.

At last the ceremony was over and she was free to start the walk back down the crimson carpet. When the gilt doors had closed behind her she let out a long breath of relief.

"You did excellently," Randolph said. "You looked right and you had the perfect distant manner."

It was modest enough praise, but she felt a small glow of satisfaction. She guessed Randolph wasn't a man who paid lavish compliments.

"I feel like a puppet whose strings have been suddenly let go. They don't like me."

"They were all very impressed by you."

"Not Sophie Bekendorf and her brother. Did you see the way he looked at me? Like I was dirt?"

"Their position is...peculiar," Randolph said awkwardly. "They too have had to adjust to circumstances."

His tone warned Dottie to inquire no further. As if to keep her off the sensitive subject he hurried on, "Tonight I thought you and Mike would like to see some of the sights. The city is beautiful by floodlight."

So Mike wasn't to be kept entirely apart from her, she thought with relief. Perhaps Randolph had accepted that he couldn't win.

Aunt Liz turned her out in style in a silky, flowing creation in pale blue, with a solid silver pendant.

"Enchanting," she enthused. "And this afternoon you were just perfect. I know His Roy— That is, Randolph was thrilled with you."

"He didn't exactly put it that way," Dottie demurred.

"Of course not. You must understand that his standards are of the very highest. For his country, nothing is too good. You won't find him an easy taskmaster. What did he say to you?"

"He said I had the right distant manner."

"Excellent. He must be really impressed to be so warm in his approval."

"Yes, but... Oh well, never mind."

Tonight she could be alone with Mike and tell him of the British ambassador's promise that her reward for holding the fort would be enough money to buy the garage. They could start making plans at once.

Mike too had been newly outfitted and appeared before her in a dinner jacket and black tie. She stared at him, impressed, and he returned the compliment.

"You look great, Dot. Real great. I've got a couple of friends here, who are going to show us the sights." He turned to a handsome young couple in their twenties, who had come in with him. "Harry and Jeanie."

"Count Heinrich and Countess Eugenia Batz," Aunt Liz supplied, while the couple bowed and curtsied.

"You told me Harry and Jeanie," Mike complained to his new friends.

"And so we are," the man said merrily. "Your Royal Highness—"

"Oh no, please," Dottie protested. "I can't stand any more of that. It's such a mouthful every time."

"Isn't it?" Jeanie said gaily. "Protocol is that we just say it once a day, when we first meet you. After that it's ma'am."

"We're all going to have a wonderful night out," Harry said.

So she and Mike weren't to be left alone together, Dottie thought wryly. Randolph had thought of everything.

"I see you're all ready. Splendid." Randolph's voice from the door made them all turn.

Like the other men he was wearing a dinner jacket, and Dottie had to admit that he put them into the shade, not just by being taller, but by a certain air of natural authority, the conviction that wherever he was, he was at home. It had been born and bred into him, and she guessed that he would never lose it now.

His gaze fell on her. She had the feeling that he checked slightly and a faint warmth crept into his eyes.

"Will I do?" she asked, and held her breath for the answer.

"Admirably. You begin to look like a queen."

"Thank you," she said, deflated.

"Tonight you will enjoy yourselves. Harry and Jeanie will show you the best time you've ever had."

"Are you coming too?" Dottie asked.

"No, for once you'll be spared my company. Other duties demand my attention. But I'm leaving you in safe hands."

"Eee Dot, it's gonna be great," Mike enthused.

"You forgot my royal dignity," Dottie teased him. "You should have said, 'Eee *ma'am*, it's gonna be great.'"

Mike roared with laughter, and in the general mirth they all swept out of the door. Dottie tried not to mind that Randolph wasn't coming too, but it was natural, being used to his undivided attention, to feel a little put out.

In minutes the sleek, black limousine had reached the suburbs of Wolfenberg, the country's capital city. Although not large it was elegant and beautiful, with a Parisian air. The great buildings were constructed from pale gray stone and so cleverly built that the heavy material seemed to take wing. It was growing dark and the floodlights were already on.

"There's the parliament building," Jeanie pointed out, "the town hall, the cathedral and there's the great fountain that was built to commemorate the battle of…"

For Dottie these things were interesting, but she

knew that Mike would be going glassy-eyed with boredom. She asked him about his day and he needed no encouragement to talk about the Ferrari. Since Harry too was a car fanatic the conversation became mechanical, and they soon abandoned sightseeing.

"There's a little place just ahead that I think you'd like," Harry said and soon the car swung into a pretty piazza. A short flight of steps led to a picturesque café with tables outside.

The place specialized in ice cream, and since Dottie was an ice-cream addict she felt she was in heaven. It was a warm evening. In the piazza just below them were trees hung with colored lights, beneath which couples strolled.

"This is the center of Wolfenberg," Jeanie explained as Dottie tucked into a huge confection of chocolate, coffee and vanilla ice cream, studded with nuts and doused in cream. "People congregate here before and after the theater, and sooner or later everyone comes past."

As if to prove her right Dagbert appeared from under the trees, and hailed them. "My friends! How nice to see you!"

He was full of bonhomie, demanding an introduction to Mike, bowing very correctly to Dottie. She greeted him coolly, remembering his air of dismissive contempt earlier that day, but tonight Dagbert was on his best behavior. He began to tell Dottie about the city, especially the cathedral, "where your coronation will be held." She began to wonder if she'd misjudged him.

"It's getting a little chilly," Harry said at last. "Perhaps we should find some entertainment indoors?" He smiled at Dottie. "We also have excellent nightclubs. Robin Anthony, for instance, is singing at The Birdcage.''

''Robin Anthony?'' Dottie exclaimed in delight. ''I've been madly in love with him for years.''

''You never told me,'' Mike observed mildly.

''Yes I did. You took me to one of his concerts for my seventeenth birthday, and snored all the way through.''

''Oh yeah, I remember now.''

''But could we still get in?'' she asked anxiously. ''His concerts were always sold out.''

''They won't be sold out for you,'' Dagbert observed.

''Oh yes, I forgot. Maybe, I'm going to enjoy this.''

Dottie wasn't sure what he told the manager but they were ushered to a table at the front, and she was treated with a discreet deference that she had to admit was pleasant.

''The trouble is,'' she confided to Mike in an undervoice, ''that after one day I'm already becoming spoiled. I warn you, when we get home I'll expect it.''

''Don't you worry Dot. I'll bring you a cuppa in bed every morning.''

Dottie squeezed his arm, overwhelmed by tenderness and affection for him. How could she have imagined anything would be better than being married to Mike?

Robin Anthony was a disappointment, past his best, putting on weight and living on his reputation.

''Oh dear!'' Dottie sighed as he bowed his way off. ''Goodbye my teenage dreams.''

"May I have the honor of dancing with my future queen?" Dagbert asked as the band struck up.

"I never learned posh dancing," Dottie protested.

"It's only a waltz. I'll teach you."

She let him lead her onto the floor. As he'd promised she found the steps easy, and was beginning to get the hang of waltzing, even to enjoy it.

"Don't keep looking down at your feet," Dagbert urged her. "Have confidence. Head up."

She raised her chin and her feet seemed to find their way of their own accord. The glittering lights of the club spun around her, tables, faces. Two faces that she knew.

"Steady!" Dagbert said. "You nearly tripped."

"I—just missed my footing," she stammered.

Another turn of the dance and the little scene passed before her eyes again. A far table, discreetly near the wall, a man and a woman, holding hands, leaning forward so that their heads were almost touching, talking intimately. Randolph and Sophie.

"I'd like to sit down now," she said.

"But I thought you were enjoy—"

"Now," she said sharply. All her original distaste for him was rushing back. This might have been a coincidence, but she would have bet her kingdom on Dagbert having known where his sister would be tonight.

He'd counted on being the king's brother-in-law, and probably milking that for all it was worth. This was a warning to her that he wanted the old order restored, and the battle wasn't over.

But then, she too wanted the old order restored, so there was nothing to mind about. And if Randolph's "other duties" included a romantic dinner with his fiancée, that was just fine by her.

Just the same, she suggested that they all return to the palace, and since her word was law, everyone agreed.

Over her breakfast the next morning, Bertha informed her that Randolph would wait on her to discuss the day.

"You mean he'll come and tell me what I've got to do?" Dottie asked wryly.

"Well, His Roy— I mean, Randolph—"

"Why did you stop yourself?"

"He isn't a 'Royal Highness' anymore," Bertha confided.

"What is he?"

"Nothing. Nobody. It's hard to know how to treat him. We all keep curtsying out of habit, but he gets very cross and tells us not to."

How much self-discipline would that take? Dottie wondered. Perhaps a royal upbringing helped you to go through life smiling when you had to, behaving beautifully when your heart was breaking and concealing your thoughts and feelings. She tried to imagine herself acting so coolly, and retired, defeated.

Emerging from her bath she found Aunt Liz ready with a riding habit, "for your first lesson."

"Am I going to learn to ride?"

"Those are my instructions."

So Randolph gave orders over her head and relayed them to her via a third person. Dottie reckoned you didn't have to be a queen to be annoyed at that. But it was hard to stay cross when the snugly fitting habit showed off her trim figure and neat behind. She was admiring herself in the mirror when Randolph's voice said, "You are one of those rare women who can wear tight pants."

"I can, can't I?" she said gleefully. This was no time for false modesty.

His own riding pants were also snug-fitting, confirming what she'd only suspected before, that his hips were narrow, and his stomach flat. His long legs, the thighs heavy with muscles, might have been created for such a garb. He was standing in his shirt-sleeves, leaning against the wall, smiling like a man without a care in the world. But who could tell? she thought, remembering Bertha's words.

"Why riding?" she asked.

"Riding is a social grace, like dancing. When a foreign head of state visits you, you dance with him, and ride with him."

"Then I'll need dancing lessons as well."

"Yes, I heard about last night. I gather you managed very well."

"Didn't you see me fumbling around? You were there with Sophie."

"Yes, I was there with Sophie. Is there any reason why I should not have been?"

His eyes had lost their warmth and become as bleak and chilly as a moorland fog. For a moment she had a glimpse of a hostility that was all the more alarming for being usually hidden.

He seemed to realize that he'd given himself away for he recovered at once, and smiled. "Forgive me. I'm just not used to having my actions questioned."

"But I didn't question your actions," she said indignantly. "I merely mentioned having noticed you. There was no need to get fired up."

"True. I'm a little oversensitive. I apologize if I offended you."

The face was friendly but the tone was formal, and it impelled her to say, "Don't talk like that."

"Like what?"

"As though I was the queen."

"But you are the queen," he said quietly, "and I never can forget it."

"Then the sooner I'm gone the better. I couldn't live like this, people treating me as one person when I feel like someone else inside."

"Not a person, a monarch."

"Well a monarch's still a person."

"No, a symbol," he said quickly. "And if behind that symbol a person lurks, then she—or he—must keep that a secret, and never allow it to influence their behavior. The only thing that matters is what's good for your country. For that good, you must learn to be ruthless, to yourself first of all. Sometimes also to others, but mostly..." his voice grew heavy, "mostly to yourself."

But in a moment he became cheerful again. "But that's enough dull stuff for today. Just now I want you to enjoy your new life."

"So that I become so seduced by the goodies that I can't bear to give them up?" she said cheekily.

"Remind me never to underestimate you," he growled. "Enough. Your instructor is waiting at the stable. Let's go."

Dottie's nerves about riding vanished with the first lesson. Helmut, an elderly army sergeant who'd taught Randolph to ride, had a fierce aspect but a gentle manner. He'd found a docile little mare called Gretel for her. She was a pale honey color, with a soft nose that nuzzled Dottie in an eager search for tidbits, in a way that won her heart.

She didn't fall off, and by the end of the lesson Helmut declared that she had a natural seat and good hands. The next day he said she was ready for a gentle ride through the grounds, accompanied by a proper escort. He indicated eight soldiers standing ready with their saddled horses.

"I don't need that many," she protested.

"We're going out into the country," Helmut explained. "The queen must be properly escorted."

The soldiers were young, with bright faces, and they saluted her with a combination of respect and merriment that put her at her ease. At least three of them managed to suggest that they would have wolf whistled their queen if it wasn't treason. She took her place in the center, and they set off. Helmut stood in the stable yard watching until they were out of sight.

Before long her companions complimented her on having acquired skill so soon.

"You have really never ridden before?" asked one called Heinz.

"Just once," she said. "When I was a little girl in England we went to the seaside for a vacation, and there was a man with donkeys giving children rides along the sands. Grandpa put me up on a donkey, and I rode it for about three feet. Then I fell off and bawled the place down, and that made all the other kids cry in sympathy, so they lost their balance, and the donkey owner told Grandpa to get me out fast before he lost his livelihood."

They rocked with laughter, and she discovered that she was really enjoying herself.

They were gone over an hour. As they slowly returned to the stables Randolph watched them from an upper window.

"You chose the escort well," he observed.

"According to your instructions, sir," Helmut observed. "They're all young, cheerful and every one speaks perfect English. As far as Her Royal Highness knows they're simply there to keep her company. We might be doing Prince Harold an injustice. He'd be mad to try anything."

"But if he does," Randolph murmured, "We're ready for him. Protect her, Helmut. Nothing must get in the way of that."

"But sir, there's a rumor that she'll be leaving soon."

"Just do as I ask, Helmut. Protect her at all costs."

It was time for her first official public appearance, which would establish her in the eyes of the world. There had been a photographic session, with the pictures designed to stress her likeness to Queen Dorothea II. The palace PR office had been working overtime getting the news out to press agencies.

There would be a short reception, and the presentation of a bouquet by a little girl.

"She will make a little welcome speech," Aunt Liz explained, "and in your honor it will be in English."

"I have picked up a few words of German," Dottie said defensively.

"How many?"

"Two," Dottie confessed. "Who is she? How was she chosen?"

"Elsa Bekendorf. You've met her sister and brother. Little Elsa is such a sweet child. And of course the honor had to be given to a family of their standing.''

Dottie was silent, thinking of Sophie's head close to Randolph's, at the nightclub, and wondering whose idea it had been to thrust little Elsa forward.

Then she pushed the thought aside to enjoy her fitting for the elegant dress Aunt Liz had chosen. It was wild silk in a deep peacock blue which made Dottie stare a little.

''There's a time for restraint and a time for being eye-catching,'' Aunt Liz said. ''This is a time for being eye-catching. It's a pity that Your Royal Highness lacks just a little bit of height.''

''You mean I'm short,'' Dottie said gloomily.

''There's always very high heels, but wearing them is a skill.''

''You leave that to me. When you're my height you learn heels as a matter of self-defense.''

The heels they chose were not merely high, they were suicidal, and Dottie earned Aunt Liz's admiration by being able to manage them without a care. They were both pleased with the result.

When the day came, Dottie listened just ''off-stage'' as the prime minister explained her to the world's press. He described her background accurately enough, but with rather more emphasis on her ''position of authority'' than she thought entirely honest.

''What they would say if they saw The Grand!'' she chuckled to Randolph who was waiting with her behind the curtain.

''That's why we haven't named the place,'' he murmured. ''Although I suppose they'll find it eventually. I'm afraid journalists may track you down there.''

''Pardon?''

''When you go home. You did say you were going soon.''

''Oh yes, of course. I forgot for a moment.''

Durmand reached the end of his speech. The curtains parted. Dottie walked out on Randolph's arm to face a barrage of flashing lights. He led her to the throne, then gently detached himself and moved to the side.

She tried to concentrate on the cameras, turning this way and that so that everyone could get a good view. She became aware that a little girl was approaching her with a bunch of flowers. Elsa Bekendorf was only about four years old, and it was clear that she was very nervous. Dottie's heart went out to the child.

Scowling with concentration Elsa made her way up the three steps to the throne, clutching her posy to within an inch of its life, and embarked on her speech of welcome.

But almost at once she was in trouble. Dottie guessed that her English was poor and she'd been taught the words parrot fashion. When she broke down she had no knowledge to fall back on. There was a faint hiss from Sophie, who was watching her baby sister, full of tension. That wouldn't help the poor little thing, Dottie thought.

Elsa must have realized the same, for she cast a beseeching look at Sophie, made as if to run to her for comfort, but checked herself at once. With nowhere to turn she became overwhelmed, sat down on the lowest step and howled.

In a flash Dottie was down the steps, kneeling in front of the little girl, giving the child her best smile. "Hey, come on. It's not so bad. You should see how scared I am."

Elsa sniffed and looked at her woefully. She hadn't understood the words, but Dottie's kindly tone had gotten through to her. She managed a half smile and raised the posy, somewhat bedraggled now.

"For me?" Dottie asked. Suddenly her two German words came back to her. *"Fur mich?"*

Elsa nodded. The next moment she was swept up in an exuberant pair of arms as Dottie rose to her feet, hugging her and kissing her cheek. Elsa's confidence came back and she beamed at Dottie, receiving a big, laughing smile in return, and for a moment they were blinded by flashbulbs going off madly. And from somewhere behind the bright lights came the sound of applause.

"You, Elsa?" Dottie asked, and the child nodded.

"Mich, Dottie," Dottie told her firmly.

"Dottie?" the little girl echoed. Then she seemed to understand and gave a chuckle. *"Prinzessin Dottie!"* she caroled loudly, and there was more applause, mingled with laughter.

Somewhere Dottie was aware of Sophie covering her eyes in disgust. Probably a lot of other people felt the same. She didn't care. She was going to do this her way.

Aunt Liz came forward to take charge of Elsa. Sophie might have seemed the most suitable person, but hell would freeze over before Dottie delivered this moppet into the hands of her hard-faced sister. Despite her bright professional smile, Sophie was furious, though whether because she felt the family dignity had been damaged, or because Dottie had scored a success it was hard to say.

At last it was over. She raised her eyes to meet Randolph's, expecting to find condemnation in them, and determined to outface him.

"Who says I can't be Princess Dottie?" she asked defiantly.

Then she saw that his eyes were warm and smiling. "You can be anything you wish," he said, offering her his arm. "Well done, Dottie. You've staked your claim to the hearts of your people."

Chapter Six

Within hours the press conference had beamed around the world. Television channels showed it again and again, always focusing on the wonderful moment when Dottie had lifted little Elsa in her arms.

The Ellurian newspapers hailed her as Our Laughing Princess. Some played up the family resemblance. Others claimed she'd already showed how she would be "A true mother to her people."

"On the basis of one incident?" Dottie demanded over breakfast two days later.

"But it was great, Dot," Mike said. He'd dropped in to tell her he'd be out sailing all day. "Just fancy, your grandpa being right all along!"

"Did he bend your ear with those stories, too?"

"Only the once. He took me to the pub. We got real plastered, and he came out with all this stuff about Duke Egghead."

"Egbert. What did he say about him?"

"Well that's it, after I'd sobered up I couldn't remember, and I never have. When I get tiddly again it starts coming back to me, but it goes again."

Those who'd feared, or hoped, that Dottie's unorthodox ways might bring her down were confounded. She was a darling. That was official. Her oddities were no more than charming eccentricity, only to be expected in one who'd been reared "with wider horizons than royalty normally enjoys."

Even Randolph raised a smile at that. He was delighted at the way people were determined to see the best in her, even though the facts behind the headlines sometimes made him tear his hair.

He hadn't, for instance, been amused when Dottie vanished again, and turned up in the kitchen, chatting happily with the cooks and eating ice cream "like a greedy child," as he caustically put it.

"Well, I tucked in because I was sure you were going to arrive any minute and spoil the party," Dottie told him, adding gloomily, "And you did."

She didn't mention the fun she'd had reducing Fritz, the head chef, to jelly. But Fritz invented a new ice cream which became known as The Dottie Special, despite horrified attempts by the palace old guard to quell the name.

Dottie fell on it with delight, even ordering it for breakfast one morning, and sending down a note with the empty dishes saying. *Dear Fritz, terrific as always. How about doing one with peaches? Ever yours, HRH, Dottie.*

Somehow the story got into the papers and vastly increased her popularity, which might, or might not, have been the intention of the person who leaked it.

Messages of congratulations began to flood in from governments and royal houses, including one from Prince Harold of Korburg, that made Randolph snort with disgust.

He had an air of tension these days, the reason for which everybody guessed, although it was spoken only in whispers. Dottie's acceptance as the true heir had finally broken the patience of the Bekendorf family. Sophie's father had stormed in to see Randolph and finally broken the engagement. The Bekendorfs did not marry nobodies.

Hearing the story, Dottie winced, imagining what that cruel barb must have done to a man of Randolph's pride.

"Don't believe the lurid tales," Aunt Liz advised. "Randolph's valet is married to my maid, and I can tell you that Randolph did *not* knock the man to the floor, nor did he make a noble speech about true love conquering all, which is the other version doing the rounds. He merely observed that he had already freed Sophie from all obligation to him, and asked Bekendorf to leave."

"Poor Randolph," Dottie murmured. "How terrible he must feel."

Aunt Liz shrugged. "I suppose he must, but he'll never tell anybody."

Dottie nodded, thinking of the magical evening they'd spent together, when she'd seen only what he wanted her to see, the smiling charm, the pleasure in a shared joke. And all the time...

She tried to remember his eyes, and could recall only their warmth. Even his remoteness had been hidden that night, while he'd encouraged her to open her mind as she'd done to nobody else. And she felt again the little flame of resentment against him.

The days began to merge into each other, and slip away, each one too packed with activity for Dottie to think. When she wasn't being fitted for new clothes and wearing the triumphant results at receptions, she was discovering Elluria on horseback. Now it was Randolph who escorted her through the countryside, full of spring blossoms. He often smiled at her eager pleasure in her surroundings.

"Anyone would think you'd never seen the countryside before," he said once.

"In a way that's true. I've always lived in London. I never knew anything as beautiful as this."

They had dismounted to let their horses drink from a stream that ran through a small wood. When the beasts were satisfied, Dottie and Randolph tied them to a tree and wandered away by the water. Ahead of them the sunlight slanted between the branches, and the light seemed to mingle with the sound of birdsong and the soft crunch of their feet against the earth. At moments like this she wished it would never end. There was peace here, something she dimly recognized that she had never found before.

Randolph walked beside her in silence, handsome and maddeningly unreadable. Dottie longed to say something to comfort his sadness, but she guessed he would hate for her to introduce the subject, and she couldn't risk it. Lacking any other way to reach out to him, she showed her sympathy by a careful gentleness. At last he said, wryly humorous, "Dottie, please don't treat me with kid gloves. I promise you it isn't necessary."

"I can't help it. I heard what happened."

"It was bound to happen. Bekendorf couldn't let the situation continue. No father could."

"But doesn't Sophie get a say?"

He looked across the water. "Sophie has been more loyal to me than I deserve. She would have abandoned everything to marry me, even as a commoner. I can't accept her sacrifice, although I honor her for her generosity."

"But do you lo—"

"Please can we discuss it no further? The matter is ended."

"If you can end it just like that, then..." She stopped at the look in his eyes.

"Yes," he said dangerously, "Go on. Am I in for some sentimental psychobabble about not having loved her? The only true feelings are the ones that are paraded to the world? Because I don't bare my soul on *Oprah,* I *have* no soul? Isn't that how it goes?"

She didn't answer, only stood looking at him. He sighed and calmed down.

"I'm sorry. I shouldn't have lost my temper with you."

"Probably did you good," she said. "I can't see you blurting it out on *Oprah* either, but keeping it all in isn't good for you. All right, that's psychobabble, but sometimes even psychobabble gets it right. You're too controlled."

"Control was instilled in me as a child. It's too late for me to abandon it now."

"But don't you ever want to be simply happy?"

His answer was an eloquent shrug, and suddenly, as if a window had been opened, she saw into his mind. "You don't think happiness matters, do you?"

"Not for me," he said in a matter-of-fact tone that had no trace of self-pity.

"What does matter to you?"

"My duty to the people of this country, in one way, if not another."

"You mean teaching me to take your place?"

"Of course."

"But doesn't that hurt terribly?"

"It doesn't matter," he shouted. "Why can't you understand that? Whether it hurts me or not is unimportant. Let me tell you—" he checked and took a deep breath.

"Tell me what?"

"That life is a great deal easier this way. There's nothing worse than constantly fretting over your own feelings. There's no happiness in that either. But if you do what has to be done, there can be a little satisfaction."

Something was aching inside her, almost too much for her to speak. "And that's what you're going to live for?" she asked at last. "A little satisfaction from doing your duty."

"It's all that's left for me, Dottie."

"But you can't say that," she cried. "It's giving up on life."

"I shall live a life—"

"No you won't, except on the surface. Inwardly you'll have crawled away into a cave where you think nobody can find you. You say that being hurt doesn't matter, but actually you plan to protect yourself by not having any feelings that *can* be hurt. It looks brave and noble but actually it's cowardly."

"Thank you," he snapped. "If you've finished…"

"I haven't. There's something else."

"Get it over with."

"All right," she said breathlessly, and kissed him.

She did it quickly before she lost her nerve, but she was driven by a need so strong that it created a kind of courage. The last time her lips had lain against his had been in the park on her final day in England. The memory had been with her every moment since, and now there was something she had to know. Seeking the answer, she pressed her mouth more urgently against his, and felt his tremor, his indecision. He wanted to draw back but couldn't make himself do it. She sensed that much. But what else was there?

His hands were on her shoulders, neither pushing her away nor drawing her close. In a troubled voice he murmured, "Dottie..."

"I'm not going to let you hide in that cave."

She had a glimpse of his face, harsh and cynical as he said, "Perhaps that isn't your decision."

"I'm the crown princess, I'm making it my decision."

She silenced him before he could answer, kissing him again with purpose and urgency. Her life hadn't taught her to be a skilled lover, but she had something better than skill, a need to communicate with him through her flesh, and a feeling in her heart that she wouldn't acknowledge, but which drove her none the less.

She could feel him trembling with the struggle going on inside, and she sensed the exact moment when he stopped struggling. He'd been holding himself taut in defense against her, but suddenly the tension went out of him and his body seemed to relax against her. Then his arms went around her and he had taken charge, full of anger and resentment at how she'd broken through his guard, but unable to prevent it.

"You're playing a dangerous game, Dottie," he growled.

"Who's playing games?" she whispered against his mouth. "Kiss me."

She barely got the last word out before he smothered her mouth again, kissing her with a fierce skill that showed her she was just an amateur. But she was learning fast. Sliding her hands along his arms, feeling the swell of muscles, it was as though she'd never touched a man before. Nor had she. Only boys, as unskilled as herself, callow lads who'd deferred to "Steamroller Dottie." But this man had deferred to nobody until she came along, and now he was in no mood to defer to her. She'd unleashed something she couldn't control, and it was the most thrilling event of her life.

Her heart was hammering. Briefly, it was alarming how everything was slipping out of focus, but then she didn't care anymore. Nothing mattered beyond this moment, her old life, her new life, Mike…

Mike!

She pulled back, gasping as the world returned abruptly. "Oh no, I can't…please let me go."

He did so, staring at her with a brow of thunder. Even so, he was more in command than she.

"I shouldn't have done that," she said in horror. "Why didn't you stop me?"

"Her Royal Highness's word is law," Randolph said ironically.

"Is that the only reason why you kissed me back? To humor me?"

"Is that why you think I did?"

"Don't confuse me with questions. Oh, I'm terrible. How could I do that to poor Mike?"

Randolph made a sound of disgust. "Do you realize that's how you always talk about him? To you he's always *poor* Mike. If a woman's really in love with a man she doesn't talk about him like that."

"That's not true," she flashed. "I've always been in love with Mike."

"Perhaps that's why you aren't anymore," he suggested, his eyes full of the things she was trying to pretend weren't true.

"You know nothing about it."

"I know how you kissed me just now. I know that it was *your* kiss. What more do I need to know?"

"That's right, jeer at me."

"I'm not jeering, merely pointing out that all this maidenly reticence is a little out of place."

"Because I came on to you, right? Well, I shouldn't have done, and I wish I hadn't. I'd forgotten what you're really like."

"And what am I really like?"

"Everything's planned, isn't it? Draw people in so that you can use them, and then fend them off when they try to be nice to you. Oh boy, am I glad I'm going home soon!"

"Dottie, listen—"

"No, I'm going back. Don't come with me."

"I have to."

Suddenly inspired she flashed, "Then you can follow me 'at a respectful distance.' There! Is that royal enough for you?"

She fled back to her horse, so furiously upset that she actually managed to mount without assistance, which she usually couldn't do. By the time Randolph reached his own horse she was far ahead, galloping madly.

All over Elluria the mail deliveries were being watched with feverish excitement. A grand ball would put the seal on the new queen's acceptance, and not to be invited meant social death. As the last of the invitations arrived there were sighs of relief and groans of despair.

The chandeliers in the great ballroom were taken down and each tiny facet washed separately. The finest crystal was retrieved from cupboards. The palace gardeners worked overtime tending hothouse blooms to adorn the public rooms.

Dottie's dress was a masterpiece of blue satin, heavily embroidered and studded with jewels. On her head she would wear a diamond tiara that had been in the family for three hundred years. A matching diamond necklace and bracelet completed her adornment.

"You look gorgeous, Dot," Mike breathed when he looked in on a fitting. Aunt Liz had stepped out for a moment and they were alone.

She wondered fleetingly how she would look to Randolph. Would he think her beautiful? He'd been away for the past couple of days, and she didn't know when he'd return. That was good, she told herself. The thought of their last meeting still made her go hot and cold with shame.

"Dot? Are you there?"

"Sorry," she said hastily, returning to the present. "How are you managing, darling? I gather they're fixing you up with white tie and tails!"

He made a face in which disgust and unease were

mingled, and she burst out laughing. Then she kissed him more tenderly than usual. She was feeling guilty about Mike these days.

"And I'm having dancing lessons," he said. "I told them I didn't need that. A waltz is easy—one, two, three, one, two, three. What else do you need?"

"I said the same," Dottie replied, carefully removing the magnificent jewelry. "But I have to learn all the other stuff, too. Fancy doing the quickstep and wondering if your tiara's falling off.

"Undo me," she begged. He pulled down the zip at the back, and steadied her as she stepped out of the dress. Still in her slip, she draped the lovely dress over the back of a chair then turned to him with mischief in her eyes. "One, two, three?" she said.

"You're on. Can I have the first waltz, madam?"

But she shook her head in mock horror. "Oh no, you have to wait for me to invite you. If I deign to honor you, a footman will approach and ask if you would like 'the honor of dancing with Her Royal Highness.'"

"Suppose I say no?"

"Then I'll lock you up for an insult to my royal person."

"You're a right idiot, you know that, Dot?"

"You only just found that out?"

They laughed together and began hopping around the room like the pair of kids they had once been.

Mike's brow became furrowed, as it always did when he tried to think. "Don't feel you have to invite me to this big 'do,'" he said. One, two, three. "I wouldn't be offended if you thought I'd be out of place."

"You're not getting out of it that easily," she said,

interpreting this generous offer without difficulty. "I'll need moral support." One, two, three.

"But Dot…"

"Be there."

"Yes, Dot. Anything you say Dot."

"And don't say it like that, as though I'm always giving you orders."

"No, Dot. Anything you say Dot."

She thumped his arm. He began to chuckle and she joined in, overwhelmed by tender affection for him. He was her Mike, as comfortable as an old slipper, and right now that seemed preferable to the turbulent sensations and feelings that awaited her if she wasn't careful. At last they stopped dancing and clung together, while peals of mirth echoed up to the elegant painted ceiling.

Their laughter reached Randolph, who was approaching along the corridor and through the outer room. The sound entranced him, catching at his heart and making him press forward to find the source without considering what it might be. The door to her bedroom was ajar and he'd pushed it open and walked in before he had time to think. That was how he saw Dottie, dressed in her slip, hugging Mike to her, her head thrown back as she laughed affectionately up into his face.

"Good afternoon," Randolph said calmly.

Dottie released herself from Mike's arms, but didn't seem discomposed at being found like this. If anything, she eyed Randolph with dislike, which puzzled Mike.

"I believe Captain Gorshin and some of his friends were hoping you would join them about now," Randolph informed him.

"Right. Fine. 'Bye Dot."

When they were alone Randolph eyed her coldly. "May I suggest that you put some clothes on?" he said bleakly. "May I further suggest that in future you pay a little more attention to the proprieties? Fooling around with young men in your underwear is not the behavior this country expects of its queen."

He spoke more harshly than he'd intended. The intimate sight he'd stumbled on had struck him like a blow in the chest. He called formality to his aid, and for once it failed him.

"And may I remind you that these are my private apartments and you should have knocked before coming in?" Dottie said defiantly. "May I further remind you that in these rooms *I* decide what's proper and what isn't?"

"Congratulations, Dottie," he said ironically. "You're beginning to acquire the tone of lofty command. It's a pity you have such a poor idea of when to use it."

"Are you telling me how to behave?"

"On the evidence of my eyes I think somebody needs to."

"Oh stop being so stuffy. Mike's seen me in less than this—"

"I don't want the details."

"—when I stayed with his family once, and we all had to fight over the bathroom." She met his eyes innocently. "Everyone saw everyone in everything…or rather in nothing. Or anyway, not much." Seeing no yielding in his face she said coaxingly, "Can't you see the funny side?"

"I suppose I might have expected that from you,"

he said bitterly. "The funny side. Always the funny side. You're incurably frivolous."

"Rubbish. I can be serious when the situation is serious. But this one isn't."

"You're the queen. If you let a man see you wearing only a slip and—" he stopped, feeling his breath coming unevenly.

Dottie looked down at herself, following his gaze. "Yes, I'm not wearing a bra," she said. She couldn't resist adding, "Have you only just noticed?"

He'd been trying not to. The top of her slip was lacy and full of little holes, giving tantalizing glimpses of her otherwise bare breasts. They were as firm and uptilted as he recalled from that first morning when he'd been granted a brief, forbidden glimpse of her lovely nakedness. His brow was damp.

"Are you so shameless that you don't cover yourself?" he demanded coldly.

Dottie herself couldn't have explained what had gotten into her to make her goad him like this, but the little devil that was urging her on gave another prod with his trident.

"Why should I? It's only you."

"Meaning that I'm some kind of eunuch?" he demanded dangerously.

"I was thinking more of a father figure. And what's a eunuch?"

"A eunuch would be a man who could see a woman dressed as you are and feel no response," he snapped. "A eunuch would observe you half-naked *and see the funny side.*"

"But you don't?"

A pit yawned at his feet. Just in time he saw it and swerved.

"I cannot be amused," he said bitingly, "when a woman to whom I must swear allegiance as my queen behaves in a way unsuitable to her station."

The effect of these words on Dottie was so swift and dramatic that it took Randolph aback. He couldn't know that any reference to his lowered position cut her to the heart. He only knew that the fun drained out of her face, leaving only a sad dignity behind.

"Perhaps you're right," she said, pulling on a robe and turning away from him.

"Dottie, I was only—"

"It's a rotten situation for you. I should have remembered."

"Let's not discuss that."

"No, we don't need to discuss anything. I'll go and get dressed now."

She hurried away, leaving Randolph displeased with himself. He'd acted correctly and it had been a disaster. She was no longer joyous, therefore no longer Dottie.

And that was all wrong.

The rules stated that royalty arrived last and departed first. So on the night of the great ball Dottie stood, with Randolph, behind the huge mirrored double doors that led into the ballroom, knowing that on the other side were gathered two thousand people.

She would have liked to grasp his hand, but although he was beside her she couldn't make herself do it. Everything was wrong between them now.

The moment came. From behind the doors she could hear the orchestra play the national anthem. The doors opened on the glittering scene and they stepped forward.

At once she was engulfed in a wave of applause. Everywhere people were smiling at her. She knew a stab of pleasure, but hard on its heels came indignation. Why didn't they hate her for displacing the man whose life was dedicated to their service? Why didn't they spare a thought for his suffering? Burning with pity for him, she failed to notice her progress until she found herself at the foot of the stairs leading to her dais.

Randolph led her to the top, inclined his head and withdrew. The Master of Ceremonies caught her eye. She nodded, he signaled to the orchestra conductor, her partner presented himself and the ball began.

Deep in the crowd, Mike had watched Dottie's arrival with fond admiration, glad to see that she didn't seem to need his help. Then a footman approached him, but the words weren't the ones he'd expected. "Would you like the honor of dancing with the Countess Sophie Bekendorf?"

Mike looked around wildly at some of his officer friends, but they slapped him on the back and urged him on. Sophie was magnificent in dark red velvet, her shoulders bare but for the famous Bekendorf rubies. Feeling like a lamb being led to slaughter Mike followed the footman toward her, not in the least comforted by her brilliant smile.

But Sophie was charming. She greeted him warmly and was even understanding about his dancing. After a couple of turns around the floor she said sympathetically, "Why don't we sit this one out? I'm a little thirsty."

Mike found himself in a small conservatory just off the ballroom, a drink in his hand, and Sophie's ardent eyes turned on him.

"I really only drink beer," he protested.

"But this wine is practically our national drink," she said, sounding hurt.

So he tried it, and had to admit that it wasn't bad after all.

"Everyone wants to talk to you," Sophie said admiringly, "because nobody knows our new queen as well as you. We're all so glad to have her. She's refreshingly natural."

"Aye, speaks her mind, does Dot," Mike confirmed.

"So I've observed. Tell me, did her royal birth really come as a surprise to her?"

"Oh yes. She had no idea. Mind you, her grandpa always knew. Used to say all sorts when he'd had a few."

Sophie gave a tinkling laugh and Mike began to feel that perhaps he was a heck of a fellow after all. He drained the second glass and a third appeared as if by magic. Or perhaps it was the fourth.

"But I don't suppose he knew very much," she said.

"Well, he had some very strange stories. Nobody believed a word of them, mind." Mike held out his glass to Dagbert, wondering why he'd ever been worried. A glow of content was settling over him.

Deep in the ballroom Dottie was beginning to feel relieved. So far she'd managed without mishap. Every foreign ambassador had to be honored with a dance in strict order of importance. Somewhere near the lower end of the list was Count Graff, the ambassador from Korburg, who danced correctly, spoke like a robot and barely bothered to conceal the fact that he was looking her over with mingled interest and contempt.

Sometimes she caught sight of Randolph, splendid in dress uniform. He too was doing duty dances, although her quick eyes never saw him in Sophie's arms. Why? she wondered. Had they made a pact to avoid each other in this public place? Or was Randolph simply too heartbroken to be near her?

Then she realized that he never looked at her. She'd dared to be pleased with her own appearance. She knew that she really looked like a princess. And for all the notice he took she might as well not have bothered.

At last her duty dances were done, and she could sit on the plush chair on her dais, and wiggle her toes. Randolph would approach her now, but he seemed deep in conversation with a general, so Dottie set her chin and summoned a footman.

"Inform my cousin that I would like to speak to him," she said, sounding more imperious than she felt because she felt uneasy behaving like this.

After a moment Randolph approached her and bowed correctly. His air was polite but formal. He bowed again when she indicated the chair beside her, and took it.

"Is there some way I can be of use to you?" he asked.

"You can tell me how I've offended you."

"Your Royal Highness has not offended me."

"Oh stop that!" she said, letting her temper flare a little. "Why haven't you asked me to dance?"

"Because it's not my place. I've already explained that it's for you—"

"But surely that doesn't apply to you?"

"I'm afraid it does."

"Then I'm asking you to dance with me."

He rose and extended his arm. "As Your Royal Highness commands."

She was about to speak to him crossly again but she noticed how sad his face was, and it silenced her. They danced together correctly for a few minutes, and Dottie became more depressed every minute. When had they ever been correct? Perhaps his misery over Sophie was more than he could conceal. Whatever the cause, he seemed to have become almost a stranger.

He saw her looking at him and smiled self-consciously. "I trust you're enjoying your first ball?" he said.

"Thank you," she said. "I'm enjoying it extremely." She thought that sounded about right.

Randolph heard the elegant phrasing and his heart sank. For some reason tonight he found himself remembering their first evening in London, when she'd laughed and talked outrageously. At first he'd been shocked, but shock had passed as he became charmed by her springlike freshness. And all the while he'd been deceiving her, and he knew that she'd never quite forgiven him.

Now a change had come over her. She was beginning to learn her role, to dress correctly and speak elegantly. But, inch by inch, she was ceasing to be Dottie, and he didn't like it.

He reminded himself that to her this was just a game, that she was looking forward to calling a halt and returning home to marry Mike, the man to whom her heart clung with a stubbornness that drove him wild. He thought of the secret action he'd taken to ensure that her dream would never come true. He was deceiving her again, and his guilt tormented him.

For a moment her attention was distracted, and he followed her gaze to where Sophie was floating by in the arms of the Korburg ambassador, the third time she'd danced with him.

Oh, no! he thought in dismay. *Please Sophie, not that!*

He didn't blame her. He knew the family pressure she was under to find a royal husband, and Harold was now the most eligible. But he felt sick at the thought that she might ally herself with a man he despised. Then he realized that Dottie was watching his face, and he hastily smiled.

The dance was coming to an end. He led her back to her dais, bowed and excused himself. Suddenly feeling very lonely, Dottie looked around for Mike, but there was no sign of him. What she did see was Randolph approaching Sophie and firmly cutting out the Korburg ambassador. She watched miserably as they circled the floor, until Aunt Liz touched her arm and indicated somebody that she really ought to honor with her attention.

For a while Randolph and Sophie waltzed in silence. But at last he could contain himself no longer and said in a soft, urgent voice, "Don't do it, Sophie. For pity's sake, don't do it."

"Are you the man who should say that to me?" she asked softly. "What else should I do? Wear the willow for you?"

"No, not that, but how could we marry when I have nothing to offer? There was no choice for either of us. Your father made me see that."

"I understand. Forgive me for what I said, beloved. You're a good man. I know your heart too is broken."

A frisson of unease went through him. Perhaps she sensed it, for she gave a beautifully modulated sob.

"Sophie, please," he murmured. "Don't cry here."

Swiftly he danced her out onto the terrace. She was still weeping, and he felt vaguely embarrassed, and then ashamed of his embarrassment. Once he'd thought her cool, composed, a good friend but no more. Her apparent desolation at his loss made him awkwardly conscious that his own feelings had always been weaker.

"Sophie, my dear," he said as they slowed to a halt, "what do you want me to do?"

"I know you can't change anything," she sobbed. "I accept it, but you mustn't blame me for what I do."

"How could I ever blame you? But it hurts me to think of you as that man's wife."

"And yet you yourself will soon be married, won't you?"

"Hush," he placed his fingertips gently over her mouth. "Don't speak of that."

"No, there's nothing more to say, for either of us. Kiss me goodbye."

Saddened by her grief, and what he felt to be his own inadequate response, he drew her close and laid his lips tenderly on hers. It was the kiss of a generous friend, but from a short distance it could have had the appearance of a lovers' embrace.

At least, that was how it seemed to Dottie, standing at a window, looking out with bleak eyes.

Chapter Seven

Mike appeared in her room at noon next day, hungover and apologetic.

"Don't know what was in that stuff I drank," he said. "Maybe I should have stuck to beer." He rubbed his head.

"What made you change the habits of a lifetime?" Dottie asked. She too wasn't feeling at her best today.

"I didn't want to offend Countess Bekendorf. Mind you, she wasn't so bad."

"What on earth did you find to talk about?"

"It was some of the stuff your grandpa told me, about your royal ancestors."

"But you told me you couldn't remember that."

"I can't when I'm sober, but last night I wasn't sober."

"So what was it?"

Mike looked rueful. "Sorry Dot, I'm sober again now."

"Oh well," Dottie sighed, "she was bound to try to find out if I'm an impostor. So now she knows that I'm the real thing. Not that it matters. They'll find someone else soon, and then you and I can go home and get married."

She was eager for their departure. There was something about this place that made her behave unlike herself. It wasn't Dottie who'd insisted on kissing Randolph. Nor was it Dottie who'd teased him with her half-clad body, determined to get a response from him and bitterly satisfied when she received one. Dottie would never behave like that because she loved Mike, and it was love that mattered, not lust.

Lust. She considered it, trying to see it in relation to herself. All right, she admitted at last. She fancied Randolph. Fancied him like mad, if the truth be told. But that wasn't real life.

She didn't see him for a couple of days. He'd left in the early hours after the ball and gone to an estate he had nearby. She left a message for him, and he came to her as soon as he returned.

"You should have found another heir by now," she said quietly.

"But I haven't. There's only you."

"But I have to go back to England."

"Are you going to abandon us?" Randolph demanded fiercely. "You have a short memory if you can forget how the people of this country have welcomed you. You know what our fate will be if you desert us."

"They can put you back on the throne," she said

desperately. "It should be you by rights. I'm all wrong. You've said so often enough, and it's true."

"Yes, it is, but it doesn't matter. I'm illegitimate and therefore barred from the throne."

"Well, they can have a what d'you call it? Referee—"

"Referendum."

"Referendum. People can vote for you to be king and then you can marry Sophie and everything will be all right." She hadn't meant to add that last bit.

"If I tried to claim the throne, even with the consent of parliament and the people, Harold would use that as an excuse to start a war. And if I stand back and let him become king, he'll plunder the country and crush its people. The only person who can stop that is you."

"And where does Mike come in your grand scheme of things?"

"He doesn't. You can't marry him. Surely you've realized that?"

"You mean I should just dump him? Oh, lovely. Sorry Mike, it's been nice knowing you but something better has turned up. A nice opinion of me you have! Remember how it felt to lose Sophie?"

The bleak, guarded look that she dreaded appeared in Randolph's eyes. "Why don't we go and talk to Mike?" he asked smoothly. "He's surely entitled to express an opinion."

"I see your game. You'll give him the fancy speech you've just given me, and then you think he'll make the grand sacrifice."

"I admit I don't associate him with grand sacrifices. He impresses me as a very down-to-earth young man, doing everything for prosaic reasons."

"Right! And he'll tell you to jump in the lake."

"I'm trembling."

"And then *I'll* tell you to jump in the lake, and since I'm the crown princess you'll have to do it."

"At Her Royal Highness's command I'll jump in any lake you care to name. Would you like me to wear a lead weight about my neck?"

"Don't be funny with me, buster!"

As they talked Randolph had contrived to urge her out of the door that led to one of the hidden corridors. Dottie followed him, furiously angry. At last she found herself on a little landing, outside a nondescript door. Randolph took a key and unlocked it, ushering her forward. She strode into the room, ready to confront Mike, but the sight that met her eyes drove everything else out of her mind.

Stretched out on the grandiose bed, her eyes closed in pleasure, lay a naked young woman. The rest of her face was obscured by the back of Mike's head. He was also naked, and far too occupied with what he was doing to realize that his fiancée had entered the room. Only drastic action was going to get through to him, so Dottie took it, raising her hand high above her head and bringing it down hard on his vigorously working rump.

His yell of surprise and outrage hit the ceiling. Wriggling away to escape, he contrived to fall right off the bed, landing in an undignified heap at her feet, and revealing the identity of his companion, who screamed as she saw Dottie's doom-laden face.

"You've got a nerve, Bren," Dottie told her. "But I'll come to you later, when I've thumped *him* to kingdom come and back."

"Now, Dot," Mike said from the floor where he

was haplessly trying to cover himself and squirm away from her at the same time. "Don't lose your sense of proportion."

"I don't have one," she growled. "As you're about to discover. Oh, get up for pity's sake!"

He did so, his hands clutched protectively in front of him, his eyes fixed warily on Dottie. Randolph had been discreetly locating Brenda's robe and helping her put it on. Mike's clothes were scattered about the room, suggesting some urgency in their removal, which did nothing to improve Dottie's temper.

"What are you doing here anyway?" she demanded of Brenda.

"I won a holiday," Brenda said sullenly.

"Oh really!" Dottie turned her fire on Randolph. "Courtesy of the Ellurian Tourist Authority, I suppose? You weren't offered a honeymoon as well, by any chance?"

"None of your business!"

"Oh yes it is," Dottie said wrathfully. "You forget you're talking to the queen."

"Not quite yet—" Randolph murmured.

"You hush!" she told him firmly. "You've told me often enough about my power. Well, how's this for power?" She swung back to the other two. "I could have both of you arrested, locked up and nobody would ever hear of you again."

Brenda gave a little squeak, and Mike edged closer to her. "She can't do it, love," he muttered. "We haven't broken the law."

"Think treason," Dottie suggested dangerously. "Think firing squad."

"Her Royal Highness is naturally disturbed by this breach of protocol," Randolph said smoothly, "and she desires only to find a way out of the unfortunate situation.''

''A firing squad,'' Dottie said stubbornly.

''Aw, c'mon Dot,'' Mike said placatingly. ''You'd finished with me anyhow. You just hadn't gotten around to telling me yet.''

Before she could answer Randolph drew her aside. ''Perhaps you shouldn't blame him too much,'' he murmured. ''After all, you too have permitted yourself—shall we say the odd moment of dalliance?''

She met his eyes and saw in them something that made her gaze fall. He was reminding her of scurrying excitements that he could cause in her, thrills that she'd never known with Mike. They were starting again, reviving the memory of the kiss that had made her feel so guilty. But she'd fled temptation, she remembered. Mike had embraced it full-on.

''That's different,'' she muttered. ''I didn't go in for…what they were doing.''

''Are you sure it might not have happened, if the circumstances had been right?''

''Quite sure.''

His eyes called her a liar. She whirled away from him and confronted Mike, who'd hastily resumed his clothes, and with them, some of his confidence.

''What do you mean by saying I'd finished with you?''

''You've belonged here from the start. And you knew it really. What would you do in Wenford after this? Besides,'' he indicated Randolph who was talking kindly to Brenda, and dropped his voice to say, ''you've gotta marry him.''

''I—he—what are you talking about? I'm marrying

you. At least, I was before you turned out to be a devious, treacherous, unfaithful..."

Mike gave her his sweet smile. "I'm not really, Dot. I'm just an ordinary feller, who wants an ordinary home and an ordinary wife. Thing is, you ain't ordinary."

Randolph returned to them. "The kindest thing you can do for Mike is to let him go back to England, where he can marry Brenda, and settle down with his own garage."

"He hasn't got a garage," Dottie pointed out grumpily.

Randolph held up a set of keys. "These keys unlock the place you had your eye on, Mike. It was purchased last week by the Ellurian embassy, and can be transferred to you whenever you wish, together with a check that I believe will be sufficient for you to make whatever improvements are needed. There is, of course, a condition."

He eyed Mike significantly. Mike eyed Dottie nervously. Reading resignation in her face he changed from nervous to sheepish.

"Sorry, love," he said, accepting the keys. "But it's better this way. You're a smashing lass, but you're like a steamroller." He added confidentially to Randolph, "You'll find that out."

Randolph grinned and nodded.

"I suppose you're going now," Dottie said.

"Well, we're a bit in the way, aren't we?" Mike suggested.

"Yes," Randolph said, "but it has been a pleasure knowing you. A car will take you to the airport. Just pack your immediate necessities. The rest will be sent on."

An historian would have been intrigued by the way Her Royal Highness bid farewell to her victorious rival. But he wouldn't have understood a word.

"You always said you'd have him off me," Dottie said. "I suppose I should have listened. But you be good to him, or you'll have me to deal with."

"Honest Dot, I'll make him happier than you would have."

"Bet you don't!"

"Bet I do!"

"Bet you don't!"

"We'll call our first girl Dottie." Brenda patted her stomach. "She should be settling in nicely by now."

"What?"

"Well, I have been here for two weeks."

"Two—I see." Dottie cast Randolph a look that boded ill for him.

For her final words to Mike she drew him aside, out of earshot of Randolph.

"What were you on about, saying I was marrying Randolph? You're daft, you are."

"No I'm not. Everyone knows he has to marry you so that he can be king, like he was supposed to be. That's what it's all about." He kissed her cheek. "'Bye love. It was great knowing you."

She kissed him back and said goodbye, but by now she was functioning on automatic. Mike's last words were whirling in her head. She'd been brought here to marry Randolph, and everyone knew it, including Randolph.

While Randolph escorted the lovers to the waiting car, Dottie stormed back to her own apartments. None of this was Mike's fault. He'd been *manipulated* into betraying her. Just as she herself had been manipulated.

From her balcony she watched as the car drew away, taking her old life with it. She was here for good now, because she had nothing to go back to. Randolph had seen to that.

As he returned to the building he glanced up at her and she summoned him with a small movement of her head, something that once she would never have done. He arrived a few minutes later, looking like a man bracing himself. "All right. Say it."

"Say it," she seethed. "You mean say it and get it over with, so that you can brush it aside. Because you don't actually mean to take a blind bit of notice."

"I'll do whatever you wish. Shall I fetch Mike back?"

"You know it's too late for that."

"It was always too late," he said flatly.

"Only because you've been pulling strings."

"I didn't force him to make love to Brenda."

"You put her there."

"I put her into his room, not his bed. That was up to him. I suppose he could always have controlled himself."

"She'd been here two weeks," Dottie said, choosing to ignore this. "What a time you must have had keeping us apart, making sure I never suspected anything. Quite a conspiracy. You've been determined to break us up since we arrived."

"Since before that."

She gasped. "You admit it?"

"Why should I deny it? There's no place in your life for Mike. You have to realize that."

"Oh really? Well, maybe being princess has some

advantages, and one of them is that I don't need to let you tell me what I have to do. I'm the one who says whether Mike has a place in my life.''

''Doesn't he have a say? He turned away from you to Brenda.''

''Only because you fixed it.''

Randolph gave a snort of impatience. ''I fixed it so that you wouldn't walk into the wrong marriage. He wouldn't have been happy with you. You're too much for him.''

''That's not true. We were perfectly happy before you came. All I wanted was a cozy little home—''

''And a cozy little husband,'' Randolph finished. ''Don't you realize your destiny is greater than that?''

''What I realize is that you've been conniving to get your own way, and never mind how I felt.''

''That's right,'' he said in a harder voice than she'd ever heard him use before. ''Never mind how you felt, or how I felt. Never mind anything except the welfare of your people. You disappoint me, Dottie. I thought you were a woman of your word, but you're backing out on the deal. We've found nobody and never will. That means, it ought to mean, that you stay here for good. But you're chickening out.''

''I'm doing no such thing. I just don't like the way you did it.''

''All right, you don't like my methods. I don't like a lot of the things that have happened to me recently, but I don't complain because my feelings aren't what it's all about. And nor are yours. That's the fact, whether you like it or not. From the moment we knew who you were, your marriage to Mike was impossible.''

''Why? Because I'm being set up to marry you?''

She hadn't meant to blurt it out like that but she was too angry to think straight.

Randolph drew in a sharp breath of surprise, and his face was very pale. "That's something we had best not discuss for the moment," he said curtly.

Dottie's head went up and her eyes glinted. "*I* will decide what we discuss," she said regally. "It's the truth, isn't it? All this training me to be a queen is just so much hot air because the real plan was to marry me and take the throne back that way. I certainly think we should discuss the idea, if only so that I can tell you where to put it."

"You're angry—"

"Hey, you noticed!"

"—and therefore you're bound to put the worst construction on this. When you've thought it over you'll see that neither of us has a choice."

"Wanna bet?"

He regarded her in tight-mouthed silence, and Dottie realized that she'd never before seen him as bitterly angry as he was at this moment.

"I think we should both calm down," he said after a while. "A little time to think—"

"Will just give me the chance to recall all the ways you've pulled my strings," she flashed. "Starting with the very first evening. You set out to charm me. I realized long ago that it was calculated, but I thought you were simply doing it to get me here. Only you were looking right ahead and doing a number on me."

"Doing a—"

"Work it out. You thought I was such an idiot that you could dazzle me until I lost all judgment. And who knows how well it might have worked if Mike hadn't opened my eyes today? What next? Would you have been crass enough to try to make me think you were in love with me? I suppose I should be grateful to have been spared that piece of dishonesty.''

He stepped closer to her, his eyes very hard. ''Be quiet,'' he said. ''You make your glib judgments and you think you know everything. Try looking at the reality.''

''The reality is that you want your throne back and there's only one way of getting it without starting a war,'' she flashed.

''And you think I'm low enough to cheat and deceive you to get it.''

''That's exactly what you did at the start. Mr. Holsson and the tourist authority. You've won a prize to sunny Elluria. I wonder you can look me in the face.''

''I did what I had to do,'' he shouted.

''That's a rotten excuse and you shouldn't hide behind it. You did what suited you and called it duty. That's what being royal means, isn't it?''

''Being royal means doing what you have to, whether it's what you want or not. It means giving up what you love and settling for what you can get.''

''So you give up Sophie and settle for me? Do I congratulate you?''

He didn't know how to answer her in this mood. Dottie's eyes warned him to be careful. She was bitterly, wretchedly angry, in a way that was new to him. Where was the chuckling pixie who'd enchanted him? This woman looked as though she'd never laughed in her life.

While he stood there, dumb, she walked away to the window and stood looking out at the avenue of limes. After a moment he went up behind her, and spoke softly.

"Do you remember what you said to me that first evening by the Thames?"

"Don't," she said huskily, putting a hand over her eyes. "Don't ever mention it again."

"I must, because that night you opened your heart and spoke to me out of your true self. You said that you'd dreamed of being a children's nurse. Now I know why. It's in you, that instinct to care for those weaker than yourself. Now you have three million children looking to you. 'A true mother to her people,' they called you. Who will care for your children if you don't?"

"Oh, you know all the right things to say, don't you?" she cried in despair.

"No, it's you that says the right things. I merely remind you of them. That night you spoke of fate and destiny, and how there was a niche waiting for you somewhere in the world, that only you could fill. Those were your very words."

She turned. He met her eyes, hoping to see in them understanding and acceptance, but there was only the dread of a trapped animal.

"Dottie," he said gently, touching her.

But she sprang back at once as though his touch was hateful to her. "Keep away from me," she said hoarsely. "I can't bear to look at you. *Keep away.*"

He put out his hand but he was too late to stop her. She evaded him and darted for the door, then outside, and he heard her footsteps along the corridor. After a moment she appeared on the ground, racing along the long drive where Mike's car had departed, as though she had some wild hope of calling him back. But then she turned aside. Randolph's last view of her was disappearing into the trees.

For an hour Dottie wandered beside the lake, her thoughts too jumbled to make any sense. Sometimes it seemed that she wasn't thinking at all, just feeling. But feeling hurt too much. Randolph was right. It was better to do without it.

She hoped he wouldn't send anyone after her. She needed the solitude of this place, to be away from him. She'd relied on Randolph every moment since she came here, and now she didn't know how she could ever rely on him again.

Looking around, she realized that she was in the place she'd seen from her window the night she came to Elluria. In this spot Randolph had wandered with the woman he loved, his arms around her, thinking himself hidden by the darkness.

It was a long time before she returned to her room. He was no longer there and she sat for a while, not allowing anyone in. Just now she needed solitude. After a while she rang the bell and summoned Aunt Liz.

She had much to keep her occupied for the rest of the day. Her dressmakers brought several half-finished outfits to be fitted and there were decisions to be made. What should she wear for this reception and that? What shoes went with what? She was meeting an ambassador and must wear the jewels that had been a gift from his country.

It was strange how rivetingly interesting new clothes could be one day, and how depressing another.

It was silly to quarrel, she thought, as her anger

evaporated. This was what he'd meant when he'd talked about realpolitik. It was the real world of royalty.

She didn't like this world. It was a place where she was expected to marry Randolph and be satisfied with the outward show; a world where her heart and feelings had no place.

But she couldn't afford to be at odds with her chief advisor. She would smooth it over somehow. She called his room on the internal phone, and his valet answered.

"Prince Randolph isn't here," he said. "He left the palace some hours ago to visit his estate. Do I understand that he left without informing Your Royal Highness? Oh dear."

"No," she said quickly. "He did mention it of course. I forgot."

"Do you wish him to be notified that his presence is required?"

"No, that won't be necessary."

As she went to bed that night Aunt Liz mentioned that she'd left her "a little light reading," on her table. This proved to be a scholarly history of Elluria, and a reference book on the country's constitution.

She discovered that the sovereign's power was considerable. Elluria had an elected parliament from which most of the cabinet were drawn. But she could appoint anyone as a minister, elected or not. Also she could, at any time, declare a state of emergency and rule by decree. No wonder she scared them. She scared herself.

Now more than ever she needed Randolph here to explain everything and reassure her. But he was also the last person she would trust, because it all added up to a reason why she should marry him.

And pigs would fly first.

Next day Aunt Liz was bubbling over with excitement.

"Are the rumors really true? You're going to stay? Oh, that's wonderful!"

Dottie was touched by the older woman's obvious delight. But perhaps Liz was only pleased because she foresaw a marriage. A different candidate might have been a man, or already married, leaving Randolph out in the cold.

Was this what it meant to be a queen? To be suspicious of everyone who was nice to you? If so, it was a bleak prospect. And now there was nobody to help her. She was truly alone. The aloneness of royalty.

She soon realized that the news that she was staying had changed everything. Now she must appoint ladies in waiting, meet her cabinet and have in-depth discussions with her prime minister.

About what for heavens sake? Somebody tell me what I'm supposed to be doing.

"Of course you met your chief ministers when you arrived," Aunt Liz reminded her. "But today it will be the full cabinet. I think your clothes should be slightly severe, your hair up, just one piece of jewelry, this brooch that bears the coat of arms of Elluria."

As she dressed for her first cabinet meeting Dottie's thoughts swung about like a pendulum.

He's left me like this to show me that I can't manage without him. I didn't think he'd descend to that.

It seems I got him wrong. Well, he got me wrong too. Do I need him?

The meeting was in the parliament building, in the city. At noon Dottie was ready, pale but determined. She heard the faint knock at the outer door, but barely registered it until Bertha hurried in to say, "Prince Randolph asks leave to attend you, ma'am."

She discovered that she could assume the royal mask, so that nobody could suspect the way her heart leapt. Nor did her voice quaver as she said, "Please ask him to enter," although she was trembling inside.

Randolph looked like a man who'd spent a desperate, sleepless night. Dottie had meant to stay angry with him but she couldn't. In another moment she would have opened her arms, apologized for her angry words and asked him to be friends again. But before she could do so he bowed and said, "I am at Your Royal Highness's service."

His cool politeness was more hurtful than a slap in the face. He was doing his duty. No more.

"I thought you would be away for several days," she said quietly.

"Forgive me for leaving without first informing you," he responded. "That was improper of me."

She wanted to cry out, *Don't talk to me like that. This is me, Dottie.*

But it was too late. There was no going back to the old days: happy days, she understood, now that they were gone.

"Are you coming with me to the cabinet meeting?" she asked.

"If that is what you wish."

"I can't manage it without you."

"Then I shall certainly be there. It won't be very

terrible. Remember they're more nervous of you than you of them.''

''Impossible.''

''You can dismiss them at will and appoint your own nominee.''

''Yes, that's what the book said. It doesn't sound very democratic.''

''It isn't, but it can be very effective.''

''Then why don't I just appoint you prime minister? That would be fair, wouldn't it?''

It was a mistake. If possible his face closed against her even more firmly, and his voice seemed to come from an arctic cave.

''It would be far from fair to dismiss Jacob Durmand, one of the best prime ministers this country has ever had. Nor do I wish to be the subject of your charity. I trust I make myself clear.''

''Perfectly. Shall we go?''

''Wait one moment,'' he said imperiously. ''There are things to be said between us first.''

''You're angry about what I said yesterday, but—''

She stopped, for Randolph had held up his hand as if warding her off. He didn't deny that he was angry, she noticed. He merely consigned the subject to the realms of the unimportant—as feelings were, to him, she reminded herself.

''Listen to me,'' he said quietly. ''And heed what I say, for I have never been more serious in my life. Once you've attended that meeting, you're committed, finally and irrevocably to the people—*your* people. After today a door will slam shut behind you.''

''Oh no. The door slammed shut yesterday. You must have noticed. You did it.''

"I think it could be opened again. You could return to England, reclaim Mike."

"How could I ever do that?"

Randolph put his fingers beneath her chin and lifted it. "Remember what you told me once? 'A smile usually does it.' In London I watched you turn the chef into your slave. And Fritz in the kitchens here—he'd lay down and die for you. You have the gift of winning hearts, Dottie. You could win Mike's back. You could win…any man's." The last words seemed to come from him reluctantly.

She scanned his face in wonder at this strange talk. His expression was gentle, but beyond that she couldn't read.

For a moment the temptation dazzled her. To regain all she'd lost and return to her contented life.

Then reality kicked in and she gave a little sigh. "It's no use. Mike never really loved me. He just thought he did because—" she gave a jerky little laugh, "because I kept telling him. Like he said, I'm a steamroller."

"A sovereign needs to be a bit of a steamroller. But she also needs the gift of winning hearts, which you have. I'll help you all I can, but you must give me your word that you're totally committed. We can accept nothing less."

"We?"

"Your subjects," he said quietly.

"But—"

"That's what we are," he interrupted her. "Every one of us. We've given you our hearts, and all we ask in return is—everything. Your life, your freedom, your independence, your time. We ask you to think of us day and night, to put us first no matter what your own feelings dictate. In other words, we ask your love.''

''Everything,'' she whispered.

''Yes, it's a lot to ask. This is your last chance to escape. After today there's no going back.''

Dottie gave a wry smile. ''There never really was, was there?''

''No. There never really was.''

She put her hand in his.

''I think we should go now,'' she said. ''They're waiting for us.''

Chapter Eight

Two cars left the palace for the parliament building. In the second was Aunt Liz and another lady-in-waiting. The leading vehicle was a black limousine that had been specially constructed for the purpose of transporting a monarch. The entire rear was one huge window made of bulletproof glass, so that the sovereign should be easily visible.

Dottie sat there by herself. Randolph had chosen to sit in the front, beside the chauffeur, and by now she was sufficiently attuned to protocol to understand that this detail was significant. On this important day her people would see her alone.

She couldn't know that Randolph had another reason. He sat apart from her because he needed time to sort out the turmoil of his feelings.

Dottie's harsh judgment of him had briefly been right. He'd left the palace in a mood of bitterness, and headed for his estate, meaning to stay there. Dottie's mistrust, her accusations that he'd acted from base motives, infuriated him, and the look on her face when she'd said "I can't bear to look at you," had struck him like a blow. He'd put as much distance between them as he could.

But he'd barely arrived at his country house when his more generous self reclaimed him. He'd brought her here, dumped her in the middle of a crisis and then abandoned her. And why? Because his pride was hurt. He, who'd always said that feelings didn't count beside his duty to his country, had done something so cruel.

He'd spent the night pacing the floor, and next day he'd returned to the palace, arriving just in time. He'd searched her face as he entered, for any sign that she was pleased to see him, but her manner had all the regal austerity that he'd tried to teach her. It should have been a triumphant moment.

Now they were entering Wolfenberg, drawing up before the parliament building, an elaborate edifice that looked incongruously like a wedding cake on the outside. But inside it was redolent of history. Tapestries, depicting battles, hung on the walls. Statues of monarchs stood gloomily in niches. Red tiles streamed across the floors.

In a small chamber that led directly to the cabinet room Randolph said to Dottie, "Would you oblige me by waiting here a moment, while I go in first, to make sure everything is in order for you?"

She nodded and he strode into the next room. The ministers were already in place, and they greeted him with relief.

"If you're going to direct proceedings, sir, we'll

all be very relieved,'' Sternheim announced. He was one of the few who hadn't warmed to Dottie.

"I'm not,'' Randolph announced flatly. "And you must put any such thought out of your head.''

There was a universal groan.

"A woman,'' Sternheim said. "And a stupid, ignorant foreigner at that.''

"Keep your voice down,'' Randolph snapped. "That is exactly the kind of attitude I came to warn you about.''

"Be assured we shall observe all proper respect,'' Durmand said soothingly.

"I meant more than that,'' Randolph told him. "Let me tell you something about your crown princess. She might be naive but she isn't stupid, especially about people. Don't ever make the mistake of underestimating her, because she'll pounce on any slip you make like a ferret up a drainpipe.''

Sternheim was aghast. "Like a what?''

"Never mind,'' Randolph said hastily. He didn't know what had made him say that, except that Dottie's rich language had come back to him suddenly, and it was catching.

Next door Dottie walked up and down, increasingly nervous at the delay. Aunt Liz had opened the door a crack and was shamelessly eavesdropping.

Dottie couldn't bring herself to do the same but "stupid, ignorant foreigner" reached her clearly.

"If he just went in there to stir them up he needn't have bothered,'' she muttered.

"Of course not,'' Aunt Liz said. "He's trying to ensure that they show you respect.''

"Then he's doing a lousy job. And I'll fight my own battles,'' she added illogically.

At last Randolph returned, to lead her into the cabinet room. It was lined with bookshelves weighed down by learned-looking tomes. In the center was a heavy table, large enough to seat fourteen people. Randolph led her to her seat, and when he had solemnly presented her he stepped back and to the side, moving his chair to where she could just see him out of the corner of her eye.

Durmand gave a speech of welcome, then he courteously asked if she had anything to say to her ministers.

"Yes," she said. "I have. Please sit."

When they were all seated she felt horribly exposed, the only one on her feet. Until today it had been a kind of game. Suddenly it was for real.

"I think none of us really expected this moment to come," she said in a voice that surprised her by being steady. "I thought you would find somebody more suitable, and you must certainly have hoped for it."

Perceiving that their sovereign had made a witticism the ministers permitted themselves a few smiles.

"But here we are, and must make the best of each other," she continued. "I know I can rely on your loyalty both to me, and to Elluria. And you can rely on my loyalty to my new country."

That pleased them and she was able to smile as she seated herself, asking, "What do we do now?"

It seemed there were many matters requiring her attention. Since it was her prerogative to appoint the cabinet every minister resigned and was immediately reappointed.

"But I may wish to make a few changes later," Dottie observed. "I notice that there are no women here."

"There are only six women in parliament," Sternheim noted caustically.

"And how many men?" Dottie wanted to know.

Sternheim gave a snort of impatience. "I don't recall the precise figure."

"But you're my chancellor. If such a simple sum is beyond you, perhaps I should think again."

There were smothered smiles. Sternheim snapped. "Eighty-two."

"And only six women? Well, there'll be time for me to put that right."

Bernhard Enderlin, minister of the Interior, coughed gently. "Strictly speaking, ma'am, that's my province."

"Certainly it is," Dottie agreed warmly. "I look forward to discussing it with you. Shall we say sometime next week? That will give you time to work out your plan. How lucky that I'm here."

"I see that you believe in taking the bull by the horns, ma'am," Enderlin said, accepting defeat with grace.

"Otherwise known as being a steamroller," Dottie murmured. "Is there any other business?"

"The Korburg ambassador is agitating for his master to be invited for a private visit," Enderlin said. "It hardly seems advisable in the circumstances."

"I disagree," Dottie said at once. "Do you want him to think you're so unsure of me that you're hiding me from him? Nothing could be more dangerous. Never mind a private visit. Let's invite him for a *state* visit."

There was consternation around the table.

"The more fuss the better," Dottie rattled on before anyone could speak. "Let him *see* that the throne of Elluria is occupied. That'll teach him."

Consternation changed to smiles as her meaning got through, and there were murmurs of approval.

"Bull by the horns, gentlemen," Dottie said. "Boldness is best. Harold and I can get a good look at each other. He'll spit feathers, I'll say 'Get knotted!' and that will be that. All right, don't faint any of you. I'll just smile sweetly and do my stuff."

Everyone sighed with relief. Durmand, seeming to feel that the sooner the meeting ended the better for everyone's nerves, murmured, "In that case…"

"One moment," Dottie stopped him. "I have another appointment to make. You all know how unprepared I am for all this. Some people think I'm no more than a 'stupid, ignorant foreigner.'" She waited for the nervous frisson to die down. Out of the corner of her eye she saw Randolph give a faint smile. "Maybe I am, but it's not all I am, and to prove that I need help. Nobody can help me better than Prince Randolph, which is why," she took a deep breath, "I'm asking him to be my confidential, private secretary."

There were smiles of pleasure and relief. Dottie turned to Randolph, expecting to see approval, perhaps even a smile, but at once she knew she'd misread him. Of everyone in the room, he alone was not pleased, although good manners prevented him from saying so. He inclined his head and murmured something about wishing only to serve her, but his heart wasn't in it.

On the journey home he joined her in the back, shutting the partition so that they could speak privately.

"You had no right to do that without consulting me first," he growled.

"I only thought of it at the last minute. Besides, it's perfect. You can keep me from making mistakes."

"Like the one you just made?"

"I'm sorry for the way I did it, but that's all."

"Then let me give you my first piece of advice as your confidential, private secretary. Don't ever, *ever* take me by surprise again."

His reaction gave her a sense of disappointment that cut sharply and made her snap back, "I'm the crown princess. I can do anything I like."

"Not anything."

"Yes, anything. If you don't believe me, read the constitution. And if you say another word I'll declare a state of emergency."

That silenced him. They spoke little on the way back to the palace, and Dottie had supper alone, feeling let down. She confided in Aunt Liz, and was surprised when the older woman seemed troubled.

"You don't think I did the right thing?"

"It depends what you were trying to tell people," Aunt Liz said cautiously. "Naturally you need Randolph at your side, but people were thinking... That is they hoped—"

"That I would marry him? Suppose I don't want to?"

"Then the sensible option is to keep him by you as a servant. Which is what you've done."

Dottie's hand flew to her mouth in horror. "A servant? Oh no! That's not what I meant at all. I meant to honor him."

"You think he's honored to be a secretary? A royal

prince? Not that he's a royal prince now. Or any kind of prince.''

''What is he then?'' Dottie asked curiously. ''Surely he has some other titles?''

''He lost all his titles since he was illegitimate.''

''What, everything? And what about his estate? I know he still has that.''

''That was a personal gift from his father years ago, so it's safe. But it's all he has now, and it's a very small place. Just a retreat, really.'' She considered Dottie before saying casually, ''Of course, you could always make him a prince again. Not a royal prince, and it wouldn't make him legitimate, but you could give him a courtesy title that would make his life a lot easier.''

''Did he ask you to suggest that?''

''Oh my dear, if you haven't understood that he'd go to the stake rather than ask, even indirectly, then you haven't begun to understand him.''

''No, I suppose I don't understand him. But he doesn't want me to, I understand that much. He'd see it as a sort of invasion. Oh heavens! I've done it all wrong. I'm always going to do everything wrong. Why didn't I think? Because I never think. I'm an idiot, a clown. I have no right to be here. Oh *damn!*''

Of the twelve candidates to be her ladies-in-waiting, the only one Dottie knew was Jeanie, Countess Batz, whom she'd met when they'd all gone to the nightclub. The others had briefly passed before her and been lost in a blur. Dottie immediately picked her.

''A good choice as a lady-in-waiting,'' Aunt Liz

enthused, ''although perhaps a little young to be your *chief* lady.''

''I suppose I'll see more of the chief lady than the others?''

''Certainly.''

''Then I'll have Jeanie. I like her. Besides, her English is perfect.''

''They all speak perfect English,'' Randolph remarked from a nearby table, where he was making notes. He didn't raise his head or look at her.

''I want Jeanie,'' Dottie said stubbornly.

''As Your Royal Highness commands,'' Aunt Liz agreed.

''Oh, don't give me that,'' Dottie said crisply. ''I did exactly what the two of you meant me to do. I'll bet you put your heads together and said, 'How can we make her choose Jeanie for chief lady? Oh yes, tell her Jeanie's unsuitable and watch her take the bait.' You were like a pair of sheepdogs corralling me into the pen.''

They were both looking at her now. She looked back, not defiantly but evenly, like a businesswoman setting out her terms. ''Okay, it worked. Just don't kid yourself that I didn't see it happening. I may be ditzy but I'm not daft.''

''Of course you're not,'' Liz enthused. ''That's just what Randolph told your ministers. 'Like a ferret up a drainpipe,' he said.''

''Did he indeed?'' Dottie murmured. ''How interesting. It seems I'm not the only one learning things.''

Randolph gathered his papers and prepared to depart, but paused beside her first to murmur, ''Well done, ma'am. You're getting good at the game.''

''You mean the game of never trusting anyone?''

she murmured back. "Yes, I was sorry to learn that one, but I manage better now that I have."

She met Randolph's eyes. His fell first. These days it seemed that every conversation between them ended in some awkwardness. The gap between them yawned, unbridgeable, heartbreaking.

But Dottie was getting good at the nuances of court life. When she made her next move it was carefully planned.

She had just taken part in her first investiture. In front of a small audience twenty people came before her, bent one leg onto a small stool so that they were half-kneeling, and just the right height for her to pin on a medal, or bestow a title.

Randolph stood beside her, telling her who each one was, and how they had deserved honor, and when it was over and they were walking back to her apartments, she said casually, "Harold will be here soon. I'm working hard to learn everything I need to know, but I'm still floundering. Never mind. You'll be there to look after me all the time, won't you?"

"I'm afraid not," he said.

"But why?" she asked in apparent surprise, although she already knew the answer.

"Because I'm only your secretary, and you can't keep me by you on state occasions. Naturally I'll help you behind the scenes—"

"No good. I want you 'on stage' with me."

"That honor belongs to someone from a titled family. This is a very old-fashioned court, still. Tradition prevails. Only those of the highest rank may attend the monarch in public."

"Then the solution's easy. I just restore your titles. Plus all," she began to quote frantically before she could forget, ''appurtenances and privileges theretofore, not withstanding, herinafter, thingywhatsit and howsyourfather.''

His lips twitched. ''You've been doing your homework very well.''

''And landed estates,'' she finished triumphantly.

''No, that you can't do. They are crown heritage and must belong to you. But the rest—'' he broke off, sorely tempted.

Then he remembered the ceremony he'd just witnessed. He thought of kneeling before her; he who'd kneeled to nobody in his life, and his pride revolted. He was about to tell her stiffly that he would prefer not to receive her charity, but he saw her watching him anxiously, and realized how hard she'd worked to make this easy for him. His heart softened.

''Thank you, ma'am,'' he said gravely. ''It's a kind offer, and I accept.''

Her smile of relief told him how nervous she'd been of his reaction, and he was shocked at himself. He couldn't match her generosity. He could only pretend to and hope she didn't suspect.

She arranged the ceremony so quickly that he guessed she'd had everything planned. There was a small crowd, a few of the highest ranking families, the women in evening gowns and jewels, the men ablaze with decorations. Dottie was glittering with diamonds from the crown jewels, retrieved from the bank that morning under armed guard.

Randolph himself was in full dress uniform and Dottie, watching him walk toward her, thought he'd never looked so splendid. She knew this must be painful for him, but if only he would smile at her they could share the moment and turn the pain aside.

But he gave her no smile. His face remained stern and set as he neared the steps that led up to the throne, beside which she was standing. He climbed the steps, his eyes searching for the stool on which he must bend the knee.

It wasn't there.

His eyes met hers, registering his surprise that this detail had been forgotten. Then he saw her smile, saw her shake her head slightly and understood that this was no accident. The next moment she confirmed it, reaching out her hand to draw him to stand at her side.

She began to read from the letters patent that returned his status. Inwardly Randolph flinched, waiting for the words, "our loyal and most devoted servant." It was foolish to be so troubled by a few words, after what he'd already endured, but every pinprick seemed to pierce him twice now.

She was nearly there. As if from a distance he heard Dottie say, "our loyal and most devoted cousin and friend..."

A frisson went around the crowd. She'd departed from the traditional words of the letters patent, words that had been carved in stone for centuries. She'd simply dumped them to spare the feelings of the man beside her. Randolph stared at Dottie, shock warring with gratitude.

Next moment she had another shock for him. Refusing to let him kiss her hand she reached up and kissed his cheek. Then she took his hand and gestured to the applauding crowd, presenting him to them, inviting them to share her pleasure.

Randolph was aware of a dangerous ache in his throat. It mustn't happen. He had to speak. Somehow he managed it. The discipline held, the words came out, meaningless because all he was aware of was Dottie's hand still holding his.

It was over. He turned, went down the steps and walked away. But before he did so he tightened his hand on hers and felt the answering grasp of her fingers. They felt so small against his big hand, but their grip was surprisingly strong.

That was how they communicated these days; through public gestures filled with unspoken emotion, while their private conversations were awkward and uneasy.

Everyone agreed that inviting Harold for a state visit had been a brilliant idea, but it resulted in Dottie needing a crash course in ''royal'' behavior.

She, who'd never been to a formal dinner in her life, must become familiar with a whole array of cutlery, wineglasses, finger bowls. That was the easy part. It was the conversation that drove her distracted.

''Can't I just smile and say, 'My, how interesting'?'' she begged.

''Certainly,'' Jeanie agreed. She'd entered into her new duties, and her youth and fun-loving nature were just what Dottie needed.

''You can say, 'My how interesting' when you're visiting a hospital or meeting a line of actors after the theater,'' she explained now. ''But in a longer conversation it's not enough. You have to introduce a new topic now and then.''

''But why can't other people do that?'' Dottie demanded distractedly. ''Then I could just float with the tide, and say 'My, how interesting!' at short intervals.''

"Because only you can change the subject."

"*What?*"

"Nobody but you can introduce a new topic. If the sovereign wants to discuss one-legged spiders all night then that's what everyone has to do."

"I'm outta here."

"Now don't panic."

"Panic? I'm in a state of stark terror. You're all crazy."

The other thing she had trouble with was the royal "we."

"You're not just one person," Randolph explained. "You represent the state. In fact, you *are* the state. So you're speaking for both of you."

"Both of who?"

"You and the state."

"But you just said I *was* the state. So that's just one of us, isn't it?"

"In a sense. But you are you and the state is the state."

"Except that I'm the state, and the state is me."

To her surprise he beamed. "Excellent Dottie. Louis XIV expressed it in those very words. *L'etat c'est moi!*"

"Why didn't he speak English?"

"Because he was French."

She tore her hair. "How did he get into this conversation?"

"Because you used the very same words, thus proving that you really do belong in the great line-up of rulers. Just remember, you use the royal 'we' to indicate that you speak for your country as well."

"But I'll sound daft saying, 'We would like another slice of toast.' I'll probably end up with two."

Randolph closed his eyes. "It's only for use in public," he said with difficulty. "'We are delighted to declare that...' or 'It is our wish that...' And so on."

"Okay, I'll try to get the hang of it. Now, would you mind going because it's late and *we* would like to do our toenails before *we* go to bed?"

In between learning the proprieties, she interested herself in politics in a way that set her ministers' nerves jangling. At the earliest possible date she carried out her threat to summon Enderlin to discuss the low number of women in parliament.

"There really is nothing to be done about it," he protested. "Women aren't applying to stand for seats."

"But they might if the hours weren't so long," said Dottie, who'd been studying hard. "If you reorganized the debates so that the votes were at a reasonable hour I think the women would come forward." After a moment's thought she mused, "With a little encouragement."

Enderlin turned a hunted look on Randolph who was sitting to one side, but he seemed preoccupied with his notes.

"Do I understand that you intend to provide the encouragement, ma'am?" Enderlin asked faintly.

"Could be."

"Might I suggest that these interventions would be more appropriate when you've been here a little longer?"

"You mean when the election's over?" Dottie asked mischievously. "I did know that there was one due in a year. I want things done before that."

He made one last effort. "Such matters take time—"

''Not if you have the power of decree,'' Dottie reminded him mischievously. ''We'll have to move fast if we're to get things changed before then, but I know I can leave that to you. Randolph is always telling me how efficient you are.''

When Enderlin had bowed himself out Randolph said grimly, ''Do you mind leaving me out of your assaults on the executive? I value my skin.''

''Coward.''

''Yes, I am a coward,'' he said after a moment. ''More than you know, ma'am.''

''Don't call me that.''

''It is appropriate.''

''I mean when we're alone. I'm still Dottie.'' There was almost a plea in her words.

''No,'' he said at last. ''Dottie has gone a long way away, and how can I complain? It was I who sent her away.''

He walked out without the usual punctilious request for permission, leaving her wanting to burst into tears. Or throw something. Either one would have been better than the ache she felt all the time nowadays, and which she'd soon realized had nothing to do with the loss of Mike. It was the loss of Randolph that hurt.

It had been building up since that night in London when he'd whisked her away from her ordinary life, thrown magic into the air so that it dazzled her as it fell, and then...

''And then he made me fall in love with him,'' she mused. ''Dirty, rotten swine!''

Her feelings for him had always been there, from the first evening. No, from the first moment when she'd seen him in the café and known that he was unlike all other men. He was thrilling and dangerous, and he'd aroused her senses as Mike never had. She'd called him a magician, too ignorant and unsuspecting to know that the spell he cast was the oldest one in the world.

She would have seen the truth earlier if there hadn't been so many things in the way. But she saw it now, and it made her so angry with him that sometimes she could hardly bear to be with him. But when she wasn't with him it was worse.

Most painful of all was the knowledge that she could marry him tomorrow. A man as shrewd and subtle as Randolph would know the right words to convince her, because she longed to be convinced. Just let him once guess her feelings for him, and she would be lost. They would embark on a marriage of love on her side and duty on his. And in no time at all she would hate him.

Sophie had left the palace now and was living at the Bekendorf family mansion in Wolfenberg, at which, it was rumored, a stream of gifts arrived each day from Korburg. But she still had the freedom of the palace park, and arrived there most mornings for a ride.

Sometimes Randolph joined her, for it suited his pride to have the world see that they were still on good terms. And Sophie, still doing a hopeful juggling act, always welcomed him warmly.

One morning when he didn't appear she went to seek him out in his office. Strictly speaking she should have been properly announced before walking in on the crown princess's private secretary while he was reading the royal correspondence. But while Sophie stuck rigidly to protocol for others, she blithely ignored it to suit herself.

"My dear," Randolph said, rising to kiss her cheek. "It's good to see you looking so well."

She was at her best, blazing with life and health, and elegant in her riding habit. She kissed him back, cheekily, on the mouth, lingering just a moment too long, so that he gently disengaged himself.

"Prince Harold would not approve," he said lightly.

She shrugged. "Oh, nothing's settled. But he'll be here soon."

"Sophie be careful," he said, meaning only to be kind. "Harold is a cold, unscrupulous man. He won't treat you well if it suits him not to."

"Whatever do you mean?"

"I mean he may be after bigger fish. He still wants the throne of Elluria."

"As do you," she said with a brittle laugh. "You'd better marry the silly creature quickly before she realizes what you're really after."

"Don't talk like that," he said in a voice he'd never used to her before. "I forbid you ever to mention the subject again. It's an insult to her and an insult to me."

Sophie shrugged, not disconcerted, as Dottie would have been, by the bleak winter that had come over Randolph. She'd miscalculated, but she would recover. She perched on a corner of his desk and glanced over the letters there. Randolph didn't notice, being occupied in arranging coffee for her, to atone for his ill temper. By the time he dismissed the servant and looked back into the room Sophie was tearing open a small packet.

"What are you doing?" he demanded. "You can't open her letters."

"Why not? It's from England. You couldn't have given it to her anyway. It's probably from her lover. Read it and throw it away."

Examining the wrapping Randolph saw, with a sinking heart, that it was postmarked Wenford.

Sophie gave a shriek of laughter. "Listen to this…'Dottie, love—'"

"Give me that," Randolph snapped, tearing it from her hands. "How the devil am I going to explain to her that it's been opened?"

"I thought it was your job."

"Not her private letters."

"She shouldn't be getting private letters from her lover. Just don't give it to her."

"I shall give it to her, because I won't betray her trust."

"She wouldn't know."

"She would if you grew careless and—shall we say?—let it slip."

"*Me?* Do such a thing?"

"I'm not sure, but I'm beginning to realize that I never really knew you Sophie." He gave her a level gaze that would have alarmed a more perceptive woman. "Perhaps you and Harold will go well together after all."

She smiled. "Don't you think I'll make a splendid Princess Consort?"

"Only for him. Not for me. I don't think you should come here again."

There was no mistaking his meaning. Sophie scowled, understanding that this game, at least, was lost.

"I'll leave you then," she snapped, snatching up her riding hat and marching out so forcefully that the servant, bringing coffee, was forced to flatten himself against the doorjamb.

Chapter Nine

Left alone with the letter in his hands Randolph clenched his fingers slowly so that the paper was scrunched and only *Dottie, love* was showing.

It wasn't too bad, he told himself. Mike might have written "My darling," or something intense. On second thoughts, no. Intensity wasn't his style. For him, "Dottie, love" was the height of passionate abandon. And she would understand it that way.

If he gave it to her.

He shut off the thought at once. She'd already made it insultingly clear that she didn't trust him. This would simply prove her right, and if she didn't know it, he would.

Without further delay he went to her apartments, marching in without waiting to be announced. Dottie had been contentedly munching breakfast, wrapped in a large pink toweling robe. She choked over her coffee and drew the robe more firmly around her. Her movement was just fast enough to leave him in doubt whether she was wearing anything underneath.

Inwardly he cursed the bitter fate that had made her a sexy imp who could get under his skin without trying to. What was a man to do who'd had one glimpse of the loveliest body on earth, and then been haunted by it, day and night, ever since. The sight was there in his dreams, and with it a rich chuckle at some absurdity of life that he'd never noticed before, but would never forget now, because it reminded him of her. He would awaken to find himself trembling, aching in his loins with a deprivation that only one thing could ease. And that was something he couldn't have.

By day it was even worse, for he would be with her, always at a disadvantage, struggling not to let her suspect feelings that shocked him because he couldn't master them. A lifetime of discipline and control, all set at nothing because this exasperating creature had a smile of wine and honey and a wicked gleam in her eyes. But she hadn't overcome him yet, and he would make sure she didn't.

He coped by keeping their meetings brief, businesslike and sometimes harsh on his side. It frustrated him, but it was his only protection.

"Do you mind?" Dottie asked belligerently.

"I shan't disturb you for long. I merely wished to give you this," he held out the letter, "and to apologize for the error which led to it being opened. It fell in with all the other official correspondence."

"Oh yeah?" she said, looking at the postmark. "You saw Wenford and assumed it was 'official correspondence'?"

"It was an accident, ma'am, but one for which I wish to apologize."

Dottie was examining the rest of the packet, which turned out to contain a piece of wedding cake, and some wedding photos.

"He didn't waste much time," she murmured. "Nice of him to send me some cake."

"May I suggest that letters from your ex-fiancé are inappropriate?" he said, putting as much frozen propriety into the words as he could manage.

She didn't answer at first. She was studying a picture of the bride and groom, happily lost in each other. Looking over her shoulder Randolph felt nauseated by Mike's gaze of foolish fondness for the commonplace creature he'd preferred to the magical Dottie. It made no difference that he himself had pushed them together. Mike should have treasured his enchanting fiancée, and never looked at another woman, no matter what the provocation.

Dottie's face bore a look of sadness. "They look very happy together," she said wistfully.

"Would it have been that way with you and him?" Randolph couldn't stop himself asking.

"Oh no, you were right about that. And he was right, too. She suits him better. It's just, they're daft about each other, like people should be on their wedding day," she added wistfully.

"You speak like someone who's given up on happiness."

"On that kind, yes. You shouldn't be surprised. You brought me to a place where it doesn't happen anymore."

He knew his next words were unwise but all the wisdom in the world couldn't have stopped him saying them. "That's not true Dottie. This can be a happy place."

"It'll never be happy for me," she said quietly.

There was an ache in her voice that he couldn't bear. He would have given anything, if only she could smile again. But she was looking into the distance, murmuring, "A cozy little home and a cozy little husband. This place isn't cozy."

"No, it's not. But as I told you before, you're meant for something bigger."

"It's all right, I'm not fighting anymore. At least, I'm not fighting my destiny, or whatever you want to call it."

"Then what?"

"You. I'll always fight you."

"Because you don't trust me?"

"Because I thought I *could* trust you, before I discovered that I couldn't. That's worse than knowing from the start. But it doesn't matter, does it? Because feelings don't matter and people don't matter."

"I never thought I'd hear you talking like this. I don't like it."

"Well you did it," she said with a little sigh. "I learned my lesson well, didn't I? But this—" she held up the letter and an edge returned to her voice, "this is out of order. Don't you ever dare read my private letters again."

Her swift change from wistful to autocratic caused a revulsion of feeling in him. "I did not read your letter," he said, tight-lipped.

"Oh yeah? You opened it and you didn't read it?"

"I didn't—" He stopped, realizing that the truth would lead to more trouble.

"Didn't what?" Light dawned. "You didn't open it? Then who did."

"It was an accident."

"Who opened it?"

"Sophie," he said unwillingly. "She was trying to help. She didn't know—"

"You let Sophie read my correspondence?"

"I didn't mean it to happen."

"Oh please!" she said bitterly. "Did I give the pair of you a good laugh?"

"Don't call me a liar," he said in a dangerously quiet voice. "Don't ever do that."

"You're saying that you haven't read one word of this letter?"

"Only the first two, which strike me as highly unsuitable for you to receive from your ex-lover and a married man. If that had fallen into the wrong hands—"

"As far as I'm concerned it already has."

"She only saw the start, I'm sure of it."

"Yes," Dottie said in a strange voice, "Now I'm sure of it, too." She was reading the letter. "I think you should hear this."

"There's no need," he said tensely. "I don't want to know what passes between you." If only this were true!

"Oh, but I think you should hear every word," Dottie said, with a light in her eye that troubled him. "Then you can tell me how 'unsuitable' it is for me to receive it." She began to read. "Dottie love, thought you'd like to know the end of the story. Wedding went off great. Hope you like the cake. Garage is smashing. Am definitely pregnant. Love from 'all three' of us. Best, Brenda."

When she'd finished there was silence. Randolph looked at her while his reactions warred in him. He felt foolish for having been so completely caught out, but greater still was the feeling of joy. She wasn't exchanging love letters with Mike.

But he couldn't read her. He knew Dottie's gift for "seeing the funny side," but would it rise to this?

"I think perhaps I'll publish this in the court circular," she said with grim hilarity, "so that everyone can see what an efficient secretary I have."

He gave a small, formal bow. "That, of course, is Your Royal Highness's privilege."

"Don't you dare talk to me like that!"

"Well, anything I say or do now is going to be wrong, isn't it?"

"And stop trying to cut the ground out from under my feet."

"I had it cut out pretty comprehensively under mine. Let's face it, Dottie, the joke's on me. Why not just enjoy it?"

As the import of these words dawned on her she felt her anger drain away out of the soles of her feet. It was unbelievable, impossible. "Randolph, are you actually going to stand there and tell me that you've seen a joke against yourself? *You?*"

"I suppose I am. It must be your influence." His lips twitched. "I'm sorry, Dottie. I really am."

"So you should be. Oh heavens!" She finally yielded to her laughter, and he joined in. Laughing at himself was a new experience, but he found he got the hang of it fairly easily.

"That's better," she said. "You see, you can do it." She put her hands on his shoulders and gave him a little shake, and the next moment he'd enfolded her in a bear hug.

"Dottie, Dottie…" He scarcely knew what he was saying, only that it was wonderful to hold her close in a moment of affectionate companionship.

If he tried hard he could believe that was all it was, but in no time he knew it had been a mistake to hold her against his body. The toweling robe was thick, but not thick enough to make him unaware of her nakedness beneath, or to stop him responding to it. He began the movement that would push her away, but it turned to a caress so light that he hoped she wouldn't feel it.

Dottie was so happy to have gotten rid of the hostility between them that she tightened her arms, hugging him with all her might. In return she thought she felt the lightest touch on the top of her head, as though a kiss had been dropped there. She looked up quickly, finding his face just above hers, and it seemed to her fancy that he looked like a man who'd just kissed someone and wanted to do so again. He was trembling, but not as hard as she was.

But then his hands were firm on her shoulders, pushing her away. "I'm sure you have a busy day ahead, ma'am."

"No I haven't. I've got a free morning. Let's go riding."

Her eyes were wide and hopeful, full of an offer to forget their quarrel, and return to the time when they had been at ease. Wouldn't a good secretary accept that offer and be on friendly terms with his future sovereign? For the sake of the country?

The temptation hung before him, dazzling him with offers of beauty and excitement: to ride with her under the trees, to walk beside the water where she'd once kissed him, in the days when he'd still been blind to what was so clear now, to laugh and be happy and forget duty.

With a sigh he came down to earth. She was dangerous. She threatened his control.

"It sounds lovely, but your secretary must spend the day serving your interests."

"Oh, all right. Spoilsport. Now push off while I get dressed."

"Of course." He extended his hand. "Friends?"

She took it. "Friends."

It came nowhere near the truth, but it would have to do for now.

The state visit was arranged for six weeks ahead. While preparations went on behind the scenes Dottie's ministers decided to capitalize on her growing popularity by introducing her to the country. She found her schedule full of visits to hospitals, factories, schools.

Often she had to stay overnight. These were fun occasions that she used to get to know her ladies, who were mostly young and lively. The exception was Duchess Alicia Gellin, an elderly widow with a reputation as a battle-ax. Dottie's sharp eyes saw the loneliness beneath the crusty surface, and insisted on appointing her.

It turned out to be an inspired choice. Alicia knew more gossip than the rest of the court put together, and she kept Dottie in the know better than any security service.

On one hospital visit she outlined the timetable, ten minutes for this ward, fifteen minutes for that, five minutes with the matron and an hour with the governors. But Dottie was unable to leave a children's ward in less than half an hour. She started singing a children's song from her own childhood and soon they were all singing it. Every verse ended with a command to start again from the beginning, and it seemed as if they would be there forever. Patients who could walk wandered in to see what the noise was about, and stayed to sing. Young doctors joined in with gusto. One of them winked at Dottie, and she winked back. The song ended only when they were all too weary to go on.

After a while the visits blended seamlessly into each other, the same rides through the streets, the same smiles and cheers. Then there would be dinner with the local dignitaries, during which Dottie could practice being the one to direct the conversation. This was mentally exhausting as it was always up to her to produce new ideas. Luckily Alicia seemed to have relatives wherever they stopped and was a mine of local information. Of course, her secretary would have been even better, but Randolph had contrived to excuse himself on the grounds of pressing work.

After dinner she would sit up with one or two of her ladies, chatting with the top level of her mind, while the rest of it wondered what Randolph was doing at this moment.

One day her driver, confused in a strange place, took a wrong turn and went too far down a narrow street to be able to turn around. Seeking a way out, he drove on and on, until Dottie found herself in a nightmare place.

"It looks as though they've had a fire," she said,

getting out. "At least three streets have gone. But why don't they do something?"

"Because the council's taken all the money," said a surly voice nearby. It belonged to a shabby man who seemed to be living in the ruins of a house.

"Tell me about it," Dottie said at once.

The houses belonged to the local council, and had caught fire years ago. The government had voted money to rebuild but the council bickered endlessly about which department had the right to spend it, while the inhabitants stayed homeless. As the man spoke, more and more people came close and stood listening. Soon there were enough to form a dangerous mob, had they been so inclined. But none of them moved. They were watching Dottie. They knew her face from pictures. Suddenly they had new hope.

By now her official escort had managed to catch up with her, full of profuse apologies, eager to whisk her away, the story half-told. Dottie saw the expressions in the crowd change to cynical. Now she would leave and forget them. She couldn't bear it. Impulsively she spread her hands.

"Don't worry," she told. "I'm going to get this sorted."

There was a sharp intake of breath from close by, but it was drowned by the cheers from the crowd. They believed her.

"Now you've got a tiger by the tail," Alicia observed as they talked that night. "Sternheim is the local 'great man' around her. The ruling clique on the council are mostly his buddies. He protects them and they do as they like."

"Why doesn't the local newspaper make a fuss?"

"He owns it."

It didn't surprise Dottie to find, on arriving home, that Sternheim had been in urgent consultation with Randolph.

"Don't tell me," she said, holding up her hands at the sight of Randolph. "The future queen isn't supposed to make promises, but I've made it now and I have to keep it and that means—"

"Dottie—"

"—that it doesn't matter what Sternheim or anyone else says."

"Dottie—"

"I don't even care what the rules say because—"

"Dottie, will you pipe down and let someone else get a word in edgeways?" he roared.

"Just as long as I've made myself clear."

"Blindingly. Now will you please tell me what happened and how you managed to get Sternheim so rattled."

"He's rattled? Great!" She told him the whole story. "Alicia says he's the local great man. Local pig if you ask me. Anyway, he's got them all by the short and curlies." Randolph winced. "You know what I mean."

"Yes I do, and I beg you not to use that expression to anyone but me."

"Never mind that," she told him impatiently. "Tell me what I can do. What about a decree?"

"No decrees," he said at once. "A decree is a blunt instrument. Save it for a big occasion."

"I only—"

"Button it, and listen. Sternheim will be here in a minute. He'll have heard you're back and he won't waste time."

"Good. I want a word with him."

"No!"

"Yes."

"Dottie, you can't accuse him. It would cause a scandal. He mustn't even suspect that you know of his involvement. There are other ways. I'll talk to him. You don't say a word."

"Oh don't I?" she said, bristling.

"No, because if you do you'll ruin everything, and the people who will suffer will be the ones you've promised to help."

That silenced her, he noticed with a touch of respect. "You leave it to me," he said.

The last words were spoken in a tone that brooked no argument, and for a moment she could see Randolph as the king he should have been. But she couldn't say anything because Sternheim appeared at that moment, bristling with barely suppressed annoyance. But Randolph would put it right, Dottie thought with a surge of confidence.

When the civilities had been gotten out of the way Randolph said, in the smooth voice of a diplomat, "Chancellor, I'm sure you appreciate that our princess is young and unfamiliar with her new duties, and she was wholly unaware of the impropriety of her..."

He managed to make it last for five minutes, during which Dottie stared at him, sick with disillusion. How could he be doing this? Not to her, but to the innocent victims of fire and corruption.

Sternheim was relaxing visibly as the emollient words poured from Randolph. Gradually a smile spread over his smug features.

"I'm sure we can all consider the matter settled," Randolph said at last, "once we've dealt with the small matter of presentation."

"What's that?" Sternheim demanded.

"Her Royal Highness gave a promise in public. People will be watching to see what happens, so we must make it seem as if things are being done. I suggest a commission of inquiry, with full powers to investigate and summon witnesses. They'll speak to the unfortunate residents and everyone on the council, and the accounts department will explain exactly what's happened to the money, and the world will be satisfied."

As he listened to this speech Sternheim's smile had faded and his skin turned an ugly gray. Watching him, Dottie realized that Randolph had pulled a masterstroke. Without uttering a single accusation he'd lured the minister into a trap from which there was only one escape.

"A commission of inquiry," Sternheim said, almost stuttering. "But that'll take time."

"Months," Randolph confirmed. "Since every detail must be uncovered."

"But where are these poor people supposed to live in the meantime?" Sternheim blustered.

"In the ruins, where they're living now," Dottie couldn't resist saying.

"Shocking! Shocking!" Sternheim stammered hastily.

"Your concern does you credit," Randolph told him, "but what else can we do?"

"I know a few people on that council," Sternheim said. "I could put a rocket behind them."

"And get rebuilding started quickly?"

"In a few days. And temporary accommodation for those poor unfortunates in the meantime. Much better than a lengthy commission. Leave it all to me." Sternheim looked at Dottie who was giving him an alarming smile. "Happy to, er, be of service."

"I'm sure Her Royal Highness won't object if you left now," Randolph said. "You'll be wanting to get on with things."

Sternheim mopped his brow and bowed himself out. Randolph turned to Dottie with an air of triumph, and their eyes met. *Yes!*

"You did it," she crowed.

"No, we did it," he said firmly. "I did the talking but you provided the substance."

"Will it work?"

"I think we can look for the bulldozers to start clearing the site double quick, and the building work to proceed soon after. And when things are well under way, and it's too late to stop them—" he looked at her with almost a touch of mischief.

"What?" she breathed.

"Then we'll send in the commission."

Her eyes widened. "But... Didn't you just make a deal with Sternheim?"

"No, but I let him think I did."

"Oh, Randolph," she breathed in awe, "you really know how to fight dirty."

"Thank you, ma'am," he said, correctly interpreting this as a compliment. "I think we've got him by the, er, short and curlies."

She crowed with laughter, then sobered and admitted, "You do this better than me."

"Let's just say we're a good team."

"The best."

She moved toward him, her hands outstretched. In another moment she would have thrown her arms about his neck, forgetting everything except that he was wonderful. But then it seemed to her that he flinched and took a half step back. His eyes were fond and smiling, but there was no doubt that he had avoided making contact with her. After their perfect communication it felt like a snub, and her happiness faded.

But not entirely. The moment might have been brief, but it had happened, and she could treasure it.

Even with a kind of truce things were never going to be smooth between them. He was naturally imperious and she was learning fast. Power, Dottie discovered, was the sweetest thing in the world. Better even than ice cream.

Her intervention about the rebuilding had been a triumph. The papers carried the story of, "I'm going to get this sorted," and the sudden activity next day was proof, as though anybody needed it, that Princess Dottie kept her word.

Her success gave her an appetite for more intervention, with varied results. Sometimes she achieved something, more often she misread an unfamiliar situation and put her foot in it. Randolph always managed to smooth things over, but her ministers were beginning to regard her with alarm, and Randolph told her crisply that while she might think of herself as Joan of Arc she actually resembled a loose cannon, blundering across everyone's toes. After that the atmosphere became chilly again.

There was so much to be put right about this country, she decided. Increasing the numbers of female politicians was more complicated than she'd thought. It wasn't just the outdated parliamentary hours, but beyond them a whole raft of laws and social conditions that created pointless obstacles to women.

At least, Dottie thought they were pointless. Enderlin spoke of tradition and the need to move slowly. She spoke of the twenty-first century and the need for Elluria to get there without delay. He clutched his head. She poured him cups of strong tea, which he drank and felt better. He was a courtly, gracious man who never allowed their battles to affect his liking for Dottie, nor allowed that liking to make him yield easily. Soon they could exchange prejudices freely, while staying friends. When things reached crisis point Randolph was called in to referee.

He did so reluctantly. "Can't you cope with her yourself?" he demanded.

"Nobody can cope with her," Enderlin groaned. "Her new idea is to reorganize the civil service training so that everyone can learn to do gardening, which, apparently, is good for the soul."

"She's winding you up," Randolph said, exasperated. "Can't you recognize it yet? If you react she just gets worse."

"I am not used to being 'wound up' by my sovereign," Enderlin replied with dignity. "And I'm too old to start now."

"Nonsense! My father enjoyed practical jokes."

"So he did," Enderlin said, much struck. "I'd forgotten. It's just that from a woman it somehow sounds strange."

"Don't say that to her," Randolph begged in alarm. "She'll give you a speech about equal rights, and this time she *won't* be joking."

"I have to admit that she brightens the place up. I accompanied her on a recent trip to my hometown and she insisted on walking through the streets and talking to the crowd. She noticed a child in a push chair, who'd lost a shoe, and blow me if she didn't pick the shoe up from the pavement and put it on the kiddy's foot herself, then chat to the mother for five minutes about the outrageous price of children's clothes.''

''She didn't promise to 'sort' them as well did she?'' asked Randolph, alarmed.

''No, I managed to intervene just in time. But, to be fair, it's not anything she says. It's what she is. She gives them that smile…you know the one.''

''Yes,'' Randolph said quietly. ''I know the one.''

''It seems to bring the sun out for them. Mind you, I'm not sure if that's what a monarch is supposed to do…''

''Could a monarch do better than make the sun shine on her people?'' Randolph asked, still in the same quiet voice. ''It's a great gift, and she has it.''

''Well, I don't deny that she's lovable, and maybe that's important.''

Randolph nodded. ''And maybe it's the only thing that matters.''

''If only somebody could reign her in.''

His significant voice and look brought Randolph out of the semitrance in which he'd been wandering. A horrible suspicion of having betrayed himself made him explode, ''Forget that idea now and never mention it again.''

''But your duty to your country…''

Randolph said something very rude about his duty to his country. Enderlin shook his head, trying to believe he'd really heard what he thought he had, but he couldn't manage it.

"You've never failed in your duty before," he pleaded.

"Ideas of duty vary, Enderlin. I'm doing mine now by trying to teach this crazy woman how to occupy the throne without blowing it up. But I recognize no duty to marry someone who goes through life like a jumping bean. And if my countrymen think otherwise, they are welcome to try it for themselves. Let me make it quite clear to you that she is the last woman I would ever dream of marrying. And that's official."

Then, calming down just a little, he added hurriedly, "But you'll never repeat that to anyone."

Enderlin promised and kept his word. But walls have ears and the story reached Dottie by the end of the day, and duly affected the atmosphere. It was a measure of how far she'd traveled that instead of treating Randolph to her frank opinion of him she merely smiled sweetly at their next meeting, and left him wondering.

Chapter Ten

The first time Dottie saw a picture of Prince Harold she thought there had been a mistake.

"But he's supposed to be a monster. Wow, what a hunk!"

The man in the picture had everything to attract the female fancy, including a brilliant smile, regular features and eyes that seemed to gleam with fun. His mouth was full and sensual, and his body, as another picture revealed, was tall and lean.

"He looks good on horseback," she observed, picking up a third. "You did say that I'd be going riding with him, didn't you?"

"I don't believe your schedule includes it, no," Randolph said coldly.

She looked at him but he didn't return her gaze. His attention was absorbed in some papers and even the set of his shoulders seemed forbidding. She grew cross. Which of them was the boss here?

"Better fix it so that it does," she said coolly.

"That is impossible. The schedule has been laid down and agreed with the Korburg embassy. It cannot be changed now."

"Rubbish, you changed it only yesterday. I know you did."

He still didn't look up but the back of his head clearly revealed his irritation. "And I'm not changing it again," he said through gritted teeth.

"You're not? Don't I get a say?"

"You get too big a say as it is."

"My people have no complaints. Ask them."

"Oh yes, I've seen the latest opinion polls. They see you visiting sick children and homeless shelters, and they adore you because you do it wonderfully well."

"That's not all I do."

"No, some of your meddling has been lucky."

"Meddling? How dare you!"

"What about the mayor of Sellingen?"

"I apologized for that."

"And the wretched little man whom you decided was running a disorderly house?"

"It was a misunderstanding. He forgave me. Those roses over there come from his garden."

Yes, that was it, Randolph thought, exasperated. She made the most outrageous mistakes, brought them all to the edge of disaster and her victims sent her roses.

"You jump in with both feet, never stopping to ask questions first, and count on people only remembering your successes," he said. "There are rules that govern these things, just as there are rules that govern every aspect of your life now. The sooner you get used to that the better.''

"Oh, I know about the rules. It doesn't mean I'm going to lie down under every single one. Maybe I can change some of them.''

"Then you will do it after due consultation with me,'' he said bluntly. "And don't threaten me with a decree or any of that nonsense.''

"I've never actually issued one yet, just talked about it.''

"Yes, because you rely on the threat to bring people to heel. I give you credit for trying. But often you're not trying in the right way.''

"You mean I'm not doing it your way. But why should I?''

"Because I happen to know a great deal more about what this country needs than someone who's still playing games.''

"If that's what you think I wonder you tolerate me here at all. Send me back and have Harold. I'm sure he knows what he's doing.''

She could have bitten her tongue off as soon as the words were out. Randolph's eyes grew cold with contempt.

"I thought better of you than that. Blackmail. Cheap, and despicable.''

She knew it and would have given anything to unsay the words. But she couldn't admit it to the bitterly contemptuous man who turned his scorn on her now.

"You're playing at being queen, Dottie. No more than that. Don't turn away from me.'' He seized her arm as she turned and pulled her unceremoniously back to face him.

"Let me go," she snapped.

"Not till you've heard me out."

"Let me go at once, or I'll scream and bring the guards in."

"I'm trembling."

"You should. 'Laying unauthorized hands' on the monarch is high treason. You taught me that."

"Why, you cheeky little—"

"Calling the monarch names is probably treason, too. I'm sure I could find a law about it somewhere. But I won't need to. You won't risk me calling the guards. Think how undignified it would be."

In the silence his hand fell from her arm. Nothing in his lifelong training had prepared him for this situation, and his outrage and confusion were almost tangible.

Dottie took advantage of it to say, "You have our permission to leave."

"What?"

"The crown princess gives you her permission to leave."

"Dottie, you're beginning to do it very well but—"

"You will address me as Your Royal Highness, and you will not approach me again until I say so."

She was shocked by her own temerity. After a stunned moment Randolph stepped away, bowed his head, clicked his heels and departed without a backward glance.

Everybody knew. In less than an hour the news of the breach had gone through the palace. By the next day everyone knew that it was worse than that. Prince Randolph had waited one day to give her the chance to summon him. When she didn't, he'd taken off to his estate in a terrible rage.

"He was just like this as a boy," Aunt Liz recalled. "There were dreadful storms, when it was best to keep out of his way. But don't worry. Just give him a little time to calm down, then send for him again."

"In a pig's eye I'll send for him."

"Then you seem condemned to perpetual stalemate," Aunt Liz said crossly.

"No way. He'll bring me the papers tomorrow as usual, and I'll let him know that he's forgiven."

"For what?"

"For incurring my royal displeasure," Dottie said with a chuckle.

There was something to be said for being royal. You could win every argument.

But next morning there was no sign of Randolph. His assistant appeared with a message to say that he'd been called away unexpectedly to settle a matter of administration in the princess's service. He would deal with it speedily, and on his return would give himself the honor of reporting to her, etcetera. Dottie made a suitable response, and wished she could have Randolph there for just five minutes, to tell him what she thought of him.

He was gone four days, then five, then a week. Dottie, who'd prepared a dignified speech, grew infuriated at never being able to deliver it.

When he did return after a week, and a servant came to say that he would wait upon her, she was so annoyed that she sent a message to say that she would inform him when it was convenient for her to see him.

After that there was silence.

"Why doesn't he report to me?" she demanded of Aunt Liz.

"Because you told him not to. Do you think a man of Randolph's pride is going to risk another snub?"

"Okay, so he can just sit there and sulk."

"Yes, and you can sit here and sulk. And that'll make two of you sulking while the country goes to rack and ruin. I've no patience with either of you. Call him up and tell him how much you've missed him."

"No way."

"Dottie, why ever not?"

"Because I'm the crown princess," she said miserably.

Somehow being royal was no guard against feeling that the world was empty because one man wasn't there. There had been nothing between them but kisses, anger and the half-admitted flaring of desire, but now she longed for more. Kisses weren't enough. She ached for him.

She wanted to know if his body, beneath his clothes, was as hard and athletic as she suspected. She'd had so little opportunity to find out, and the thought tormented her night and day. She wanted him to kiss her deeply, powerfully, and then do more than kiss her. She wanted him to take her wherever passion could lead them. She wanted him to show her the whole world.

But he wasn't there.

As Harold's visit neared, there was a series of meetings between politicians and civil servants, which Dottie insisted on attending. She wanted to know every detail of the arrangements. There were receptions, a state banquet and a ball in Harold's honor. There would be a performance at the State Opera House, and Harold would be asked to give a speech to parliament. So far so good.

But Harold also wanted to visit Korenhausen, a magnificent country mansion, where his grandmother had been born.

"He couldn't stand the old lady," Sternheim snapped. "What's he playing at?"

"I suppose he wants to stand there looking 'deeply affected' for the sake of the photographers," Durmand said. "And to remind everyone that he has Ellurian royal blood."

"So have I, and I come from an older line, which is why I'm here and he isn't," said Dottie, who'd been studying hard. "Let him do what he wants. Is there anything else?"

"Just one thing ma'am," Durmand said. "It'll be hard to—"

"What is it?" Dottie asked. Not only had Durmand stopped but his eyes, and those of every other man in the room, were riveted on the door. Turning, she saw Randolph standing there with a brow like thunder.

"Out, all of you," he said curtly.

His manner was so grim and purposeful that every man around the table forgot that Randolph was officially a nobody, and rose to leave the room. Dottie rose too, to confront him indignantly. But instead of being impressed by his sovereign's wrath he took firm hold of her arm.

"I didn't tell you to leave," he said.

"What?"

"I said stay here."

The door closed behind the last man.

"And just what do you think you're doing?" she demanded.

"I came to commit high treason," he said, pulling her into his arms and silencing her mouth with his own.

The sudden granting of what she'd yearned for was a stunning shock, obliterating everything except sensation. It was glorious to have his lips against her own again, thrilling to feel the implicit promise in his movements, and despite her indignation she felt herself yielding to temptation.

But then, having let her glimpse wonders, he slammed the door again, drawing back a few inches, but keeping hold of her shoulders.

"Don't you ever keep me out again," he growled.

Her temper flared. "And don't you tell me what to do. I'm the queen."

"Not until your coronation, and not if I wring your neck first."

"As if!" she scoffed.

He was holding her just far enough away so that she could see his intense, blazing eyes. This wasn't the Randolph she knew, the urbane, worldly wise aristocrat, or the friend and mentor whose exasperation with her was usually tinged with wry amusement. This was a man driven beyond endurance, no longer in command of himself. Something stirred in her— not quite alarm, but certainly a feeling of danger. She realized suddenly how helpless she was, alone with him, now that he was too angry to be careful. She hadn't known that danger could be so thrilling.

"I have spent the last two days twiddling my thumbs, waiting for *Your Royal Highness* to deign to remember my existence." Randolph said the words with savage emphasis. "Do you really think you can treat me like that and get away with it? Because if so, you're living in cloud-cuckoo-land."

"Is this the man who told me to remember my royal dignity?"

"Not with me—"

"Yes, even with you."

"Careful Dottie. You're letting power go to your head."

"That's what it's for!" she yelled.

"You have so much to learn. Don't ever insult me like that again, because I promise you I won't be a gentleman about it."

"Is this you being a gentleman?"

"This is me letting you know what I will and will not put up with, and what I will *not* put up with is being ignored by you while the entire court sniggers at me. Do you understand?"

"I would have seen you any time the week before, but you weren't there," she cried. "You were sulking at your estate."

"I do not sulk."

"Well, it sure looked like it to me."

His eyes glinted. He'd spent the past few weeks learning deference to this maddening woman, but the lessons had come very hard to him. Suddenly it all fell away and he was once more *Prince* Randolph, reared to pride and arrogance from the day of his birth. "I don't let anyone talk to me like that," he said softly.

"I just did."

"And you won't do so again. Not if you know what's good for you."

She grew lofty. "Have you forgotten who you're talking to?"

"*I* haven't forgotten, but I think *you* have—Dottie Hebden, who used to be charming but has gotten much too big for her boots."

"No, I'm just wearing bigger boots. Why should you complain? You put them on me. I'm not 'little Dottie Hebden' anymore, Randolph. She vanished. If you don't like the new me, tough. You created me. I'm Crown Princess Dorothea, soon to be Queen Dorothea III, and you could get a life sentence for assaulting my royal person!"

"Then I may as well be hung for a sheep as a lamb," he muttered, tightening his grip.

"How dare you—"

"Shut up." He covered her mouth again.

This time there was no doubt that her royal person was being assaulted. He was doing what he wanted, and to hell with her objections! She should have been full of righteous indignation at this disrespect, but she wasn't. She didn't want respect. She wanted excitement. She wanted to be made aware of her own body as never before. She wanted what he was doing now, forcing her to recognize him as a man responding to her as a woman.

It was the first unambiguous proof she'd had that he desired her as much as she desired him, and she rejoiced in it. He wasn't faking the fierce movements of his lips, and the knowledge went through and through her with thrills of pleasure that seemed to be everywhere at once.

He wore no jacket, and through the thin material of his shirt she could feel his heated body, hard as a rock. There was no way she could have struggled against the strength in his arms, even if she'd wanted to. There was more than desire in this. He was showing her where the power really lay, so that she wouldn't kid herself about it. But there were other ways to demonstrate power. He'd chosen this one because he wanted her as much as she did him, on a basic level that had nothing to do with their fights. And he, too, was kidding himself if he thought he could kiss her like this and forget about it. There was no going back now.

Randolph couldn't have defined what had overtaken him, except that it had been a long time coming. He'd taken other orders from her and learned to grin and bear it. But no more!

"You can keep anyone else out," he growled. "But not me."

"You won't get in here another time," she murmured, deliberately provoking him.

"I'll get in no matter how many doors I have to break down. Why don't you call your guards and have me arrested?"

"For what?" she whispered.

"For this," he said tightening his arms again and kissing her lightly, swiftly, caressing her face with his lips while he murmured to her, "You're a fool, Dottie—but I'm a fool, too...."

His tongue was flickering against her lips, until she let them fall open. She was winning. At any moment—

And then she felt him stiffen, heard the swift muttered curse as he drew away from her, and her hopes came crashing down.

The door had opened, and all the men who had so spinelessly abandoned her to this predator were creeping sheepishly back, having belatedly remembered which one of them was the monarch. Now they looked distinctly nervous at the prospect of challenging Randolph.

"It's all right," he said. "I'd finished." He released Dottie abruptly. His face was pale and his chest was still rising and falling, but he'd regained control of himself. As he made his way to the door, there was a touch of nonchalance in his manner.

"You can get on with your meeting now," he said. And he walked out.

Korburg was a small state just over the border, and unlike Elluria it was not a kingdom, only a principality. As such, it was a "poor relation" and not strictly entitled to the full panoply of honors for a state visit. But Dottie insisted on them. She had a point to make.

On the day of Harold's arrival she was waiting on the carpeted platform as his train glided in, to the accompaniment of the Korburg national anthem. The double doors of the special train slid open, and a man stepped out who was everything his picture had suggested, and more.

Dottie advanced the length of the red carpet to greet him. Flashbulbs went off as the press recorded their meeting. He took her hand in both of his and gave her a big, charming smile. For a brief moment she was overwhelmed by this dazzling, attractive man.

But the moment passed. Dottie hadn't been a waitress and a barmaid without learning how to read men's smiles. The mouth stretched but the eyes calculated. Will she, won't she? Fair game, anyway. Despite his splendid looks there was something disagreeable about him.

I'd enjoy slapping your face, my lad, she thought.

But for the moment she had to defer that pleasure, and greet him with the appearance of friendliness. Then they must sit side by side in the open carriage, drawn by four white horses, and parade through the streets of Wolfenberg while crowds waved and cheered.

"Already you have won your people's hearts," Harold said. "I congratulate you on your success."

She responded appropriately, but she wasn't fooled. He was here to look her over and if he could find any sign of weakness he would pounce. But Dottie was equally determined that he would find nothing.

He was there for three packed days. That night there was a state banquet at which they sat side by side through six courses and ten speeches. They toasted each other. He smiled. She smiled. Randolph did not smile.

Harold paid a sentimental visit to Korenhausen, where he made a short, touching speech. He addressed parliament, with Dottie sitting in the gallery to lead the applause. They didn't ride together because, despite her command, Randolph had mysteriously forgotten to include it in the itinerary. But Harold was her host at a banquet at the Korburg embassy. She was his hostess for a performance of *The Marriage of Figaro* by the Ellurian State Opera. Dottie had gone glassy-eyed at this prospect, having never seen an opera before, but knowing it was bound to be boring. But halfway through the overture she found herself tapping her foot in time to the music, and after that everything was fine.

Harold was charm itself, playing the gallant to Dottie, and kissing her hand at every opportunity until she wished he would stop. He had a big, apparently genial smile which he turned on everyone, but above it his eyes were calculating and he missed nothing. Most of all, he saw that she was popular.

On his last evening there was a ball at the palace. They led the dance while the onlookers applauded.

"I've been eager for this moment," he said.

"But of course. We are both heads of state. It's only proper that we dance together first."

"That's not what I mean, and I think you know it. You're a beautiful woman, and now I have my arms around you, where they belong."

"You're too kind," she murmured. "Of course, I know that your position obliges you to pay me compliments, prince."

"To hell with my position. You inflame me to madness."

Dottie fought down a desire to laugh. Was she supposed to take this stuff seriously?

"I underestimated you," Harold went on, visibly preening himself. "Now that I know you better I believe we can do business."

"Business?" she considered the word. "You mean the kind of business you've been doing with those international companies who want to get at Elluria's minerals?"

"I? How could I do that? The minerals are yours to sell, not mine."

"That's right. So it isn't true?"

"True?"

"That you've been accepting money on the promise of concessions to be delivered when you take over as king of Elluria?''

His face became gray with temper, but Dottie's sunny gaze at him never wavered, and after a moment he laughed.

''Of course it's not true.''

''And it's not true either that certain people are pressing you to cough up or repay the money?''

''Pardon? Cough up?''

''Never mind. I'm sure it's a terrible slander.''

''You know how rumors get around. That wasn't the kind of business I had in mind.'' He tightened his arm about her waist.

''Prince, please,'' she murmured modestly. ''We are observed. People will talk.''

''Underlings. What do their opinions matter? I wish I could make you realize what this visit has meant to me. I'm thinking and feeling so many strange, unexpected things. Do you understand me?''

Perfectly, she thought with grim humor. *I know your kind. Flash Harry! All teeth and trousers!*

But she met his gaze, wide-eyed, and shook her head.

''I thought you wouldn't. You're so new at this game, that's what's enchanting about you.''

She nodded. ''Everyone finds me enchanting since I became a crown princess,'' she confided innocently.

That threw him because he wasn't sure how serious she was. He gave an uncertain smile, wondering if she was daring to make fun of him. Dottie's answering gaze was as guileless as a baby's, and she saw him relax, reassured that she really was as stupid as she'd allowed herself to seem.

"We can't talk now," she murmured, "but later perhaps...on the terrace?"

The music ended. She gave him a dazzling smile and departed for her next dance. For an hour she passed from one distinguished nonentity to the next, making conversation with the top layer of her mind, while the rest noticed when Sophie danced with Harold and when with Randolph.

At last she had a moment to sit down. She leaned toward Jeanie, who was in attendance on her that night. "Ask Prince Randolph if he would like the honor of dancing with me," she commanded regally. She then spoilt the effect by adding, "And tell him he'd better, or else."

A moment later Randolph appeared. "I am bowed down by the honor," he said as he extended his arm.

"I'll stamp on your toes if you talk to me like that," she threatened.

"I see that we still understand each other," he said ironically.

Being in Randolph's arms was nothing like being in Harold's. One man was full of lush compliments, overpoweringly attentive. The other was like a hedgehog. Yet with Harold she'd thought constantly of the moment of escape. With Randolph she thought only of Randolph, of how it would be if he held her close, so that she could feel his body move against her own.

The last time he'd held her was the day he'd stormed into the meeting, when he'd abandoned all control. But now his control was perfect again, and he danced as he did everything, correctly.

"How am I doing for my first state visit?" she asked.

"You're overdoing it," he replied coolly.

"Is that all you've got to say? And I was trying so hard to please you."

"What does it have to do with me?"

"Well, you're my mentor. Practically my father figure." The sudden tightening of his hand in the small of her back was almost imperceptible, but she felt it nonetheless, and it eased her heart. She turned the screw a little. "I rely on your fatherly advice."

"You wouldn't take any advice I could give you Dottie, and if you think I'm going to help you play off your tricks, you're mistaken."

"I don't know what you mean."

"You know exactly what I mean. There's a very shrewd brain underneath that blond fluff. And don't look at me like that either."

"Like what?"

"Bland and innocent."

She laughed. "Perhaps I really am bland and innocent."

"Not you. You're a witch. Dottie, stop it! I told you not to look at me like that."

Her laughter rang out. "Just ignore me. It's easy."

He eyed her with grim appreciation of these tactics. "Be careful," he said softly. "Harold is a dangerous man. If you're doing what I think you are, let me warn you, your people won't stand for it."

"Randolph, you have absolutely no idea what I'm doing, so don't kid yourself."

And he really didn't know, she thought. He was that blind. In fact, he was probably so blind that he wouldn't notice when she slipped away onto the terrace with Harold.

The moment came an hour later, when everyone was being refreshed with champagne. In honor of her distinguished guest Dottie carried two glasses out herself and they sat side by side to toast each other.

"To you, Dottie," he said. "You don't mind if I call you that?"

"No, I still answer to it, with my friends." She didn't say whether he was one of them.

"You've come a long way."

"And I'll bet you know just how far."

"It wasn't easy, but my researchers managed to track down The Grand Hotel. Manageress, eh?"

"Haven't your researchers found out any more?"

"Oh yes. I know you were nothing but a glorified barmaid. Who cares? You are a shrewd, ambitious woman, and I think we understand each other."

"You keep my secret and I keep yours?" she asked archly.

"Precisely. And the best way for us to do that is—" abruptly he pulled her into his arms.

She had to fight not to gag. He was disgusting. She made a movement to box his ears, but stopped herself in time. Don't spoil it now, she thought. She laid her hands gently on his shoulders, as though she was willing but restrained by modesty.

They were like that when Randolph came to find Dottie.

Nothing could have gone better, she thought, lying in bed that night, looking into the darkness. Harold had been nonchalant, the very picture of a ladies' man caught in the act and loving it. Randolph had been furious and unable to say so, although there had been a look of angry reproach in his eyes that thrilled and hurt her at the same time.

She stretched and was about to settle down to sleep when she heard a noise at the French doors that led onto the balcony. She sat up and it came again, the soft movement of the latch, and then the sound of the door being opened, and somebody slipping quietly in.

"What are you doing here?" she cried.

"Sssh!" Harold said urgently, hurrying across the room to the bed. As he reached one side she slid out of the other.

"Keep away from me," she said, feeling around for her robe without taking her eyes from him. Too late she realized that the robe was close to Harold.

He followed her eyes and whisked it up.

"Can I have that please?"

"Of course." He began to move forward.

"Just throw it to me, and get right out."

"You want me to walk out of that door?" he said indicating the door to the outer chamber.

Dottie froze. Out there was a lady-in-waiting, on night duty, and in the corridor outside were two footmen. No way could they be allowed to see Harold leaving her bedroom.

"Leave the way you arrived," she insisted. "Come to think of it, how did you arrive?"

"You don't pay your maid enough."

"You bribed her?"

"It's the simplest way. I got here before you, using the rear corridors. She let me in, I went out to wait on the balcony and she left the windows unlocked, I just crouched down behind the parapet. I thought we could talk better like this."

"I have nothing to say to you."

"I think you have. You like being crown princess,

I've seen it. As my consort, you'll still enjoy all the goodies. We'll both gain.''

"Marry you?" she said in a voice of pure scorn. "You're the last man I'd ever marry."

"My dear, I'm the last man you'll have the chance to marry. Soon everyone will know that I'm here. You'll have no choice. But let's make quite sure, shall we?"

He moved fast but Dottie was faster, slicing her hand across his nose in a swift movement that made him squeal like a pig.

"Right," he said, speaking rather nasally, "if that's how you want it I'm happy to oblige."

Ducking her second blow he grasped her shoulders and pulled her hard against him. At such close range she couldn't fight effectively, and it seemed that nothing could stop him lowering his mouth to hers. He was getting nearer...

"Leave her alone." It was Randolph's voice that cracked like a whip from the shadows.

He stepped forward into the light, his face livid. Behind him Dottie could see four other men.

Time stopped. Dottie freed herself from Harold's frozen hands and stepped back. Cornered, Harold stared around at them all with loathing.

"You're fools, all of you," he raged. "You give your loyalty to that?" He pointed at Dottie. "That? A queen? She's a barmaid, that's all. A cheap, jumped-up little barmaid, giving herself airs. And you fell for it."

Randolph started forward with murder in his eyes, but Dottie moved first.

Her knee came up sharp, hard and aimed with deadly accuracy. Harold fell onto the bed, clutching himself and moaning, while she regarded him with satisfaction.

"I wasn't a barmaid for nothing," she observed.

A cheer went up from her defenders. They laughed and applauded while Dottie clapped a hand over her mouth in horror.

"I shouldn't have said that," she squealed, looking in horror at Randolph.

But he too was laughing. "We are all your friends here," he said. "And we're all proud of you."

As if to prove it the men applauded some more. Looking around she recognized them all as soldiers who'd been her escorts at various times.

"They volunteered," Randolph told her, reading her expression. "Your whole army is loyal to you, but these are 'your' men in a special way." As he spoke he was slipping a robe over her disheveled nightgown.

"How did you all come to be here?" she asked.

"Bertha is more loyal than she seemed. Having pocketed Harold's bribe she came straight to me. I told her not to breathe a word to you, and when you'd gone to bed she let us all in. You were never in any real danger."

"Thank you so much, all of you," she said, spreading her arms wide to the soldiers.

"Don't think you really needed us though," one of them said, provoking a laugh.

Harold was still writhing and choking. Two of them raised him to his feet and would have removed him, but Randolph stopped them.

"My dear cousin," he said tenderly to Harold, "don't go without being the first to congratulate us. Princess Dorothea has honored me by agreeing to become my wife." He turned swiftly to Dottie. "I know you'll forgive me for announcing it like this, but there are reasons why Harold should be the first to know."

The soldiers were in ecstasies. Dottie regarded Randolph with a fulminating eye, but there was nothing she could say in front of an audience.

What had she expected? Moonlight on a rose-strewn balcony? A tender declaration? This was a marriage of state. Yet his kisses had surely told her of something more, and she felt a quickening of excitement, even through her indignation at his high-handed behavior.

At last they were alone, and she confronted Randolph.

"'First to know' is right," she seethed. "Harold knew before I did."

"Nonsense Dottie, you've always known that our marriage was inevitable. You promised to do whatever your country needed. Now you know what it needs, and quickly. We can't take chances. He'll try something else, and we have to spike his guns."

"Of course," she said in a colorless voice.

That was how he saw their marriage, she realized—spiking Harold's guns.

Chapter Eleven

Elluria had never known such celebrations. Two royal weddings, one after another. First Prince Harold of Korburg would marry Sophie Bekendorf in Wolfenberg Cathedral, and the very next day their own Princess Dorothea would be united in wedlock to Prince Randolph. A few weeks after that there would be the coronation. The makers of royal souvenirs were working overtime turning out mugs, tea towels and anything else that they could think of.

Much as she disliked Sophie, Dottie felt sorry for her as she flaunted Harold's huge engagement ring, and boasted of his passionate proposal. Did she know, Dottie wondered, that her future husband was saving face, having failed to seduce Elluria's future queen?

The only story that came out of that night's events was her own betrothal. Randolph had scotched the scandal very effectively. Dottie only wished she knew what other motives he might have had.

These days every spare moment was taken up with preparations for their wedding, and they hardly saw each other except in public. She kept promising herself that she would talk to him privately, but what was there to say? This was a state marriage, and all the talking in the world wouldn't change it.

When they'd discussed a honeymoon he'd suggested Venice, Rome, New York and several other glamorous places. But Dottie had turned them down.

"Too public," she said. "I'd rather go somewhere quiet in Elluria."

Several of his friends offered her the use of their country houses, but Dottie claimed that all of them were too large, too palatial.

At last Randolph said hesitantly, "There's my own estate of Kellensee, but it's little more than a farm."

"Then it'll suit me better than a palace," Dottie said at once.

If he noticed that after raising difficulties about the others she fell in with this suggestion at once, he never said so. A message was sent that night, ordering Kellensee to be prepared.

The question of who was to give her away had caused a few headaches. As she had no close male relatives it was the prerogative of the chancellor, Sternheim. Dottie had groaned and prepared to dig her heels in, but then she'd noticed Sternheim looking at her like a dog expecting to be kicked, and realized that he was terrified of a public rebuff.

Her reaction was to advance on him with hands outstretched, smiling as she said, "Shall we call a truce? You can hardly give me away if we're not speaking, can you?''

Stripped of his usual self-possession, Sternheim stammered out something about being honored, glared furiously at everyone around him and hurried away. The last citadel had fallen to her. Durmand, watching from the sidelines, murmured, ''That's a very clever lady.''

''No,'' Randolph said quietly. ''That's a very kind lady.''

But Dottie heard none of this.

On the day of the first wedding Randolph and Dottie drove together through the streets of Wolfenberg to the cathedral. Soon Harold arrived and took his place before the altar, waiting for his bride.

Dottie had to admit that Sophie was magnificent as she walked down the aisle on her father's arm, her long train streaming behind her. She wondered if Randolph was thinking that this was the day Sophie should have become his wife, but when she stole a glance at him he was brushing something from his sleeve.

It was much worse at the wedding reception when protocol obliged her to dance with Harold while Randolph danced with the bride. Dottie refused to look their way even once, but she couldn't stop her thoughts following them jealously around the floor.

And then the next day it was all to do again, except that this time she was the bride, despairingly conscious that a person of only five foot one could never match Sophie in splendor.

Her snowy dress was lace, specially woven by Elluria's famous lace makers. Her veil was held by a pearl tiara, part of the crown jewels. More pearls hung about her neck and from her ears. Queen Dorothea II had worn these same jewels to her wedding in 1874. Now they adorned Queen Dorothea III, as she would be known after her coronation.

Sounds below told her that Randolph was leaving for the cathedral. She would have stolen a glimpse but a shocked Aunt Liz barred her way to the balcony, uttering dire warnings about "bad luck."

A message from the stables gave her details of the horses that would draw her carriage, led by Jack, the oldest animal in service and coming to the end of his working life. To be drawn by Jack was a promise of good luck.

And she was going to need good luck, she thought. She'd taken a huge gamble to marry the man she loved, uncertain of his true feelings for her. And perhaps she would never truly know. That was the real gamble.

But she would take it and risk the consequences. What was life if you were afraid to seize your chances?

Her procession was a long one. As she stepped outside to be handed into her carriage by Sternheim, proud to bursting point, the leading horsemen were already turning out of the main gates. They were followed by two open carriages containing the six bridesmaids, then a division of the royal cavalry and finally the bridal carriage, escorted by outriders.

And all this was for her, little Dottie Hebden, from Wenford.

She never forgot that drive to the cathedral. She'd known her people had accepted her more readily than she'd dared to hope, but now, as she went through streets lined with cheering crowds, smiling, wishing

her well, she understood how completely they'd taken
her to their hearts. She'd come home. She was eager
to accept this place as home, as hers. She could embrace them, as they had embraced her.

She thought of Randolph and the embrace they
would share that night. And then surely she could win
his heart as he had won hers? She would banish his
last regret about Sophie. At that moment she came
within the sound of the cathedral bells, greeting her
with a wild, joyous clamor, and she smiled in response. Her heart was high and her courage was
enough to dare anything.

In a few minutes they drew up outside the cathedral. Her bridesmaids were waiting to assist her with
her train and the long veil, and then they were all
ready for the walk down the aisle.

The cathedral was large enough to seat over two
thousand, but Dottie saw only one man as she moved
along the red carpet that led to the altar. Randolph
stood, tall and proud, his face turned in her direction.
He didn't smile. If anything, his face was rather stern,
and gave no clue to his thoughts. Perhaps he saw her,
or perhaps he saw another woman, the one he'd really
wanted.

Seeing him from a distance she understood that he
was imposing, not because of his rank but because of
himself. Even without a title he would always draw
the attention of men and women, especially women.
It wasn't merely his fine looks, the handsome set of
his head and his dark, expressive eyes that would attract them. They would look at him with calculating
eyes, reading the promise of pleasure in those long
limbs and hard, narrow hips. They would understand
the power, no less fierce for being concealed by his

formal clothes, and also by the innate restraint of his nature.

She herself didn't fully understand that power, but she suspected it, and the suspicion gave an edge to every thought, every feeling and sensation. As she stepped forward to stand by his side she had never felt more alive.

The ceremony was long and impressive, but it reached her from a distance. All that she was really aware of was Randolph stepping forward, his face paler than she'd ever seen it. He took her hand and for a moment she thought that his was shaking. But she must have imagined that.

In ancient, traditional words they took each other as man and wife. At last the priest smiled, looking from one to the other.

"You may kiss the bride," he said.

Strangely, this was the moment for which she'd been nervous, for she still didn't know on which ground this marriage stood. But when Randolph lifted her veil it was as though the white gauze shut out the world, leaving only themselves. His eyes were kind, full of a question, and she understood, with astonishment, that he was as uncertain as herself.

His lips lay gently on hers for only a moment, but as he drew back they shared a smile that the congregation, murmuring with pleasure, couldn't see.

The organ burst into joy overhead as they turned to go back down the aisle, united.

As they stepped out into the sunlight the crowd cheered their relief. Now they really felt safe from Harold.

The cheering became deafening when Dottie tossed her bouquet high into the air, to go sailing over the crowd and land in a confusion of excited squeals. It was something royal brides never did, but she did it anyway.

As they drove back to the palace she thought ahead to the reception. So many long speeches, so much protocol, so many hours before she could be alone with him. After weeks of fencing she would find out what kind of man Randolph really was. What would she find? Would she be glad or sorry?

The reception moved too slowly for her. At last came the moment she had looked forward to, when her groom led her onto the floor and took her in his arms for the first waltz. They had danced before, but not like this. Now they were husband and wife.

"Are you sorry?" he asked, oddly grave for a bridegroom.

"Should I be? Only you know the answer."

"Trust me, Dottie," he said abruptly, as though she'd touched a nerve.

"I have another wedding present for you. I was saving it for later, but I want to tell you now. I've signed the letters patent."

"You've what?"

"The ones that make you officially Prince Consort. I didn't like leaving it up in the air."

She thought he would react. After all, this last step was the one he'd really wanted, but he only looked at her with an odd little smile.

"Randolph?"

"I'm sorry. I was thinking how lovely you look."

"Did you hear what I said?"

"Yes. Thank you. When can we escape and leave them all behind?"

"I don't think they'd mind if we went soon."

There were grins and kindly laughter when the bride slipped away to change. Their entourage, which had gone on ahead, was minuscule by Dottie's usual standards; just Bertha, being rewarded for dealing cleverly with Harold, and a valet. Randolph drove the car himself.

It was dark when they reached Kellensee and she formed only a brief impression of the building, solid and comfortable, but not palatially huge. To please the servants they sat down to a small meal and toasted each other in champagne, but at last the servants melted away, and Randolph said, "Come with me."

Taking her hand he led her, not upstairs, but to a room at the back of the house. It was an oak paneled room, dominated by a large bed, with a few small rugs on the floor and the bare necessities of furniture.

"Not what you expected?" Randolph asked, a little wryly.

"I love it. It's cozy and friendly. Just like a real home."

She knew she'd said the right thing. His face broke into a smile of real warmth. "If you feel that, then all is well."

"Wasn't it well before?"

He took her face between his hands. "Things will always be well between us, Dottie, I promise you."

"You can't," she whispered longingly. "Nobody can promise that."

"I know that there's been much between us that has been difficult. So many quarrels, so many times when we couldn't be completely honest with each other, so much anger and mistrust. But those things have no place here, now. Let there be just us, and as long as we live, I'll never give you cause to regret that you married me.''

''I shall start regretting it soon if you don't kiss me.''

He paused just a moment, searching her face for something that he might or might not have found there, she couldn't tell. Then his mouth touched hers and all thought stopped.

Throughout their short engagement he'd maintained a correct distance, so that this was their first kiss since the day he'd burst in on her. That had been an assertion of power, and it was a million miles away from the gentle coaxing she felt in his lips now. She let her mouth fall open, inviting him, eager for the feel of his tongue, relishing its purposeful movements against the soft inside of her cheek, feeling her whole body turned to molten liquid.

His kisses changed, became more demanding and her blood leapt in response. She began to explore his mouth as he had explored hers. She was filled with urgency. With every inch of her she wanted what came next, and when she felt his fingers at the fastening of her dress she moved quickly to help him. When it had slipped to the floor he dropped his lips to the hollow of her neck, teasing her with such skill that she felt the beginnings of a slow burning fire deep inside her. Its soft intensity seemed to possess her so completely that she noticed only vaguely that he was removing the rest of her clothes.

He threw aside his shirt and drew her against him gently, so that the hair on his chest rasped slightly against her breasts. She put her arms around his neck in a gesture of abandon that seemed natural now.

She felt his hands at her waist, lifting her off her

feet and raising her so that the distance in height between them was canceled, and it was she who looked down on him. She took his face between her hands and rained kisses on it, willing him not to delay any more. Her excitement was growing by the minute.

She didn't know when he'd moved to the bed, only that they were suddenly there and he was lowering her, tearing off the rest of his clothes, then lying beside her.

Her caressed her everywhere with his hands, his lips, until the sweet torment grew almost unbearable. She wanted to urge him on, yet at the same time she was content to leave this to him, because only an expert could bring those sensations into magical being.

She thought she knew her own body, but now she realized they'd been only casually acquainted. It had been something to be scrubbed down in the bath and toweled quickly to keep warm. Randolph was intent on revealing her to herself, a desirable woman, all the more desirable because of her response to his maleness.

There was a whole world between men and women that had been hidden from her. As she discovered it now she wondered how she'd lived so long in ignorance. Because he hadn't been there was the answer.

He slipped his knee between her legs, which parted for him easily so that he could move over her. The feel of him coming into her was almost shocking in its beauty and she drew a long breath, willing it to go on and on. This was the meaning of the obscure yearnings that had troubled her. All this time she'd wanted Randolph inside her, and nothing else would do. Now that she'd experienced him, she wondered how she'd endured the wait.

She moved back against him, claiming, releasing, instinctively in harmony. As if by a signal he tossed aside the last of restraint and drove into her vigorously and she cried out with the sharpness of her pleasure. And after that it grew stronger until it enveloped her completely and there was nothing left of her, except that she was reborn and found herself back in his arms, where she had always belonged.

Dottie awoke first and sat up gently so as not to disturb Randolph. That wasn't easy as his big body was sprawled all over the bed. In the night she'd discovered the true Randolph, not the disciplined person of the daylight, but some other man who could abandon himself heart and soul. He'd held nothing back, pleasing her and showing her how to please him, until they were both drained.

Just for now she wanted solitude, to come to terms with the new person she'd become, so she eased herself gently out of bed and looked around for her clothes. There was her dress, just as he'd removed it and tossed it away, too urgent in his desire for her to care if it was ruined. And it was ruined, she saw, noticing a small rent with delight. As she drew the dress against her body every silken movement felt like a caress, bringing memories flooding back. She smiled blissfully...

As he was still sleeping, she found her nightdress, pulled a robe over it and opened the French doors.

They led straight out into the garden, and now that it was daylight she saw for the first time how small a place this was. Not to her. After Wenford everywhere looked spacious, but to a man raised in palaces this was tiny. Yet it was his retreat, his refuge.

The house might have belonged to any solidly prosperous country gentleman. Outside was a small park with a pond on which ducks glided contentedly. She went down to the edge and at once they swam toward her, then away again, quacking with disgust because she was empty handed. She laughed and turned back to the house to find Randolph watching her. He opened his arms and she ran into them.

For a moment they held each other close, in silence. There was nothing to say. What had happened last night was too deep for words.

"I was afraid you wouldn't like this place," he said after a long time.

"I love it. I want to stay here forever. If only we could."

"If only." He kissed her lightly. "Let me show you my home, and make it your home, too."

Over breakfast he told her to wear casual clothes, which would once have been easy, but nothing in Dottie's wardrobe was really casual now. She compromised with a silk shirt and a pair of elegant tweed pants, but Randolph was in the authentic gear, shabby jeans and an old sweatshirt. After one look Dottie burst out laughing.

"I never wear anything else while I'm here," he said.

Kellensee was a working farm, just large enough to be self-supporting. Randolph raised cattle and sheep, and although he had a manager it was clear he was closely involved.

"It belonged to my father," he said as they wandered hand in hand through meadows filled with wild flowers and alive with butterflies. "He used to use it as a retreat for his less admissible hobbies. That's why he had his bed installed on the ground floor. He said it was easier to get to when you were legless. Of course, beer wasn't his only 'hobby.' There were various easygoing ladies, and he could let them in and out discreetly through the French windows."

"What about your mother?"

"They were fond of each other, but they led their own lives. She didn't mind his friends, and he was discreet. I was only fourteen when she died, but I somehow knew the truth for a long time before that. What is it?" He'd seen a shadow come over her face.

She shook her head without answering and instead of pressing her he went on, "I'm afraid I was a disappointment to my father. His way of life shocked me a little. He thought I was very odd."

"That's what royal marriages are like, though, aren't they?"

"Some of them. It wouldn't have suited me."

"But," she knew it was risky to pursue this but she didn't seem able to stop, "if you had to marry someone you didn't really want to, it would be forgivable, wouldn't it?"

"No it wouldn't," he said, so forcefully that she jumped. "If you're hinting about lovers Dottie, let me warn you to forget it. I won't be a complaisant husband."

"Don't be silly," she said, coloring and trying to hide her pleasure. "Anyway, who says I was talking about me?"

"Didn't we agree to leave the baggage of the past behind? Don't do this Dottie, please." He laid his fingertips across her mouth. "There are some subjects we should never mention."

She longed to say, "What about Sophie?" but she couldn't get the words out in the face of his determination to silence her. And wasn't he right? If they could leave their awkward beginnings behind and start a new page, mightn't there be happiness that way?

Taking her hand, he led her deeper into the wood until they reached a place among the trees where the land sloped down then rose gently on the other side. The little valley was a mass of plants and small bushes, and on this side stood a small building made of heavy logs. He took her inside and Dottie looked around in delight.

"It's like a little cottage," she said.

"It's a 'hide' where you can watch animals and birds. My father had it built. Our happiest times together were spent here. And since he died I've sometimes come here alone. It's quiet and blessedly peaceful, and the noise of the world can't touch you." He indicated a rustic bed by the wall. "Sometimes I stay all night. The best time is in the dawn."

There was a large window where watchers could sit in the shadows, and Dottie went to sit by one, looking out ecstatically at the quiet scene. Now and then a soft rustle in the undergrowth revealed the presence of an animal. Sometimes she actually saw one. Or a bird hopped close, never knowing itself to be watched.

"Time for supper," Randolph murmured, close to her.

"It can't be, it's only...good heavens, we've been here hours."

"Yes, that's how it is. This place casts its spell and you forget everything else...almost everything else." He took her hand. "Come, let's go back to supper, and afterward, we will sit chastely holding hands."

"You dare and you're dead."

It was wonderful to hear his laughter echoing up into the branches, and see the flock of startled birds rise into the air.

The days passed in a haze of summer. Once it rained and they stayed indoors, leaving the French windows open, lying in bed, watching the shower. The nights merged into one night.

One morning she awoke in the early hours, and lay for a moment without opening her eyes. She was lying on her face and she could feel a slight chill on her back that told her the bedclothes had been removed. Fingertips were sliding softly across her skin, touching her so lightly that she could hardly feel them, but there was no doubt about the sensations they were creating. She gave a deep sigh of pleasurable content.

His fingers had reached her spine, moving down it in a leisurely, lingering fashion until they reached the small of her back. There they suddenly vanished, to be replaced by his lips, beginning the return journey. She shivered with delight and tried to turn over, but he prevented her.

"Keep still," he whispered. "I haven't finished yet."

"Just keep on as long as you like," she murmured blissfully. "At least...no, I don't mean that, because sooner or later I want you to do something else."

His lips were working on the back of her neck

while his hands traced her spine down and cupped her behind.

"I've wanted to do this," he said, "ever since the day I found you naked in the cupboard." She gave a deep throated chuckle that shivered through him, straight to his loins and made him take a sharp breath.

"I remember that day," she said. "You were so shocked."

"Shocked at myself. You were so lovely. I tried not to notice, but I couldn't manage it. And now, here you are, and you're all mine."

"Getting possessive, eh?"

"Any man, looking at you, would get possessive."

She rolled onto her back so fast that she took him by surprise. "Men aren't the only ones who get possessive," she said as her arms closed around him with a strength born of newly discovered passion. "Come here."

"My darling—"

"I said come here."

They had been married a week, just a few days, but long enough for her to change into a woman of fierce needs, determined to fulfill them. This was her lovemaking and with her words and her movements she let him know what she wanted. Having seized the initiative, she kept it. Randolph grinned, understanding perfectly, and not minding in the least when she said fiercely, "Now, *now!*"

Just as she'd learned about her own body she'd also learned about his and she put her knowledge to use, demanding the power and vigor of his loins for her exclusive pleasure.

"You're wrong," she whispered mischievously. "It's you who are all *mine.*"

"Your Majesty's obedient servant," he said, falling in with her mood.

"So I should hope. Oh Randolph. *Randolph...*"

Later, remembering that enchanted time, Dottie found that it wasn't only the passion that stayed in her mind.

For one thing, there was the dog.

He appeared one day in front of the hide where they were watching together, and turned a hopeful face on them. He was a tramp among dogs, scruffy, muddy and with no one part of him matching any other. Dottie was immediately won over by his goofy charm, but she could imagine Randolph's reaction to this disgraceful creature.

Then she heard a soft whistle and looked up to see him grinning. He whistled again and opened the door of the hide. There were still scraps from their meal on the table, and he proceeded to offer these to the visitor, who wolfed them down. Seeing her regarding him with raised eyebrows, Randolph colored and said self-consciously, "I had a dog like this when I was a child."

"You? Like this?"

"Yes, he was a stray that I adopted, but only for five minutes. My mother didn't like dogs, said they were messy creatures, and made me get rid of it."

"What did your father say?" Dottie demanded indignantly.

"Nothing. He never interfered in domestic matters. That was her price for turning a blind eye to the way he lived. He sent him to the stables where he probably had a happier life than he would have done in a palace."

"Perhaps it was because it was a mongrel. Maybe a pedigree dog would have been better."

"She disliked all dogs. But I wanted a mongrel. Everything around me was pedigreed. My friends were chosen for me from among the aristocracy. Some of them I liked well enough, but it's not the same as choosing for yourself. And 'royalty must keep a proper distance,' even from friends."

"That's terrible," Dottie said, aghast. "No wonder you're so…so…"

"Yes, no wonder," he said, understanding what she couldn't say. "Fritz, my dog, was everything the others weren't. He came from the wrong side of the tracks. He didn't have a bloodline—not a respectable one, anyway. He was spontaneous and he didn't understand rules. I can't tell you how attractive that was to a boy who was just beginning to understand how rules had to govern his life, and there was no escape for him."

The light was fading fast but Dottie didn't light the lamp they sometimes used. She had a feeling that the darkness was helping him. This was a man who didn't confide his feelings easily, but today something had made it happen.

"What a pity that your mother couldn't ease up," she said slowly, "just to make you happy."

"She loved me in her way, but to her everything was subordinate to being royal. When I was old enough I had to give her a formal bow when we met in the morning. She was the queen, and only after that was she my mother. It wasn't her fault, it was the way she was raised."

"Poor little boy!" Dottie murmured.

"It's sweet of you to say so, but don't feel sorry for me. That little boy doesn't exist anymore."

He was so wrong, she thought. That lonely little boy was here with them this minute, so real that she felt she knew him. Such love as he'd received had come from a mother too rigid to show him real affection. His father had been kindly but weak, too selfish to limit his own pleasures to stand up for his son. Had anybody in Randolph's whole life loved him warmly, tenderly, unconditionally?

Yes.

She couldn't say, "It's all right, you've got me now," because that would be to venture onto his private ground where he was still uneasy of intruders. He'd allowed her in, just a little, but there was a long way to go yet. But she could be patient.

The dog was gulping the last of the tidbits noisily.

"I expect he'll stay with you now," she observed.

But the next moment a cry of "Brin!" came through the trees. The dog grabbed one last morsel of food, leapt onto the table and vanished through the window. From the distance came cries of welcome from childish voices.

"Obviously that was Brin," Randolph said wryly.

Dottie took his hand and squeezed it. "Never mind. *I* come from the wrong side of the tracks. Will I do?"

He slipped his arm around her, and spoke more tenderly than she had ever heard. "I think you'll do very well, my Dottie."

That night, for the first time, he slept with his head on her breast, and her arms around him.

The next day Dottie found a man who bred German shepherds and arranged to have a litter of three brought to Kellensee for Randolph's inspection. He

chose one, but Dottie fell in love with the others and
they ended up keeping them all. A visit to a local
animal sanctuary produced two cats, but after that
Randolph begged her to stop.

Then there was the time Bertha discovered a pair
of paparazzi and managed to send them both flying
into the duck pond. Grinning, Randolph complimented her, but added that her technique wasn't a
patch on Dottie's.

The newspapers arrived and piled up, unnoticed.
When she could spare time to read about their own
wedding Dottie found herself studying a picture of
the moment she'd tossed her bouquet. She was looking away from Randolph, into the crowd, but he was
watching her with an expression that made her catch
her breath.

The headline called it The Look Of Love. Underneath it the caption said, *Those who thought this was
nothing but a state marriage had their answer today
in the look of adoration the groom turned on his
bride.*

Dottie studied Randolph's face longingly. Adoration? It could be read that way. He was smiling, oblivious of everything but his bride, the very picture of a
man entering on his greatest joy.

But why did he never let her see that look?

She heard footsteps and hastily thrust the newspaper under a cushion, going quickly out to meet Randolph and be told that a deer had been seen near the
hide, and they should hurry.

By day their happiest times were spent in the hide.
Birds and animals came and went while they watched,
entranced, in silence. In those silences she felt herself
growing closer to him. She'd thought so often of what

they might say, but now she knew that words were unnecessary. He'd brought her to the place nearest his heart, and allowed her in, and that counted, even though she'd had to nudge him.

"Why were you reluctant to bring me here?" she asked once as they sat by the window in the fading light.

"That isn't true, Dottie."

"You never suggested it until I turned down Rome and New York."

"I thought you'd find them more exciting. Don't you want to see the world?"

She smiled. "Do you have a world better than this?"

"No." He smiled back. "There isn't one."

"We will come back, won't we? Often."

"That will be for Your Majesty to say," he teased.

"No it won't. You're officially Prince Consort now. And about that, you never said anything."

"I said thank you. It was our wedding day. Did you expect me to think about anything but you?" His voice became teasing. "I was a little disturbed to find my wife's mind fixed on state affairs while she was dancing with *me*. Seriously, I do thank you. It's just that such things seem less important now."

"Wait until we get home and a mountain of paperwork descends on you. I give it all back. Well, most of it. You'll run the country much better than I could."

"Dottie," he said, shocked. "Surely not because I'm a man? Don't disillusion me."

"No, you idiot," she said, laughing. "Because you've had years of training, and you know all the things about this country that I don't. I'm going back to school. I need to know Elluria's history, which means," she gave a gloomy sigh, "I need to know every other country's history, too."

"Cobblers!" Randolph said sympathetically.

"Right. Oh heck, what have I let myself in for? There's so much for me to learn, and while I'm doing that someone must keep things going. I've managed so far on a smile and a load of chutzpah, but it's not enough for the years ahead."

"What a wise woman you are," he said tenderly.

"But don't think you're going to have it all your own way."

"That thought never crossed my mind," he said truthfully.

"I still want my parliamentary reforms in time for the next election and I'll be breathing down your neck to make sure I get them."

"Just like before, really."

"But you can do as you like with the boring stuff."

"Thank you, Dottie. Your faith in me is deeply moving."

"You don't fool me."

"And *you* don't fool *me*. This is nothing but a trick to off-load 'the boring stuff' onto me, leaving you free to indulge in a good fight whenever the mood takes you. Oh no! We'll be a team. It works better that way. To be honest, I was never much good at the smile and the chutzpah."

"You're getting better at them."

"Only when you're around. But you're not getting off that easily. Stick to your studies. I hear your languages are coming on splendidly. Your tutor says you have a natural ear. Your German is excellent, your French not far behind." A sense of mischief that he'd never known he possessed made him add, "One day you may even stop mangling the English language."

She gave him a gentle thump. "I'll get you for that, just you wait!"

He murmured softly in her ear, "Must I wait?"

His breath tickled her ear and sent scurryings of pleasure through her. "Randolph, I'm trying to be serious."

"So am I. Very serious." His lips were at work on the soft skin of her neck, distracting her.

"It's important."

He rose, drawing her with him, and moving toward the bed. "What could be more important than this?"

"But we were discussing urgent matters of state."

"*Hang* urgent matters of state."

Chapter Twelve

As the summer faded people looked anxiously at the sky and feared for the weather on coronation day. But the morning dawned pale and clear, with no clouds in the sky, and the promise of warmth to come. As she was picking at tea and toast, having no appetite for more, Dottie took a phone call from her head groom.

"With Your Majesty's permission I believe we could risk the open carriage."

"I agree," she said with relief.

As her ladies dressed her Aunt Liz remarked, "People would have been so disappointed not to see you properly."

"Yes, it's really their day," Dottie agreed, turning a little to survey the coronation gown in the long mirror. It was a magnificent creation in cream satin, embroidered with the four emblems of Elluria, each one studded with tiny diamonds. More diamonds were worked into the curve of the neckline, and in the long train that stretched behind her.

"What a day!" Aunt Liz enthused. "Who would have thought it would ever happen?"

"Nobody," Dottie murmured, "because it shouldn't have."

How could she tell anyone that her heart was heavy on what should have been her day of triumph? Who would ever understand that she was miserable at what today would do to the man she loved? This should have been Randolph's coronation. Instead he would hand her to the place that should have been his, and swear loyalty to her with her other subjects. And he would do it with a smile on his face.

That smile scared her, because he never told her of the pain that lay beneath it. It was kind, tender, understanding, and it shut her out. But surely, today of all days, he would give her a glimpse of his true feelings?

"Leave me for a moment," she said suddenly.

Her ladies, who had been fussing about her, curtsied and withdrew. Dottie paced the floor, feeling a dozen years older than the unaware girl who'd arrived here six months ago. She stopped at the open French windows, looking out onto the park, where the colors of autumn were just being seen. This was the day when her future should stretch ahead, clear and triumphant. Instead it was shrouded in mist.

She turned at the sound of the door. It was Randolph, and she thought he had never looked more splendid.

"Are you quite ready?" he asked.

"I shall never be ready for this," she burst out. "It's all wrong. This should be your day."

"It is the day we shall share," he told her gravely.

"No, no," she shook her head. "That's just pretty words. I'm stealing what should be yours and I don't know how not to. I'm not really queen and we both know it."

"Listen to me," he said, shushing her as he took her hands between his. "I told you once before that you must believe in yourself before anybody else can do so. That was never more true than now. You have made the throne your own, not through your ancestors, but with your heart. You've won your people's love, and because of that they are truly your people."

"But I was given the chance. You'd have taken it, too."

He shook his head. "No, I never knew how. They respected me, but they didn't love me. I've always done my duty, and thought that was enough. It was you who showed me that duty could—should—be done joyfully, so that people's hearts reached out to you. I never had the gift of winning hearts."

"You won mine."

"Yes, and that's my best hope. When they see that you love me, they may think I'm not so bad after all."

She couldn't bear that. To the horror of both of them she burst into tears.

"Dottie, Dottie..." he drew her close. "Don't cry."

She couldn't stop. The sadness of his resignation overwhelmed her. She'd never wept for herself, but she wept bitterly for him.

"That's enough," Randolph urged her, half tender,

half commanding. And when she still couldn't stop he gave her a little shake. "Listen Dottie, for I'm speaking very seriously now. This is the twenty-first century. Kings and queens have survived a long time, but we can't go on in the old way, depending on respect, fear or power. Now our people have to want us. They have to love us. And it's you that they love. It's you that has the power to take this monarchy, this country, into the future. I know it, and your people know it. So now go out to them, and let them see that you are theirs. This is your day of glory."

"But it should have been yours," she said huskily as he dried her eyes.

"Is there only one kind of glory then? Haven't we discovered another kind?"

He spoke softly in the voice he used at night when there was only the darkness and their passion, but Dottie couldn't let herself off the hook that easily.

"Yes, we have, but you know you need more than that. You know you couldn't be happy if you weren't doing your job."

"But I shall be doing it, through you. It's the same. Hush..." he laid a finger over her lips. "There are things about me you don't know yet. They can only be told at the right time, and perhaps that time will never come. Try to trust me, and believe this, that there is no bitterness in my heart today. Only love for you. My darling, why can't you believe me?"

"Because... Oh, I can't wrap it up in posh words."

He laughed. "That's my Dottie. Blunt to the end. Be blunt then, and tell me why you can't believe that I love you."

"Because it's your duty to love me. And you always do your duty."

"Is that what you think? Only duty and no more? Dottie, Dottie what a short memory you have. Haven't there been nights when I've held you against my heart and we've been soul of each other's soul as well as flesh of each other's flesh?"

"Yes," she said wistfully. "I've felt that then, but why have you never actually said you loved me before?"

"Because I didn't want to win your contempt. Don't you remember once saying to me, 'Would you have been crass enough to try to make me think you were in love with me? I suppose I should be grateful to have been spared that piece of dishonesty.'? My darling, blinkered Dottie, how was I supposed to speak of love after that?"

"But I...I didn't mean it. I was angry. I'd have said anything."

"That I believe," he said with a touch of humor. "But when you stopped being angry, you didn't take it back."

"How could I?"

"Hush. We tangled ourselves in such a web, and words only made it worse. I tried to show you my love and hoped you'd understand, but you seemed to be pining for Mike..."

"Not really. I've loved you longer than you think. It was Sophie I was afraid of."

"Never fear, and never doubt." He drew her close and laid his lips on hers, caressing them tenderly. "Do you doubt me now...and now?"

If only they would all go away, she thought, and leave the two of them alone in the place where they could love and be happy. But the world couldn't be shut out for long. A noise in the outer room made them sigh and draw apart.

"There will be later for us," Randolph said. "Now you belong to your people."

"Not without you," she said urgently.

"I am always beside you."

She stood for a moment, composing herself. Meeting Randolph's eyes, she saw his slight gesture indicating that she should lift her chin, and did so. His smile reassured her.

Her ladies were waiting to attach the heavy ermine and velvet cloak to her shoulders. She took Randolph's arm and they walked out of the state apartments into the broad corridor. To left and right of them people were curtseying and she smiled. This was her day, because Randolph had given it to her. Now she would take what he had given, and make of it something better still.

Down the grand stairway, left along the crimson carpet to where the sun gleamed in the courtyard, then out through the wide arch to the open carriage. The waiting crowds cheered as they appeared and at first she acknowledged them, but the next moment, Dottie-like, she forgot regal dignity in the excitement of a discovery.

"It's him," she told Randolph. "It's Jack, leading the horses."

Before he could speak she slipped away to where the head groom stood holding Jack's bridle. The old horse stood proud and beautiful, a plume nodding from his head.

"It'll be his last outing, ma'am," the coachman

said proudly. "But I promised him he wouldn't miss this great day."

"I'm so glad." She planted a swift kiss on Jack's forehead. "It wouldn't have been the same without him."

"Dottie," Randolph said patiently, "I'm glad to see him too, but can we get on with the coronation?"

Smiling she took his hand and let him hand her into the carriage. The crowd, who'd understood what was happening, cheered louder than ever. That was Dottie, their queen.

The carriage door slammed behind them, then a signal to the horses and they were on the move out of the palace gates. Bunting flew in the breeze overhead, more bunting was draped from the lamp posts, almost everyone in the crowd seemed to be waving a little flag.

As they drew up outside the cathedral Randolph turned to her. "Remember," he said. "Together."

"Together."

The cathedral was cool and dark as they entered it. There was the master of ceremonies watching their arrival, clutching a mobile phone with which to alert the organist. It all went smoothly and at the exact moment that they stepped forward the organ pealed out overhead.

Dottie had expected this part to be a blur. Instead she found her senses heightened so that she could hear each note of the music and pick out individual faces. Almost every country had sent a representative to her coronation.

Near the front she saw Prince Harold and his princess, invited because diplomacy demanded it. Sophie's face was a mask, but Harold was watching the procession near, and something told Dottie that he was tensed as a coiled spring. She could almost feel the waves of anger radiating from him.

She and Randolph slowed to a halt in front of the archbishop, solemn and splendid in his golden vestments. The organ faded to silence and the archbishop raised his voice to declare, "This is a glorious day—"

"It's a day of dishonor!"

The shout died away, leaving behind a stunned silence. Into that silence Harold's voice came again.

"This is a day of dishonor, the day Elluria crowns an impostor with no right to the throne." He stepped out into the aisle and advanced on Dottie and Randolph who'd turned to face him.

"Be silent," Randolph commanded him.

"You expect me to be silent while I'm cheated of my rights?" Harold screamed. "It's a conspiracy. This woman is not the true heir."

He snatched a paper from an inner pocket and turned to face the startled congregation, waving it aloft. "She is not the true heir," he shouted again. "She springs from a bastard line, and here is the proof."

"Nonsense!" Durmand bustled forward, angry and businesslike. "This has all been dealt with. Her Majesty's line has been checked back to Duke Egbert and found to be direct."

"Direct but not legitimate," Harold sneered. "Egbert never had a child by his lawful wife. His daughter was the product of an extramarital liaison with a housemaid."

"But that is nonsense," Durmand protested. "He could never have passed her off as his wife's child."

"He could in those days," Harold snapped. "And with his wife's connivance. Don't forget what a long time it took Egbert and his wife to travel from Elluria to England. A journey of a few days took months, and why?"

"Because they lingered to enjoy themselves," Durmand said helplessly.

"Because it was easier to perpetuate a fraud in another country," Harold shouted. "The child was born in Switzerland, where nobody had ever seen either woman. They stayed in an out-of-the-way house in the country, the maid gave birth, the doctor was told he was attending the duchess. How was he to know otherwise?"

"But the duchess would never have agreed—" Durmand protested.

"Why not? People had jeered at her as too old to give her husband a child. After that the jeers stopped, and she traveled on to England with 'her' baby in her arms. The maid was bought off and thrown out. But she talked and the story has been preserved."

Enderlin stepped in, as much Dottie's champion as he had been her combatant. "But nobody heard of it until now," he said. "It's surfaced too conveniently for my liking."

"And might never have surfaced at all," Sophie said, speaking for the first time. "But for the invaluable assistant of Mr. Michael Kenton."

"Mike?" Dottie exclaimed. "I don't believe it."

"We had such an interesting talk the night of the ball," Sophie continued, turning directly to Dottie. "He repeated tales he'd heard from your grandfather, when he was in his cups, and there was enough to put us on the trail."

"But that was ages ago," Dottie exclaimed. "Why wait until now?"

"It was just a rumor," Harold said. "It's taken until now to get the proof, hidden in the Swiss archives." He waved his papers again. "But the proof is here. Examine it. In the meantime I demand that this false coronation is called off."

Through the whirling of Dottie's head only one thing was clear. If Harold was clever enough to make this credible, Randolph would lose everything for the second time. She herself would lose the friends she'd made and the country she'd come to love, but it was for him that her heart ached.

"Randolph," she said, clasping his hand.

"It's all right, my darling. Everything is going to be all right."

"But can this be true?"

"It wouldn't surprise me at all," he said calmly. "Old Egbert was very free with his attentions. I should think he had any number of liaisons. He undoubtedly married his wife for her money and she was some years older than him. It all sounds very likely. How fortunate that it didn't come to light before."

"But, Randolph…what difference does that make? It's out now, and that means I can't be the queen and—"

"It means no such thing. Trust me Dottie, I'll make you a queen before the day's out."

Sophie was regarding Dottie with a mixture of triumph and malevolence. Harold and Durmand were having a shouting match, with Harold's voice growing shriller every moment.

"This woman is an impostor. She should be arrested for offenses against the state."

"But you'll never get the king to agree to that," Randolph observed mildly.

Harold rounded on him. "I am the king."

"No," Randolph said, still in the same mild tone. "*I* am." Ignoring Harold's sneer he went on, "I have been king of Elluria since the moment of my father's death."

If Harold's announcement produced consternation this one caused turmoil. Everyone was staring at Randolph as if unable to believe their ears, but his glance was for Dottie, as though only her reaction mattered to him.

"Your researchers have been hard at work, Harold, but so have mine. And I too have found something interesting. It concerns Ellie Trentworth, the young woman with whom my father went through a form of marriage. I say 'a form of marriage' because it wasn't worth the paper it was written on. Ellie already had a husband, two in fact. Probably more than two. Goodness knows who she was really married to, but it certainly wasn't my father.

"So the 'form of marriage' had no basis in law. It was invalid, leaving him as much a bachelor afterward as before, and therefore free to marry my mother. There never was a stain on their marriage, or my legitimacy."

Harold had gone very pale but he recovered himself.

"Words," he scoffed. "Where is your proof?"

"Here," Randolph said, pulling some papers from inside his jacket. "These are the marriage certificates of Ellie Trentworth to both husbands. Since I discovered the truth I've kept them on me at all times. I had a feeling I might need to produce them at a moment's notice, especially today."

Harold snatched at the papers. The whole cathedral seemed to be holding its breath as he went through them.

"These are forgeries," he snapped. "I don't believe any of it."

But Sophie believed it. As she saw her last chance vanish she screamed and went into hysterics. Nothing else could have so effectively demolished Harold's claim, and two soldiers moved discreetly to take their places behind him. Sophie's sobs grew louder, prompting him to hiss, "Shut up!"

"This is most irregular," the archbishop said worriedly, looking at Dottie. "Is this lady of legitimate descent, or isn't she?"

"It doesn't matter, since she makes no claim to the throne," Randolph said. "Indeed, she never did make a claim to the throne. It was forced on her, and she accepted it as a duty, and from love. But it was based on a misapprehension. The mistaken belief that I was illegitimate because my parents' marriage was bigamous. These certificates prove otherwise."

Durmand was studying the papers with increasing delight. "Then the marriage was valid, and your claim to the throne cannot be challenged," he told Randolph. "You are, and have always been, the rightful king."

"You need never have brought me here at all," Dottie breathed. "Randolph, how long have you known about this?"

"I discovered soon after you arrived in Elluria."

Her brain whirled. "You mean...before we married?"

"Yes."

She couldn't speak. The implications were so enormous, so wonderful, that she didn't dare believe them. "But why did you keep quiet?" she asked at last. "If you'd spoken then you wouldn't have needed to marry me."

He put his hands on either side of her face and spoke in a voice deep with tenderness. "Darling, beloved Dottie, I wanted to marry you. I *longed* to marry you. I've loved you since the day we met in London, when you took me out of the narrow, constricted world I'd known, and showed me another world that could be mine, but only if you were there. Since then I've plotted and schemed, pulled strings, behaved unethically, broken rules, all to keep you with me. You made the sun shine for me, and I knew if I lost you the sun would never shine again.

"I was afraid that if you learned the truth, you'd pack your bags and go. I couldn't face the thought of losing the only woman I have ever loved. It was a deception, but one for which you will, perhaps, forgive me?"

"But you could have been king all this time," she breathed, still not daring to be convinced by the love she saw in his eyes, a love that more than matched her own.

"Earlier today I told you that there were things you don't know about me, and perhaps never would, because they could only be told at the right time. Now that time has come." He raised his voice. "I call on everyone here to witness that I would rather be your consort than king, and married to any other woman."

The congregation broke into loud applause. The royal guests in the front row rose to their feet and were followed by row after row behind them, clapping and cheering. High up aloft the choirboys joined in.

But Randolph and Dottie saw only each other. His gaze said that this was the measure of how much she mattered to him. She was more to him than his duty, more than his life. She *was* his life. She was awed by the sacrifice he'd been prepared to make, rather than lose her.

The archbishop's worried voice broke in on them. "But can we have a coronation or not?"

"Of course we can," Dottie told him. "The coronation of Elluria's rightful monarch, King Randolph."

"And his consort, Queen Dorothea," Randolph put in, "who reigns as supremely in her subjects' hearts and she does in her husband's."

Taking her hand in his he stepped forward and they stood side by side as the archbishop raised his voice, calling to the people.

"I present to you, Randolph, your sovereign lord, rightful king of Elluria, and his lady..."

She barely heard the rest. The mist that had shrouded the path ahead had lifted now, and she could see clearly at last. This was the world they would share; years of work and duty, made sweet to each by the presence of the other. Behind them stretched the way back out of the cathedral, and beyond that lay the sunshine.

* * * * *

The Royal MacAllister

JOAN ELLIOTT PICKART

JOAN ELLIOTT PICKART

is the author of over eighty-five novels. When she isn't writing, she enjoys reading, gardening and attending craft shows with her young daughter, Autumn. Joan has three all-grown-up daughters and three fantastic grandchildren. Joan and Autumn live in a charming small town in the high pine country of Arizona.

For my dear friend and agent,
Laurie Feigenbaum,
with special thanks for
understanding that authors
are mommies, too.

Chapter One

Alice "Trip" MacAllister stood outside the five-star restaurant engaged in a heated argument with her toughest opponent...herself.

She did *not*, she fumed as she began to pace, want to be here, taking part in the huge family dinner that would include the royal family of the Island of Wilshire.

Royal family. Her cousin Maggie was going to marry an honest-to-goodness prince, for crying out loud. Maggie had met Devon Renault on New Year's Eve while on duty in the emergency room at the hospital, and it had been practically love at first sight for the dewy-eyed pair.

It was now the first week in March, and Devon's family had finally managed to make all the necessary arrangements to enable them to travel to Ventura, California—the upscale city where the MacAllisters lived.

Unbelievable, Trip thought, continuing her trek. Ever since Maggie was a little girl she'd dreamed of marrying a prince, had made it her wish each time she blew out the candles on her birthday cake, and—ta-da—she was going to do exactly that...marry her Prince Charming.

She was happy for Maggie, she really was, but... The wedding would be held on the island in six weeks, and would be a gala affair with all the royal pomp and circumstance. And she, Trip MacAllister, in what must have been a mentally diminished state at the time, had agreed to attend.

But that was a nightmare to think about later. What had her nerves jangled to the point of near-hysteria now was that she was expected to attend the dinner inside this restaurant, was in fact late in showing up.

But she didn't want to be here. Family gatherings were not her thing, per se, hadn't been for as long as she could remember. She always felt uncomfortable, edgy, constantly ticking off the seconds until she could leave whenever she was surrounded by the multitude of MacAllisters.

And *this* dinner also included a royal family, for Pete's sake, who had just arrived early this morning. Devon's father, King Something...oh, what was his name? Chester. King Chester had decided it would be best to get acquainted with his son's fiancée and her family in a more relaxed setting rather than amid the hoopla surrounding the wedding.

Dandy, Trip thought with a sigh, as she stopped wearing a path in the sidewalk. But why hadn't she begged off? Even worse, she was wearing a dress she'd borrowed from her sister Jessica. A slip dress, Jessica had called it. It was skimpy and clingy and made her feel like a little girl playing dress-up.

She'd recently worn the one nice outfit she owned to Jessica and Daniel's wedding and couldn't show up in the same thing. The remainder of her wardrobe consisted of jeans, shorts and casual tops. Oh, yes, and the tacky polyester number that was the color of Pepto-Bismol that she wore when waiting tables at the café. Asking Jessica to loan her a dress had seemed like a good idea at the time, but this creation was absurd.

She was going home, Trip decided. She'd send

a message inside to her parents saying she had the flu, or a killer headache, or the chicken pox, or some lame thing, and hightail it out of there. Yes.

No, she thought in the next instant. That wasn't fair to Maggie, or to the rest of the family she was attempting to mend fences with after years of keeping emotional and physical distance between them. A goal that, in her opinion, wasn't going too well so far.

Get a grip, Trip told herself, patting her cheeks. *March in there, and smile while you're marching.*

Trip took one step toward the door of the restaurant, then halted in her tracks as a man came striding past, obviously not seeing her as he fumbled with a tie while muttering under his breath. He stopped two feet beyond where Trip stood.

"Dumb," he said. "Why does a man have to put on a tie to eat dinner? Who made up these rules? And who invented these god-awful things? It must have been a woman who hated men." He flipped one end of the tie around the other, pulled it through, then turned slightly as he shoved the knot to the top of his shirt. "There."

"It's lumpy," Trip said. "And the tail is too long and…you'd better start over."

"Well, hell," the man said, yanking the tie apart. "For two cents I'd ditch this shindig."

Trip laughed. "I'd ditch my party for one cent."

"Oh, yeah?" he said, looking at her for the first time. "Would you be dead as a post if you did?"

"In spades," Trip said, matching his smile.

Good grief, she thought, he was handsome. He was grumpy as all get-out, but he was drop-dead gorgeous, that was for sure. He was tall, probably six foot or more, had thick, black-as-midnight hair, rugged tanned features and the bluest eyes she'd ever seen, surrounded by long, dark lashes a woman would kill to have. Broad shoulders, long muscular legs, dark suit custom-fitted to perfection... Absolutely gorgeous.

"Well, I guess I've put this off as long as I can," Trip said with a sigh. "I'd better go in there, apologize for being late, and smile, smile, smile."

"Wait," the man said quickly and a tad too loudly.

"Wait?" Trip said, cocking her head slightly to one side. "Could you add something to that command so I know what you're talking about?"

"What? Oh. It wasn't a command, it was a plea. Would you help me with my tie? Then I'll go find my group, too, I guess. I'm already late, I'm probably in hot water and I don't dare show up without a tie."

"Well, I..." Trip started, then shrugged. "Sure. Why not?"

The man stepped closer, and Trip gripped the tails of the tie, her eyes widening for a moment as she saw that her hands were trembling slightly. She drew what she hoped was not an obviously steadying breath, then completed the task, giving the knot a pat when she finished. Before she could drop her hands, the man grasped them between both of his.

"Thank you," he said in a raspy voice. "I mean that. Thank you very much."

"You're welcome," Trip said, then met his gaze.

Dear heaven, she thought, she couldn't breathe. The heat from the man's work-roughened but gentle hands was traveling up her arms and across her breasts, causing them to feel heavy and achy.

Oh, mercy, now the heat was swirling throughout her, lower, hotter, pulsing deep. Those eyes. Those incredible blue eyes were like a mysterious ocean holding secrets yet to be discovered. They were pulling her in, making it impossible to move, or to think clearly. This man, this stranger, was...was dangerous, so blatantly, sensually masculine it was overwhelming.

"I..." Trip started to say, then realized she didn't have enough air in her lungs to speak.

"Look," the man said, his voice rather gritty,

"we're about to go our separate ways, now that we're going inside the restaurant, but I'd really like to know your name. Please? I'm Brent Bardow."

Brent Bardow? Trip thought. Why did that sound familiar? No, forget it. If she'd met this man before, she most definitely would remember.

"I'm Tr— I mean, I'm Alice," she said, after drawing in much-needed air. "Alice MacAllister."

"You're kidding," Brent said with a burst of laughter. "Did my name ring a bell?"

"Yes, but..."

"I'm Devon Renault's cousin from the Island of Wilshire." Brent's smile grew bigger. "Shame on you, Alice MacAllister. You don't want to go to the party set up for our families to meet before the big wedding bash."

Trip pulled free of Brent's hold, took a step backward and planted her hands on her hips.

"Shame on *me?*" she said. "I seem to recall that two cents would have been enough to get you to head south rather than go in there."

"Guilty as charged," Brent said. "Well, you and I are obviously the black sheep of the family. Black sheep who are very late in showing up for this shindig. Shall we go face the music? Everyone will be on their best behavior tonight so maybe we won't catch too much hell."

Trip laughed. "Don't count on it." She paused. "Okay, partner in crime, let's go."

The private dining room reserved for the party was enormous, yet managed to maintain a rather cozy atmosphere with its dark paneling. The crystal chandeliers were dimmed just enough to add soft light to the candles on the long, gleaming table, which boasted the restaurant's finest china and crystal.

When a still-smiling Trip and Brent entered the room, an immediate hush fell and close to forty pairs of eyes were riveted on the pair.

"Sorry I'm late," Trip and Brent said in unison, then looked at each other and burst into laughter.

"Your tardiness is not excused, Brent," Byron Bardow, Brent's father, said, scowling at his son.

"Well, they're here now," Jillian MacAllister said as she directed a rather speculative look at her daughter. "Dare we ask where you've been?"

"It was my fault," Brent said. "I was faced with a crisis situation." He ran one hand down his tie. "Alice was good enough to assist me in rectifying the dilemma." He grinned. "How's that?"

"Not worth a plugged nickel," Brent's mother, Charlane, said smiling. "But your excuses for being late, or not showing up at all, rarely are, dear." She swept her gaze over everyone seated at the table. "This is our son, Brent, who should be introduced to the members of this gathering, then given a test on the names to see if he'll be allowed to have dinner."

"Thanks a bunch, Mother." Brent chuckled. "I assume those two empty chairs are for Alice and me?"

"Indeed they are," King Chester said from the far end of the table. "Your salads are there. Sit down and eat and catch up with the rest of us."

Robert MacAllister, Trip's grandfather, had the place of honor at the head of the table, at the opposite end from the king.

"You look lovely this evening, Alice," Robert said. "That dress is very becoming."

Forrest MacAllister frowned. "I think she forgot to put *on* her dress. She's wearing a slip."

"Got it in one, Dad," Trip said, sitting in the closest of the vacant chairs. "It's all Jessica's fault. She loaned me this slip, then got in a huff about something and wouldn't give me the dress to wear over it." She shrugged. "What can I say?"

Brent settled on the chair next to Alice, mentally thanking whoever had arranged the seating for the evening.

"That's not true," Jessica said, laughing, then

looked at her husband, Daniel. "See what I went through growing up? This is a recording…it's all Jessica's fault. Trip was a master at getting me into trouble."

"Amen to that," Emily, the third member of the MacAllister triplets, said. "Remember the puppy Trip found and dragged home, not caring whether he wanted to come or not? Then told Mom and Dad that the mangy beast had followed *me*?"

"Let's not get started on those kind of stories." Robert laughed. "It's a pleasure to meet you, Brent. Let me introduce my family. As for a test on who is who, that's still open for discussion."

Brent nodded and smiled as Robert delivered the multitude of names.

Trip? he thought, only half listening to the names to go with the faces. Alice's grandfather had called her Alice, but her sisters had used the strange title of Trip, which must be some kind of rather weird nickname. To him she was Alice, because that's what she'd called herself outside the restaurant.

Alice, he mused. Like Alice in Wonderland, who embarked on a mystifying journey when she'd fallen down the rabbit hole and had no idea where she was going? Interesting thought.

He didn't want this beautiful woman to disappear, never to be seen by him again. She was exquisite. Tall, slender, about thirty years old, he'd guess, and she had big, brown eyes that were accentuated by her peaches-and-cream complexion. Her hair was blond, very short and just wavy enough to be extremely feminine.

That dress. Whew. It clung…what there was of it…in all the right places and seemed to change colors as she moved like…yes, like a lovely pastel opal.

He had a great deal to learn about the enchanting Ms. MacAllister and could not deny that he was looking forward to discovering the pieces to the puzzle.

Conversation around the table resumed, and the noise level was high as Trip and Brent concentrated on eating their salads.

"Trip?" Brent said quietly to Alice.

Trip flipped one hand in a dismissive manner. "Old news. Long story."

"I'm interested. Will you share your old, long story with me?"

Trip popped a radish cut to look like a flower into her mouth and shook her head.

"Ah, a secret, is it? This will be challenging." He stared into space for a long moment, then looked at Alice again. "Try this on for size. Trip is a nickname you were given at some point in your life before you became the lovely, graceful creature that you are. You were in a stage where you constantly fell…tripped…over your own feet. Did I nail it?''

"Not even close," Trip said, then followed the radish with a cherry tomato.

"Well, damn, I'll give this more thought. Unless, of course, you want to put me out of my misery and just tell me what the deal is.''

"Nope."

"How's the food at the Pop In Café, Trip?'' her cousin Bobby asked.

Trip shrugged. "No one has died from it in the two months I've been waiting tables there. The only thing I've tried is the homemade pie and it's delicious.''

"Maybe I'll stop by and sample the pie," Bobby said. "If I eat in your area do I have to tip you?''

"Big time, cousin." Trip smiled.

"Forget it," Bobby said. "You still owe me two dollars and twenty-two cents for the lizard I sold you when we were kids.''

"I'm never paying for that crummy lizard." Trip laughed. "You failed to mention that it had been dead for a week before you convinced me to buy it. I thought it was sleeping in that shoe box you toted it around in, but the poor little thing had croaked.''

''That's why I gave you such a smokin' deal on it,'' Bobby said, grinning at her. ''My original asking price was five bucks when it was still breathing. Hey, I'm about to become a father. I need that two twenty-two to feed and clothe my firstborn child, Trip.''

Trip rolled her eyes heavenward. ''I moved back to Ventura over the Christmas holidays, and I already know that some things have not changed during all the years I was…where I was. I am not giving you the money, Bobby MacAllister, so put a cork in it.''

Laughter erupted around the table, and Brent smiled politely while gathering his data about Alice from what he had heard.

Curiouser and curiouser, he thought, was that Alice was a waitress at a place named the Pop In Café. A waitress? There was certainly nothing wrong with that profession, but it was hard manual labor as far as he was concerned. Not only that, it didn't fit the picture of the MacAllister family that King Chester had painted.

The MacAllisters, Brent thought, reaching into his mental memory bank, were highly respected in many areas of the professional careers arena. Their reputation was one of power, wealth, intelligence, indisputable honesty, and they also were known for giving back to their city by being involved as volunteers in various charitable activities. The name MacAllister had clout. They were upper-crust, movers and shakers.

But Alice was a waitress?

Oh, yes, curiouser and curiouser. And very intriguing was the lovely Ms. Alice. A mystery waiting to be solved. A puzzle, he'd dubbed it earlier, beckoning to him to piece it together. A delectable package that would be unwrapped very carefully, one layer at a time.

Brent frowned slightly as he pushed his salad away and slid a glance at Alice.

A mystery, a puzzle, a delectable package? he thought. He sure was getting poetic in his thirty-second year, which was very out of character for him.

Maybe…yes, this thought had merit…maybe his determination to learn all there was to know about Alice MacAllister was due to his having jet lag from the flight over from Wilshire. His tired brain was a tad fuzzy.

And maybe…but somehow he doubted it…his sexual attraction to Alice was a product of his fatigue, as well. When he'd held her hands as she stood so enticingly close to him after she'd fixed his tie, he had been consumed with desire so explosive, so hot, wild and burning, that he'd felt as if he were going up in flames.

There had been a crackling...something, a nearly palpable entity, weaving back and forth between them like nothing he'd ever experienced before.

Jet lag? No, forget that. It was something else, something more, something that needed to be explored and defined.

"Brent?" Trip said, bringing him from his rambling thoughts.

"Yes? What? Pardon me?" he asked.

"Did I wake you?" Trip said, smiling. "The waiter wants to know if you're finished with your salad. I realize it's a major decision in your life, but..."

Brent laughed. "Yes, I've had enough salad, thank you. The major decision I was facing was whether to eat those radishes or put them in a vase. Heavy stuff, so I'll just pass and have the plate removed to give my beleaguered brain a break."

"Oh, okay," Trip said, unable to keep from laughing as the waiter picked up Brent's salad plate.

Wonder of wonders, she thought. She was having a good time, was actually enjoying herself, having fun.

Because of Brent Bardow.

He was just so...so real. He was a member of a royal family, was the nephew of the king and cousin to the heir to the throne, yet he wasn't acting pompous or putting on airs. He obviously had a comfortable and loving relationship with his parents. Brent had a quick wit and caused her to laugh right out loud, something she didn't do easily.

Yes, she liked Brent Bardow.

But...

Trip smiled at the waiter as he placed a plate in front of her that held a fluffy baked potato smothered in butter, French green beans with slivers of almonds and a succulent slice of roast beef.

But, she thought, resuming her train of thought, she mustn't forget that Brent was capable of rendering her speechless, hardly able to breathe, when he pinned her in place with those incredible blue eyes of his.

She had to remember how off kilter she'd felt as the heat of instantaneous desire had whipped throughout her. When she'd stood close, so close, to him, it had felt like a fire raging out of control.

She must keep—front-row center in her mind— the fact that Brent was dangerous, a threat to her focus, should she succumb to his blatant sexuality and masculinity. Nothing, no one, would be allowed to keep her from accomplishing what she was setting out to do.

She could enjoy Brent's company while he was in Ventura if he chose to spend time with her, but she would keep him at arm's length, both physically and emotionally.

No problem. She had it all figured out.

"Very good," Trip said, nodding decisively.

"How do you know?" Brent said. "You haven't tasted anything on your plate yet."

Trip was saved from replying by King Chester getting to his feet.

"If I may have your attention for a moment, please," he said. "Your glasses are being filled with the newest and finest wine from Wilshire, the Renault-Bardow, which was created by my nephew, Brent. As you all know, it was while Devon was in this country marketing the wine that he met his Maggie. I hereby propose a toast to Maggie and Devon. May they have a long and happy life together and be blessed with the babies I've been waiting to bounce on my knee." King Chester raised his glass in the air. "To Maggie and Devon."

"Hear, hear," Robert MacAllister said.

Everyone at the table raised their glasses, then took a sip of the wine, which resulted in a buzz of compliments about the flavor as King Chester sat back down.

"You created this wine?" Trip said to Brent. "It's delicious. Very different. Special. Congratulations, Brent."

"Thank you," he said, touching his glass to hers. "It was several years in the making, but I finally accomplished what I set out to do."

"You were obviously focused on your goal, your dream."

Brent laughed. "I think it was closer to being possessed, like a mad scientist. I exhaust myself whenever I look back at the long hours I put in each day for all that time." He took another sip of the wine. "But it was worth it."

"Heartfelt dreams are worth that kind of sacrifice," Trip said quietly.

"True. Do you have a heartfelt dream, Alice?"

"You betcha," she said breezily, averting her gaze from his. "I'm going to get the owner of the Pop In Café to change the uniforms the waitresses have to wear even if I have to nag the man to the point of insanity."

"There you go. Good luck."

"Thank you very much," Trip said, then picked up her fork and began to eat.

That was it? Brent thought. That was her agenda

for the future? She didn't have some secret passion that would consume her, keep her separated from those around her who cared about her? Could that actually be fantastically true?

"Brent," Charlane Bardow said, "did the airlines call you back about that flight you wanted to be on tomorrow to return to the island?"

Trip's head snapped up and she stared at Brent. He was leaving Ventura? she thought. Tomorrow? But he had just arrived here and...

"No," Brent said. "They're supposed to contact me if they get a last-minute cancellation but..." He turned his head to smile at Alice, then redirected his attention to his mother. "I believe I was a bit hasty in saying I would only stay the one night here."

"Oh?" Charlane and Byron Bardow, as well as Jillian and Forrest MacAllister, all said in unison, their gazes darting back and forth between Trip and Brent.

Trip felt a warm flush of embarrassment creep into her cheeks, and for the lack of anything better to do, drained her wineglass.

"Well, I..." Brent cleared his throat. "Witnessing Uncle Chester toasting Maggie and Devon with the Renault-Bardow wine makes me realize that I've earned a little time off from the vineyards, should have a vacation, of sorts. I'll call Peter and tell him to cover for me. He's a top-notch foreman, so... He can always contact me if there's a problem or..."

"You're babbling, dear," Charlane said. "We're delighted that you're staying on, considering I had to resort to motherly tears to get you to make this trip at all. You deserve to relax and enjoy yourself."

"Right," Brent said, cutting his meat. "Enough said on the subject."

Jillian and Forrest, and Charlane and Byron, exchanged smiling, speculative glances, but didn't say another word, per Brent's instructions. The noise level in the room increased again as everyone ate the delicious meal and carried on conversations around the table.

"You didn't want to come to Ventura?" Trip asked Brent.

"No."

"Why not?" she asked, frowning slightly.

"To quote you, Ms. MacAllister, it's old news, long story. There's something far more important on my mind at the moment."

"Which is?"

Brent smiled. "Would you pass the salt, please?"

Chapter Two

By the time the dessert of red raspberries nestled in rich French vanilla custard was served, Trip mentally marveled at how the royal family and the MacAllister clan interacted as though they had known one another for years, rather than mere hours.

It wasn't just Brent. Maggie was marrying into a wonderful family, no doubt about it.

The conversations during the meal revealed that the visitors would stay in Ventura for two weeks, then Maggie and her parents would accompany the Renaults and Bardows on the return trip to prepare for the royal wedding. The remainder of the MacAllister family would travel to the island for the affair a month after that.

Two weeks, Trip mused, sliding a quick glance at Brent. It would appear, from the attention he'd shown her all evening, that Brent intended to see more of her while he was in town.

Two weeks. She could handle that. If Brent did seek her out, she was perfectly capable of enjoying his no-strings-attached company. She would not become another of what was probably a long list of women who had succumbed to his good looks, charm and sensual masculinity, topped off by those incredible blue eyes.

And a good time was had by all, Trip thought, rather smugly, then took a bite of the delicious dessert.

"What do you think? Do you want to go with us, Brent?" Charlane said.

"No, thanks," he said. "I've been there a couple of times, so I'll pass."

Oh, dear, Trip thought, she'd been so busy carrying on a conversation with herself that she had no idea what everyone was talking about.

"Are you going to tag along on the great adventure?" Brent asked Alice.

"I...um...can't. I haven't been working at the

café long enough to have any vacation days on the books. So, I... No, I won't be going to...nope.''

"Our triplets have been to Disneyland more times than I can count," Forrest said.

Oh. Disneyland, Trip thought. Thank you, Dad, for clearing that up.

"There was a string of years while they were young girls," Forrest continued, "that they'd put their three heads together and decide that was where they wanted to go for their birthday. I used to have nightmares about spinning teacups.''

"Triplets?" Brent said, raising his eyebrows, then looking at Alice. "You're one of a set of triplets? I didn't know that." He glanced at Jessica and Emily. "Well, sure, I can see it now. I knew you three resembled one another but...I'll be darned. You are identical triplets."

"It's hard to tell," Emily said, "because I weigh far more than Jessica and Trip. Do note, though, family, that I did not have dessert, nor did I put sour cream on my potato. I am on a very serious diet and ten pounds are already history."

"Well, good for you, Emily," Charlane said. "I shouldn't have eaten my raspberries and custard, either, because I probably gained a pound just looking at it, let alone gobbling it up." She sighed. "I ate every delicious bite. Oh, shame on me."

"This is a special occasion, darling," Byron Bardow said, smiling warmly at his wife. "Besides, I'd love you no matter what you weighed."

"Well, bless your heart." Charlane laughed. "In that case, maybe I'll ask for another serving of dessert. No, no, I'll hold myself back."

"Maggie," her mother, Jenny, said to the bride-to-be, "have you given fair warning to Devon that twins and triplets run in our family in vast numbers?"

"She has," Devon said, nodding. "When it comes to babies...the more the merrier."

"Easy for you to say, Devon." Jillian laughed. "I lugged around triplets for nine months. It's no picnic, believe me. I completely forgot what my feet looked like. Grim."

"You were gorgeous," Forrest said, giving his wife a quick kiss on the lips. "I predicted you would have triplet girls and...bingo...you did. That was way back when I was the baby-bet champion of this family. Man, I was good, unbeatable for a very long time." He chuckled and shook his head. "It's hard to believe how many years have passed since then. But we're getting off the subject. The issue at hand is who wants to travel down the coast to Disneyland?"

Everyone suddenly seemed to start talking at once about the proposed journey.

"You've been to Disneyland?" Trip asked Brent.

He nodded. "Yep. I attended college at UCLA. Unlike Devon, this is not my first time in the United States. I lived here while I got my degrees in agriculture and viticulture, then returned home to the Island of Wilshire where I intend to live out my days messin' around with my grapes."

"Messin' around with your grapes?" Trip said, with a burst of laughter. "That's pretty high-tech jargon you're using there, Mr. Bardow."

"And you, Ms. MacAllister," he said, lowering his voice so only she could hear, "have the most beautiful laughter I have ever heard. It's like wind chimes. It would fill the cloudiest day with sunshine, and it makes those gorgeous brown eyes of yours actually sparkle with merriment. I do...oh, yes, I do like the sound of your laughter."

"Oh, well thank you," Trip said. "No one has ever commented on it before. I guess I've never given it any thought, either. Laughter is laughter."

"Wrong. Some people force it, make it part of a phony facade. Some people laugh too loud because they're attempting to become the center of attention. Yours is just right."

"Are you doing your own version of the three bears?" Trip said, smiling.

"Nope. You can't be Goldilocks, you're already Alice in Wonderland. I think your cousin Maggie is Cinderella because she's going to marry the prince. I wonder who else is in this room?" He glanced around. "Ah, I have it. Your sister Emily is Sleeping Beauty. She said she was on a serious diet, so she'll eventually wake up the woman within her and be who she really is and wants to be."

"You're very perceptive, very…sensitive," Trip said. "I doubt that anyone could put anything over on you that you didn't pick up on right off the bat."

"Don't bet the farm on that one," Brent said, a slight edge to his voice. "I'd like to think that I've learned how to read people correctly due to… I'll sure as hell give it my best shot now, believe me." He paused. "So! What's your favorite thing at Disneyland, Alice?"

"The boat ride through the It's a Small World castle," she said. Secrets. Brent Bardow had more than his share of secrets. "And you?"

"Ears."

"Pardon me?"

Brent laughed. "The best part is buying one of those Mickey Mouse hats and walking around all day with those dynamite ears perched on the top of my head. Hey, we're talking way cool here.''

''You're crazy,'' Trip said, her laughter mingling with Brent's. ''You're fun and funny, and totally nuts.''

''You would be, too, if you spent your life talking to grapes.''

''But you love your work *and* the Island of Wilshire. Right?''

''Yes. Yes, I truly do,'' he said, nodding. ''You'll see how beautiful Wilshire is when you come for the wedding. Who knows? Maybe you won't want to leave...ever.''

''Oh, I couldn't stay on the island,'' Trip said, attempting to ignore the funny little two-step her heart suddenly executed.

''Why not?'' Brent said, raising his eyebrows.

''I don't know diddly about grapes.''

''Well, I'd just have to teach you all I know about—'' Brent looked directly into Alice's eyes ''—grapes.''

''That might be—'' Trip started, unable to tear her gaze from Brent's ''—interesting.''

As though pulled by invisible threads, Brent leaned closer to Alice, his gaze shifting to her slightly parted lips.

The sound of her grandfather clearing his throat

caused Trip to jerk. She glanced around and felt an instant flush on her cheeks as she saw that everyone at the table was staring at her and Brent. She looked at her grandfather, who winked at her, then got to his feet.

"It's been a marvelous evening," he said, "but it's time for Margaret and me to head for home and our soft pillows. As the senior member of the MacAllister family, King Chester, let me say what a pleasure it has been to get to know you and yours. We're all very pleased that you'll be staying in Ventura for a while."

"I'll second that," Forrest said, then pushed back his chair. "Ready to go, Jillian?" He rose, then looked across the table. "Trip, is your car still being repaired? Do you need a ride home?"

"Yes, my poor clunker is being held captive by the mechanic. I came here in a taxi, and I'll just take another one home, Dad. My place is miles out of your way."

"That's no problem," Forrest said. "Your mother and I will see you safely home."

"Forrest," Jillian said, laughing as she got to her feet, "you're slipping into your protective daddy mode. The night is young to the next generation in this room. Trip might not be ready to end the evening."

"She's not," Brent said quickly, then looked at Alice. "Are you? Would you like to go dancing?"

Trip frowned. "Dancing? Goodness, I haven't danced since I was in high school."

"It's like riding a bike. It will all come back to you when the music starts. Are you game, Alice?"

"Oh, well..." she said. No, she had to get up very early to be at work for the breakfast crowd at the café. The sensible thing to do was to accept her father's offer of a ride and get a solid night's sleep. She was not, however, in a particularly sensible mood at the moment. Brent was making her feel so alive, young and carefree, and... "Yes, I'd like to go dancing, very much."

"Who wants to join us?" Brent said, sweeping his gaze over the group.

No one accepted the invitation due to a host of excuses.

Brent shrugged. "Guess it's just the two of us, Alice in Wonderland."

"Don't you have to work in the morning, Trip?" Forrest said.

"Say good-night, Forrest," Jillian said, poking him in the ribs with her elbow. "That's your line. Good night, everyone."

Forrest sighed. "You're right. I'm sorry. Old

habits just don't dissolve that easily. Good night, everyone. This was a terrific evening.''

A flurry of farewell hugs were exchanged by all, and ten minutes later Trip and Brent were in a taxi headed for a popular nightclub.

''I've got it,'' Brent said, snapping his fingers. ''You use the nickname Trip because you like being a triplet. Right?''

''Not exactly,'' Trip said, frowning as she shook her head. ''I detested being a triplet when I was growing up, having people ask which one I was. When I was eight or nine years old, I announced that people might as well just call me Trip because they didn't view me as an individual but one of an interchangeable set. The name stuck. Everyone except my grandfather still calls me Trip.''

''Oh,'' Brent said, nodding. ''Being a triplet wasn't fun and games, huh?''

''Not for me,'' Trip said quietly. ''It never seemed to bother Emily and Jessica, but… So! You solved that mystery. You owe me one.''

''One what?''

''Answer to an unsolved mystery,'' Trip said. ''Why didn't you want to make the trip? And why did you plan to only stay long enough to attend the dinner tonight?''

Brent stared out the side window of the taxi for a long moment, then shifted his gaze back to Alice.

"Let's just say that I don't have particularly fond memories of my years here in the States and I didn't feel like reliving them." He paused. "But now I've met you, I'm looking forward to my stay in Ventura. I hope you'll agree to spend time with me while I'm here, Alice. I really do."

"I'd like that, but I don't think you answered my questions."

"I was close enough. And right on time because we're here. Ready to rock and roll, or hip-hop or whatever they call this stuff these days."

"Mmm," Trip said absently. Brent had just done some very fancy verbal footwork. What had happened to him during the years he'd attended college in this country? Oh, yes, the man definitely had secrets.

But then, she thought, as Brent assisted her from the cab, so did she.

Due to it being a work night, the club wasn't crowded and Trip and Brent had their choice of several tables edging a large dance floor. A waitress appeared wearing a short fringed skirt, a vest over a tube top, boots and a white Stetson perched jauntily on her head.

"It's country-western night," she said, smiling,

"in case you didn't figure that out already." She laughed. "Y'all. What can I get you?"

Both Trip and Brent ordered soft drinks.

"Got it," the waitress said. "Oops. Almost forgot to say 'y'all.' On hip-hop night I call everyone dude. Drives me nuts. Back in a few."

"Oh, dear," Trip said, looking at the people who were dancing. "They're doing that western thing… you know, the two-step or whatever it is. I'm definitely out of my league here."

Brent shrugged. "We'll just wait for a slow song and they won't know we don't have a clue as to how to do line dancing, or whatever." He paused. "You moved back to Ventura over the holidays. Where were you living before you returned home?"

"San Francisco. I was there for three years. Before that? Here, there and everywhere."

"Do I detect a wanderlust spirit?" Brent said, frowning slightly.

"No, not really. I'm back in Ventura to stay…I hope."

The waitress returned with their drinks, told them to give a shout, y'all, if they wanted refills, then hurried off.

"You *hope* to stay in Ventura?" Brent said. "It's your choice to make, isn't it?"

Trip sighed, then poked at the ice in her glass with the straw.

"It's rather complicated, Brent," she said, looking at an ice cube bob up and down. "I'd rather not discuss it, if you don't mind. Let's just say that I'm waiting to discover if the old cliché, you can't go home again, is true, and leave it at that."

"Sure. Okay. Well, one thing is a given. You have a great family. I imagine they're delighted that you decided to move back here."

Trip shrugged as she continued to dunk the ice cube.

"Aren't they?" Brent said, leaning slightly toward her. "Alice?"

Trip met Brent's gaze. "Brent, don't push. Please. I said I didn't want to talk about this."

"Hey, I'm sorry," he said, covering her free hand with his on the top of the table. "I just…well, I want to get to know you better." He rolled his eyes heavenward. "Oh, man, I can't believe I said that. Corny to the max. The thing is, it's true. I *do* want to understand who you are, what makes you tick, because I…I like you, Alice." He smiled. "Y'all."

"I like you, too, but… The band just started a slow song," she said. "Vince Gill's 'Look at Us.' Do you know the words? It's beautiful."

"I don't think I've ever heard it."

"It's about a man marveling at how much he still loves his wife. Even though they've been together such a long time. He still sees her as being pretty as a picture. In this sad age of married today, divorced tomorrow, I think this song is so lovely, so meaningful and romantic."

"Then let's dance to it."

"I'd like that."

Trip walked in front of Brent to the dance floor, then turned and moved into his arms. He nestled her against him as they swayed to the music, holding her not too tightly, not too far away, but just right.

She was dancing with a magnificent man, Trip thought dreamily. Oh, he felt so good, so strong and powerful, yet had such a gentle aura. He smelled good, too, like fresh air and soap and something that was just him, the man, Brent.

"Ah, Alice," Brent said quietly, "look at us."

Trip tilted her head back to gaze into the depths of Brent's blue eyes and smiled at him. In the next instant her smile faded as she saw raw desire change the hue of Brent's eyes to a smoky gray at the same moment she felt the heat of her own desire begin to pulse low within her.

Oh, yes, she thought, look at us. They wanted

each other, wanted to make love for hours and hours. It didn't seem to matter that they'd just met...the want, the need, the fire within them was there, burning hotter with every beat of their hearts.

The beautiful song ended, and the band launched into a loud, wild version of ''Boot Scootin' Boogie.'' As the other dancers on the floor whirled and twirled around them, Trip and Brent continued to dance slowly, oblivious to their surroundings, as they gazed into each other's eyes.

Time lost meaning.

One song led to another, then yet another, and still they danced, hearing their own music and the words to ''Look at Us'' over and over again.

''Last call for drinks,'' someone yelled.

Trip and Brent were jerked from the misty, sensuous place they had floated to. They stumbled slightly, then stopped dancing. Brent slowly, and so reluctantly, released his hold on Alice.

''I...'' Trip started, then averted her eyes from Brent's as she busied herself smoothing nonexistent wrinkles from the skirt of her dress. ''I had no idea it was so late. I...I have to get up early in the morning for work and...''

''Alice,'' Brent said, his voice husky.

''Hmm?'' she said, lifting her head slowly to meet his gaze.

"There is something totally terrifying happening between us."

Trip's eyes widened. "Totally terrifying? Dangerous and...oh, thank goodness. This is wonderful."

"Huh?" Brent said, frowning. "Come on, let's go back to the table where we can discuss this privately before they toss us out of here and close for the night."

When they were seated again, Trip smiled at Brent.

"Okay," he said. "You have the floor. What's wonderful about this totally terrifying whatever it is?"

"That fact that we're on the same wavelength, Brent. The same page, as the modern jargon goes. Oh, don't you see? We're very aware of the incredible sexual attraction between us. It's...it's like nothing *I've* ever experienced before, that's for sure. But since we both feel it's a tad terrifying, dangerous, even overwhelming at times, we can decide...together...what we want to do about it, knowing that neither of us can be hurt because it's all temporary and—"

"Hold it," Brent said, raising one hand. "You're making sense, but I'd like to clarify one thing you said. This is more than just sexual attraction. That term edges toward lust, Alice, and that is very tacky. There are emotions involved here, too, caring, wanting to know who the other person is, how we feel about things, and...understand? Are you with me here?''

Trip nodded slowly. ''Yes, all right, I'll go with that. Fine. But my point is, whatever it is that's throwing us so off kilter isn't totally terrifying or dangerous because we both know it's there.

''We also know that you're only in Ventura for two weeks, then later I'll be on the Island of Wilshire for the wedding, and...and that will be that. We have the data, the facts, Brent. There is absolutely no chance of either of us being hurt, or one of us having our heart smashed to smithereens, because we're dealing up-front with how things stand.''

Brent stared into space. ''Oh.''

''That's it?'' Trip said. ''I just delivered one of the longest speeches of my entire life, and all you have to say in response is...oh?''

''I'm digesting your dissertation,'' he said, looking at her again. ''I have jet lag, remember? My brain isn't operating at full power.'' He leaned back in his chair and folded his arms across his chest. ''So, what you're saying...bottom line...is that whatever decisions we make as consenting adults regarding what we do as…as consenting adults isn't risky business because we're consenting adults who have analyzed the damn thing to death.''

''What are you getting so crabby about? And don't say consenting adults again, because it's getting on my nerves.''

Brent laughed and moved forward again. ''I'm a consenting adult who is very rattled at the moment.'' He paused. ''Seriously, I do understand what you're saying and it's very valid. A little cold, a little clinical, but it has merit.''

''It certainly does.''

''Head 'em up and move 'em out,'' the bartender yelled. ''Y'all.''

Brent got to his feet and extended one hand to Alice. ''We're outta here.''

Trip placed her hand in Brent's and allowed him to draw her up and close to him.

''Will you have dinner with me tomorrow night?'' he said, then glanced at his watch. ''Well, technically it's already tomorrow, but…seven o'clock?''

''I…yes, I'd like that. Since you'll have a taxi waiting, I'll be in the lobby to my building at seven.''

Brent nodded and they started toward the door of the club with the other people who were leaving.

Outside a line formed as waiting taxis collected fares and drove away. When it was their turn, Brent reached for the handle of the back door of the vehicle, then hesitated.

"What's wrong?" Trip said.

"This cab has tinted windows that are acting almost like mirrors."

"That's nice. Open the door. It's chilly out here in my slip."

"In a second," Brent said, encircling her waist with one arm and pulling her close to his side. He cocked his head toward their reflection in the window of the door. "Look at us, Alice in Wonderland."

Chapter Three

Trip yawned as she hung her sweater on the designated hook in the rear of the kitchen of the Pop In Café early the next morning. Her hand lingering on the sweater, she stared into space, a soft smile forming on her lips as the lilting melody of the song "Look at Us" floated dreamily through her mind.

Last night, she mused, had been...well, heavenly. She'd had such a marvelous time with Brent, had thoroughly enjoyed the entire evening. She'd even been more relaxed while in the company of her huge family.

And dancing with Brent? Oh, gracious, there

were hardly words to describe how feminine, cherished and desired she'd felt, while held in Brent's embrace. The sensual mist that had encased them in their private world had been like nothing she'd experienced before.

It had taken every bit of her willpower to firmly state that Brent was to remain in the taxi when it stopped in front of her apartment building. She'd blithered on about how late it was, how early she had to get up, how she was perfectly safe going inside alone because there was a security guard on duty at a desk in the lobby. So, thank you, Brent, for a lovely time and…

And then he'd kissed her.

Trip sighed.

That kiss, she thought, had been incredible. Brent had slid his hand to the nape of her neck, lowered his head and claimed her lips with his…right there in the taxi for anyone who cared to look to be a witness. Mmm. That kiss. Heat had coursed through her with such intensity she was convinced that her bones were dissolving and she'd just slither into a puddle on the sidewalk when she attempted to walk to the door of the building.

That kiss had caused her to desire Brent Bardow to the point that she had instant visions of making sweet, slow love with him through the remaining hours of the night. She'd managed, somehow, to sort of slide out of the cab, dash across the sidewalk and into the lobby.

Oh, my, that kiss had been so...

"Say goodbye to your sweater, Alice," a voice said. "There are hungry customers in your station."

Trip jerked and returned to the reality of the shabby little café, pulling her hand quickly away from the silly sweater.

"Hi, Hilda," she said to a plump woman in her forties who was wearing the same bright pink uniform Trip was. "I was daydreaming, I guess. Sorry."

Hilda laughed. "You were hanging on to that sweater like it was an adult form of a security blanket."

"I just forgot to let go of it," Trip said, smiling. "I'm a tad tired this morning. Why does this place have to start serving breakfast at 6 a.m.?"

"Because that's when people get hungry," a man said, then turned bacon on a griddle. "You ladies ready to earn the big bucks I pay you?"

"Big bucks?" Hilda said with a hoot of laughter. "You're so full of bull, Poppy. This must be a labor of love on our part, because we sure aren't doing it for the money, you tightfisted bum."

Poppy, an extremely skinny man in his sixties,

chuckled. "Labor of love? That I know to be the truth. The ladies have been after my body since I hit puberty. What can I say? I'm irresistible. But instead of ravishing me, go wait on the customers. Shoo."

"Going, going, going," Trip said, then hurried across the room and through the swinging doors leading to the outer area of the café.

She zoomed past the counter where several men were sitting on stools covered in red leather, and headed for the booths she was in charge of. Then she stopped so quickly she teetered, her eyes widening.

"Brent?" she said, walking forward slowly. She stopped next to the booth where he was sitting. "What...what are you doing here?"

"Having breakfast," he said, smiling up at her.

"Here?" Trip said incredulously.

"Why not?" he said, lifting one shoulder in a shrug. He retrieved the plastic-covered menu from behind the metal napkin holder. "What's good?"

"I have no idea," she said, still staring at him. "I've only eaten the pie, remember? I...you really want to have breakfast...here?"

"What I really want," he said quietly, meeting her gaze, "is to say good morning to you, see you, hear your laughter, share another kiss with you."

"Shh." Trip glanced quickly around. "Go back to the breakfast thing. Coffee?"

Brent nodded. "And a number three, with the eggs over easy."

"Right," Trip said, then turned and rushed away.

Alice was flustered, Brent thought, watching her. He was obviously the last person she expected to find in this crummy place this morning.

But...so, okay, he'd admit it to himself. He just didn't want to have to wait until their dinner date tonight to see Alice MacAllister. The image of her in his mind had caused him to toss and turn through the few remaining hours of the night when he'd returned to his hotel. The remembrance of the kiss...

That kiss, Brent mused, looking out the grimy window of the café. That kiss he'd shared with Alice in the cab had been sensational. And *shared* was an important word there, because Alice had returned his kiss in total abandon. Sensational. Man, oh, man, how he'd wanted her, wanted to make love with her for hours, wanted...

Brent shifted in the booth as heat rocketed through his body and looked up to see Alice approaching with a coffeepot and a mug. She plunked the mug on the table and began to fill it.

"I would have thought you'd be sleeping. I mean, you were suffering from jet lag, then we were out late dancing and... You should have done that, you know. Slept. Not gotten up at the crack of dawn and—''

"Alice..." Brent said.

"—and come to this place for breakfast when you could have had room service in your hotel, I assume, and rested because—''

"Alice," Brent said, grabbing a handful of napkins out of the holder, "the mug is overflowing."

"Oh!" she said. "Oh, dear me, I'm so sorry. I wasn't paying attention and...I'll get you a clean mug and wipe up the table and..."

"Am I upsetting you by being here?" Brent said, raising his eyebrows.

"Of course, you are, you dolt. I mean, for Pete's sake, members of royal families don't eat in this dump. And I was just thinking about you, and then here you are, and it's like I conjured you up by mentally dwelling on the kiss and the dancing to our song, and the..." She smacked her free hand against her forehead. "I can't believe I just said all that." She sighed. "Okay, fine. I'm totally mortified. I'll go get your number three, and I hope it tastes terrible."

"*Our* song? Hey, I like that. It's kind of teenage corny, but...I really like that. We have a special song that is ours. And I'm delighted to hear that you were thinking about me, the dancing, the kiss. We're still on the same wavelength the morning after.''

"This is not a morning after," Trip whispered, leaning toward him. "You're making it sound as though we... What I mean is... You know."

"Alice," Poppy yelled through the pass-through window to the kitchen. "You want this number three, or what?"

Trip glared at Brent, spun around and stomped off, a shiver slithering down her spine as she heard his throaty chuckle behind her.

"Who's the hunk of stuff?" Hilda said as Trip retrieved Brent's breakfast plate from the ledge.

"A member of the royal family of the Island of Wilshire. He's the cousin to the prince, who is the heir to the throne."

"Oh, okay," Hilda said, laughing. "Can I be Madonna? No, wait. I'll be Julia Roberts because she's got that cute guy, what's his name. Who are you this morning?"

"Me? Oh, what the heck. If you can't beat 'em, join 'em. I, my dear Hilda, am Alice in Wonderland."

Hours later, refreshed from a nap and a long soak in a bubble bath, Trip smoothed the waistband of a red string sweater over her navy blue slacks.

At the café that morning, Brent had said he was hungry for some good ole U.S.A. pizza and they'd agreed that they would go to a pizza place for dinner. He'd then declared that his breakfast was delicious, an announcement that had caused her eyes to widen in surprise.

Trip walked from behind the decorative screens that created the sleeping area of her loft, then stopped, sweeping her gaze over the large expanse.

A chill coursed through her, and she wrapped her arms around her elbows.

No, she thought. She was not emotionally prepared, just not ready, for anyone in her family to see this. And she most definitely didn't intend to invite Brent Bardow to enter her sanctum.

Trip sank onto the puffy sofa and sighed as she leaned her head on the top and stared at the ceiling.

But, she thought, how many excuses could she come up with as to why Brent should bid her adieu out in the hall?

How many times did she *wish* to end an evening with the lingering feel of Brent's lips on hers, just that kiss and nothing more? How many times? None. She wanted Brent. She wanted to make love with him, hold and kiss, touch and taste him.

"You're a wanton woman, Trip MacAllister," she said, raising her head.

But she didn't care how brazen and out of character her passion for Brent was. It was there, it was real, and it made her feel alive and vital, acutely aware of her womanliness.

She and Brent were on measured, borrowed time, with a date clearly marked on the calendar saying when he would return home. Even though she'd travel to the island a month after that, her stay there would be short, and it might even be impossible to escape from the families and be alone with each other.

She'd never been in a situation like this before, Trip mused. She'd never engaged in an affair that would be over because one of the participants flew off to the other side of the world.

She was usually the one in the few—very few—relationships she'd engaged in in the past to end things when they became too serious, when she began to feel pressured, smothered, was having more asked of her than she was willing, able to give.

Actually, there was nothing *ordinary* about this…this whatever it was…with Brent, Trip thought, getting to her feet. From the very moment she'd seen him fumbling with his tie, it was as though everything was magnified and moving at fast forward. So, it stood to reason that her determination to make love with him, a man she'd known such a short length of time, was out of the ordinary as well. That made sense. It really did.

"Fine," Trip said, planting her hands on her hips. "I want to make love with Brent, but I can't invite him into my home, and I really don't want to share that intimate act with him out in the hall."

But...but she wasn't ready to have him come through that door and see...

Trip glanced quickly at her watch, her mind racing. She ran to the door, then down the hall to the next one, knocking loudly when she arrived. The door was opened by a nice-looking man in his mid-thirties.

"Hey, Trip," he said, "what's doin'?"

"I'm about to ask you for a really big favor, Denny," she said. "I need your muscles and some space in your loft to stash some stuff...now. I'm in a major rush."

"May I ask why?" Denny said.

"No."

"Got it." Denny shrugged. "Okay, whatever. Let's do it."

"Oh, thank you," Trip said, grabbing his arm and hauling him forward. "Thank you, Denny."

Trip was waiting for Brent in the lobby of the building as planned and went outside when she saw him start to get out of a taxi that had arrived at the curb.

"I'm ready to go," she said, as Brent rose to stand in front of her. "Pizza. Mmm. I'm starving, too."

"Well, okay," he said, frowning slightly, "but I would have come in and gotten you at your apartment, you know." He smiled. "My mother would give me a stern lecture on my gentlemanly manners because I didn't collect you at the door to your home."

"We won't tell her," Trip said, matching his smile. "Your mother is so nice. She's fun and—"

"Trip," a voice called, causing Trip and Brent to turn in the direction the sound had come from.

Bobby MacAllister came trotting down the street, stopped in front of them and took a much-needed breath.

"Whew, I'm sure out of shape," he said. "Okay, I can breathe again. Look, Trip, I know you told the family that we shouldn't just drop by your new place unannounced, but this is an emergency. Besides, you're not *in* your place, you're standing on the sidewalk *outside* your place, so…"

"Bobby, what's wrong? What's the emergency?"

"Oh. Diane went to the doctor today and he said the baby could come any time now. So, I went out and rented cell phones for everyone in the family who doesn't have one so I can contact you when the big event happens." He extended one hand toward Trip. "Here's your phone. Man, I'm a wreck. I am coming unglued. Diane is so calm it's driving me crazy. She just pats her stomach and tells the kid to come on out whenever it's ready. I swear, Trip, I'm not going to survive this."

Trip took the cell phone and put it in her purse. "This is a marvelous idea, Bobby. I'm…I'm very touched that you thought of me when you…thank you."

"Hey, sweet cousin," he said, "you're a very important part of this family. We've really missed having you with us all these years, and Diane and I hope you'll stay on in Ventura and be a spoil-you-rotten auntie-type person to our child. Nobody is torked at you about the past. This is now. Okay?"

"Yes," Trip said quietly. "I'm struggling with that theory, but I'm trying to fit in, Bobby. Tell Diane I'm thinking of her. I'll be waiting for this phone to ring and…my goodness, this is exciting. This is the first time I'll be going to the hospital for the birth of one of the MacAllister babies."

"Yep. Nice to see you again, Brent. For the record, I can't say I'm surprised you're with Trip. That won't be a big news flash to anyone in the family after last night at the restaurant and… Hey, I don't have time to chat. I've got phones to deliver, then I gotta get home and have Diane hold my hand so I'll get it together. Bye.''

"Bye, Bobby," Trip called, as her cousin sprinted off down the sidewalk in the direction he'd come from.

"You folks going someplace, or what?" the taxi driver yelled.

"Oops," Trip said, then slid onto the back seat of the cab. She leaned forward and gave the driver the address of the restaurant as Brent settled next to her and pulled the door closed.

"Wasn't Bobby cute? Talk about a flustered daddy-to-be."

"Mmm," Brent said.

"Bobby has had months to prepare for the arrival of the baby and now he's a blithering idiot. I think that's so adorable."

"Mmm."

"I wonder if it's a girl or a boy?" Trip rambled on. "If it was me, I wouldn't care either way if it was healthy and… But I don't envision myself getting married and having babies, so that's a moot point. Bobby and Diane have a long list of possible names for their firstborn. Some were very strange. I wonder what they'll—"

"Alice," Brent said quietly.

Trip turned to look at Brent questioningly. "Yes, Brent?"

"Could we back up here a bit to some of the things your cousin said?" he said. "Like...your family is not to drop by your new place. No one is holding a grudge about the past. They all hope you'll stay on in Ventura, but apparently they're not convinced you will." Brent paused. "Let's toss in why you don't see yourself marrying and having babies, too, while we're at it."

A flash of anger coursed through Trip, then kept right on going and disappeared, leaving her feeling very vulnerable and exposed. Her shoulders slumped and she sighed.

"I was hoping you wouldn't pick up on all of that," she said, not looking at Brent as she fiddled with the clasp on her purse. "I *could* say it's none of your business."

"Yes, you could," Brent said, nodding, "but that sure would build a high wall between us, Alice, that you'd be hiding behind. Getting to know each other better would stop right here and now. That's not good. Not good at all. But, well, it's up to you as to whether you wish to share more of who you are with me. I can't force you to do it."

"Pizza," the taxi driver said, coming to a

screeching halt. "Hey, buddy, all women have secrets. You're better off not knowing what they are
the majority of the time, because then you're supposed to automatically know how to deal with their
feminine person, or whatever the hell they call it."

Brent leaned forward and gave the man a bill.
"Keep the change."

"The advice was free," the man said. "Thanks
for the nice tip, though. Enjoy your pizza, folks."

Right, Trip thought dryly, as Brent assisted her
out of the vehicle. There was now a bowling ball
in her stomach and no room left for any pizza. Two
more minutes and Bobby would have missed catching her in front of her building and Brent wouldn't
have heard her cousin chattering like a magpie.
Darn, darn, darn.

The restaurant was fairly crowded, but Trip and
Brent found an empty booth, agreed on the toppings
for their pizza, then Brent went to place their order.
He returned with a pitcher of cola, sat down opposite Alice and filled their glasses.

"Here's to—" he said, lifting his glass "—sharing and caring."

Trip stared at Brent's raised glass, at her own that
she hadn't touched, then back at Brent's.

"All right," she said, her voice not quite steady.

She lifted her glass and clinked it against Brent's. "To sharing and caring."

They each took a sip of the cold, sweet drink, then set their glasses on the wooden table. Brent leaned back and spread his arms along the top of the leather booth.

She didn't *have* to tell Brent Bardow anything she chose to keep to herself, Trip thought, frowning slightly as she met his gaze. This wasn't a long-standing relationship with a hoped-for future together that would crumble into dust from the weight of secrets kept. This was a very short-term whatever it was, that had a beginning, middle and an ending already marked on the calendar.

There was no reason to bare her soul to Brent.

But yet...

She wanted to.

She didn't like the image in her mind of the wall between her and Brent that he had spoken of. She already had a barrier between herself and her family that was proving difficult to demolish. She had, in fact, kept an emotional distance from everyone she'd met since she'd left home years before. That's how she conducted her life, which meant she would never fall in love, marry, have babies, because it was too late to change who she was.

But if she lowered that barrier just a tad, answered just some of Brent's questions, it would be a...yes, a safe way to sort of practice at least peeking over the wall she'd erected around herself. Safe because what she had with Brent was temporary. It might enable her to make more positive overtures toward her family.

As far as stepping from behind the wall completely to enable her to fall in love? No. She'd be kidding herself if she thought she could ever do that. It was just too big, too frightening. No.

"Alice?" Brent said quietly.

"What?" She took a deep breath and let it out slowly. "Yes, all right. It's not all that complicated, Brent. I told you that I didn't like being one of the MacAllister triplets, and I did a bang-up job of rebelling against that role when I was a teenager.

"Jessica and Emily were excellent students, so I slacked off and just squeaked by as far as my grades went. They had oodles of friends, so I was a loner, kept to myself. They enjoyed nice clothes, so I wore funky junk from used-clothing stores. They obeyed every rule our parents had set in place, so I broke them all, like coming in later than our curfew. Nice kid, huh?"

Brent lifted one shoulder in a shrug. "You were establishing your own identity."

"In spades," Trip said. "I left home right after

high school graduation, refused to even talk about going to college. Not me, not the rebel. I went to New York and pursued... Well, anyway, I lived in New York City for several years, then went to Colorado, then on to San Francisco. I never told my family when I'd be home, I'd just show up from time to time. I...I hurt some wonderful people very, very much by the way I conducted myself.''

''But now you've come home.''

Trip nodded. ''I'd like to think I've finally matured to the point that I realize that what I did was wrong. I've missed my family and want to be a part of the MacAllister clan...but it might very well be too late.''

Brent leaned forward and folded his arms on the top of the table.

''I find that hard to believe after meeting your family. They're warm, honest, open. I heard what Bobby said. No one is dwelling on the past.''

''That may be true, but they're tense around me, afraid they might say something to upset me, cause me to pack it up and leave town again. I find it hard to relax around them, too. It's been so many years and... I don't know. I guess maybe it *is* complicated.''

''Why don't you want them to drop by your apartment when they're in your neighborhood? Casual visits like that are often more comfortable than scheduled gatherings.''

''No,'' Trip said quickly. ''What I mean is, I'm not used to that, and the thought of it makes me edgy. I don't want to open my door and find a MacAllister standing there out of the blue. No.''

''I see,'' Brent said, nodding slowly. ''I guess. Okay, go on to the part about why you'll never marry and have kids.''

''It should be clear to you by what I've just explained. If I am struggling to connect with a group of people who love me unconditionally, it's far too late to let down my guard entirely, not protect myself in any manner, which is what is required to be an equal partner in a loving relationship, a marriage. I just wouldn't be able to give enough of myself to another person, risk that much.''

''But...'' Brent started, then cocked his head to one side. ''That's our number for the pizza. I'll be right back, Alice.''

Trip nodded, then Brent started to slide out of the booth. He stopped and looked directly into Alice's eyes.

''I think you're giving up on yourself too easily,'' he said. ''You know, saying you can't change enough to be an equal partner in a relationship and what have you. You should give yourself credit for what you just did here…with me.''

"What do you mean?"

"You talked to me, Alice, and I listened, really heard what you said," Brent said. "You did the sharing and I did the caring. You can't beat that combination.''

Chapter Four

To Trip's heartfelt relief, when Brent returned to the table with the pizza, he launched into a discussion about a bestselling novel that was to be made into a movie. They engaged in a game of selecting what actors should play the roles of the various characters, which was rather silly but definitely fun.

When they left the restaurant, they stopped at an ice-cream store, bought two-scoop cones, then strolled along the sidewalk and window-shopped as they ate their creamy dessert. Brent pointed out that they both kept pushing the ice cream down so that the very last bite of the sugary cone would be filled.

"There's probably some scientific, psychological meaning behind that," Brent said, after popping the tip of the cone into his mouth. "Gives great insight into our personalities, which are, once again, on the same wavelength. Maybe I'll research it on the Internet."

"Oh, for heaven's sake," Trip laughed. "Emily used to bite the end off her cone and practically stand on her head to use it like a straw. I wonder what the shrinky-dinks would say about that?"

"Don't have a clue," Brent said, chuckling, "but I'm sure it's very important in regard to the identity of Emily's inner child. Speaking of child types, Emily has a son, right? He was sitting next to her at the dinner? Trevor. Yes, that was his name. He looked to be about twelve, or thirteen. Nice kid. I assume since there wasn't a dad on the scene at the party that Emily is divorced?"

"No," Trip said, tossing her napkin in a trash barrel as they walked past it. "Emily has never been married. She had Trevor when she was eighteen and has raised him alone."

"Whew, that's a tough job," Brent said, "especially when you take it on that young."

"The family was very supportive, there for her when she needed them," Trip said. "I honestly don't know what happened between her and

Mark…Trevor's father…because they had been to-gether all through high school, then he suddenly left Ventura for college back east and…

"Well, the truth is I took off, too, so I never heard whatever explanation there was for their split. As time passed and I came home to visit, the opportunity to ask for details didn't present itself, nor did it seem to matter by then. I do know she named her baby Trevor *Mark* MacAllister, so she didn't end up despising Mark for leaving."

"Interesting."

"Trevor is a nice kid from what I gather," Trip continued, "although I guess he gives Emily a bad time about being overweight. He's at an age that having a…well, chubby mother embarrasses him, and he's rather vocal about the subject."

"Teenagers are not known for their diplomacy and tact at times. That statement doesn't include yours truly, of course. I was a prize, a peach of a teen, never gave my parents a moment of grief."

"Is your nose going to grow?" Trip asked, smiling up at him.

Brent laughed. "From here to Chicago. I was, shall we say, busy at that age. Poor ole Devon had to toe the line because he was the prince, the heir to the throne, but I was removed from that just enough to raise hell without lightning striking me dead.

"I got lots of lectures about behavior befitting a member of the royal family, but I wasn't under a microscope the way Devon was, and still is. Maggie will have to get used to that when she marries Devon and lives on the island, but I get the feeling she'll handle it just fine."

"I'm sure she will," Trip said, nodding. She glanced around. "Goodness, we've really trekked on and on here. We're only about a block from my apartment building. There won't be a need to hail a cab to see me home, Brent."

"Are you trying to tell me something, Alice? Like you're ready to end the evening?"

Trip stopped walking and met Brent's gaze, seeing the frown that knitted his brows.

"No," she said quietly, "I don't wish to end the evening yet, Brent." She paused and sighed. "I'm not very sophisticated, I guess. I don't know how to play the dating game, don't know all the rules and... You'll see me to my door, then I envision an awkward moment where I'm supposed to either say good-night, or invite you in. Right?"

Brent nodded. "That's how it generally goes."

"And if I invite you in on the pretext of having

coffee, I'm actually indicating that I want to…that I want to make love. Am I still right?''

''As a rule, yes. But if you invite me in and tell me it's for a cup of coffee and nothing more, I'll accept that. I won't like it, you understand, but I'll be a gentleman about it to the point of ad nauseam.''

Trip wrapped her hands around her elbows. ''So, it's up to me, isn't it? To decide how this night will end. That is a tremendous responsibility, Brent, and…'' She shook her head.

''Hey,'' he said, gripping her shoulders. ''It doesn't have to be like that, Alice. Everything about us is different, special, rare. We're not going to do that come-in-for-coffee nonsense. We're going to talk it through, discuss this like—''

''Consenting adults,'' Trip said, rolling her eyes heavenward. ''Blak.''

Brent encircled Alice's shoulders with one arm and they started off down the sidewalk again.

''I've definitely overused that term,'' he said, smiling. ''I won't say it again, I promise.'' He paused, his expression now serious. ''Okay, we'll discuss this. I'll go first to make it easier for you.''

''Thank you,'' Trip said. A silent minute went by, then two, then three. ''Brent?''

''I don't know how to do it,'' he said, raking his

free hand through his hair. "I'm programmed for the come-in-for-coffee bit.

"What am I supposed to do? Just open my mouth and tell you that I desire you more than any woman I've ever met? That I want you so badly I ache? That making love with you is never far from my thoughts, and I think we should sprint the remaining distance to your apartment so I can take you in my arms and...cripe. It's all true, but...damn it, Alice, help me out here."

Trip stopped walking and stared up at Brent with a rather astonished expression on her face.

"I don't believe this. You, Mr. Worldly and Wise, who probably has broken hearts across the globe, is admitting that you're feeling a tad awkward, rather jangled, shall we say, by this exchange we're having?"

Brent frowned. "I do not have a reputation for breaking hearts, my dear Ms. MacAllister. But as far as the rest of what you said...yeah, okay, I'm a little flustered, due to the fact that I've never taken part in a conversation like this one." He smiled. "But then, I've never met a woman like you before, either, so I guess that makes sense. Okay. I've bared my soul. The ball is now in your court."

Trip stared at Brent for another long moment, then she smiled. It was a lovely smile, a warm, womanly, I'm-glad-I'm-me-and-you-are-you smile. She reached up and framed Brent's face with her hands.

"I absolutely adore you, Brent Bardow," she said, the smile still firmly in place. "You're just so real, so down-to-earth. You take things that could become uncomfortable and complex and just smooth them out and make them seem so easy, simple, without diminishing their value. That's a gift, it truly is."

"Oh," Brent said. "You have such soft hands. I'll give you three years to get your dainty paws off my face."

Trip laughed in delight.

Brent had done it again, she marveled. He'd made her feel so young and carefree, happy and just plain old glad to be alive.

"I want to make love with you, Brent, very, very much. There. I said it out loud, just as you did. It feels right, the way it is meant to be. I'll have no regrets about taking this momentous step with you." She dropped her hands from his face and took off at a run. "You said we should sprint to my apartment," she yelled. "I'm leaving you in the dust."

"Hey!" Brent said, starting after her. "You

cheated, Alice. You're supposed to say ready, set, go.''

Brent's long legs covered the distance between him and Trip in short order. They entered the lobby of her building together, their laughter dancing through the air and accompanying them into the elevator.

A few minutes later, Brent was sweeping his gaze over Trip's apartment. She'd left one small lamp on, creating a warm, golden glow.

''A loft,'' he said. ''Dynamite. I really like your home, Alice.'' But how did she pay the rent for this place on her current salary?

''Thank you,'' she said, her gaze lingering on the screens she'd moved from in front of the bed to the opposite side of the expanse. ''I was lucky to find it when I moved back here. It's perfect for...my needs.'' She paused. ''Would you like something to drink? Oops. I think I'm supposed to ask you if you want coffee.''

''No, I don't want any coffee.'' Brent closed the distance between them. ''I want—'' he cradled her face in his hands and dipped his head to outline her lips with the tip of his tongue ''...you.''

Shivering at the sensuous foray, Trip whispered, ''And I want you.''

Trip stepped back, causing Brent to drop his

hands from her face. She took one of his hands in hers and led him across the large room to the double bed that was streaked partially with shadows. She turned to him, her arms floating up to encircle his neck. He wrapped his arms around her and claimed her lips in a searing kiss.

Brent ended the kiss slowly, reluctantly, savoring the taste of Alice, the feel of her breasts crushed against his chest, her aroma of spring flowers and woman. He drew his hands down her arms, then kissed the fingers of both of her hands before releasing them.

Trip swept back the blankets on the bed, then lifted her chin and met Brent's smoky gaze. With hands that were not quite steady, they removed their clothes, fumbling at times, Brent swearing under his breath at the repeated motions and wasted time. Then they stood there...naked before each other, drinking in the sight of what was displayed for them, only them.

"You're exquisite, Alice." Brent's voice was raspy with passion.

"So are you," she said, hearing the thread of breathlessness in her voice.

She moved onto the bed and waited...an eternity...for Brent to retrieve a foil pack from his wallet. He stretched out next to her, propping his weight on one forearm.

"Alice," he said huskily, "we are going to go to Wonderland together."

And they did.

They kissed and caressed, explored and discovered the mysteries being revealed to them of a body so soft and feminine, and one so rugged and male, etching all they found indelibly in their minds...and hearts.

Brent drew the lush flesh of one of Trip's breasts into his mouth, laving the nipple with his tongue. She sighed in pure pleasure, closing her eyes for a moment to savor every heated sensation consuming her. He moved to the other breast to pay homage there, as her hands slid over his moist back, his muscles bunching beneath her palms. He skimmed one hand across her flat stomach, then along her slender hip and leg, his lips soon following the heated path.

"Oh, Brent, please," Trip said, her voice holding an echo of a sob. "I want...need...now...I..."

"Yes," he said, hardly recognizing the gritty sound of his own voice.

He took the necessary steps to protect her, then his mouth melted over hers once more before he entered her with a deep, powerful thrust, filling her, bringing to her all that he was.

She gripped his shoulders as he began the rhythmic tempo, slowly at first, then increasing it, faster, harder, thundering. Trip matched him beat for heart-stopping beat in perfect synchronization.

Higher they went. Heat coiled and tightened, sweeping through them in waves of ecstasy that held the promise of the moment yet to come, the place they would be flung to. Wonderland.

"Brent!"

"Alice. Oh, Alice."

There was a kaleidoscope of colors, so vivid, so rich, swirling around them, encasing them in a cocoon where no one else was allowed entry. It was theirs. They spun out of control, clinging to each other, knowing they were safe as long as they were together. They hovered there, shifting, drifting, feeling the last ripples of release whisper throughout them.

Brent collapsed against Alice, spent, sated, then gathered the last ounce of strength he possessed to move off her and roll to her side, tucking her close to him, lips resting on her damp forehead.

Trip splayed one hand on the moist, dark curls on Brent's chest, feeling his heart begin to return to a normal beat just as hers was. Their bodies cooled, and Brent reached down to pull the blankets over them.

Neither spoke.

They searched their minds for the proper words to describe the beauty of what they'd just shared, the awe of it, then gave up in defeat as they realized that the words they needed had not yet been invented.

"Will you stay?" Trip finally said. "The night? With me?"

"I'll stay. This is where I want to be, Alice."

"This is where I want you to be," she said, then closed her eyes and slept.

Brent woke to the sound of water running in the shower, and the warmth of sunlight tiptoeing across his face. He laced his fingers beneath his head on the pillow and stared up at the ceiling.

Incredible, he thought. That was just one of the words he could use to describe the lovemaking shared with Alice. But the memories themselves were far better than any adjectives he might come up with.

Heat rocketed through Brent's body, and he shifted slightly in the bed, telling himself to change the mental subject.

Okay, he thought, he wouldn't dwell on making

love with Alice, he'd think about Alice herself, the woman. Man, she was something, really fantastic. Yes, she was complicated, had an intense side to her that caused her to scurry behind her protective wall if she began to feel pressured or pushed.

She also had a rather disturbing attitude about not being capable of being in a serious relationship.

Why that bothered him, he didn't know. Heaven knew he wasn't in the market for a serious relationship. He'd been down that road once and had vowed never to retrace those steps. He should count Alice's stand as more points in her favor but...forget it. That was too heavy a subject before morning coffee.

Alice, Brent mused on. There was also a fun, whimsical part of her that surfaced when she relaxed and just enjoyed herself. Her dark eyes sparkled, and her smile and laughter were real. She had a what-you-see-is-what-you-get honesty that he cherished, that he knew was very important to him. She was a waitress in a crummy café and if anyone had a problem with that...tough. Yes, she was reluctant to talk about herself to any great degree, but that would come in time.

The bathroom door opened and Alice appeared wearing her pink uniform. Brent drank in the sight of her, and vivid, sensuous images of the previous night formed in his mind's eye.

"Good morning," he said.

"Hello," Trip said, smiling. "I'm sorry I woke you, but I have to be at work at six, so we need to get ourselves in gear."

Meaning, Brent thought, that she preferred not to leave him here in her apartment when she left. Fair enough.

"I'll take a quick shower," he said, flipping back the blankets and leaving the bed.

"Brent, I just want to say… What I mean is…last night was…thank you."

Brent gathered his clothes from the floor, then walked past Alice and dropped a quick kiss on her lips.

"Ditto," he said. "I'd kill for a cup of coffee. Do we have enough time?"

"Yes."

Heat slithered down Trip's spine as she swept her gaze over Brent's naked body as he walked toward the bathroom. When the door closed behind him, she took a quick breath, realizing she'd nearly forgotten to breathe as she'd stared at him.

"Oh, my," she said rather dreamily. *"I will never, ever, forget last night."* She paused. *"Coffee. Make coffee, Trip. Right now."*

She had just poured two mugs full of the steaming drink when Brent emerged from the bathroom, his hair damp, his face still stubbled in a dark beard.

"I don't look too presentable," he said, running his hand over his chin, "but I'm squeaky clean. Ah, coffee. I'm forever in your debt." He took a sip of the hot brew. "Hello, my name is Brent Bardow and I just woke up."

Trip laughed. "You're so crazy. I think I've laughed more since meeting you than I did in the six months before we met."

Brent sat down at a small table and Trip settled in the chair opposite him.

"I should offer you some breakfast," she said, "but I can't because I don't have any breakfast-type food in the house and I don't have time, anyway."

"This coffee will hold me until I get back to my hotel. May I see you tonight, Alice?"

"I...I have an...appointment this evening, Brent," she said, tracing the edge of the mug with a fingertip. "I'm not certain what time I'll be free."

"An appointment? At night?"

Trip met his gaze. "Yes."

"All right," he said. "Try this on for size. I'll stay put in my room at the hotel, and you come by when you're finished with your…appointment. We'll have a late dinner. Sound feasible?''

''I'd like that.''

''All the Bardows and Renaults are staying at the Excaliber. I'm in room 610.''

Trip nodded. Brent drained his mug and got to his feet. ''I'm outta here,'' he said. ''I'll see you tonight. Walk me to the door?''

At the door Brent kissed Trip so intensely that her knees began to tremble.

''Tonight,'' he said when he finally released her.

''Yes,'' she said with a little puff of air.

When the door closed behind Brent, Trip stared at it for a long moment, then started back toward the table and her unfinished coffee. Halfway across the room she stopped, her gaze pulled to the screens on the far wall.

Secrets, she thought, walking to the screens, then behind them. She was still keeping secrets from Brent, from her entire family. Well, Brent had secrets, too. He hadn't yet told her why he had dreaded returning to the States, hadn't shared what had happened to him in the past to evoke that negative emotion.

So many secrets.

Trip stared at what she had hidden with the screens.

There they were. The easel, the paints and brushes, the few small framed paintings she'd left there when she'd taken the large ones to Denny's.

There they were. Her hopes, dreams, the focus of her existence.

There they were. Her secrets.

And tonight she and the agent she'd hired upon returning to Ventura were meeting with the owner of a prestigious gallery to discuss the possibility of an exclusive showing of her work. Trip had already sold some of her pictures on the beaches and in small galleries up the coast, and that money allowed her to pay the rent on her loft. But this could be her big break.

Her work. The paintings she signed with an *A* in the lower right-hand corner. An *A* for Alice, because when she painted she was no longer the rebel Trip, the confused and angry Trip, searching for her own identity. When she painted she was free in her mind, her spirit, her very soul. She was Alice, and when she painted she embraced the very essence of who she was.

Just as she had done when she'd made love with Brent Bardow.

But the majority of the time, she thought with a sigh, walking slowly back to the waiting coffee, she was still Trip and had been for many, many years.

Trip, who didn't even know how to reach out and embrace the unconditional love of her family, let alone lower her self-made barriers enough to give her heart to a special man.

She sank onto the chair at the table, then stared across to where Brent had sat.

When she was with Brent, she mused, she was vitally alive, free of her inner ghosts and demons. When she was with Brent, her smiles were real and genuine laughter flowed easily from her lips.

When she was with Brent, she was beautiful and acutely aware of her own femininity, her woman-liness.

"Caring and sharing," Trip said aloud.

Brent was teaching her how to do that and it felt like a warm, comforting blanket she could wrap around herself and savor.

Chapter Five

Trip walked slowly along the crowded sidewalk leading to the Excaliber Hotel, attempting and failing to blank her mind.

She'd had the taxi let her out two blocks away with the hope that the added distance would enable her to settle down to earth after the exciting meeting with her agent and the owner of the art gallery.

She'd even gone home to change into jeans and a nubby, lightweight white sweater before starting out for the late dinner with Brent. But even that diversion hadn't stopped her mind from replaying every word that had been spoken at the gallery.

"Unbelievable," Trip whispered.

In a little more than two months, she was to have a private, invitation-only showing of her work at one of the most prestigious art galleries in Ventura, California.

A shiver of pure joy coursed through her and she wrapped her hands around her elbows to hug the wondrous sensation, to keep it safely within her so she could savor every precious moment of it.

After so many years of pinching pennies to buy supplies needed for her work, of spending endless hours alone concentrating on her painting, cutting herself off from her family, as well as the people she'd come to know, the solitary life she'd led had finally resulted in her being recognized as a talented artist.

"Unbelievable," Trip said again, but in the next instant she frowned as a chill swept through her.

Her heartfelt dream, her deepest desire, was coming true, she thought, and she had no one to share the glorious news with.

She just couldn't envision herself calling a meeting of the MacAllisters and saying, "Guess what? I know that I haven't acted like a member of this family for many years, but now I want you to forget all that and be sincerely thrilled for me. I've accomplished what I set out to do, which was, of course, something you knew absolutely nothing about.'' No, that was asking far too much.

Trip sighed, glanced at her watch, then quickened her step when she saw that it was nearly nine o'clock.

Sharing and caring, she thought. Brent placed great emphasis on that, but she couldn't tell him what had transpired this evening, either. It was all too new and she felt so fragile, as though she was hanging on to what had happened by her fingertips, afraid it would somehow disappear into oblivion and not really be true.

Trip entered the hotel and started across the expensively decorated lobby, headed toward the bank of elevators. And ran smack-dab into King Chester, Charlane and Byron Bardow, Maggie and Devon and Maggie's parents, who had just walked out of the restaurant on the main floor.

Oh, good grief, Trip thought, where was the rabbit hole to fall into when Alice needed it?

''Trip,'' Maggie said, smiling. ''What are you doing here?'' She laughed. ''That was a silly question. You must be meeting Brent.''

''Who refused to have dinner with us,'' Charlane said pleasantly, ''because he said he already had plans for a late supper. The salmon was delicious, dear, and came with a dill sauce to die for. You might mention that to Brent. He enjoys salmon when it's cooked to perfection the way they do it here.''

''I'll...tell him,'' Trip said, acutely aware of the flush of embarrassment staining her cheeks. ''Salmon and dill sauce. Got it.''

''Did Bobby find you and give you a cell phone?'' Maggie said. ''My brother is coming unglued about this baby that's about to arrive. It's so cute. I've never seen him so jangled.''

''There's a lot of 'being jangled' going around these days,'' Trip said, producing a small smile. ''Yes, I have the phone and... Oh, good grief, this is mortifying. I mean, heaven knows what all of you must be thinking about me and Brent and my arriving here at this hour and...'' Her voice trailed off and she threw up her hands.

King Chester smiled. ''I do believe we're thinking that you and Brent intend to share a late dinner, my dear. There's really nothing mortifying about having salmon and dill sauce in the company of someone you enjoy being with. It's a rather common occurrence.''

''Oh,'' Trip said.

''Trip, I hope you didn't mind that Bobby gave you the cell phone,'' Maggie said. ''If you'd rather not be disturbed at heaven only knows what time when the baby decides to come into the world, I can tell him not to call you."

"No, no, I want to be called. Really." There it was again, the walking on eggshells around the unpredictable and here-today-and-gone-tomorrow Trip. "I was very pleased that Bobby included me."

"Well, if you're sure," Maggie said.

"Positive," Trip assured her.

"We've kept you from your dinner long enough," Charlane said. "I know my son. He's a grumpy bear when he's hungry. It was lovely seeing you again, Trip. Alice."

"It was nice to see all of you, too." Trip edged around the group. "I'd better be on my way so the bear doesn't get any grumpier. Bye."

Trip rushed to the elevators, silently thanked one that was standing open as she entered it and pushed the button for the sixth floor with more force than was necessary.

Mortifying, she mentally repeated, then stared into space. Except…now that she thought about it, *she* had been the only one who had been embarrassed when she'd encountered the Bardows, Renaults and MacAllisters.

Oh, would she ever be able to relax and just…

just *be* around her family and those connected to it? She was beginning to doubt it would ever happen.

Brent spun around from where he'd been staring out the window when he heard the rather tentative knock on the door of his suite.

"Alice," he said, aware that his heart had increased its tempo. "She's here, at long, long last."

He strode across the room and flung the door open, not taking the time to look through the safety hole.

And then he just stood there, drinking in the sight of Alice.

She was here, after a day that had seemed like a week. She was here, looking so lovely, delicate and feminine. She was here, and if he didn't take a breath in the next two seconds he was going to pass out cold on his face.

As Brent filled his lungs with much-needed air, he extended one hand to Alice. She placed her hand in his and allowed him to draw her into the room.

Brent closed the door behind Alice, then dropped her hand and moved close, causing her to bump into the door. He braced his hands on either side of her head and looked directly into her eyes, his body only inches from hers.

All the thoughts in Trip's mind disappeared into

a sensuous mist as she gazed into Brent's blue eyes. The tips of her fingers tingled with the urge to touch him, but she kept her arms at her sides.

Time lost meaning as they stood there, not moving, hardly breathing, anticipating the moment when their lips would meet. Heat began to churn low and hot within them as the tension built and their desire soared.

Then Brent slowly, very slowly, lowered his head and brushed his lips over Alice's. Once. Twice. Then returned to claim her mouth in a kiss they had waited an eternity to share.

Brent groaned deep in his chest.

A whimper of need caught in Trip's throat.

Brent broke the kiss and spoke close to Alice's lips, his body still inches away from hers.

"I missed you." His voice was rough with passion. "I thought about you all day. It's corny, it's nuts, but it's true. I am so damn glad you're here, Alice."

"This—" she drew a shuddering breath "—is where I want to be, Brent."

"Same wavelength. Perfect."

"I...I bumped into our families in the lobby," Trip said. "They know I'm here. With you. I was embarrassed, flustered, because it's so late at night, and I was obviously heading for your room and...

But they all acted like it was the most natural thing in the world, and your mother suggested you have salmon for dinner.''

Brent chuckled, and the rumbling, male sound caused a shiver to course through Trip.

''Salmon with dill sauce?'' he said.

''Dill sauce,'' she said, nodding. ''She said it was delicious and... If you don't take me in your arms right now I think my bones are going to dissolve from the heat, the incredible heat that's...oh!''

Trip's startled ''Oh!'' was followed by a gasp of surprise as Brent swept her up into his arms and carried her across the living room and into the bedroom beyond. He placed her on the bed, then followed her down, his mouth melting over hers. She wrapped her arms around his neck and returned the heated kiss in total abandon.

When they separated only long enough to shed their clothes, Trip felt as though she was floating above herself, watching Trip remove what she'd chosen to wear, then be magically transformed into Alice. Alice, who could simply *be*.

Their joining held an edge of urgency, of need so powerful it consumed them beyond reason. It was earthy and rough, wild and real. It was ecstasy. And heat. Burning. It was wave after wave of sensual sensations that carried them over the top and flung them into glorious oblivion as each called out the name of the other, the only one who could go with them to that private and magnificent place.

And then they stilled, and savored and stored memories in chambers of hearts that began to return to normal tempos. They drifted down from where they had been to realize that where they now were was also theirs alone to embrace.

"You," Brent said, lying close to Alice, his lips resting lightly on her forehead, "have woven a spell over me, Alice."

"That's because I'm Alice in Wonderland," she said dreamily. "I followed the white rabbit into a world of magic."

"Tell the rabbit to get his own woman. You're mine."

Trip stiffened slightly, then relaxed again, refusing to allow anything to mar the sweet bliss of the moment.

"Yes, I'm yours," she said, then paused. "For now. For the time we have while you're here and…"

"Shh," Brent interrupted. "Don't go there."

"You're right. Shh."

A lovely, serene silence fell, and sleep began to creep over their senses. Then Brent's stomach rumbled, causing a bubble of laughter to escape from Trip's lips.

"You're hungry. Your mother told me that you turn into a grumpy bear if you're not fed regularly, or something like that."

"A grumpy bear?" Brent said, smiling. "What kind of a thing is that for a mother to say about her darling kid? However, the truth of the matter is...I need food. Want some salmon with dill sauce? I'll call room service and tell them it's an emergency rush order."

"Go for it."

Less than half an hour later, Trip and Brent were dressed, seated at the table by the windows and taking their first bites of flaky salmon.

"Delicious. Your mother is a wise woman, sir."

Brent nodded. "Yep, she is. Most of the time. She gets kind of freaky on the subject of my providing her with a slew of grandchildren, though. I told her not to hold her breath and she threatened to do exactly that and her death would be all my fault."

"You don't want to have children?" Trip said, cocking her head to one side.

Brent sighed. "At one point in my life I wanted

the whole nine yards. A wife, kids, a home. But then..." He shook his head.

"Brent, does the 'but then' have something to do with why you didn't want to make this trip with your parents? You haven't...well, shared that with me, the reason you didn't wish to return to the States. We do sharing and caring, remember?"

Brent looked at her for a long moment, then nodded.

"You're right, that's part of our program. So, yeah, okay. When I was in college I was in what I believed to be love with a woman who was getting a degree in psychiatry. I assumed, which was my first mistake, that we would marry and live on the Island of Wilshire. I later realized we hadn't discussed that in any depth, that I had just taken that fact for granted.

"Brittany, that was her name, was assuming a far different scenario. She thought that I understood she couldn't make a name for herself on a dinky little island in the middle of nowhere."

"Oh, dear."

"Brittany had it all figured out," Brent continued quietly. "I should return home long enough to train one of my men to take over the vineyards, then come back to California and get a job with one of the big outfits here. That last scene with Brittany is not a fond memory, believe me.''

"I'm sorry, Brent. It's no wonder you didn't want to make this trip, return to a place that would bring back painful memories. But…well, I'm very glad you did.''

"So am I,'' he said, producing a small smile. ''But what happened with Brittany made me wary of getting into any kind of serious relationship again. She had an agenda, a plan, that didn't include my wants, my needs.

''For the last few years I haven't even dated because I found myself wondering if the woman might have a secret agenda, a dream to leave the Island of Wilshire for the excitement of the world beyond it. What if I came to care for someone, only to discover…

"You know what Brittany told me, Alice? During that last ugly scene with her she said I was out of step with the times, that I'd expected her to put her career on the back burner. That I should go home to my fantasy island and find someone to wait on me hand and foot.

''She said I'd better make certain that the next woman in my life didn't have any hopes or dreams of her own. According to Brittany, I was so selfish and self-centered I couldn't deal with a woman needing more than just me to feel fulfilled.

"I've never forgotten those words she hurled at me. They leveled me like physical punches. Secret agendas. I made up my mind I'd never run the risk of going through something like that again. There you go. The great tale of woe."

"I'm...well, sad, that you had such a devastating experience. It obviously hurt you very much."

"On a much brighter note," Brent said, "my mother promised to bring me some of those dynamite Mickey Mouse ears when they all go trekking down the coast to Disneyland. Cool, huh?"

"Majorly way cool," Trip laughed. "Is that how the teenagers say that these days? Or is it awesomely majorly way cool? I'll ask Trevor and get back to you so you can refer to your new ears in the proper manner."

"Your assistance in the matter will be appreciated."

They burst into laughter, the joyous sound pushing aside the shadows of the past with the sunshine of the present, but giving no space to thoughts of the future.

They completed the meal with lively chatter that flowed easily from one topic to the next, then settled onto the sofa and began to watch an old movie on television. Trip curled up close to Brent, resting her head on his shoulder. He wrapped one arm around her, absently stroking her arm as they yelled at various people who might be the villain and cheered on the hero.

"I am *not* spending the night here," Trip said during a commercial. "I mean, good grief, with my luck I'd find your family in the elevator in the morning when I left."

Brent chuckled, then kissed her on the forehead. "They'd probably just smile and ask you to join them for breakfast. They're...wait a second, I have to say this right...they're awesomely majorly way cool people."

"Well, *I'm* not," Trip laughed. "I'd die on the spot. Nope, I'll wait until this movie is over, even though I already know the butler did it, then I'm definitely going home."

"The butler did it?" Brent said, frowning. "No, he didn't. He's not the one who tried to kill the hero. The butler is an undercover agent for the FBI. The gardener did it."

"He did not," Trip said. "He was planting marigolds when the shot was fired. The butler is really the hero's long-lost sister, posing as a man, and she wants to ice the hero before he can marry the heroine so she can inherit the family fortune."

"Have you seen this movie?"

"No." Trip laughed. "Have you?"

"Nope. Okay, now this is getting interesting. I'll bet you five bucks that the gardener did it."

"Oh, easy money. You're on, Bardow. It was the butler in drag, or whatever."

"I don't accept credit cards, MacAllister," Brent said, with a hoot of laughter. "I want my five smackeroos in cold, hard cash."

They both moaned in dismay when it turned out that the cook did it. The hero's father, long since deceased, had jilted her in her youth and she was out for revenge, deciding the son would repent for the sins of the father.

"Boo, hiss!" Brent yelled.

"Who wrote this thing?" Trip said, dissolving in a fit of laughter. "No wonder they showed it late at night. No one would waste their leisure time in the early evening to watch it. I give it a thumbs-down."

"Ditto." Brent pressed the remote to turn off the television.

"I've got to go home," Trip said, not moving. "It's already tomorrow, and I have to get up so early."

"I wish you'd stay." Brent pulled her even closer to his side. "I want to wake up next to you."

"I..."

"Hey, it's okay," he said quickly. "I understand where you're coming from. I might add, however, that Maggie is spending the night in Devon's suite and my clan knows it. That's just a little bubblegum for your mind to chew on. Data."

"Maggie and Devon are engaged to be married," Trip said, wiggling out of Brent's embrace and getting to her feet. "Big difference there."

"I won't argue the point," Brent said, rising. "This time. But it's going to be a trade-off. Don't give me grief over the fact that I'm going with you in the taxi, will see you safely home, then I'll come back here."

"But—"

"It's not open for discussion, Alice," Brent said, then paused. "The cook did it. Man, talk about having a secret agenda." He wrapped his arms around her and nestled her to his body. "You will never know how glad I am that you don't have a secret agenda, Alice. That means more to me than I could even begin to tell you."

People in general, Trip thought, would probably view her as being terribly dishonest with Brent because she hadn't told him about her art, the scheduled showing, her hopes and dreams, her secret.

But what those who would pass censure on her

actions wouldn't understand was that her *agenda,* to use Brent's word, wasn't something that would cause him to feel betrayed if he knew about it.

No, it wouldn't be like that at all, because if she and Brent were actually moving toward having a future together, her secret agenda would fit in perfectly with his lifestyle on the Island of Wilshire, where he intended to live out his days. If she told Brent about her painting, he would be so happy as he realized she could be very contented on his peaceful, beautiful island.

Trip sighed.

There was no point in telling Brent about her painting, as they were *not* viewing what they were sharing as possibly being permanent.

Besides that she hadn't yet gathered enough courage to tell Brent, or her family, about her work. Every time she envisioned herself doing that, she was consumed with icy fear, a feeling of being so exposed, so vulnerable to opinions and attitudes.... All those years of being alone still held her in an iron fist from which she was unable to break free.

Chapter Six

For Trip, the following week seemed to fly by with a speed that made her head spin at times. She should, she knew, be thoroughly exhausted from the pace she was keeping, but she was, instead, bursting with energy that kept her moving at top speed.

Life, she decided at one point, was glorious. Working at the café was something she did by rote, then her afternoons were spent painting more pictures for the gallery showing…sometimes in her loft, other times in a nearby park…and her nights were focused on Brent.

She'd gotten her car back from the repair shop

and taken the pictures she'd had stashed at Denny's to the gallery, where decisions were reached on the types of frames to be made for each. She had only three more pictures left to paint to complete the agreed-upon number for the showing of her work.

One week plus a day since the night she and Brent had eaten salmon with dill sauce in his hotel suite, they stood in line at a movie theater, waiting to inch their way forward to purchase tickets.

"Missed you today, per usual," Brent said, one arm encircling Alice's shoulders to keep her tucked close to his side. "I went to a museum this afternoon and kept seeing things I wanted to share with you, ask you what you thought, while knowing we'd be on the same wavelength. I toyed with the idea of calling and asking you to join me, but I know you need to sleep so you'll be ready to rock and roll with me in the evening."

"Mmm," Trip said.

She'd put the finishing touches on a painting this afternoon, had *not* been napping as Brent assumed she'd been, she thought.

"Is something wrong, Alice?" Brent said, bringing Trip from her troubled thoughts.

"What? Oh, no, no," she said, smiling up at him. "I'm just a little tired. I'll relax during the movie and be fine."

"Didn't you get enough sleep this afternoon?" Brent said. "We can make an early night of it if you like so you can get the rest you need."

"Feed me popcorn during the movie," she said, "and I'll be as good as new."

"You've got it, my sweet," Brent said, dropping a quick kiss on the top of her head. "I'll buy you the biggest bucket of buttered popcorn they make." He tipped his head to the side to see what was taking so long to get to the ticket window. "If we ever get into this place, that is. We're going to miss the start of the movie if they don't hustle up. Time is marching on."

Time is marching on, Trip mentally repeated. Time was the enemy. Time was going to run out and Brent would get on a plane and fly to the other side of the world, out of her life.

Yes, she'd see him again when she went to the island for the wedding, but she'd already told herself not to count on being able to spend many private hours with Brent there because of the festivities scheduled.

Dear heaven, the very thought of Brent leaving made her feel so hollow, so bleak and chilled to the core. She would reach across the bed in the darkness of night and he wouldn't be there. She'd sleep alone. She'd eat alone. She'd spend her days and nights alone.

And she would be so very, very lonely.

She felt such a sense of rightness when she was with Brent, of being complete, whole, of having found the masculine counterpart who fit so perfectly with the new awareness of her womanliness she now possessed. She cared so much for him that the thought of his leaving her made her feel cold and empty, and a breath away from bursting into tears.

Good grief, Trip thought, frowning. If someone could read her mind they might very well come to the conclusion that she was in love with Brent Bardow. But she wasn't. Dear heaven, no, of course she wasn't. Falling in love was beyond her grasp, was an emotion she wasn't capable of.

If she didn't have the courage to show Brent, or her family, her dream, her art, she was definitely not able to run the risk of allowing herself to do something so emotionally momentous as falling in love, giving her heart to someone to do with as they may. God, what a terrifying thought.

Trip gazed up at Brent, who was once again looking at the line ahead of them.

Brent was going to get on that airplane, she thought, and he was *not* going to take her heart with him. No. The deep feelings she had for him, the caring, would fade in time, dim, then be gone. She was *not* falling in love with Brent.

"Ah, here we go," Brent said. "Some guy was buying about fifteen tickets for the group with him so that took a nice chunk out of the line."

"I...oh, good heavens," Trip said, jerking in surprise. "My purse is ringing." She rummaged inside and snatched up the cell phone.

"Hello, Bobby," she said tentatively as she pressed the tiny device to her ear.

"It's happening, Trip," Bobby said. "Finally. The baby. We're at the hospital. I'm petrified. I can't breathe, Trip. I swear I...gotta go. Bye."

"Bye," Trip said, her eyes widening. "Brent, the baby is...Bobby can't breathe," Trip said, then took a sharp breath. "I can't, either. Now what?"

Brent laughed. "Now we go to the hospital and wait for the newest MacAllister to come into the world."

"You don't have to spend your evening pacing around a hospital waiting room," Trip said as they left the line of people and started down the sidewalk. "You can just drop me off if you like."

"No way. I wouldn't miss this for the world. It's not every day of the week that a person gets to be involved in a miracle."

"What a lovely thing to say," Trip said, as Brent assisted her into the car he'd rented.

Brent splayed one hand on the roof of the car and gripped the edge of the open door with the other. He bent down to look directly into Alice's eyes.

"That's what babies are, Alice," he said quietly. "Miracles. Two people made love, shared the most intimate act known to humanity and created a new life. Oh, yes, babies are miracles."

"Yes," Trip said softly. "You're right, and you're also very special for having said so."

Brent leaned far enough into the car to kiss Alice, then stepped back and closed the door. He jogged around to the driver's side and slid behind the wheel.

"Buckle up," he said, "and send messages to the stoplights to turn green as we approach them." He turned the key in the ignition. "Oh, this is great. I have no idea where the hospital is."

"I'll direct you," Trip said. "Go straight ahead for two blocks, then turn right. The hospital is where Maggie and Devon met, you know."

"Yeah, I heard the story of how they connected there. Well, that hospital is definitely a miracle-making place," Brent said as he pulled away from the curb.

A baby, Brent mused, as he maneuvered the car through the heavy traffic. A miracle. What would a baby created by Alice and him look like? Would he, or she, have blond hair like Alice's? Or black hair like his? Maybe nature would combine the two and their baby would have brown hair. Yeah, that would be nice...a blend of his parents.

Oh, man, Alice would be so exquisitely beautiful while she was pregnant with his child, and he'd be by her side every step of the way. He could envision himself placing his hand on her rounded stomach, feeling the baby move within her. What an awesome and humbling thought.

Brent blinked, then frowned.

What a ridiculous thought, he admonished himself. Where had all that nonsense come from?

He and Alice weren't going to create a baby when they made love.

They weren't going to get married and raise a family. They weren't even going to see each other again when he left Ventura, except for whatever time together they could steal when Alice came for the wedding.

And the most important "weren't" on the list was the fact that he and Alice *weren't* in love with each other in the first place, an ingredient that should definitely be in the mix.

Yes, that's what it was. A recipe. Two people met, were attracted to each other. Add sharing and caring, respect and honesty, blend well while spending as much time as possible together. Sift in smiles and laughter, and lovemaking so incredibly fantastic it defied description.

Simmer until hearts melted, then meshed into one entity strong enough to withstand the rigors of time.

Whoa, Brent thought, rolling his eyes heavenward. That was so corny it was a crime. Since when did he indulge in such romantic gooey garbage like that? Well, it wasn't really garbage, it was sort of poetic. Love, forever and ever love, was a carefully attended-to recipe that two people concentrated on making together and...

"Oh, for Pete's sake," he said, shaking his head in self-disgust.

"What's wrong?" Trip said, looking over at him.

"Huh? Oh, I got caught by this red light, that's all," Brent said.

Trip smiled. "I don't think the baby will be born before we get to the hospital." She paused. "Will it? It's overdue, I guess, so maybe it will be in a big hurry now and...forget it. I have no idea what I'm talking about. Brent, the light is green."

"Oh," he said, pressing on the gas pedal. "Alice, did you ever think about the fact that love is like a recipe? There's a whole bunch of ingredients that have to be there in the right amounts, then blended together just so. And they have to be continually tended to so that it doesn't go stale like something you baked would if you just ignored it once you... Never mind. I'm blithering like an idiot."

"No, you're not," Trip said thoughtfully. "I think you expressed that very well. Very romantically, too, I might add. Yes, love could be compared to a recipe." She smiled. "I think one of the ingredients is magic."

"Mmm," Brent said, nodding.

Like the magic he and Alice shared. Oh, Bardow, cut it out. He was not giving one more moment's thought to love and the stupid recipe and...because he wasn't in love, had no intention of ever falling in love again and that was that.

The fact that he felt sliced and diced whenever he thought about leaving Alice was because...was because he *cared* for her. A lot. More than a lot. Very deeply. Very, very deeply and...

"Turn right at the next corner," Trip said, bringing Brent from his jumbled thoughts.

"Thank you," he said, more than happy to direct his attention entirely to following the directions to the hospital.

"Thank you?" Trip said, laughing. "For telling you to turn right? Gosh, do I get a hug when we actually arrive in the parking lot of the hospital?"

"Sure," Brent said, chuckling.

"It's that tall building in the next block," Trip said, pointing. "See it?"

"Yep. I imagine the waiting room is going to be packed with MacAllisters."

"I don't know. I have no idea if the clan turns out in force after all these years and all the babies that have arrived. Maybe they just stay home and wait for a telephone call."

The MacAllisters definitely did not wait at home for news of the birth. The waiting room that Trip and Brent were directed to was crowded to the point that Trip's cousin, Ryan, and his father, her uncle Ted, were leaning against the wall outside the room.

"Hey, Trip, Brent," Ryan said, then shook Brent's hand. "Nice to see you here."

"This is exciting," Trip said. "How long do you think we'll have to wait before the baby is born?"

Ryan shrugged. "Don't have a clue." He laughed. "My famous top-cop dad here delivered my sister himself because she was in such a rush. Then? I was six months old before they came to Korea to adopt me. I think they were still worn out from the way Patty popped into the world four years before that.''

''Very funny,'' Ted Sharpe said, chuckling. ''Not funny was the fact that you took one look at me and started wailing your head off.''

''You're a scary guy,'' Ryan said, smiling at his father. ''Lean and mean.''

''Yeah, right,'' Ted said. ''As for Bobby and Diane's baby? It's anyone's guess how long we'll all be here. Babies start running the show from the very beginning, that's for sure.''

Trip poked her head into the waiting room. She felt a little shiver of nervousness slither down her spine at the size of the group, who were all suddenly looking directly at her.

Now, she supposed, they would all make a big fuss over the fact that she was there, was joining the family for this special event. She'd become so uncomfortable that she'd want to leave in about three minutes flat and...

''Hi, sweetheart,'' Forrest MacAllister said, then resumed his conversation with his brother Michael.

''Hello, darling,'' Jillian called to her daughter. ''I'm afraid there's nowhere to sit in here so you'll have to stand for now.'' She redirected her attention to Margaret, who was sitting on the sofa.

Trip opened her mouth, then closed it again, allowing a genuine smile to form on her lips.

No one was going cuckoo because she was here, she realized. It was as though they simply expected her to be among them because…well, because she was a MacAllister. Oh, this was nice. Very, very nice.

"You look pleased about something," Brent said, sliding one arm across Alice's shoulders.

"I'm just glad to be here," Trip said, smiling up at him.

"Alice," Robert MacAllister said, coming out of the room.

"Hello, Grandpa," she said, kissing him on the cheek. "Did you enjoy visiting Disneyland…again?"

"It brought back fond memories," he said. "Alice, remember when I announced at Christmas that I would be meeting with each of my grandchildren at a time that I chose to give them a special gift?"

"Yes, of course I remember. I thought Jessica was going to pop a seam waiting for her turn. She was always begging to open gifts early when we were growing up.

"I know that the beautiful chess pieces that Jessica put on the top of her and Daniel's wedding cake were from the gift you gave her, but she's been very secretive about the meaning behind it. In fact, I have no idea how many of your private meetings have been held.''

''That's not important,'' Robert said. ''What is of importance is that it's your turn. Are you free any time tomorrow?''

Trip's eyes widened. ''I'm next to receive my surprise? Oh, I'm getting goose bumps. Yes, tomorrow is my day off. What time would you like me to come? I don't mind getting up early and... Stop laughing, Brent.''

''I can't help it. A little eager, are you? To get this special present?''

''Well, yes. This is March, and Grandpa made his announcement at Christmas, and...just hush. Grandpa? What time?''

''Nine o'clock tomorrow morning?'' Robert said. ''In my study at the house.''

''I'll be there,'' Trip said quickly.

''Bets, bets, baby bets,'' Forrest said, coming out in the hall with a fistful of money. ''It's time to put the old tradition back into action. I was champion for a long spell, Brent, way back when, until that darn Ted Sharpe blew me out of the water. I'm figuring on regaining my title. I'm predicting a girl born within the next hour. Five bucks, folks. Let's see the green.''

"It's a boy," Brent said, pulling his wallet out of his pocket. He glanced at his watch. "In no more than twenty-two minutes from now."

"Oh, yes, easy money," Forrest said, snatching Brent's bill.

Ted, Ryan, Robert and Trip all made their predictions and produced five dollars with Trip choosing a girl in two hours and fifteen minutes. Forrest scribbled all the data on a piece of paper, then disappeared back into the room.

"I'm part of the baby bet," Trip said, smiling. "Just like—"

"One of the family," Robert said, winking at her, then returning to join Margaret on the sofa.

"Yes," Trip whispered, "just like one of the family. Just like a real MacAllister."

"Good for you," Brent said quietly, then kissed her on the temple. "You *are* a MacAllister, Alice. And you're also the most *real* woman I've ever had the pleasure of getting to know."

A warmth suffused Trip from the top of her head to the tips of her toes. She savored it, memorized how it felt, then tucked it away in the special place in her heart.

Brent won the baby bet.

With only two minutes to spare of his predicted twenty-two, Bobby came running down the hallway dressed in green scrubs.

"It's a baby!" he said. "It's a boy. Seven pounds, three ounces, fingers, toes, nose, everything. He's beautiful. He's... Diane was fantastic and..." Emotions choked off his words and he shook his head.

Hugs, handshakes, slaps on the back took place, then Forrest smacked the wad of money into Brent's outstretched hand.

"I was really starting to like you, Brent," Forrest said, "but forget it. No, you're okay. I won't be a bad sport. Man, you nailed it. How did you do that? Being the baby-bet champion will just have to be a fond memory of mine, I guess. I've lost my knack."

"You're pouting, Forrest," Jillian said, coming to where they all were standing and slipping her arm through his. "You had your days of glory. Congratulations, Brent, you're the new baby-bet champion."

"I can live with that," Brent said, stuffing the money into his wallet. "When can we see this little miracle who just earned me a bunch of bucks?"

"I'll go find out," Bobby said.

"Wait, Bobby," Trip said. "You didn't tell us what you and Diane named your son."

"I didn't?" Bobby said. "Man, I'm so frazzled, exhausted, excited and..."

"His name, Daddy." Trip laughed.

"Oh," Bobby said. "Well, Diane and I decided that we're about to add a bunch of more people to the family when Maggie marries Devon. So, in honor of those new folks we're naming the baby Joseph Devon."

"I'm honored," Devon said, from where he was standing in the doorway to the waiting room. "I really am. I can't begin to tell you what this means to me. Thank you, Bobby, and express my gratitude to Diane, too."

"Sure thing," Bobby said.

"Baby MacAllister is ready to receive his admirers," a nurse said as she approached the crowd. "I've lost count of how many times I've said that. If you'll all follow me, please?"

A few minutes later it was Trip and Brent's turn to step close to the window to peer into the bassinet that had been moved next to the glass.

"Oh," Trip said, awe very evident in her voice. "Oh, Brent, look at him. He's beautiful. Such perfection in a tiny package and...you're right he's a miracle. Hello, Joseph Devon. Welcome to the world, and welcome to the most wonderful family in the universe." She sniffled. "I'm going to cry, no doubt about it."

Brent stared at the sleeping infant, his heart thundering as he drank in the sight of the baby. The achy sensation in his throat told him that it wouldn't take much for tears to fill *his* eyes, too.

A son, he thought. A miracle. He'd long ago buried the dream of being a father, having a son or daughter, created with the woman he loved. But that dream was front-row center again and was strong and solid, refusing to budge.

Brent slid a glance at Alice and saw her dash two tears from her cheeks as she continued to smile at the baby.

A baby, Brent's mind echoed. His and Alice's child. That image was settling in right next to his heartfelt desire to be a father. Whew. He was on emotional overload.

What did they mean, these new and foreign thoughts and feelings? Did his *caring* for Alice run much deeper than he'd realized? Or was he just caught up in the moment of seeing Joseph Devon within minutes of his arrival?

Damn, he didn't know what was happening to him, but he knew that somehow, *somehow,* he had to find out what all this meant.

Brent hardly remembered the farewells exchanged in the hospital, nor the drive to Alice's apartment building. She had chattered on about the new baby, about how special it had been to be a part of the family as they all saw him for the first time. He assumed that he had commented in all the right places as Alice hadn't asked if something was wrong, or remarked that he was acting strangely.

As the couple entered the loft, Brent pulled himself from his tangled and unsettling thoughts, then realized that Alice had spoken to him and was now looking at him questioningly.

"Pardon me?"

"I asked if you wanted something to eat or drink?"

"Oh. No. No, thank you," he said, then glanced around. "It still smells like paint in here, doesn't it? The little table you mentioned that you painted is sure taking a long time to dry, I guess."

"Yes, it is," Trip said quickly. "That's because I used oil-based paint. Smelly stuff. I wasn't aware of the odor because I'm so used to it. I'll open a window."

Trip hurried across the area and fiddled with the locks on one of the windows on the far wall.

Tell him, her mind shouted. *Tell Brent about your paintings. Take him behind the screens and...no. No, not yet. Not yet. But soon. I'll share it all with him very soon. But, oh, God, I don't have the courage...not yet.*

Brent sank onto the sofa. "Joseph Devon. That was really a fantastic thing that Bobby and Diane did...naming their baby after my cousin. What an incredible honor. What a gift, a touching and important way to make it clear that we're all part of a big and unique family."

Trip opened the window, then walked slowly back and settled next to Brent on the sofa.

"Yes, it was an extremely nice thing to do," she said. "Maggie was on her third tissue the last time I looked at her, and Devon was a tad misty himself."

"Mmm," Brent said, nodding. "Just think, Alice. Tomorrow, or the next day, whenever, Bobby and Diane will take the baby home and lay him in the crib they've surely gotten ready for him. They've waited all those months and he's finally here. If it was me, I think I'd probably just stand there and watch him sleep, not want to move, not leave the nursery, or... Man, a baby. A son. They're really a family now."

"Yes," Trip said softly, "they are." She swept her gaze over the loft. "I can't envision a baby in here. It's not cozy enough."

"What about in your heart, your mind?" Brent

shifted on the sofa so he could look directly at her. "Can you envision a baby there?"

"That's not a fair question at the moment, Brent," Trip said, clutching her hands in her lap and staring at them. "We just came from seeing a newborn baby, Bobby and Diane's miracle. Something like what we experienced tonight might create emotions, yearnings, that will disappear in the dawn's light of the next day."

"*Might* is the important word, Alice. But it doesn't stop there. The emotions, the yearnings, when examined in the morning light might *not* have disappeared at all. They could very well be here to stay."

Trip frowned as she met Brent's gaze. "Why are you doing this? Pushing about emotions, yearnings, regarding a baby, being a family... What are you doing?"

Brent stared up at the ceiling for a long moment, then looked at Alice again.

"I don't know," he said, sounding suddenly weary. "I saw that baby and I...I thought I'd buried those kind of dreams deep enough that they'd never be able to surface again, but...

"Alice, whenever I think about leaving you in a couple of days I feel as though I've been punched in the gut. You mean so much to me, so damn much.

"Then when I saw Joseph Devon I...I wondered what a baby you and I would create, together, would look like..." He dragged both hands down his face. "I'm a mental mess. I don't know what's happening here, what it all means, but I really can't bear the idea of walking out of your life and never... Ah, hell, I don't know."

"I don't want you to leave, either," Trip said. "We'll see each other at the wedding, but it just won't be the same. These days...and nights...with you have been so... When you go I'll miss you..." She drew a wobbly breath that held the hint of tears. "I think I just joined your mental-mess club."

"Do you...do you think we're falling in love with each other, Alice?"

"No. No, absolutely not. We'd know it if we were." She paused. "Wouldn't we? Well, yes, darn it, of course we would, and we're not. I'm just now making progress with opening my heart to my own family. I'm not even capable of the intensity of man-and-woman love, for heaven's sake. Brent, please, let's change the subject. You *are* leaving. There's no purpose to be served by having this insane conversation."

"Isn't there? Don't you want to know what's really happening between us? Don't you?"

"No," Trip said, getting to her feet. "I'm going to have a glass of orange juice. Would you like some?"

"No, thank you." Brent rose and gripped Alice's shoulders. "I *do* want to know what this is we're sharing. So, okay, I do, you don't. It calls for a compromise, I think."

"No, I don't want to think about—"

"Compromise," Brent interrupted. "Just listen, all right? I won't bring up the subject again while I'm here in Ventura, if you promise to think about it, us, during the month we're apart before you come to the Island of Wilshire for Maggie and Devon's wedding.

"The old cliché will apply, per se. The distance, the separation, will either make our hearts grow fonder, or we'll look at each other when you arrive on the island and realize what we had here was special, but...well, temporary, and that it's over. The month apart will, hopefully, supply us with the answers we don't have."

"But—"

"Alice, please promise me you'll think about us, what might be happening here. God, what if we're soul mates, meant to be together, and we let it slip through our fingers because it's so damn terrifying, and we're still held in the grips of our past pain, our ghosts, or—''

''I…I don't know what to say, Brent,'' Trip said, unwelcome tears filling her eyes.

''Just say yes. Agree to this compromise. Say you'll think about it, us, relive the memories we've made, get in touch with your hopes, dreams, yearnings, look into the future. Please.''

No, Trip thought, feeling a rush of panic consume and chill her. She couldn't handle this. Couldn't do what Brent was asking of her. She wasn't strong enough, brave enough. She was too fragile and vulnerable.

''Please, Alice,'' Brent said, a catch in his voice. ''Say you'll do it. Say yes.''

Trip stared at Brent and saw the shimmer of tears in his beautiful blue eyes, heard the edge of desperation in his voice, felt the trembling in his hands where they were splayed on her shoulders, and knew she was defeated.

''Yes,'' she whispered.

Chapter Seven

"I'm not even going to attempt to chat with you for a while, Alice," Robert said, smiling at his granddaughter the next morning. "The meetings I've already had with my grandchildren to present them with my specially selected gift have shown me that the recipient is eager to get down to business."

Trip laughed. "Guilty. I've been awake since dawn, and it seemed as though the clock was refusing to move forward so I could come over here, Grandpa."

Robert chuckled, then got to his feet and crossed

the room to a closet on the far wall. He returned, sat down, then handed Trip a framed picture face-down that was about fourteen inches square. She took it, turned it over, then the color drained from her face as she stared at it.

"Yes," Robert said quietly, "it's one of your paintings. I've had it for about two years now, although no one has seen it but me, not even your grandmother."

"But how..." Trip started, then leaned the picture against the fireplace and met Robert's gaze. "I don't understand this. I mean..."

Robert raised one hand for silence. "Alice, I couldn't bear not knowing where you were beyond the postcard you would send. I didn't know what you were doing, if you were safe, happy. It was very difficult for all of us to cope with that."

"And I'm so sorry," Trip said. "It was so selfish and self-centered of me. I'm trying to make amends to the family for the way I behaved all those years but..." She shook her head.

"But you were pursuing your dream of becoming an accomplished artist."

"Yes, but how did you—"

"I hired a detective," Robert said. "Now, before you get angry that your privacy was invaded in that manner, please understand that I did it out of love and concern for you. Once I knew you were safe, knew what you were doing, I simply waited for you to come home, having told no one what I discovered.

"That was a hard decision to make because at times I felt your parents had the right to know that you were fine, but I kept silent. If there had been any hint that you were in trouble, needed help, I would have told Forrest and Jillian. The detective bought this picture from a group you were showing on the beach up the coast and brought it to me. You're very talented, Alice, and I'm extremely proud of you."

"Thank you," Trip said softly. "I'm…I'm going to have a private, invitation-only showing of my work at a gallery here in Ventura in a couple of months, but no one in the family knows that."

"Don't you think it's time you told those who love you what you've been doing all these years? Why the secrecy, Alice?"

"Oh, Grandpa," she said with a sigh, "it's all so complicated. Mom and Dad were aware that I liked to draw and paint when I was a child, and they always put my pictures on the refrigerator. But when I started high school, they told me that even though I obviously had artistic talent it would be best to have a marketable skill. They insisted I take computer classes, things like that.''

''And?''

''They did that out of love and the worry that I might become a starving artist or whatever if I concentrated only on my painting. I realized that years later, but at the time, in my rebellious teenage mind, I viewed it as a put-down, a rejection of my talent, as a statement that I wasn't talented *enough*.''

''Oh, my dear child,'' Robert said, frowning and shaking his head.

''I was wrong. I know that now. But that was my mind-set for so many years. So many, Grandpa, and I built such high, strong walls around myself, keeping everyone at bay. I want to really come home, be a part of this family, tell everyone about my painting, the showing I'm going to have and…but I'm terrified. Grandpa, I'm so scared. If I do that I'll be stripping myself bare, will have no more walls to hide behind.

''I'll be Alice. What if I fail, don't reach the level of success I dream about? What if I tell the family about the showing and it's a flop, none of my pictures sell, people take one look and turn around and walk out of the gallery and…''

''Alice—''

''No, Grandpa, I'm Trip.'' Tears filled her eyes.

"It's safer being Trip, don't you see? I know how to protect myself when I'm Trip."

"And Trip is lonely," Robert said.

"Oh, God," Trip said, then pressed trembling fingertips to her lips to stifle a sob, "yes."

"It *is* time to come home," Robert said gently. "It's time to be Alice, my darling." He paused. "I'm going to give you your special gift now."

Robert reached down along the side of the chair, retrieved a tissue-wrapped square object and handed it to Trip. She sniffled, accepted the gift, then placed it on her knees and removed the paper.

"Oh, it's beautiful. A pewter picture frame and it's exquisite."

"It's also empty," Robert said. "It's waiting for an eight-by-ten-inch picture to be placed in it. I want you to do a self-portrait."

"What?" Trip said.

"I want you to paint a picture of yourself to be placed in that frame," her grandfather said. "But with one stipulation. It must be a portrait of Alice. Not of Trip. Alice. It will reveal who Alice really is by the expression on your face, the emotions in your eyes. Our Alice. Understand?"

"I can't do that!" Trip said, shaking her head. "No, I..."

''Shh, shh,'' he said. ''Take the frame with you. When the time is right, you'll paint the portrait.''

''But...''

Robert got to his feet, then bent over and kissed her on the forehead. ''I love you, my darling. Your entire family loves you unconditionally. Remember that.''

Robert left the study and closed the door behind him. Trip wrapped her arms around the lovely pewter frame, hugging it close. She drew a shuddering breath, then gave way to her tears and wept.

The next night Trip stood in front of the mirror over the bathroom sink in the loft and practiced smiling, finally sighing and leaving the small room in defeat. She sank onto the sofa with another sigh.

She didn't feel like smiling, she thought miserably. This was the last night she was to have with Brent. The airplane flight the royal family was booked on was scheduled to leave very early tomorrow morning.

Then Brent would be gone.

Dear heaven, it was so stark, so harsh, the reality of that thought.

Trip got quickly to her feet as she felt the sting of threatening tears in her eyes. She wandered around the loft, then went behind the screens and stared at the empty pewter frame she'd hung on the wall.

A self-portrait, she thought. That's what she was supposed to paint and place in the lovely frame. But it had to be a picture of Alice, not Trip. Oh, why was her grandfather doing this to her? Didn't he understand that she just wasn't ready for this? She couldn't do it, she just couldn't, because...

A knock on the door caused Trip to jerk, then she spun around and hurried to answer the summons.

Brent, her mind hummed. He was taking her out to dinner at a fancy restaurant. She would have to reach deep within herself for the fortitude to be cheerful and pleasant, not put a damper on this special evening.

Get it together, Trip, she told herself, then opened the door.

"Hi," Brent said quietly, no hint of a smile on his face as he stepped into the room.

"Hi," Trip said, closing the door behind him. "I was going to go shopping for a new dress for tonight, but I just didn't have time. So I'm wearing the one I had on the night we met, and I'm sure that's breaking some sort of rule in the dating book for you to see me in the same dress so soon...oh, Brent, I don't want you to leave Ventura."

"Ah, Alice," he said, wrapping his arms around her, "I don't *want* to leave Ventura."

Trip encircled Brent's waist with her arms and leaned her head on his chest. They just stood there, savoring the feel and aroma of each other, holding fast, not wishing to let go.

"We're a fine pair, aren't we?" Brent said finally. "We're supposed to be going out for a night on the town, and we're acting as though we're headed to dentist appointments. For root canals."

Trip laughed, a rather wobbly, tear-filled laugh. "I know. I'm trying very hard to be bubbly, shall we say, but I'm failing miserably."

"We won't think about the fact that I'm leaving tomorrow," Brent said firmly. "As of right now it's erased from our minds. What did your grandfather give you yesterday morning for your gift?"

Trip stepped back and out of Brent's embrace and met his gaze.

"Oh, you're sneaky," she said, actually producing a genuine smile. "You just slid that in there so smoothly, hoping I'd answer without thinking first. I told you last night that it was a private, sort of secret thing that is just between me and Grandpa."

"I know, I know," he said, matching her smile, "and I respect that, I really do. But a part of me is so curious I can't stand it. Mature, huh?" He glanced at his watch. "We'd better go. I made reservations."

Trip picked up her purse and shawl from the sofa and they left the loft.

Don't think about tomorrow, Trip told herself.

Just concentrate on tonight, Brent ordered himself.

The restaurant was one of Trip's favorites and was where her parents had taken their triplet daughters to celebrate their sixteenth birthday.

"Are you a mind reader?" Trip said when they were seated at a small table. "I adore this restaurant. It's so elegant and the food is delicious."

"No, I didn't read your mind," Brent said, then cocked an eyebrow at her, "but it's an interesting idea. There are times I do believe that would come in very handy in regard to you. But the truth of the matter is, I called your mother and asked her where she thought I should take you tonight. She told me to bring you here."

Trip's eyes widened. "You went to all that bother? Well, my goodness, I feel very special."

Brent looked directly at her, his expression now serious. "You *are* special, Alice, more than I think you even realize. These two weeks with you have been... I'll be counting the days until you arrive on the island and I can see you again, hold you again.... Do you suppose I should change the subject?''

"It would be a good idea," Trip said, nodding. "Oh, here we go. There's a waiter zooming this way. We'd better decide what we want to eat."

"I'm not very hungry."

"Brent," Trip said, leaning slightly toward him, "we're going to have a lovely time this evening. That will start with us enjoying a scrumptious meal. Pick something from the menu."

"What are you going to have?"

Trip sighed. "I'm not certain I can swallow one bite." She paused and flipped open the menu as the waiter stopped at the table. "Cancel that. I'm starving. I'm going to eat every bite of—" she swept her gaze over the selections "—shrimp scampi."

The waiter took both of their orders, including the request for a bottle of Renault-Bardow wine, then hurried away. Across the room a man slid onto the bench in front of a piano, then began to play and sing along.

"Isn't that music nice?" Trip said. "They didn't have that before, but it has been years since I've been here. He has an excellent voice, and he's singing so you can hear him but it doesn't intrude on conversation."

"Mmm," Brent said, poking a fork in his salad. "They didn't make flowers out of the radishes here like they did at that other restaurant. On the night we met." He lifted his head slowly to look directly at Alice. "The night that changed my life as I've known it to be for so many years. A night I will never, ever forget."

"I'll never forget that night, either, Brent," Trip said. "Nor any of the nights, days, hours or minutes that followed. I—"

"Ladies and gentlemen," the piano player said, "please excuse the interruption, but I have had a request for a special song to be sung to a special lady." He paused. "Alice in Wonderland, this is for you."

"What?" Trip said, stiffening in her chair.

"Just listen," Brent said.

Tears misted Trip's eyes as she heard the first words of the song "Look at Us" being sung...just for her.

"*Our* song," Brent said.

"Oh, dear God," Trip said, as she dashed two tears from her cheeks. "I'm going to fall apart. Thank you, Brent, for... No, I just want to listen to...*our* song."

With the music came the magic.

All gloomy thoughts were whisked into oblivion

and replaced with a rosy mist that seemed to swirl around Alice and Brent. They weren't in a bustling restaurant, they were in a land of wonder that had been created just for them. The song ended but they still heard the lovely, romantic words and the lilting melody that floated over and through them with a gentle, warming touch.

They finished their meal but couldn't have said what they ate, nor did the Renault-Bardow wine prompt them to remark on its excellence. Nothing had meaning or importance beyond the one they gazed at, drank in the sight of, cherishing and savoring every detail, look, smile, brushing of hands that lingered.

Alice in Wonderland borrowed the magical flying carpet from Aladdin and transported them back to her loft, where clothes were whisked away by the wave of Cinderella's fairy godmother's wand. They tumbled onto the bed that the Three Bears had declared to be just right, then Alice reached for Brent and he gathered her into his embrace.

Their lovemaking was slow and so very sweet, familiar, yet new. The rosy mist took on a deeper hue as their desire consumed them.

Their joining carried them up and away to the glorious place that was meant only for them, flinging them into the land of ecstasy at the very same time.

And through it all...it was magic.

They slept, only to waken again as Snow White and Sleeping Beauty had done from the kiss of the prince. Through the hours of night they tucked beautiful memories away in private chambers of hearts filled with the essence of the other.

The light of dawn tiptoed into the room with a hush and nudged them awake to face the truths of reality.

"I have to go," Brent said, his lips resting lightly on Alice's forehead.

"I know," Trip whispered.

"Stay right where you are. I want to remember you just like this, take this memory of you with me."

"Yes, all right, but I should say goodbye to your family."

"No. They wouldn't expect you to get up this early to see us off," Brent said, then paused. "Alice, I know I said I wouldn't bring this up again, but I need to hear you say it. Say you'll think about what this might be that is happening between us. Promise me. Please."

"I promise." She splayed her hand on Brent's

chest so she could feel the steady beat of his heart beneath her palm. "I promise, Brent."

"Good. That's good. Thank you."

She sighed. "I...I believe it would be best if we didn't speak on the phone, or write letters, during this month we'll be apart. We need to focus inward, look for the answers to the questions... God, a whole month until I see you again, then when we're on your island everyone will be there, and we'll be so busy with the festivities and..."

"We'll find a way to be alone," he said. "We will. I have to go. I don't *want* to go. That settles it. I *refuse* to go."

Trip laughed softly. "You sound like a spoiled brat, Mr. Bardow."

"Oh, yeah, Ms. MacAllister?" he said, chuckling. "If I flop on the floor and kick my feet will I get to stay?"

"Tantrums are not rewarded by the tantrumee getting what he's after."

"Well, damn." Brent tightened his hold on Alice, as though he intended to never again let her go. "Ah, man, this is awful. Just terrible. The bummer of the century. Grim, really grim. And if I don't get out of here I'm going to miss that plane and be murdered by people who will forget that they love me."

He eased back so he could look directly into Alice's eyes, then groaned aloud when he saw tears shimmering in their beautiful brown depths.

"Oh, don't cry," he said. "You'll rip me to shreds. Cry later, or something. I...hell."

Brent captured Alice's lips with a searing kiss that held an edge of roughness and desperation, of emotional need so intense, it stole the very breath from their bodies.

With all the willpower he possessed, Brent broke the kiss and left the bed. He dragged on his clothes, extended a trembling hand toward Alice, then snatched it back and strode across the room and out the door, closing it behind him with a click that seemed to echo like a jarring explosion through the loft.

"Goodbye, Brent," Trip whispered, then gathered his pillow to her, closed her eyes and buried her face in it, savoring his aroma and the warmth from where his head had lain.

And then she cried because she already missed him, was already lonely, was already aching for the sight of him. She already missed his touch, his smile, the sound of his laughter and that throaty chuckle of his that never failed to cause shivers of desire to slither down her spine.

Trip cried because now she was left with only

her own thoughts and emotions that were so confusing and so very frightening.

She cried until there were no more tears left to shed, then she slept, her head nestled on Brent's pillow, which was now damp from her tears.

Chapter Eight

By the end of the following week, Trip was so tired she knew she could not continue on with the plan of working at the café from early morning to midafternoon, then painting during the remainder of the day and into the evening.

Adding to the exhausting schedule was the fact that she wasn't sleeping well. She only dozed, then woke with a start and reached for Brent, who was never there.

Memories of their wondrous time together would tumble through her mind, causing her to stare up into the darkness, missing Brent.

Each time she attempted to get in touch with herself, to think about what might be happening between them as she'd promised him she'd do, she skittered emotionally away, telling herself she didn't yet have the courage to find the answers to those questions.

Her mind often played a torturous game of tug-of-war that was also depleting.

One minute she believed that she was not capable of giving her heart to a man for all time.

Then another argument would push its way forward: since she was definitely making progress in her quest to be comfortable with her family, wasn't it also possible that she might be capable of falling truly and deeply in love?

Was she in love with Brent Bardow?

No, no, she couldn't, wouldn't, examine her inner feelings too closely. Not now. Not yet. It was too frightening. Just too terrifying.

She'd drift off into a restless slumber, only to wake and repeat the turmoil, so acutely aware through it all of how much she missed Brent, and of how very, very lonely she was.

When she fell asleep in a chair in the kitchen of the café during her break a week after Brent had left, Trip knew she had to quit the waitressing job. She was running the risk of becoming physically ill from exhaustion and would be unable to complete the required number of paintings for the gallery showing.

Trip told Poppy she was sorry she couldn't give him two weeks' notice but she wouldn't be back the next day. She mentally crossed her fingers that none of her family would drop by the café for the pie she'd recommended and discover that she no longer worked there.

That night in her loft Trip stared, as she did every night, at the empty pewter frame hanging on the wall. She shook her head and started to walk away, then stopped and looked at the frame again over her shoulder.

She could, she supposed, sketch a basic outline of her head, hair, the shape of her face. That might ease her guilty conscience as far as not even attempting to paint the portrait as her grandfather had instructed her to do. She loved her grandpa so much, hated the idea that she might fall short in his eyes by not fulfilling his request.

Yes, this was a good idea, Trip thought, settling on the stool in front of the easel.

She tacked in place a sheet of special paper she used when she decided to draw a particular picture first, instead of reaching for a brush right from the beginning as she did most often. She definitely did *not* have the courage to begin the self-portrait without the safety net of sketching it first.

An hour later Trip had completed the basics of the portrait, not even considering adding her features. She nodded in approval.

She could, she decided, do this much in oils now, too, and would begin tomorrow night. The rest of this evening had to be spent on a seascape she was doing for the showing. Next would be the craggy, weather-beaten face of an old fisherman she'd seen in a small town up the coast and whose image was vividly alive in her mind.

And so was Brent.

Trip removed the paper from the easel, then put the canvas she was working on in place. She stared at the picture but saw only Brent in her mental vision.

What was he doing now, right now? she wondered. Was he thinking about her? Yes. Yes, he was, she just somehow knew that at that exact moment, Brent Bardow's mind and, well, maybe even his heart, was focused on her. She could feel his presence as though he was right there next to her about to reach out and draw her into his arms, then lower his head and kiss her and...

Trip blinked, then drew a shuddering breath as heat suffused her, swirling low and hot within her and causing her breasts to ache for the soothing touch of Brent's strong but gentle hands.

"I miss you, Brent," she whispered.

At that same moment, the first streaks of a gold and crimson sunrise were inching from the horizon as Brent stood on a hill above the vast vineyards of Wilshire, his hands shoved into the back pockets of a faded pair of jeans.

"I miss you, Alice," he said aloud, staring at the sky as the glorious colors grew bigger, pushing away the darkness of night.

He jerked and snapped his head to the side, having felt for a second that Alice had actually tapped him on the shoulder to get his attention, to let him know that she was there next to him, waiting for him to take her into his arms and kiss her, hold and touch her.

A chill swept through him as he faced the stark reality of his aloneness, knew that Alice was far, far away, the distance perhaps measured not just in miles, but in Alice's emotions as well.

What was she thinking? Brent wondered. About them. About what was transpiring between them, what it all meant. Had she already reached the conclusion that what they had shared had been special, but was now over? Was she giving way to her ghosts and hiding behind the walls she'd built around herself, her heart? No, please, no.

Brent turned and swept his gaze over the lush land behind him.

Here, he thought, nodding. This was the place. This was where he wanted to build the house that would become a home filled with love and laughter, children, the little miracles created with the woman who had stolen his heart for all time.

For him the questions were answered.

He was deeply and irrevocably in love.

With Alice.

And he was filled with the greatest joy and the greatest fear he had ever known.

Because he didn't know if Alice MacAllister was in love with *him.*

Brent sighed and dragged both hands down his face.

Man, he was tired, he thought. The day had just begun and he was weary to the bone starting out. He'd hardly slept since he'd returned to the island, had spent his nights tossing and turning, and missing Alice. But here, in the place where he belonged, his world, his little slice of heaven, he'd discovered the truth and the incredible depth of his love for his Alice.

God, how he missed her. Ached for her. Wanted,

needed, to feel her nestled close to his body, hear her laughter, see her smile, inhale her aroma of fresh air and flowers.

Alice. His soul mate. The woman he'd come to believe he'd never find but *had* found, and had envisioned as his wife, the mother of his children, his partner in life until death parted them.

Three weeks, he thought as he began to walk down the rise. There were three hellish weeks left before he would see Alice again, before he could declare his love to her, then hope and pray that she loved him in kind. Three agonizing weeks.

"I'm not going to survive this," Brent muttered. "Alice will arrive on the island and find a blithering idiot. Me. I will have slipped over the edge of my sanity and…"

Damn it, he fumed. Why had he agreed that it would be best for Alice and him to not have any contact during the month they would be apart so they could think clearly and… Wait a minute.

He *hadn't* agreed to that condition of no contact between him and Alice. He had memorized every detail of his last night with Alice, remembered when she'd made that statement and also recalled that he hadn't commented on it, one way or another. He couldn't be held to something that he hadn't really agreed to.

Brent stopped so suddenly that he staggered, then smacked into a tree, bumping his head and swearing loudly as he rubbed the throbbing spot.

"Cripes, I'm losing it," Brent said, shaking his head. "My poor parents. Their only kid is not the brightest crayon in the box. I am, actually, edging very close to being certifiably insane."

"You won't get any argument from me about that statement," a man said, coming through the trees and startling Brent. "You're to be commended for figuring that out all by yourself, Brent. It will save a hassle when they come to carry you away."

"Not cute, Peter," Brent said to the foreman of the vineyards.

Peter chuckled and the two men fell in step and walked in silence for several minutes.

"Tell me something, Peter," Brent finally said. "How long have you been married?"

"Thirty-seven years this summer," Peter said, smiling, "and I'm alive to say that because I never once forgot Lynn's birthday, or our anniversary. Oh, and Valentine's Day. That's a biggie for women."

"But there's a helluva lot more to it than just presents on the appropriate day," Brent said. "Love is...love is like a recipe and all the ingredients have to be there in the proper measure with both people working together to produce the desired result.''

''Well,'' Peter said, running one hand over his chin, ''that's a tad flowery for my way of thinking, but I get your drift. All I know is that I love Lynn even more today than when I married her. She's my wife. She's my life. Pure and simple.''

''Ah, that's really nice,'' Brent said, punching Peter on the arm. ''She's my wife. She's my life. Man, that is something.''

''Yeah,'' Peter said, eyeing Brent warily. ''You sure are in a weird mood this morning, boss. If I didn't know better I'd think that you're... Well, for heaven's sake, that's it, isn't it? You're in love. I'll be damned. Who is she? The island gossip mill says you haven't even dated anyone on Wilshire in a couple of years.''

Peter paused and his eyes widened. ''But you just got back from Ventura, California. But, hell's fire, even an old guy like me knows that long-distance relationships are not the way to work together on your recipe for love.''

''I realize that, Peter. But she doesn't have a secret agenda that would make her insist on living in the States. She could be happy here, I just know it. What I *don't* know is if she's in love with *me*.''

Peter shrugged. ''So, ask her.''

"I can't. Not yet. It's rather complicated but I sure as hell can tell her how I feel about *her*. And I'm going to."

"That's a start."

"Yeah, well," Brent said wearily, "I have a knot of cold terror in my gut that it might be the finish because it won't be what she wants to hear." He narrowed his eyes. "I think I'll wait a few hours before I telephone her because with the time difference from here to there she'll be asleep when the call comes. If she's sort of foggy I have a better chance of getting to say what's on my mind, in my heart, without her cutting me off. You know what I mean?"

"That's sort of sneaky."

"Desperate men take desperate measures, Peter," Brent said. "And I'm definitely desperate."

Trip was sleeping so close to the edge of the side of the bed where Brent had slept that when the telephone rang she jerked awake, then with a shriek fell off the bed and landed squarely on her bottom with a painful thump.

The telephone shrilled again.

"Ow. Darn it, that hurt," Trip said, crawling back onto the bed, then across it to snatch up the receiver of the telephone on the nightstand next to her side of the bed. "What!"

"Uh-oh," a deep voice said. "This isn't starting out so good."

Trip snapped on the small lamp on the night-stand, then flopped onto her back, deciding that the caller obviously had the wrong number but sounded so much like Brent that her heart had done a funny little two-step. This was not fair, not fair at all.

"You have the wrong number," she said, with a sad little sigh.

"I do? No, I don't. That's you. Ah, man, it's so great to hear your voice, Alice."

Trip sat bolt upright on the bed, her eyes widening. "Brent?"

"Yes, it's me. But listen a minute, okay?" he said quickly. "I want to be very clear on this issue. *You* stated we shouldn't have any contact during this month we're apart, but *I* didn't agree to that. Believe me, Alice, I remember our last night together and I *did not* comment one way or the other when you presented that plan."

Trip narrowed her eyes and mentally relived that last night with Brent.

"You're right," she said slowly. "You didn't say anything about—"

"Alice," Brent interrupted, "why are you so

wide awake? I mean, it's the middle of the night there and I thought you'd be rather...zoned if I called now.''

Trip glanced over at the edge of the bed she'd tumbled off.

''It was a rather...startling awakening,'' she said. ''Brent, you're making it sound as though you planned this call to come when I'd be at a...I don't know...disadvantage, so to speak, spacey, or something.''

''Yes, that was the idea, which obviously failed miserably.'' Brent paused. ''Alice, I miss you so much. I can't sleep, have to force myself to eat...I'm a complete wreck.''

''Me, too.''

''You are? You're a wreck? Oh, man, that's great to hear.''

''Thanks a bunch,'' she said, sinking back onto the pillow.

''Alice, I know we're supposed to be using this month to attempt to determine what's happening between us. The thing is, I've already figured it out...for me, at least. I have the answers to the questions. I know exactly how I feel about us.''

''You do?'' Trip said, a shiver of cold fear coursing through her.

Oh, dear heaven, she thought frantically, had

Brent purposely telephoned when he thought she'd be half asleep so he could tell her that what they'd shared had been no big deal? Would he then hang up before she could react and cause a messy, emotional scene?

"Yes, I do," Brent said. "I know without the slightest doubt in my mind."

"Well...that's...interesting," she said, her hold on the receiver tightening. "I guess."

"Okay, here I go. I'm going to tell you now, so just hear me out. Okay?"

Trip nodded, then shook her head slightly in self-disgust as she remembered that Brent couldn't see her.

"Yes," she said, "I'm listening."

"Alice MacAllister," he said, then cleared his throat, "I, Brent Bardow, am totally, completely, irrevocably, forever and ever in love with you."

Trip opened her mouth, closed it, blinked, then tried again. "I beg your pardon?"

"I love you, Alice in Wonderland," Brent said quietly. "I love you with all that I am as a man. I want to marry you, create little miracle babies with you, live out my days with you, here on the Island of Wilshire."

"But—"

"No, no, don't say anything," Brent said.

"You're still to have your month to get in touch with yourself, find *your* answers. It's just that you didn't have all the proper data while you were doing that, so I called to tell you that I love you beyond measure.

"I thought if you were sleepy I could just declare my love for you and hang up. But you're wide awake so I'm begging you to please not make a hasty decision or comment, or whatever, about what I just told you."

"But—"

"I'll be waiting here for you, Alice. I'll be waiting for you and for your reply to my proposal of marriage. I'll be waiting for you on the Island of Wilshire, the place, I hope, pray, you'll view as your future home...with me. I love you so much. Good night, my darling Alice."

"But..." Trip said, sitting up in bed again. "Brent?" The dial tone buzzed in her ear. "Brent?" She shook the receiver. He'd hung up?

Sudden unexpected tears filled Trip's eyes and she didn't know if they stemmed from wondrous joy or stark terror. She placed the receiver down then had to give a firm directive to her fingers to release her tight grip. She snapped off the lamp, then slid down in the bed, pulling the sheet up and holding it tightly beneath her chin with both hands.

"Brent Bardow is in love with me," she whispered.

Then Alice MacAllister, having no idea that her emotions echoed those of the man halfway around the world, those of Brent Bardow, was filled with the greatest joy and the greatest fear she had ever known.

Chapter Nine

During the next two weeks, Trip worked diligently on her paintings for the showing. She took time off to go clothes shopping with her mother and sisters and had a lovely time with her family, a fact that suffused her with warmth and happiness. Her smiles had been genuine, her laughter real, during the day they spent together going from store to store, stopping only long enough for a quick lunch.

When Jillian had taken Trip aside that day and told her that her parents would like to purchase the expensive airplane ticket for the trip to Wilshire, Trip had been deeply touched. She thanked her mother but said she had enough money in savings to pay for the fare, plus all the clothes she was buying.

"You do?" Jillian said, frowning. "But how... never mind. It's none of my business. I'll simply take credit for having done a fine job of teaching you how to handle your money while you were growing up."

Trip had smiled and nodded, but could not ignore the icy wave of guilt that swept through her. Her savings came from the sale of her pictures.

Soon, Trip had told herself. She'd gather her courage and tell her family everything...soon.

With sheer force of will, Trip did not allow herself to dwell on Brent, on his declaration of love for her, until she was alone at night during the designated time she set aside to work on the self-portrait her grandfather had requested that she paint.

It was then that she wrapped Brent's love around her like a big fuzzy blanket with a warmth that crept within her to gently caress her heart, her mind, her very soul.

She painted by rote, focusing instead on the image of Brent in her mental vision, seeing his smile, the desire in his eyes, his thick black hair that she had sifted her fingers through.

She selected memories from the treasure chest in

her heart of time spent with Brent, and she relived the ecstasy of being with him, walking, talking, smiling, laughing and making sweet wondrous love in the darkness of night.

No doubts or fears were allowed entry into the misty, sensual cocoon that swirled around her as she painted her self-portrait.

She simply savored the nearly unbelievable knowledge that she was loved by the most magnificent man she had ever known. She kept the questions regarding her own feelings at bay, not yet having the courage to examine them, seek the answers as she'd promised Brent she would do.

Three days before the MacAllister family was scheduled to leave, Trip delivered the last of the requested paintings to the gallery and basked in the owner's praise and enthusiasm for her work.

The invitations for the showing were at the printer's, the gallery owner told Trip, and a contract had been signed with a catering service that would serve champagne and canapés on the night of the showing.

The press releases had been written and delivered to the Ventura newspapers. They included the specific date on which her work would be available to the public, the day after the private showing.

Trip's agent, Delores Dano, who was overseeing

all the details, even came to Trip's loft that night to help her select what the artist of the moment would wear to the big event.

"This is silly," Trip said, as the woman examined Trip's wardrobe in the closet.

"This is image," Delores said. "Ah, here we go. This is it." She held the hanger at arm's length and nodded in approval. "Floor-length, simple but hinting at sexy with this clingy material, sophisticated, but the rose color will make you approachable, shall we say, not standoffish like basic black can be. Perfect. Trust me. I've done extensive studies on this."

"Whatever," Trip said with a shrug. "I still think it's silly. People aren't buying me, they're, hopefully, purchasing my paintings."

"Wear the dress."

"I'll wear the dress."

After Delores left the loft, Trip decided to have some dinner before putting the finishing touches on the self-portrait. She started toward the kitchen area, hesitated, then stopped.

It would be better, she decided, to look at the painting objectively, with no thoughts of Brent cluttering her mind, see what she still needed to do to it, then mull over her discoveries as she ate.

"Good plan," she said, walking to the screens she hadn't bothered to replace by the bed.

She moved around the screens, then came to such an abrupt halt that she stumbled slightly, her gaze riveted on the eight-by-ten-inch canvas on the easel a few feet in front of her.

"Dear heaven," she whispered, the rapid beating of her heart echoing in her ears.

Trip moved forward slowly, aware that her legs were trembling and she was having to tell herself to breathe, to inhale, then exhale, producing choppy little puffs of air. She pressed shaking fingertips to her lips as she stopped in front of the easel, staring at the image of herself.

She had put on canvas who she was when she was with Brent Bardow.

And it was there, shining in her eyes, in the soft smile on her lips, in the glow of her slightly flushed cheeks.

It was there.

Her love for Brent was as clear and real, honest and deep, as if she were speaking the words, declaring her feelings for him.

She was in love with Brent Bardow.

And she was Alice.

She clasped her hands beneath her chin and closed her eyes, causing tears to spill onto her face.

Free, she thought incredulously. She was finally free of the past.

And she had fallen in love. Totally, completely, irrevocably, forever and ever in love with Brent, just as he loved her.

She was Alice in a wonderland so glorious it defied description.

· "I love you, Brent," she whispered as fresh tears fell. "I love you so very, very much. I'm Alice. *Your* Alice. Forever. Wait for me, Brent, there on your island. I'm coming home…to you."

The next morning Alice entered Robert's study and smiled at her grandfather, who was sitting in one of the leather chairs. She sat in the other, brushed back the tissue on the pewter frame, then handed Robert the picture. He held it carefully in both hands and stared at it intently.

"My darling Alice," Robert said, his voice choked with emotion as he met her gaze, "this is a portrait of a woman who is deeply in love and who is secure in the knowledge that she is loved in kind, is complete, has found her soul mate, her partner in life."

"Yes," Alice said, smiling as tears echoed in her voice. "I know. I do love Brent, Grandpa, and he loves me. He telephoned me from the island and told me that he loves me, then he asked me to marry him, but not to give him my answer to his proposal until I arrived on the Island of Wilshire.

"It wasn't until I painted the self-portrait that I knew how I felt about him. You are so wise, Grandpa. If it hadn't been for you requesting that I paint that picture, I might have remained too frightened to truly examine my feelings for Brent. The walls I erected around myself are gone. I can't begin to thank you for knowing me better than I knew myself, for...I'm Alice, Grandpa. I'm Alice."

The roar of the engines of the medium-size commuter plane the MacAllisters had transferred to for their final leg of the journey to the Island of Wilshire made conversation nearly impossible, a fact that suited Alice just fine.

Alice slid a glance at her mother, who was sitting next to her, then closed her eyes again.

She was so blessed to have her parents, as well as the entire MacAllister clan, Alice thought. She'd treated them all so shabbily for so many years, yet when she'd called a family meeting in her loft last night and expressed her heartfelt apology, they accepted it immediately, telling her how happy they were that she back among them.

With a voice that had been slightly shaky from nerves she'd then revealed her secret to them, in-

cluding the news of the private showing. She had
several paintings still in the loft that weren't going
to be in the showing, and when they had looked at
her work, the air had buzzed with excitement and
awe.

"As you can see," she had told her family, "I
sign my work with a flowing *A* in the bottom right-
hand corner. That's…that's who I am…Alice. Alice MacAllister." Her voice had quivered with
threatening tears. "I'm not Trip anymore. I don't
need, nor want, to be Trip. I'm…I'm Alice."

That announcement, Alice mused, had produced
hugs and tears and created a marvelous memory she
would never forget. Then the family had helped her
select a painting as a wedding present for Maggie
and Devon. Everyone agreed that it would be fun
not to breathe a word about her work until the bride
and groom had unwrapped the gift, making it even
more of a surprise. It had been such a very special,
sharing evening…

"Ladies and gentlemen," the pilot said over the
microphone, "please fasten your seat belts. We are
about to make our approach to the Island of Wilshire."

Brent, Alice thought, lifting her head and looking
out the small window. He was down there, waiting

for her. Her. The woman he loved and wished to marry. Brent.

Jillian leaned past Alice to peer out of the window. "Oh, my," she said, "look at all that lush greenery. The island is bigger than I thought it was. Isn't it beautiful, Tr— Alice?" Jillian laughed. "It will take a while to remember to call you Alice, sweetheart, but believe me it's music to my ears. Oh, there, that section must be the vineyards where Brent produces that marvelous Renault-Bardow wine."

Alice nodded and Jillian settled back in her seat.

"My, my," her mother continued, "won't it be lovely to see the Renaults and Bardows again?"

Alice laughed. "Yes, Mother, I'm definitely eager to see Brent. That *was* what you were asking, isn't it?"

"Guilty," Jillian said, then kissed Alice on the cheek.

"I didn't fool you for a minute, did I? You realize, of course, that your family is very curious as to just what is going on between you and Brent Bardow. That's not being nosy. It's because we care about you, love you."

"Oh, okay." Alice smiled. "Not even a little bit nosy?"

"Well..." Jillian said, then shrugged, her eyes dancing with merriment.

"When the time is right, Mother," Alice said, suddenly serious. "I'll tell you what you want to know. But I have to talk to Brent first. Please be patient."

"I will. But don't be surprised if your father pesters you for answers. He's a loving, doting daddy, and worries himself silly about all three of his daughters, forgetting at times that you're adult women. *You're* going to have to be patient with *him.*"

"That's fine," Alice said, then looked out the window again.

Brent, her mind hummed. She could see the runway now as they made their descent to the island. She was getting closer...and closer...to Brent.

Brent stood beneath the white canopy with the other members of the royal family, as well as Maggie and her parents. Off to the right was an honor guard with two men in dress uniform with gleaming sabers and two women, one holding the flag of Wilshire, the other the flag of the United States of America in honor of the bride-to-be and her family.

Brent was dressed in gray slacks, a white shirt, gray tie and a dark blue blazer with the crest of the royal family on the pocket. A cool, late-afternoon breeze ruffled his hair, but a trickle of sweat slithered down his back. A yawn threatened and Brent faked a cough to hide it, aware that his sleepless, pacing-the-floor night was catching up with him.

"There's the plane," King Chester said. "Right on time, too."

Not exactly, Brent thought. It had taken an agonizing month for that airplane to appear through the clouds and approach the runway. Right on time? No, it had taken *too* much time. And before *this* day ended, his entire future happiness, or lack of the same, would be determined by what Alice told him.

He was a wreck. Last night he'd fantasized like an adolescent about the arrival of Alice on the island. He would step past the rest of the family, breaking all the rules of protocol, open his arms to her, and she would run across the tarmac and fling herself into his embrace. Then, not caring that there were *beaucoup* witnesses watching, he would lower his head and claim her lips in a kiss that would be...

"A perfect landing," King Chester said, jerking Brent back to the moment at hand.

Get it together, Bardow, Brent told himself firmly. *Now.*

The airplane turned at the end of the runway, then taxied back to the designated place indicated by the ground crew. A man pushed a staircase toward the plane, while another unrolled a red carpet that spread like a brilliant river from the canopy to the base of the stairs. The engines of the plane quieted, the door was opened, and Brent drew a deep, steadying breath.

As the head of the MacAllister family, Robert was first to appear in the open doorway and begin his way down the stairs, followed by Margaret. The oldest son, Michael, and his wife Jenny had been there for a month already, so the next in line was Ryan and his wife Deede, then...

Come on, come on, Brent thought, clenching his teeth. Damn, they were a big family. Let's go, let's go. Hurry up, people. He wanted, he needed, to see...

Alice.

Brent stiffened, every muscle in his body tensing as Alice appeared in the doorway then started down the stairs. She was wearing a pretty flowered dress, and the breeze was swirling it around her legs and... Oh, thank God, Alice was here. She was on the tarmac now, seemed to be looking directly at him...

Before he realized he was moving, Brent stepped from behind Devon and started forward.

"Brent," his father said, "what are you doing? This is an official royal welcome that dictates that we stand here and—"

"I don't think he gives a rip, darling," Charlane Bardow said, laughing in delight. "Protocol just flew out the window."

King Chester chuckled. "Somehow I'm not surprised. Don't worry about it, Byron. There are times when royal rules need to be broken."

"Oh, look at that," Maggie said. "Brent has stopped, opened his arms, Trip is running toward him… This is so romantic I'm going to cry. Wow! She flung herself into his arms and nearly knocked him over and now,,, My stars, he's kissing her."

"That's putting it mildly." Devon laughed. "I'd hate to think what we'd be witnessing if they'd been separated for *two* months, instead of one. That is one toe-curling kiss there, folks. Dad, it's time to step forward and greet the MacAllisters."

"Oh." King Chester tore his gaze from Alice and Brent. "Yes. Yes, of course. Welcome to the Island of Wilshire, Robert," he said, extending his hand. "We extend a warm and heartfelt greeting to your entire family."

"One of said family," Robert said, smiling as he

shook the king's hand, "is in the midst of her own private welcome. Well, it's not exactly private, but... We're delighted to be here."

Brent ended the searing kiss slowly and reluctantly, but didn't release his hold on Alice.

"I can't believe I did that," he said, close to her lips. "It was exactly the way I fantasized last night when I couldn't sleep. I am no doubt in deep, deep trouble with royalty at the moment, but I really don't give a damn. Ah, Alice, I am so glad to see you, missed you so much, thought you would never get here because the days, nights, hours, seconds, dragged by and...I'm blithering like an idiot. I love you, Alice MacAllister. Ah, man, I love you so much."

"Oh, Brent," Alice said, meeting his gaze with eyes brimming with tears, "I...I love you, too."

"Wh-what?" he said as his heart skipped a beat. "Would you say that again, please?"

"Brent Bardow," Alice said, framing his face with her hands, "I've found my answers. I found myself. I'm Alice. Your Alice in Wonderland, and I love you beyond measure. I truly do."

"Oh, thank God." Brent's voice was husky with emotion. He closed his eyes and tightened his hold on Alice, burying his face in her silky hair.

"Brent, darling," his mother called. "We're leaving now. It's time to give our guests a tour of the castle, dear."

Brent raised his head and sighed. "The madness begins. Hey, if you've seen one castle you've seen 'em all. Let's go to my cottage and—"

"Brent." Alice laughed, "I've never been inside a castle."

"You haven't?" he said, raising his eyebrows. "My goodness, what a sheltered life you've led. Okay. One tour of one castle coming up. *Then* I'm going to sneak you off to my cottage and... No, I'd better not start thinking about what I plan to do to you...with you...or I'll embarrass myself. Come along, Alice. Wilshire awaits your approval."

The royal home was magnificent and looked like a castle from a book of fairy tales. With one of her hands held by Brent, as though he was afraid she'd disappear into thin air if he let go of her, Alice drank in all that she saw, making no attempt to hide her awe as they moved from one beautifully furnished room to another.

She mentally cataloged an endless list of things she'd like to paint, which caused her to frown slightly as the tour continued.

As soon as she and Brent were alone, Alice

thought, she would tell him about her lifelong secret dream. She'd share the fantastic news of the private showing of her work, admitting that she was a nervous wreck about the event, afraid that none of the pictures would be purchased.

Brent would be surprised by her news, she knew, because he believed that she did nothing more than wait tables at a dinky little café in Ventura. But he would instantly realize that she could, and would, be very content on the Island of Wilshire, painting her little heart out after they were married.

Married, her mind hummed. Oh, yes, she fully intended to accept Brent's proposal, an issue they hadn't had time to address.

Alice glanced up at Brent, who was staring into space, probably, she decided, attempting not to appear too bored as King Chester explained who was who in the large portraits of past kings of Wilshire that hung on the wall in an enormous ballroom they were presently in.

The group returned to the entryway and King Chester spread out his arms.

"And there you have it," he said, smiling. "Our humble home. By now your luggage has been taken to your rooms that I pointed out to you during the tour and everything unpacked and put away. There are fresh fruit and sweet rolls there for a snack, as well. Dinner will be served at seven in the smaller dining room.

"I suggest you nap a bit. Having made the journey you just completed, I'm very aware of how exhausting jet lag can be. After dinner we'll have a festive time watching the bride and groom open some of their wedding gifts."

The king chuckled. "Do note that I said 'some' of the gifts, perhaps only those from the immediate family. Since presents have arrived from across the globe we'd be up all night if Maggie and Devon unwrapped everything they've received.

"Again," King Chester continued, "let me say welcome to the Island of Wilshire and to our home. I hope all of you are as pleased about the forthcoming wedding as I am. I've waited a long time for this, and I truly believe that my beloved wife is smiling down from the heavens on Maggie and Devon and whispering her blessings. Until seven o'clock, then."

As the king, Charlane and Byron, plus Maggie, Devon and Maggie's parents, turned and walked down the long corridor leading away from the entryway, excited chatter broke out.

Brent took one step backward, then another, tugging on Alice's hand as he moved.

"What...?" she said, looking up at him questioningly as she was drawn in the opposite direction from her family.

"Shh," he whispered. "I feel about sixteen years old but, hey, whatever works."

Alice clamped her free hand over her mouth to stifle a giggle that was a mixture of childish, mischievous fun and pure womanly happiness.

When they reached the tall, wooden, double-front doors, Jillian stopped on the stairs and looked at them.

"Remember to return to your room here in the castle in time to dress for dinner, sweetheart," she said pleasantly, then continued on her way.

Alice and Brent burst into laughter, then dashed out the doors.

Brent's cottage was about a half mile from the castle and was nestled among tall trees, prompting Alice to declare it to be the home of the Seven Dwarfs.

"Nope," Brent said. "That would make you Snow White and you're not, because you're Alice in Wonderland."

"True."

Brent had decorated his little house simply but had managed to create a cozy aura. There was one main room that included a flagstone hearth around the fireplace, a small kitchen with a dining alcove, a braided oval rug on the hardwood floor and a marshmallow-soft caramel-colored leather sofa that faced the fireplace. The sofa was flanked by a pair of brown-toned tweed easy chairs.

The walls were white and boasted only one painting, which was of the lush vineyards on the island. A bedroom and bathroom were off a short hallway to the right.

"Oh, I love it," Alice said, her eyes sparkling as she swept her gaze over the area.

"And I love *you*," Brent said, wrapping his arms around her and pulling her close to him. "And you love *me*. Ah, Alice, this is the greatest day of my life. The only thing that could make it even more perfect is if you'll say that you'll marry me. Will you? Marry me? Please?"

Alice encircled Brent's neck with her arms and looked directly into his sapphire-blue eyes.

"Yes," she said, smiling. "I, Alice MacAllister, will be honored to marry you, Brent Bardow. Yes."

"Thank you. Oh, thank you, Alice," he murmured, then captured her lips to seal the commitment to forever they had just made to each other.

Desire exploded within them, and when Brent broke the kiss he swept Alice up into his arms and carried her into the bedroom, setting her on her feet next to the double bed.

"Brent," she said, when she could catch her breath, "we mustn't do anything to take the spotlight off of Maggie and Devon. It wouldn't be fair to them. Let's not announce our engagement until after their wedding. Okay?"

"I want to yell it from the rooftops right now for everyone to hear," he said, "but I see your point. This is Maggie and Devon's time to shine, or whatever. But after we throw politically correct birdseed at them, instead of rice, and they leave on their honeymoon, we'll make our own announcement. Agreed?"

"Agreed." Alice nodded, then paused. "I would really like to share beautiful lovemaking with you now, Mr. Bardow. Agreed?"

"Oh, lady," he said, chuckling, "I am in complete agreement with that one."

"Alice," Brent said, then kissed her lips, nose, chin and forehead. "Wake up. We fell asleep after we... Alice? Come on, my love, open your gorgeous eyes. We're going to be late for dinner if we don't get moving, and I've broken enough royal rules for one day."

Alice blinked, opened her eyes, yawned, then smiled at Brent.

"Hello," she said. "I love you."

"Hello, yourself, woman that I love," he said, then glanced at his watch. "Oh, man, we're cutting this so close. Up, up, and away we go."

They actually ran back to the castle, holding hands like children who had been turned loose to play. At the front doors to the majestic structure, Brent dropped a quick kiss on Alice's lips.

"See you at dinner," he said. "I love you. Bye." He turned and sprinted off in the direction they'd come from.

"Ta-ta," Alice said dreamily, waggling the fingers of one hand in the air.

When she entered her room, she gave it a quick and appreciative perusal, then started toward the bathroom to take a shower. It wasn't until she was standing under the warm spray of water that she realized she still hadn't told Brent about her painting. They had been concentrating on lovemaking so incredibly fantastic it was beyond description, then had fallen asleep and...

Well, it didn't matter, she thought as she shampooed her hair. In fact, this would be more fun. Brent would be as surprised as Maggie and Devon

about her work when the bride and groom unwrapped their present.

Then the light would dawn and he'd realize that
their…what had he called it?…yes, their recipe for
love was even more perfect than he'd believed it to
be, because her desire to paint made her contentment as his wife there on the island a given, was
guaranteed.

Alice turned off the water and stepped out of the
shower. She swiped her hand across the steamy
mirror to gaze at her reflection, a soft smile forming
on her lips.

There it is, she thought, for all to see, just as it
was in the self-portrait she'd painted. Love. Love
that was returned in kind by the most magnificent
man in the world.

Brent.

Chapter Ten

Dinner was a noisy, festive event with everyone sitting around a long, gleaming mahogany table in an enormous room that King Chester had referred to as "the small dining room." Roast pheasant was served with tiny new potatoes, broccoli with hollandaise sauce and a crisp, crunchy salad.

The wine was, of course, the newly marketed and highly successful Renault-Bardow, and a multitude of toasts were given after glasses etched with the royal crest had been filled.

Dessert, which Emily and Charlane politely refused, then congratulated each other on their willpower, was creamy caramel dribbled over egg custard.

The meal was concluded with brandy in wafer-thin snifters and coffee in delicate china.

None of the MacAllister children had made the trip to the Island of Wilshire. The older ones were in school and were staying with friends, the babies had been, as one of the daddies put it, "farmed out" to close friends who had young children of their own.

Alice smiled as she swept her gaze down the long table, seeing loving glances being exchanged between the various couples.

They were all treating this journey like a second honeymoon, she mused, with no thoughts of responsibilities surrounding their children or even what to cook for dinner. Therefore, the smoldering desire evident in Brent's eyes every time he looked at her was going, thank goodness, unnoticed.

"Shall we adjourn to the drawing room?" King Chester said finally.

"My dear brother," Charlane said, laughing, "you sound so pompous and stuffy, like something out of a Victorian novel."

King Chester roared with laughter. "I've always wanted to say that. It's awful, isn't it? Although it's a rather kingly thing. I usually say, 'Let's find some more comfortable chairs.' Royal antiques are all very well and good, but they're murder on the backside.''

With a great deal of laughter, the group followed the king out of the dining room, down the hallway and into a large but welcoming room where a stack of presents had been placed by a love seat. The other sofas and easy chairs were soon filled, and the remainder of the family, including Alice and Brent, settled on the floor where they were cushioned by deep, plush carpeting. Maggie and Devon sat on the love seat next to the gifts.

''Open the one from Tr...Alice first,'' Forrest said, pointing to the pile of presents. ''It's the one in the blue paper with the white doves. I'll pop a seam if I have to keep silent any longer. Go ahead, Maggie, Devon...blue paper, white doves.''

''My goodness, Uncle Forrest,'' Maggie said, ''you're making this gift sound so mysterious.'' She leaned over to retrieve the present. ''Mmm. Should I make some guesses first as to what it is?''

''No,'' Forrest said, laughing. ''I won't survive that. Just open it, Maggie.''

Alice reached for Brent's hand and gripped it tightly as she felt a bevy of butterflies swoosh suddenly into her very full stomach.

''What's the mystery about your gift?'' Brent

whispered in her ear, then paused. "I don't mean to be picky, but you're breaking my hand."

"Oh. I'm sorry." Alice released Brent's hand and drew a steadying breath. "I'm just so nervous because my gift is—"

"Oh, it's beautiful. Look at those colors," Maggie said, holding the painting at arm's length. "Isn't it an exquisite seascape, Devon?"

"It certainly is," he said, nodding. "It will have a place of honor in our home when we get it built. Do you know the artist personally, Alice? Whoever signed it at the bottom with that distinctive *A?*"

"Go over there, sweetheart," Forrest said to Alice. "Tell them who painted it and let Maggie give you a hug, which she'll definitely want to do."

"But…" Alice started, then looked quickly at Brent, who had a puzzled expression on his face. "I…oh, dear, now the spotlight is on me and…" She got to her feet. "All right, Dad, I'm going, but only for a minute."

"Mark that down somewhere, Jillian," Forrest said, chuckling. "Trip actually did as she was told by her creaky old father."

"Alice," Jillian said. "Honey, do remember that our daughter's name is Alice."

Alice stood in front of the presents stacked by the love seat so she wouldn't have her back to the others in the room. Everyone was looking at her intently.

"Maggie, Devon," Alice said, her voice not quite steady as the butterflies continued to flutter, "I'm so pleased you like the picture because I... What I mean is, the signature that consists of that flowing *A* is... I realize, Maggie, that you had no idea that I..."

"Father races to the rescue," Forrest said. "You're a tad rattled, baby girl." He paused. "Maggie, Devon, you are holding a painting produced by none other than the next artist of fame and fortune who is, I am extremely proud to add, going to have an invitation-only showing of her work at *the* most prestigious of Ventura's galleries in the very near future, and who—"

"Cut to the chase, dear," Jillian said, patting her husband on the knee.

"Oh." Forrest got to his feet. "May I present my daughter, the artist, who painted that fantastic picture... Ms. Alice MacAllister."

Maggie jumped to her feet, still holding the painting. "Oh, my gosh. Oh, Trip...excuse me...Alice, *you* did this? Oh. Oh! This is unbelievable. You're going to have a private showing of your work at... Oh, my gracious, this is so exciting."

"Well, now, let's have a closer look at this," King Chester said, getting up and crossing the room. He was followed by Charlane, Byron and Maggie's parents. "That is a truly marvelous piece of work. You are a very talented young woman, Alice."

"Thank you," she said.

"I hope you have an agent," Charlane said, staring at the painting. "You are obviously on your way to having a brilliant, highly successful career, Alice, and you must be certain that no one takes advantage of you."

"Yes, I do have an excellent agent," Alice said.

The others in the room began to converge on the area by the love seat, everyone seeming to be talking at once about Alice's work, how none of them had known her amazing secret, how proud they all were of her, and on and on. Alice attempted to get a glimpse of Brent, but couldn't see him through the crush of the chattering families.

"What are you going to wear to your showing, Alice?" Jessica said. "It has to be an absolutely stunning dress, befitting someone of your talent. Plus, there will be reporters and photographers there, I'm sure, and the dress has to be just perfect."

"Oh, well, my agent came to my loft," Alice

said, "and selected what she thought would be best and... Please, enough of this. I sincerely thank you all for your enthusiasm and support. It means more to me that I can ever begin to tell you, but we're supposed to be watching Maggie and Devon open their gifts."

Alice snatched up a present from the floor and extended it to Maggie, who had no choice but to lean the painting against the side of the love seat and accept the gift. Everyone returned to their seats, still exclaiming over Alice's marvelous surprise.

Alice started back to where she had been sitting on the floor with Brent, only to discover that he was no longer there. A chill swept through her, then disappeared in the next instant as she saw him leaning one shoulder against the far wall, his arms folded over his chest.

As a chorus of oohs and aahs filled the air when Maggie revealed the gift she had unwrapped, Alice hurried to where Brent was standing, her step slowing slightly as she saw the deep frown on his face.

"Did you get tired of sitting on the floor?" Alice said when she reached Brent.

"No," he said, no hint of a smile on his face. "That was quite a bombshell you just laid on everyone, Alice. You're a very talented artist. But you know that, don't you? After all you have an agent,

you're going to have a private showing of your
work. Oh, yes, ma'am, that is a heavy-duty secret
agenda you've been keeping under wraps. From
everyone. From me.''

''I was going to tell you about it when we were
alone earlier today,'' Alice said, ''but…well…we
had other things on our minds… But now you know
and I thought you would be pleased, Brent, but obviously you're not.''

''Pleased?'' he said, pushing himself off the wall
and planting his hands on his hips. He glanced
quickly at the group of people in the room. ''This
isn't the place. Come outside into the garden.''

Brent spun around and strode away. Alice stared
at him for a long moment, her mind racing with
confusion and a cold sense of dread, then hurried
after him.

Brent was very angry, she thought frantically.
She had seen the fury in the depths of his eyes
and…and a flicker of hurt, raw pain. Oh, dear
heaven, why was he reacting this way?

Outside on a path that led through a magnificent
rose garden, Brent turned to face Alice, a muscle
jumping in his jaw.

''I've been such a fool, it's a crime,'' he said,
none too quietly. ''It was all there right in front of
me and I was such a besotted idiot I didn't see it.

The loft with the light an artist would need to work, the smell of paint, the fact that you were living beyond the means of a waitress.'' He shook his head. ''My God, I'm stupid.''

''Brent, please, listen to me,'' Alice said, placing one hand on his forearm.

Brent jerked his arm and Alice pulled back her hand, realizing with horror that he didn't even want her to touch him.

''Here was a woman,'' he said, his voice gritty, ''that I didn't even think existed in this world. An honest woman, one who was exactly what she presented herself to be. A woman with no secret agenda to blindside me with when it was too late to protect my heart. What…a…joke.

''You used me, Alice MacAllister, to fill your idle hours until you could launch your big-time career in the artistic community. You used me.''

''No!'' she said. ''That's not true. I…''

''Why did you have to take it so far?'' he continued, pain and anger ringing in his voice. ''Did it give you a rush, a real kick, to accept my proposal of marriage, to tell me how much you love me, when you knew damn well you were just playing games?''

''I *do* love you, Brent,'' Alice said, struggling against threatening tears. ''I do.''

"Yeah, right," he said with a bitter bark of laughter. "You're going back to Ventura after Devon and Maggie's wedding to count down the days until the private showing of your work. You have an agent to take care of details even down to picking out the dress you're to wear at the gallery on the big night. Your focus is on your career, not on me, on us, on what we supposedly were going to have together. Here. On the Island of Wilshire."

"I'm going to paint here, on your island and…"

"Ah, give it a rest. I've come out of the ether, Alice. You'll have to find another toy to play with until you become one of the rich and famous. After your showing there will be interviews, talk shows, photographers wanting to take pictures of where you live and work. Between your painting and the publicity circuit, you'll be a busy little bee, won't you?"

"I…" Alice started, then stopped speaking. She hadn't given a moment's thought to what might transpire after the showing. She'd been concentrating on the hope that her work would sell that night, hadn't considered what would follow if the show was a success. "I…"

"Gotcha, lady. Your silence speaks volumes. You can't deny a word of what I'm saying. You're guilty as charged," Brent said, a rough edge to his voice. "What are you thinking right now? That maybe you should go on a big shopping spree so you'll be dressed to the nines for the cameras?"

"Brent, no, stop this," Alice said, tears spilling onto her cheeks. "You're wrong. You're drawing conclusions that aren't true. You don't understand."

"Oh, I understand perfectly. You're a master at keeping secrets. Hell, you wouldn't even tell me what your grandfather gave you as your special present. Did he know about your dandy agenda? What was the gift? A really expensive set of paints?"

"No, it was a pewter picture frame, and he requested that I... That's not important now. Oh, Brent, please, will you just hear me out? Listen to me. Please."

"No," he said, taking a step backward, his voice suddenly very low and very weary-sounding. "I don't want to hear any more lies. But you'd better listen up to everything I'm about to say. This is Maggie and Devon's special time. Nothing, nor no one, is going to put a damper on it.

"In front of the families, we'll fake it, act like the romantic lovebirds they believe us to be. Privately? Stay away from me, Alice. Just stay the hell away from me.

"I had been counting the hours and minutes until you would arrive here. Now I'm doing the same thing in reverse, ticking them off until you're on that plane and off my island, out of my life, my world. My heart? That will take some time, a long time, but I'll do it. I'll forget you even exist."

"Oh, dear God," Alice said, pressing her trembling fingertips to her lips as a sob caught in her throat. "Brent, no."

"Tell the families I wasn't feeling well," he said. "I can't handle putting on a false front tonight. But starting tomorrow we do award-winning performances. Got that? Sure you do. You've had a lot of experience pretending to be something you're not. Just look at it as another game you're playing."

"Brent, please," Alice said, dashing the tears from her cheeks. "You're wrong. About everything. I didn't tell you or my family sooner about my dream, my painting, because I was terribly frightened, so afraid of baring my soul, being vulnerable, after so many years of hiding behind my walls. I was terrified of being Alice, instead of Trip.

"Oh, don't you see? As Trip I knew how to protect myself, keep everyone at arm's length, and I needed time to gather the courage to be...to be Alice. You helped give me the strength to do that,

Brent. I was Alice in Wonderland to you. I became Alice, the woman, for me.

"I *do* love you with all my heart," she added, tears now streaming unnoticed down her face and along her neck. "I want to marry you, create the miracle of our babies with you, live with you here, on the Island of Wilshire, until death parts us. You've got to believe me, Brent. *Please.* I'll paint endless pictures *here,* be so content on your beautiful island and—"

"Until the telephone rings," Brent said, his voice flat, "and your agent tells you about the next talk show you're scheduled to be on, or the tour she's arranged for you to promote your work. Then off you'll fly without a backward glance. I don't call that loving me, Alice. Not even close.

"And our babies? Hell. You'll find a hundred excuses to postpone starting our family because, after all, your career, your damnable secret agenda, comes first.

"No, your idea of love doesn't match up with mine. We're not soul mates as I believed us to be."

"Brent..." Alice said, then stopped and shook her head, tears choking off her words.

"The game is over," he said. "You had a good laugh at my expense and now you're on your way to the spotlight of fame and all the perks that go with it.

"You don't need me to say you should enjoy yourself, do you? That's been your plan all along. In fact, you don't need me for a damn thing."

"Brent?" Charlane called in the distance. "Are you out there? I realize that you and Alice want some time to be together, but we do have guests, dear."

"I'm sorry, Mother," Brent yelled. "But I'm not feeling very well. Please extend my apologies to everyone."

"I can't go back in there," Alice whispered. "They'll all know I've been crying and...I just can't."

"Fine," Brent said tersely, "I'll bail you out tonight, but remember that starting tomorrow we put on the show they expect to see."

Alice nodded jerkily, then another sob escaped from her lips.

"Mother?" Brent called. "Are you still there?"

"Yes, I'm here. Do you need a doctor, Brent?"

"No, no, I'm just going to hit the sack. Listen, Alice is exhausted. Jet leg and all that. She's going on to her room now. I'm sure everyone will understand that it's been a long day for her. They're all probably as tired as she is, come to think of it."

"All right," Charlane said. "Sleep well. Both of you. I'll suggest we make an early evening of it in here for the sake of the travelers. See you both to-morrow."

"Good night, Mother," Brent called, then looked at Alice. "Goodbye, Alice in Wonderland. Hey, that was a perfect name for you all along, and I didn't know it at the time. Alice in Wonderland doesn't exist. She's a fantasy from a fairy tale. In the real world, there is no Alice in Wonderland. There never was."

Brent turned and strode way, disappearing in mo-ments into the darkness. Alice reached out one trembling hand toward him, then dropped it back to her side. She stumbled forward and sank onto a cement bench with intricate scrollwork on the top.

Wrapping her arms around her stomach, she rocked back and forth, sobbing openly, as she was consumed by the greatest pain and heartache she had ever known.

This wasn't happening, she thought frantically. She was in the midst of a devastating nightmare. She would wake up and find herself snuggled close to Brent in his bed in the cottage where they'd shared exquisitely beautiful lovemaking. He would tell her they had to hurry or they'd be late for the first-night-on-the-island welcoming dinner in the castle and...

Alice drew a shuddering breath, then a chill swept through her, touching her heart, mind and soul.

No, this wasn't a nightmare formed by images while sleeping. This was the nightmare of reality. She had demolished her protective walls, had emerged as Alice, had fallen in love and given her heart to Brent to have and to hold, to love and to cherish.

And he'd crushed it.

He viewed her as a scheming, devious, game-playing woman, who had used him to fill idle hours as she waited for the launching of her artistic career.

He despised her.

Brent didn't believe in her, or in her love for him. Not anymore. He'd flung hateful accusations at her that had felt like physical blows, shattering her into a million pieces. Like Humpty-Dumpty, Alice in Wonderland could never be put back together again.

Alice got to her feet, swayed for a moment, then steadied.

But Alice, the woman? she thought. She'd have to survive, move forward. Somehow. The alternative was to rebuild the walls and become Trip again, and she didn't want to do that. No, not that.

She was Alice.

She would remain Alice.

Alone and lonely, having loved and lost the most magnificent man who walked this earth. The man she would love until she drew her last breath. The man she would ache for, miss so much, cry tears for during the bleak, dark hours of the night for a long, long time.

Chapter Eleven

The next morning the MacAllisters were treated to a tour of the island while riding in a long wagon with padded seats and pulled by a team of eight sleek horses.

To Alice's utmost relief, none of the Bardows were at breakfast, although a cheerful Charlane arrived at the castle in time to accompany the group on the tour.

When Maggie commented on Alice's puffy, red-rimmed eyes, she popped on a pair of sunglasses and told her cousin that she was apparently allergic to something that was in bloom that she wasn't accustomed to.

"That's certainly understandable, Alice," Charlane said. "There's a multitude of flowers here that aren't grown in Ventura. You'll build up a tolerance for them in time, never fear." She smiled brightly. "Providing, of course, that you're in close proximity to the blossoms for a, shall we say, extended period."

Alice managed to produce a small smile, then climbed into the wagon and smothered a weary sigh.

Charlane Bardow, she thought, was about as subtle as a rock. She was making it clear that she fully expected Alice to marry Brent and live on Wilshire, which would solve the nagging little problem of being allergic to the flowers growing there.

But that wasn't going to happen, nor was the condition of her less-than-attractive eyes due to being allergic to the plants. She'd wept her way through the long night, dozing from total exhaustion at times, then waking again to cry into her pillow over the heartbreaking loss of her Brent.

Oh, dear heaven, she wanted to go home, Alice thought, as King Chester pointed out things of interest they were passing as the horses plodded along. How was she going to get through the following days without falling apart, dissolving into a puddle of tears and telling everyone that her heart was smashed to smithereens?

Get a grip, she told herself. The only thing that Brent had been right about during his tirade last night was the fact that nothing should spoil Maggie and Devon's special event. She would have to reach deep within herself for the fortitude to produce a cheerful demeanor, not give one clue that anything was wrong.

But, oh, God, how was she going to bear being close to Brent at the scheduled events and pretend they were still madly in love with each other, give everyone the impression that the next wedding on the calendar would be the exchanging of vows between Alice MacAllister and Brent Bardow?

Oh, Brent, Alice thought, blinking away sudden tears. She loved him so much. If only there was something that she could do, or say, to make him believe in her again. But there wasn't. It was hopeless. It was over.

"Alice," Jillian whispered, leaning close to her daughter in the seat they were sharing.

"Yes, Mother?" Alice said, turning her head while being very grateful that she'd remembered to pack the sunglasses she intended to wear at every opportunity.

"There are bumps in the road of love," Jillian said quietly, so only Alice could hear, "in every romance since the beginning of time. The true test of love is not to give up, not leave that road because it's painful for you at the moment."

"I never said—" Alice started.

"I'm your mother, my darling," Jillian said gently. "I know you're very unhappy right now, although your being allergic to the flowers number was very inventive. Only a woman who is deeply in love would have cried as you have. Don't give up on what you and Brent have together just because, for whatever reason, you two have hit a rocky spot in the road."

"I have no choice but to accept that it's over," Alice said, struggling against her tears. "Brent truly believes that I..." She shook her head. "I can't talk about it or I'll... I promise I won't do anything to spoil things for Maggie and Devon. That's the only thing that Brent and I are in accord about."

Jillian patted her daughter's knee. "I understand. But do remember that I'm here for you. Think about what I said, too. True love can weather many storms."

"Not *this* storm," Alice said, smiling slightly. "This is a hurricane, a tornado and a typhoon all wrapped up in a devastating package that has destroyed what Brent and I had beyond repair. I—''

"To your right," King Chester said, bringing Alice and Jillian back to attention, "as far as the eye can see are Brent's vineyards. Devon handles the paperwork, the management end of things. Brent works side by side with his employees in the fields. Brent is a man of the earth, a nurturer, who gives his heart and soul to what he loves. We're extremely proud of what he's accomplished for all of us here on Wilshire."

Yes, Alice thought, reflecting on King Chester's words. That was how he had loved her, would have loved the children they would have created together. Totally. Absolutely. A man of the earth, who worked so hard, so diligently for what he believed in and cherished. Oh, what they would have had as husband and wife, father and mother, partners, soul mates.

Oh, what would have been, but would never be.

That afternoon a final fitting of the bridesmaids' dresses took place in one of the multitude of huge bedrooms in the castle.

Maggie had chosen rainbow colors for her attendants: Jessica in pink, Emily wearing yellow, and to Alice's dismay, her dress was a lighter shade of Brent's blue eyes.

The seamstress, Ruth, was a wonder, had made the dresses from nothing more than Maggie's descriptions of her cousin's figures. Shoes had been dyed to match the material and only the hems to the dresses were yet to be done.

Emily's dress, however, had to be taken in as she had shed another six pounds during the month since the royal family had left Ventura.

"I'm sorry to cause you extra work," Emily said to Ruth, who was pinning the dress, "but I'm personally thrilled that I'm actually sticking to my diet. And this time I intend to keep the weight off permanently. I'd hate to add up how many pounds I've lost and gained over the years."

"It's no problem to fix this," Ruth said. "But I hope you don't get as skinny as your sisters. Women need to be women, not sticks."

"Hear, hear," Jessica said, laughing. "Bring on some chocolate."

"It's true," Ruth said. "You need meat on your bones so you can nurse many healthy babies."

"My baby days are over," Emily said, smiling. "My son is nearly as tall as I am already. I'm overdue to be a stick."

"You have many years left to have babies,"

Ruth said, frowning. "Why would you say your baby days are over, Emily?"

"Because," Emily said, suddenly serious, "that's…that's the way I want it. No men in my life, no babies in my future. I'm just creating a home for me and my son, running my own business. That's all I need." She smiled again. "Now, Jessica and Tr…Alice are a different story. Talk to them about putting meat on their bones so they can nurse those babies you're speaking of."

Jessica laughed. "All in good time, Emily. Do remember that I became an instant mother to Tessa when I married Daniel. One in diapers is enough to handle at the moment. There. I'm off the hook."

"For now," Emily said. "That leaves our sister Alice, the Stick. From what we all saw when we arrived at the airport here, Brent is obviously thinking about more than just grapes."

Alice sent a frantic look to her mother, and Jillian got quickly to her feet from where she was sitting on a love seat.

"I believe Emily's dress needs to be nipped in just a tad more at the waist," she said, crossing the room. "What do you think?" She swept her gaze over the other women in the room, prompting opinions to be offered.

Thank you, Mother, Alice thought, sinking onto

an easy chair. How very sad this charade was. She was once again pretending to be someone she wasn't, keeping the secret of her broken heart from those who loved her unconditionally. But she had to do it this way for Maggie's sake.

Somehow, *somehow,* when she saw Brent at dinner that night she'd appear carefree and happy, would stay close to his side, not give even one hint that there was anything wrong between them. Somehow.

"There he is," Charlane said as Brent strode into the dining room that evening. "Late, per usual."

"Sorry," Brent said, sliding onto his chair next to Alice. "I had a long-distance call at the last minute, but I'm here now. Bring on the food."

"And hungry, per usual," Byron said, chuckling.

"Hello, sweet person," Brent said. He kissed Alice on the cheek but didn't look into her eyes. "Did you have a nice day?"

"Yes," she said, fiddling with her napkin, "it was lovely."

"Good," Brent said. "Ah, here comes the soup. I am one famished man."

How on earth was she going to choke down this food? Alice thought miserably. Brent was sitting right there next to her, only a handful of inches away, yet the distance she could feel between them was like a deep chasm that could not be crossed.

She could feel, actually feel, the vibrant heat emanating from Brent's powerful body, could smell his musky aftershave and the lingering aroma of fresh soap from his shower.

Her cheek where he'd kissed her, she thought, forcing herself not to place her fingertips there, was still tingling with warmth, evoking memories of the lovemaking they'd shared.

"Didn't she, Alice?" Emily asked, snapping Alice back to attention.

"Pardon me?"

"The seamstress, Ruth," Emily said. "She was a delightful woman who decided that Jessica and you were built like sticks and needed to fatten up some so you could nurse your healthy, bouncing babies."

"I…" Alice said.

"Some women would rather focus on their careers than have babies," Brent said.

Oh, Brent, Alice thought, *don't.*

"Well, I intend to have it all," Jessica said. "A career and the roles of wife and mother. It can be done, Brent, if the couple works together."

"Amen to that." Daniel smiled at Jessica.

"We'll be the proof of that pudding, or however that old saying goes."

Brent nodded. "I agree with you, Jessica, but if the woman's career is all-consuming, there isn't room for anything else in her life."

Jessica shrugged. "I suppose you're right, but the same is to be said of the man. The couple has to be in balance, sharing, compromising, knowing when work ends for the day and family focus begins. Daniel might be called out on a case during what might be his usual time to read a story to Tessa, but the foundation is there, is in place, in the big picture of our life together."

"You're to be envied," Brent said. "Not everyone is as fortunate as you and Daniel, Jessica. For some of us, that balance, shall we say, is out of reach."

"Nonsense," Byron said. "No one is pointing a gun at your head, Brent, demanding that you put in the ridiculously long days that you do in the vineyards." He smiled at Alice. "You just haven't had a reason to cut back on your hours in the past. Things change."

"Yes, they do, don't they?" Brent said, a slight edge to his voice. "Sometimes when you least expect it, things change so drastically it knocks you for a loop. Maggie, would you pass me the pepper, please?''

Alice crossed her legs beneath the table and kicked Brent in the calf.

''Ow!'' he said.

''Oh, I'm terribly sorry,'' she said, ever so sweetly. Tit for tat. Brent had gotten in his little zinger, his dig at her, thinking she had no choice but to sit there and take it.

''Yeah, right,'' Brent said, under his breath.

''One should not push a MacAllister beyond the line in the sand.'' Jillian laughed softly.

''Where did that come from?'' Forrest said. ''Am I missing something here? Is this a woman thing I wouldn't understand even if you told me?''

''It certainly is,'' Jillian said, then looked directly at Brent. ''Men can be terribly stubborn at times, get into a mind-set and refuse to budge, won't even entertain the idea that they might be wrong.''

''Some men might do that,'' Brent said, meeting Jillian's gaze. ''I, however, make certain that I have all my data, the facts as they stand, know that I'm right.''

''I'm definitely missing something here,'' Forrest mumbled.

''My, my,'' Alice said, ''this topic is getting very

heavy, isn't it? King Chester, what…what kingly things did you do today?''

As King Chester began to reply, Alice tuned out and breathed a sigh of relief.

Her mother's protective instincts had risen to the fore, she thought, and she'd been ready to go toe-to-toe with Brent, not even knowing the full story of what had destroyed his relationship with her daughter. That was very loving of her mother, but it couldn't continue or the others would pick up on the fact that this was not just dinner chitchat.

Dear heaven, would this meal never end?

During the following days and nights preceding the wedding, the essence of that frantic plea became Alice's mantra.

Would the fancy, women-only tea in the castle garden never end?

Would the shopping trip into the quaint village in the center of Wilshire never end?

Would the agonizing tour of the winery, which was conducted by Brent, never end?

Would the music played by the string quartet that came to the castle to entertain the guests while she was sitting next to Brent on a sofa never end?

Would the formal reception to welcome the multitude of dignitaries arriving from around the world for the wedding never end?

Would the long, lonely nights spent weeping into her pillow never, ever end?

On the morning of the wedding, which was scheduled, by royal tradition, to take place at high noon, Alice woke at dawn and mentally held tight to the knowledge that early tomorrow morning she could go home.

She had to survive the wedding and the long, lavish reception following it today, then this nightmare would be over. Returning to Ventura, she knew, was not going to erase the dark, gloomy cloud that seemed to continually hover over her. But at least she would be home and could, hopefully, get at least some reprieve from her misery as she concentrated on her work.

As sunlight began to fill the lovely bedroom, Alice turned her head on the pillow to look at the beautiful bridesmaid's dress that hung on a padded hanger on an antique clothes tree.

Her cousin Maggie, Alice mused, was going to marry her prince today. It was a fairy tale come true. Maggie would be a princess and someday a queen. She and Devon were so very much in love that an aura of sunshine seemed to encase them whenever they were together.

Maggie was Cinderella, and Snow White and all the others in the whimsical stories of handsome princes claiming their brides for all time.

"And me?" Alice said aloud.

She was still dumb Alice in Wonderland, falling through the hole and tumbling down, down, down, because she'd been stupid enough to follow some idiotic rabbit who couldn't even manage to get to an appointment on time.

There was no handsome prince waiting for *her*. There was no happy ending for *her*. There was no longer magnificent Brent Bardow in love with her.

Alice drew a wobbly breath.

Stop feeling sorry for yourself, Alice MacAllister, she thought firmly. Enough of this pity party trip she was on. But, oh, dear heaven, she was just so…so sad. What a tiny little word. Three letters. Sad. But it spoke volumes with its chilling truth that totally consumed her.

And she had no one to blame but herself.

"Just like the white rabbit," Alice whispered. "I was late, too late, for the most important date with destiny of my entire life."

Alice looked again at the bridesmaid's dress.

"Always the bridesmaid," she said, then sniffled. "But I'll never, ever be Brent's bride."

In the groom's room in the church, Devon looked at his watch, stared into space, then glanced at his watch again as he realized he hadn't registered the time in his jumbled mind.

"Fifteen minutes," he said. "Why did they stick us in this room so soon?"

Brent leaned one shoulder against the wall and crossed his arms over his chest. "So you could have your nervous breakdown and get over it, cousin," he said. "Cripes, Devon, calm down. You're going to feel like the jerk of the century if you pass out cold on your face at the altar. Get a grip, man."

"Grip," Devon said, nodding jerkily. "I'm getting it. The grip. Here I am. Getting a grip. Brent, I'm about to be married."

Brent nodded slowly. "That's the plan." He paused and frowned. "This isn't a case of cold feet I'm witnessing here, is it?"

"How can you even suggest such a thing?" Devon said, none too quietly. "This is the happiest day of my life. I'm marrying my Maggie. My beautiful, sweet, wonderful princess, the woman of my dreams. I just wish there weren't five hundred people out there waiting for me to mess up what I'm supposed to say, when it's my turn to say what I'm supposed to say, when I say what I'm supposed to... Ah, hell, I'm losing it.''

"Big time," Brent said, shaking his head. "Look, try this. Tell yourself there is no one in that church except you and Maggie. Just the two of you. Focus on Maggie, on how much you love her, on the fantastic future you're going to have together. She'll be your wife, Devon, your soul mate and partner for life and..."

An achy sensation gripped Brent's throat and he stopped speaking.

Ah, Alice, he thought. Everything he was saying should be describing what they would share, what they would have together.

He loved her. He despised her.

He couldn't bear the thought of her leaving Wilshire tomorrow. He never wanted to see her again.

She was everything he had ever hoped to find in a woman, a wife. She was nothing close to being who he'd believed her to be.

"Hey, Brent?" Devon said. "What's wrong? You suddenly look like you lost your best friend."

"Got it in one, cousin," Brent said. "Forget it. I'm fine. You're the one who is coming unglued. Here. We're supposed to put these dorky boutonniere things in our lapels. Somebody nuts thought up all this junk. Why do guys need a dinky flower on their coat so they can get married?'' He opened a white florist box that was sitting on a small table.

''Oops.''

''Oops?'' Devon said. ''Don't say 'oops' when I'm hanging on by a thread here.'' He crossed the room and looked in the box. ''That's a corsage, Brent. You know, the mother-of-the-bride thing, or something. There should be two boutonnieres in that box and...oh, this is just great. Dandy. Perfect. I can't get married to my Maggie because some idiot lost my boutonniere.''

''Chill,'' Brent said, placing his hands on Devon's shoulders. ''The boxes got switched, that's all. I'll go around to the other side through the back hallway and I betcha a buck the women are in the bride's room, or whatever the hell you call it, ready to trade flowers. Okay? Say 'okay, Brent.''''

''Okay, Brent,'' Devon said.

''Good boy,'' Brent said, patting Devon on the cheek. ''I'll be back in a flash. Try not to have a complete mental collapse while I'm gone.''

''Okay, Brent.''

''Hopeless,'' Brent said, then snatched up the box and left the room.

Brent strode along the narrow, dimly lit corridor, then stopped suddenly in his tracks, his heart thundering so wildly it caused an actual physical pain in his chest.

There she was, he thought hazily. Alice. She was coming toward him, a vision of loveliness in a beautiful blue dress. There she was, walking down the aisle to take her place at his side, to repeat the sacred vows with him that would unite them in marriage. There she was. His bride. His Alice of wonder. And he loved her so damn much.

Look at us, Brent thought. As the decades went by and their love grew even deeper and richer, they would gaze into each other's eyes and say the words...look at us, after all these years together, look at you, still pretty as a picture, look at me, still crazy over you.

Oh, God, Alice.

She stopped several feet away from him.

''Brent,'' Alice said, her voice trembling, ''the flowers, this box has the boutonnieres that you and Devon... Do you have a corsage in that box you're holding?''

Do you, Brent, take this woman to be your wife, to have and to hold from this day forward, Brent's mind hummed from a faraway place.

''I do,'' he said, emotion ringing in his voice.

To love and to cherish, Alice thought hazily, in

sickness and in health, for richer, for poorer, forever, forever, forever...

Oh, Brent.

"I do," Alice whispered.

They walked slowly forward, closing the distance
between them, looking deep into each other's eyes,
hearts racing, breaths catching, unshed tears causing
eyes to sting.

It was magic, their magic, returned to them, encasing them in a mist of splendor and joy and love
so intense it was a nearly palpable entity weaving
around and through them, chasing away the chill
with a warmth that touched their hearts and souls.

"Brent!" Devon called in the distance. "Come
on. It's time. It's time."

Brent jerked and dropped the box he was holding. He leaned down, snatched it from the floor and
shoved it at Alice, forcing her to accept it.

"Brent?" she said, searching his face as she
drew a wobbly breath.

"No," he said, a rough edge to his voice as he
took the other box from her hand. "Don't say anything to me, Alice. Not anything...except...good-
bye."

The wedding ceremony was breathtaking.

Sunlight streamed through the stained-glass windows of the enormous church, creating a wondrous

rainbow of colors to cascade over the bride and groom. They spoke their vows with voices steady and sure as they pledged their love to each other for eternity. Matching rings were slipped onto fingers as visible signs of what was in their hearts, minds and souls.

As Maggie and Devon turned to be introduced as husband and wife to the multitude of witnesses, tears flowed freely from those who saw the glorious radiance of their love for each other.

Tears shimmered, too, in the eyes of Alice and Brent, but theirs were born of heartache for what would never be for them.

Chapter Twelve

As dawn crept quietly above the horizon the next morning with muted colors that grew more vibrant as they began to fill the sky, Alice stood hidden in the trees by Brent's cottage.

She'd been there an hour already, having arrived in the dark, and was chilled through, the slacks and lightweight sweater she'd chosen to wear during the flight home not warm enough for the crisp night air.

During the seemingly endless hours of the night, she'd decided that this was what she wanted, needed to do. It would probably mean nothing to Brent, but it was very, very important to her.

Giving up on attempting to sleep, she'd showered, dressed, then packed her suitcases. Feeling like a sneak thief, she'd crept down the stairs and out the front doors of the castle.

With only the stars to light the path, she made her way to Brent's cottage without a wrong turn, as though she had been there a hundred times, instead of only once.

It was as though, she thought, her heart was leading the way to the man she loved beyond measure.

A shiver coursed through Alice as a breeze rustled the leaves on the trees, then her breath caught as she saw the glow of light suddenly appear behind the curtains of the cottage. Having no idea what time he usually started his day, she had come early so she'd be certain that Brent had left the cottage and she could complete her mission.

Fifteen minutes later, the door to the cottage opened and Alice almost forgot to breathe as Brent stepped outside, clad only in faded jeans riding low on his hips.

Even from where she stood hidden in the trees, she could see that his hair was damp from a morning shower, and for a moment she was convinced she could actually smell his wonderful aroma of soap and fresh air. He was sipping from a mug, and he scanned the sky to gauge the weather for the day.

Alice drank in the sight of Brent, memorizing every detail of him, etching each indelibly in her mind. Tears stung the back of her eyes and she blinked them away, refusing to cry, wondering when she would have no more tears left.

Brent tossed the last of the coffee on the ground, then his shoulders slumped and he dropped his chin to his bare chest that rose, then fell from a deep sigh.

Oh, God, Alice thought, pressing the trembling fingertips of one hand to her lips, Brent looked so defeated, so exhausted. So very, very sad. *She* had done this to him, and the weight of her guilt was crushing.

"I'm so sorry, my love," she whispered, unable to stop the tears that spilled onto her cheeks.

Brent went back into the cottage and shut the door, emerging ten minutes later fully dressed. He strode away and disappeared in the opposite direction from where Alice was standing.

She waited another twenty minutes to be absolutely certain that Brent wouldn't return, then moved from her hiding place and ran to the cottage. She hesitated, then with a firm resolve, opened the door and entered the little house.

A short time later when Alice stepped into the entryway of the castle, she mentally moaned when she saw her family coming down the stairs.

Great timing, she thought dryly. She knew that an early breakfast had been scheduled so they could make their flight, but had hoped she'd be back in her room before the others emerged from theirs and it would appear as though she had followed the same plan as the group. Oh, well, bring on the bare lightbulb. She was about to be grilled by the pros regarding what she had been up to.

"Good morning, sweetheart," Jillian said as she crossed the entryway.

"Hi," Alice said weakly. "I..."

"I'm ready for some of those spicy little sausages," Forrest said. "I wonder if we could get the recipe for those, Jillian." He glanced at Alice. "Coming, kiddo? The next meal we'll have will be airplane food, so let's fill up while we're here."

"I..." Alice said, raising one finger in the air.

Jessica winked at her sister as she and Daniel went past Alice, then Emily beamed at her. The others strolled by, and Alice was the recipient of knowing smiles and smothered laughter.

Whatever, Alice thought, mentally throwing up her hands as she followed the family. They all believed, apparently, that she'd had a private, romantic farewell with Brent and they were going to leave it at that, no doubt feeling very sophisticated with their acceptance of her torrid affair with Brent Bardow.

My heart is smashed to smithereens, people, Alice yelled in her mind. *I'm a walking, talking, crying jag.*

Alice sniffled and six members of her family looked at her questioningly.

"Allergies," she mumbled.

"Mmm," Jillian said.

Alice poked at her food as everyone ate and chatted about the beautiful wedding of the day before. Maggie and Devon were off on a two-week honeymoon to a destination they had refused to reveal, and Forrest started taking bets on where they had gone.

Finally giving up any attempt to choke down a bite, Alice pushed her plate away and sipped her coffee. Everyone looked up as a man entered the dining room, handed a note to King Chester, then hurried away. The king read the message, then nodded.

"This is from Brent," he said. "He has things

to take care of at the vineyard this morning that need his personal attention and won't be able to see you off at the plane. He wishes you all a good journey.''

A chill swept through Alice and she set her cup back in the saucer with a shaking hand.

Brent couldn't even bear to see her one last time, she thought miserably. She'd not only destroyed his love for her, she'd pushed him all the way to actually hating the very sight of her. So many hopes and dreams, so very many, were gone…forever.

Charlane and Byron had come to the castle for the farewell breakfast, and Byron shook his head when he heard the message his son had sent.

''Brent works too hard,'' Byron said. ''We discussed that the other evening at dinner, remember? The fact that some people are too focused on their work, their careers. I thought he might be listening to me, but apparently he wasn't.''

''I…I don't believe he was referring to himself,'' Alice said quietly. ''He…never mind. It's not important. Now.'' She cringed as she glanced around the table and saw that everyone was looking at her. ''What I mean is…um…well, I…''

''What you're saying,'' Jillian said, ''is that it often takes time for change. Right, dear?''

''Right,'' Alice said quickly.

"Oh," Byron said, nodding. "Well, that makes sense, I guess. There's hope for that boy yet. He'll get his priorities straight."

"Hear, hear," Charlane said, smiling at Alice.

Brent already had his priorities straight, Alice thought. His first order of business was to erase her from his mind *and* his heart just as quickly as he possibly could.

Late that night Brent entered his cottage, stumbling slightly from total exhaustion. He'd pushed his body to the maximum and beyond the entire day with the hope that he would be so tired he would finally be able to stop thinking and just sleep, blank his mind and sleep.

He snapped on the small lamp by the bed as he tugged his filthy shirt free of his jeans, unbuttoned it and dropped it to the floor. As he unsnapped his grimy jeans, his attention was caught by a tissue-wrapped package propped against one of the pillows on the bed.

Sinking onto the edge of the bed, he frowned as he picked up the parcel, then tore away the paper, his eyes widening as what was inside was revealed.

"The pewter frame," he said aloud. "The one that Alice's grandfather gave her as her secret present. Why did she give something this special to me now?''

He sighed in confusion, then directed his attention to the painting within the frame, his breath catching as he stared at the portrait of Alice. His heart began to beat in a wild tempo and a roaring noise echoed in his ears as he drank in the sight of Alice's face, her eyes, the soft smile on her lips.

His hold on the frame tightened as his gaze stayed riveted on the self-portrait Alice had painted.

This woman, his thoughts racing, is in love. Deeply, intensely in love, and she had the glow of knowing she was loved in return. It was all there for him to see, in this portrait, in this picture that Alice had painted of herself and had now given to him.

This was the truth. This was real. This was Alice in Wonderland, whom he had come to love beyond measure. This was his future.

''Dear God,'' he whispered hoarsely, ''what have I done? Oh, my beloved Alice, what have I done to us?''

Alice entered the loft with her agent close on her heels. Alice sank onto the sofa with a weary sigh, leaned her head on the top and closed her eyes.

''That's it. That's all,'' Alice said. ''I'm done.

I've smiled so much in the three weeks since I've been back that my face is frozen in phony form."

Delores laughed and sat down in an easy chair opposite the sofa.

"You did beautifully today," she said. "The TV cameras love you, Alice. I have videos of all the other talk shows you've done up and down the coast and you're a natural in front of the cameras."

"The cameras love me?" Alice said, not moving or opening her eyes. "Hooray for the cameras. What I want is for *people* to love my work, Delores. That's what is important."

"Work they won't know about unless we get the word out about it," Delores said. "Let's see, you've done the talk shows, the radio call-in bit, been interviewed for the newspaper, plus that classy art magazine and—"

"Don't click off anymore on that list," Alice said. "I'm exhausted enough without mentally reliving it all." She raised her head and looked at Delores. "You've done a marvelous job as my agent, you really have. I know you've made an arrangement with the gallery that anything that sells during the private showing is to be left hanging there for a week, plus they have the extra paintings not being seen that first night ready to display.

"But, Delores? I've discovered something about

myself during these three weeks. When someone I know brought up the fact that I would be doing this sort of publicity I was taken off guard because I just hadn't given it any thought. But now I've lived it and I definitely don't like it, not one little bit."

Delores shrugged. "Some people do, some don't. It just depends on who you are."

Alice sat up straighter on the sofa. "That's my point. I really know now who I am in regard to this arena of publicity, public appearances, the whole nine yards. It's *not* who I am. I don't like the limelight, the personal questions, the prying. I can't, won't, do this again, Delores. Maybe it will mean I won't sell as many paintings in the future, but I want to be honest with you about this. If you'd prefer not to be my agent because I'm being uncooperative—"

"Whoa, sweetie," Delores said, raising both hands. "I'm not going anywhere. You're stuck with me. You've been a real trouper during this godawful schedule I set up for you." She shrugged. "That is that. No problem."

"My art will speak for me, reflect who I am," Alice said. "That's all that matters."

"And that's fine, just fine," Delores said, getting to her feet. "You're going to have a long and successful career, Ms. MacAllister, and you don't have to suffer through any more cameras falling in love with you.'' She glanced at her watch. ''I'm off. Don't get up. I can let myself out. You're spending this last week until the show working with the gallery owner on wall placement of your paintings. Right? Right. Okay, sweetie, I'll see you on the big night. It's going to be fabulous. Ta-ta.''

''Ta,'' Alice said, raising one hand as she sank back against the comfy cushions on the sofa. ''Ta.''

See, Brent? she thought, closing her eyes again. It would have all been so perfect.

Except it would never happen.

Because it was too late.

A star-filled sky lit the way as Brent climbed to the top of the hill where he'd stood and watched Alice's plane disappear from view, the place where he'd dreamed of building their home. He'd made this trek every night since he'd discovered the portrait in the pewter frame on his bed after Alice had left the island.

He sank onto the ground and leaned his back against a tree, staring into space.

Night after night, he mused, he came here, hoping to untangle the confusing jumble in his mind and find the answers to the heartbreaking dilemma he was facing. And night after night he accomplished nothing more than chasing his own thoughts in an endless circle in his beleaguered mind.

"And here we go again," he said aloud, his voice weary.

He loved Alice. Alice loved him. He no longer doubted that she truly loved him as much as he loved her. He had only to look at the self-portrait she'd painted to know that was true.

He also now believed that Alice *hadn't* been playing games with him, with his heart, his emotions, to fill her idle hours until her career was launched. No, she had simply been gathering enough inner courage to reveal her hopes and dreams to him, to her family. It hadn't been a secret agenda in the negative sense he'd accused her of, but a secret she'd been too frightened to make known.

Brent bent his knees, propped his elbows on them and made a steeple of his fingers, which he tapped against his lips.

He'd gotten that much straight during his nightly treks, he thought, but couldn't move forward. Still there, like an unbreachable wall standing between him and any future happiness with Alice, was the remainder of the mess in his mind.

Fact. Alice was a very, *very* talented artist, whose career was about to take off like a rocket.

Fact. Careers like hers had to be nurtured, pushed along, with publicity, interviews, public appearances, so that the public could feel a personal link with the artist of the work they were considering buying.

Fact. The necessity of being accessible to her would-be fans and supporters would result in Alice packing a suitcase and flying off to the States whenever her agent said it was time to do it again. Fly off and leave him behind to wander through an empty and lonely house that wouldn't be a home when Alice wasn't there.

Fact. The babies, the miracles, they would have created together with exquisite lovemaking would have to become a forgotten dream because there just wouldn't be room in Alice's schedule for the role of mother. Wearing the hats of wife and successful artist would be all that Alice would be able to handle.

Fact. The scenario he had just repeated…again… just wasn't enough. It was too shallow, too empty too much of the time, to fill him with the happiness that loving and being loved in return should do.

"Ah, damn," Brent said, dragging his hands down his face. "It's hopeless."

He'd just keep on as he was…alone. He'd focus

on the vineyards, start thinking of producing another new, award-winning wine with a heartfelt intensity. Just as in the past when he'd allowed nothing to keep him from achieving his dreams for the
excellence of Wilshire wines, he would once
again...

Brent stiffened, every muscle in his body tightened to the point of pain, as his heart thundered.

Wait a minute, he thought. Wait just a damn minute here. *He'd allowed nothing to keep him from
achieving his dreams.* Yet there he sat, Mr. Holier-
than-thou, passing judgment on the woman he
loved, deciding that what she had to offer him
didn't measure up, when what she was doing was
exactly what he had done. *Alice was allowing nothing to keep her from achieving her dreams.*

And she had every right to do that.

"My God," he whispered, his voice hoarse with
emotion, "I'm such a selfish jerk. We live our life
together, Alice, following only my rules, or forget
it. The hell with *your* dreams, *your* hopes, *your*
years of dedication to purpose. If they don't match
mine, they're not worth squat, lady."

Brent rolled to his feet and stared at the brilliant
sky in the direction that Alice's plane had flown
when she had left Wilshire. Left *him.*

He had been so wrong, he thought frantically. So

self-centered and wrong. The woman he loved was in love with him and he'd thrown that all away— broken a precious possession that could never be replaced.

So, okay, Alice would have to leave Wilshire to promote her work. But she'd come home. To him.

So, okay, they wouldn't have children. But they'd have each other.

So, okay, it wasn't the existence he'd envisioned them sharing as husband and wife. But it would be theirs, and with compromise, and understanding, and love, they could make it work for them. Forever and ever. Until death parted them.

It was an enormous, terrifying "if"...if Alice would forgive him for the way he'd treated her, the things he'd accused her of that weren't remotely true, if Alice still loved him despite the fact that he had been a rotten human being.

Get a grip, Bardow, get a plan, he told himself. Think. Yes. He'd catch the first plane he could find and fly to Ventura, beg...yes, *beg,* Alice to forgive him. Assure her that he would always be waiting for her to come home when she was finished with whatever promotional tour, showing, whatever, she'd had to attend to. Make her understand, some-how, that they could be happy there as husband and wife, on Wilshire. They could borrow Maggie and Devon's kids to play with or something and...

"Oh, God, Alice, please forgive me. Give me, us, another chance."

Chapter Thirteen

Forrest MacAllister stood in front of the mirror in the bathroom off the master bedroom in the home he shared with Jillian. He muttered under his breath, threw in a few earthy expletives, then...

"Jillian!" he yelled. "I can't get this damnable tie to do what I want it to. It ends up vertical instead of horizontal every time I attempt to... I need some help here. Please, dear wife, come to my rescue."

Jillian laughed and crossed the bedroom to enter the bathroom where Forrest stood scowling.

"We go through this whenever you wear a tuxedo, Forrest," she said, gripping the silky ends of the tie. "I've been coming to your rescue like this for over thirty years."

"I know, I know," he said, "but I always think that this might be the night I'll finally conquer the beast."

"I see," Jillian said, then patted the tie that was now horizontal instead of vertical. "There you are. You're gorgeous, Mr. MacAllister."

"And you are the most beautiful woman I know," he said, circling her waist with his arms. "I swear, Jillian, you don't look a day older than the first time I saw you in Deede's store autographing your newest book."

"You're such a sweet liar," Jillian said, smiling at him. "Do you like my new dress I bought for this special occasion?"

Forrest followed her and swept his gaze over her from head to toe, nodding in approval at the sea-green, full-length dress his wife wore. It had a scoop neck, cap sleeves and flared slightly from her slender hips.

"It's very, very pretty." Forrest paused. "I'm a nervous wreck about tonight. There has been so much publicity and hype about this event. What if people don't buy Alice's paintings? It will break her heart and... I'm taking a credit card with me.

I'll buy a bunch of her paintings myself if I have to and..."

The telephone on one of the nightstands rang.

"Oh, dear, who can that be?" Jillian said. "We should be leaving right now." She hurried to the telephone and lifted the receiver. "Hello?"

"Jillian? This is Brent Bardow."

"Well, my goodness," Jillian said, "this is a surprise. Are you calling from Wilshire, Brent?"

"No, I'm here in Ventura. I just checked into a hotel, and when they handed me my key card they also gave me a brochure announcing the private showing of Alice's work that's taking place tonight. I didn't know the exact date of it, but the brochure says that it's black tie, invitation only."

"Yes, that's true," Jillian said. "Then the gallery will be opened to the general public tomorrow."

Forrest began to pace around the room. "Brent Bardow. I don't know what happened between him and Alice, but I have a feeling I'm really ticked off at that guy."

"Forrest, hush," Jillian said. "Brent, I certainly don't intend to sound rude, but what are you doing in Ventura?"

"I've come to see Alice," he said. "I've been a total jerk, Jillian, and I'm hoping, praying, that Alice will forgive me. I have to see her. I have to get into that gallery tonight. But…I don't have an invitation and I sure didn't pack a tux. Will you help me, Jillian. Please?''

"What does he want?'' Forrest said.

"Shh,'' Jillian said, flapping one hand at him. "All right, Brent, I'm going to trust you. This is Alice's big night, and I don't want anything to upset her. I'll tell whoever is at the door of the gallery that you're to be allowed in with no invitation.''

"Thank you. Thank you so much.'' Brent paused. "I bet it's too late to rent a tux someplace.''

"I'm sure it is,'' Jillian said. "Don't worry about that. You're crashing the party, per se, so it stands to reason you won't be dressed appropriately. Oh, I hope I'm doing the right thing.''

"Jillian,'' Brent said quietly, "I love your daughter with my whole heart. I want to marry her, spend the rest of my life with her. She's my soul mate, my other half, my partner. I love her. I need her.''

Jillian smiled. "I'm definitely doing the right thing,'' she said, and after finalizing the details with Brent, replaced the receiver.

"Brent and Alice's love is most definitely the right thing, the wondrous thing, that has been the foundation of *our* marriage for over thirty years,'' she said, slipping her arm through Forrest's. "Brent will be coming to the gallery tonight. The rest is up to them, Forrest. Now, let's go and watch those pretty gold sold-stickers being placed on Alice MacAllister's paintings.''

Brent spoke quietly to the frowning man stationed by the front doors of the gallery.

''Oh, yes,'' the man said, ''Mrs. Jillian MacAllister made arrangements for your admittance but…'' He slid his gaze over Brent's black, long-sleeved silk shirt, sans tie, with black slacks. ''I guess exceptions are to be made for members of the family of the artist.''

''Hold that thought,'' Brent said. ''Pray about that 'member of the family' thought.''

''Excuse me, sir?''

''Never mind. Thanks for bending the rules. It sure is crowded in here. Do you have any idea where Alice…Ms. MacAllister is?''

''I believe she's being interviewed by a television anchorman at the moment, sir. Over there, where those bright lights are totally destroying the soft, gentle ambience we created for the paintings being displayed tonight.'' He sighed dramatically. ''Well, the majority of the work has already been sold, but—''

''It has?'' Brent said.

"Oh, my, yes. Ms. MacAllister's showing is a huge success, sir. A star has been born."

Brent nodded and attempted to ignore the cold fist that tightened in his gut. He made his way forward slowly, finally stopping at the edge of the group of people watching the interview take place.

Oh, man, he thought, there she was. Alice. She was so beautiful in that rose gown, her dark eyes were sparkling, and her cheeks were flushed, probably from excitement and the knowledge that she had been recognized as a talented artist. This was her night and she deserved to bask in every moment of the attention she was getting.

There she was. The woman he loved. The woman who held his future happiness in her hands. The woman who had given him the portrait in the pewter frame to tell him how much she loved him. He could only hope and pray that he hadn't destroyed her feelings for him.

"Fascinating," the man who was interviewing Alice said, bringing Brent from his thoughts. "Just a couple more questions, please, Ms. MacAllister. It goes without saying that you'll be touring with your work in the United States while you continue to establish your reputation. What I'm wondering is, do you have plans to extend those trips into Europe?"

"No," Alice said, smiling. "I'm not going to Europe. In fact, tonight will be my last public appearance for a very long time."

"I don't quite understand."

"I have no desire to be in the spotlight. Nor do I believe it's necessary. My paintings will speak for me. They *are* me. I simply want to continue to paint, that's all." She laughed. "I'll probably get labeled an eccentric, reclusive artist, but so be it. There are no publicity tours in my future. None."

"One last question—is there a special someone in your life? I'm sure our viewers would like to know."

Alice's smile faded. "I...I'd rather not discuss my personal life. What I mean is—"

"What she means is..." Brent said, making his way forward, "there are just some things that should remain private, no matter how much a successful person is in the public eye." He stopped in front of Alice, who was staring at him with wide eyes.

"I believe that answers the question quite eloquently," the man said, chuckling. He turned to face the camera. "This is Sterling Masters, Channel Fourteen news signing off and returning you to our studio."

The bright lights were turned off, Sterling Mas-

ters and his crew hurried out of the gallery, the
people who had been watching the interview wandered away, and Alice stood statue-still staring at
Brent, her heart racing.

"Brent?" she finally managed to whisper.

"Yeah, it's me," he said, attempting and failing
to produce a smile. "I crashed your party with your
mother's help. Congratulations on the success of
this show, Alice. I sincerely mean that."

"Thank you, but—"

"Is there somewhere we can talk...alone?"
Brent said. "Please?"

"Well, I... Yes, we could go into the office in
the back of the gallery, but—"

"Lead the way," Brent said, sweeping one arm
through the air.

Alice looked at Brent for another long moment,
then started across the room with him right behind
her.

"Well, Forrest," Jillian said, watching them go,
"a very important conversation is about to take
place."

"Bardow better not make my baby girl cry,"
Forrest said, frowning.

Jillian kissed him on the cheek. "Remember,
Daddy, there are such things as tears of joy."

* * *

In the small office in the rear of the gallery, Alice snapped on the desk lamp as Brent closed the door behind them. She turned to face him, lifting her chin and meeting his gaze directly as she ignored her trembling legs and thundering heart.

"I'm...I'm very surprised to see you here tonight," she said, wishing her voice was steadier.

"It took me this long to come to my senses, figure things out," Brent said, staying by the door. "It's just a coincidence that I arrived in Ventura on the night of the showing, which is why I'm not dressed properly for it." He paused. "Alice, there's so much I want, need, to say to you. I hope you'll listen, really hear, what I... Will you? Listen to me?"

"Yes," she said.

"When I saw your self-portrait in the pewter frame," he said, "I knew, with no lingering doubt, that you loved me every bit as much as I loved you. I knew that I was wrong, had accused you of things that weren't remotely close to being true."

"But, Brent, it's been weeks since I left that portrait for you."

"I know. I was still a mental mess, Alice. Yes, I knew then that you loved me, but it didn't solve the problem of your career taking you away from the Island of Wilshire, from me, for weeks at a stretch as you promoted your work.''

''Oh, but I don't intend—''

''Please,'' he continued, raising one hand. ''Let me finish.''

Alice nodded.

''I finally put the puzzle together,'' he said. ''I remembered how focused I was during all those months I was producing the Renault-Bardow wine. I was centered on my dream and spent little time with my parents, King Chester, my friends on the island. I understand about dreams, Alice, I truly do, but I was so selfish and self-centered I didn't want you to pursue yours at the cost of our being continually together. I was so damn wrong.''

''But—''

''I sat on a hill above the vineyards, the place where I hoped we'd build our home, and I realized that I needed to compromise, be willing to share you with your career, cherish the time we *would* have together. I finally knew, sitting there under the stars, that I would always be there, waiting for you to come home to me.''

''But—''

''Alice, I heard what you said to the man from the television station,'' Brent said, rushing on. ''You said you don't intend to tour with your work, that you just want to paint. But I've come here to beg your forgiveness for the horrible things I accused you of. I came here to tell you that you should never give up your dream. I came here to tell you that we could make it work by being partners, soul mates forever. I came here to ask you, again, to marry me, stay with me, until death parts us.''

''Oh, Brent,'' Alice said, tears filling her eyes.

''You believe me, don't you? You know I'm not just making this all up because I heard what you said to that guy? I swear it's true, Alice. I would be there, waiting for you, every time you came home. I even accepted the fact that we wouldn't have children because you'd be traveling so much. Oh, God, tell me you believe me.''

''I do,'' she said, a sob catching in her throat. ''Yes, I believe you.''

Brent stared up at the ceiling for a moment, to gather his emotions, then looked at Alice again.

''Thank you,'' he said, his voice raspy. ''Will you forgive me for the pain I caused you? Will you paint a portrait of us together, which we'll put in another pewter frame and hang in a place of honor in our home? Will you create babies, little miracles, with me? Ah, my Alice in Wonderland, will you marry me?''

Alice smiled as two tears spilled onto her cheeks. "Yes. Yes. Wait. Let me remember how many questions you asked. Yes. And, oh, yes, Brent Bardow, I'll marry you, be your wife and the mother of our children. Oh, God, Brent, I love you so much."

Brent let out a pent-up breath, then opened his arms to Alice. "Come here, please."

Alice ran across the room and into Brent's embrace, encircling his neck with her arms. They held fast to each other, allowing the depth and the warmth of their love to chase away the chill of loneliness and heartache that had consumed them.

"I love you," Brent said finally.

Alice tipped her head back to meet his gaze, seeing the tears that shimmered in his blue eyes.

"And I love you," she said, her own eyes brimming with tears.

Brent's mouth melted over hers and the kiss sealed their commitment to forever. Desire suffused them and hearts beat in wild tempos of want and need and love.

Brent broke the kiss and spoke close to Alice's lips.

"You'd better get back out there," he said, his voice husky with passion. "This is your night to shine and you deserve to enjoy every second of it.

I'll wait for you until the show is over. I'll wait for you, Alice.''

"I've been here long enough," she said. "I'll leave my paintings behind to speak for me. It's time for me to be with my future husband. It's time to begin our life together so that in the years to come we can stand side by side on the Island of Wilshire and say to each other, oh, look at us. My darling Brent, your Alice in Wonderland wants to go home.''

* * * * *

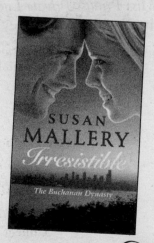

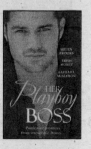

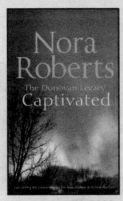
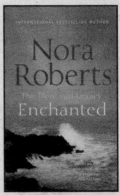
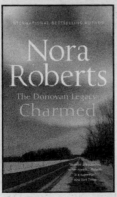